USA TODAY bestselling auth
London, England. She is mar
sons—which gives her rather
insight into the male psyche—and also works as a
film journalist. She adores her job, which involves
getting swept up in a world of high emotion, sensual
excitement, funny and feisty women, sexy and
tortured men and glamorous locations where laundry
doesn't exist. Once she turns off her computer she
often does chores—usually involving laundry!

Melanie Milburne read her first Mills & Boon novel
at the age of seventeen, in between studying for her
final exams. After completing a master's degree in
education she decided to write a novel, and thus her
career as a romance author was born. Melanie is an
ambassador for the Australian Childhood Foundation
and a keen dog-lover and trainer. She enjoys long
walks in the Tasmanian bush. In 2015 Melanie won
the HOLT Medallion, a prestigious award honouring
outstanding literary talent.

UNWRAPPING HIS NEW YORK INNOCENT

HEIDI RICE

NINE MONTHS AFTER THAT NIGHT

MELANIE MILBURNE

MILLS & BOON

First published in Great Britain 2022
by Mills & Boon, an imprint of HarperCollins*Publishers* Ltd,
1 London Bridge Street, London, SE1 9GF

www.harpercollins.co.uk

HarperCollins*Publishers*
1st Floor, Watermarque Building,
Ringsend Road, Dublin 4, Ireland

Unwrapping His New York Innocent © 2022 Heidi Rice

Nine Months After That Night © 2022 Melanie Milburne

ISBN: 978-0-263-30103-8

10/22

MIX
Paper from
responsible sources
FSC™ C007454

This book is produced from independently certified FSC™ paper
to ensure responsible forest management.
For more information visit www.harpercollins.co.uk/green.

Printed and Bound in Spain using 100% Renewable Electricity
at CPI Black Print, Barcelona

UNWRAPPING HIS NEW YORK INNOCENT

HEIDI RICE

MILLS & BOON

To the fabulous Natalie Anderson,
who is always such a joy to work with.

Let's do this again soon.

PROLOGUE

Halloween night

'Wow, THIS MUST have cost a wee fortune to put together.' Ellie MacGregor shivered in the brisk autumn breeze as she gazed out at the tiered terraces of the lavish art deco Manhattan penthouse. The staggering twilight view over Central Park was nothing compared to the Halloween decorations, which must have taken days to build and had turned the gothic apartment's roof gardens into a horror nightmare worthy of a theme-park ride. With an hour to go until the guests arrived, the set dressers were still putting the finishing touches on a haunted forest lit by glowing torches, while the catering staff were preparing a cordon bleu banquet which included a Day of the Dead graveyard sculpted in fondant icing and a punch fountain resembling the River Styx.

All just for one night!

How much did all this cost? Probably more than I'd earn in a decade.

'Haven't you heard of Alex Costa's Halloween Ball? He's one of America's hottest eligible bachelors. Him and his pal Roman Fraser vie for the top spot in *Celeb-*

rity magazine's list every year,' Carly, the wait staff's supervisor, supplied in her broad New York accent as she led Ellie past a corridor of groaning ghouls, their eyes lit a glittering green. 'For myself I think Costa's hotter—all that blue-collar sex appeal is just so...' Carly sighed '...freaking raw. But Roman Fraser's drop-dead cute too. He's got that whole classic Ivy League thing going on and the search for his missing sister totally makes you want to mother him,' Carly continued as she pushed through a door marked Keep Out or Prepare to Die.

'What search?' Ellie asked as they headed into the kitchens where the chilly calm outside gave way to frantic activity.

Carly stopped to stare at her. 'Seriously? You've never heard the story? And you're Scottish?'

Ellie shook her head, feeling even more clueless than when she'd arrived at La Guardia on her budget flight from Glasgow two days ago—after hitchhiking from the tiny Scottish island of Moira in the Outer Hebrides where she'd spent all of her twenty-one years.

She'd worked for two years in Moira's pub—after having to return her late parents' smallholding to the landowner—to earn the money to get here. She'd been looking for adventure, excitement, to see new things, meet people who hadn't known her since birth and shake off the lingering sadness of losing Ross and Susan MacGregor so close together—Ross from a heart attack and Susan from a broken heart...

Mission accomplished, she thought as Carly launched into the fantastical story of Roman Fraser and his long-lost sister.

Something about a billionaire couple from America's East Coast checking out a possible hotel purchase in the Highlands one snowy Christmas over two decades ago, a terrible car accident on a dark deserted road, the discovery of the only survivor, their little boy, Roman, barely alive hours later, and the baby who had never been found.

'You sure you never heard the story?' Carly asked, still looking astonished.

'I might have,' Ellie lied, so as not to look totally clueless.

The truth was, her job meant she often missed the TV news and the Internet only worked occasionally on Moira. Newspapers were already a day old by the time they arrived—so no one paid the news much mind. Plus from what Carly had just related about Roman Fraser's fruitless search—which had netted the poor guy loads of gold-diggers looking to become a billionaire's only relation—it had been launched a decade ago, when the guy had first come into his inheritance. She would only have been eleven years old.

'You should check the story out on your break.' Carly tilted her head to one side, considering Ellie. 'You're about her age, and you're from Scotland. You never know, you might even be her. Her name was Eloise… kinda sounds like Ellie?'

Yeah, right. Ellie kept the thought to herself.

But seriously, why did every American she'd met so far think Scotland was a country of about twenty people, all of whom she would either know and/or be related to?

'I was named after my maternal grandmother, Eleanor Fitzgerald,' Ellie said, feeling ashamed as the guilt she had struggled with ever since her parents' deaths three years ago pulsed under her breastbone.

The truth was, she'd always yearned to leave Moira, and she'd made her parents' life hell because of it. The MacGregors had been good, kind, solid, dependable island folk and she their miracle girl, because she'd been born to Susan in her forties after several miscarriages. As a kid, Ellie had bunked off school in the tiny one-room schoolhouse to roam the island and daydream about faraway places, especially New York, which her dad had once told her was exactly three thousand miles away across the Atlantic Ocean. And as a teenager she'd been even worse, hating the small-island mentality, the days spent being home-schooled with three other teens whose ambition had been to grow up to be crofters or fishermen, and all those early mornings herding sheep when she'd wanted to be somewhere cool and sophisticated and decadent, having conversations about anything other than the weather or the price of lamb. Her parents had always been so patient with her, they'd never even raised their voices, just looked at her with that combination of panic and concern in their eyes, which had only made her more ashamed of her wanderlust after their deaths.

Her need to escape had caused them so much pain. And while she'd been bound and determined to see it through, to finally leave Moira and fulfil those long-ago dreams, as soon as she'd arrived in New York she'd realised running away from one life to find another might not be enough. She'd come here to shake off that feeling of not belonging. To be anonymous, fearless, intrepid.

And while the canyons of skyscrapers, the noise and energy of the city had fascinated and excited her on one level, they had intimidated and terrified her on another. Maybe she wasn't as brave and bold as she'd thought. Or as prepared for the dog-eat-dog ethos of the people who lived here? What if she didn't belong here either?

'That's a shame,' Carly said, jolting Ellie out of her latest day dream. 'Imagine how awesome it would be to have Roman Fraser as your brother. You'd be the heir to billions. And you could totally hit on Alex Costa, because he's like Roman's BFF.'

Ellie nodded, although she didn't think it was a shame at all.

The MacGregors had been good parents. And she'd had them throughout her childhood. Unlike Roman Fraser, who had lost his parents as a little boy. The shame engulfed her again. If only she'd appreciated Ross and Susan a bit more when they were alive. And as for hitting on Alex Costa? No, thanks. The guy sounded like an entitled playboy from everything Carly had said about him already—in lavish detail. And she was still a virgin—mostly through lack of opportunity, to be fair, but she was not about to throw herself at a guy who probably had to fend off supermodels.

Way to feel even more out of my depth.

And who spent a wee fortune decorating their penthouse for a party when there were people living on the street outside?

She might have a bad case of wanderlust, but she did have some scruples, one of which was not to mess up her big adventure before she'd been in New York City for at least a week. Which meant working hard tonight, so she could get more jobs like this before her savings ran out.

Carly stopped at a rack of elaborate costumes and pulled one out to hold against Ellie's chest. 'This should fit.' She handed the costume to Ellie, which seemed to be of a demonic elf and only half there. The skirt barely reached past her knickers.

'You can change in the restroom,' Carly said, glancing at her phone. 'We start serving when the guests arrive. But they always get here super early—to check out the décor and Mr Costa, even though he's always super late. So be at your station in twenty minutes.'

'But… Where's the rest of this costume?' Ellie began.

'You want the job or not?' Carly asked.

Ellie's cheeks heated. *Stop being so small-town. You're not in Moira any more.*

'I want the job,' she replied. But as she headed off to change she decided Alex Costa was *definitely* an entitled jerk… Who else would insist the female wait staff got dressed up as hooker elves in the middle of winter?

CHAPTER ONE

Sorry, Alex, gonna miss the party. I got a better offer. Have a good one. And don't hit on anyone I wouldn't hit on.

'THAT LEAVES ME a lot of leeway,' Alex Costa muttered as he glared at the text from his best buddy, Roman Fraser—who had bailed on him. Again.

Roman's 'better offer' probably had a cute face and an even cuter figure. He didn't blame the guy for bailing though. Parties weren't Roman's thing, especially parties that involved dress-up. Truth be told, they weren't Alex's thing much either. He'd started the Halloween bash seven years ago when Costa Tech had hit the Forbes *Global 2000* list for the first time and he'd officially become a billionaire at the ripe old age of twenty-three. The themed ball had been a classy way to announce himself on the world stage. He didn't need the publicity now, but the party had become a staple of Manhattan's social calendar.

He really wasn't feeling it tonight though as he stood on the balcony of his top-floor suite and watched the festivities below. A ton of people he didn't really know and cared even less about partied in an array of pricey designer costumes while oohing and ahhing at the outdoor space, which had been transformed into a haunted house and graveyard by an A-list Broadway set designer and her crew.

He should go check it out himself—but first he'd have to put himself at the mercy of the hair and makeup team who'd been waiting for over an hour to deck him out in whatever outfit his executive assistant had ordered.

He swallowed a mouthful of the expensive Scotch he'd poured himself when he'd arrived from his downtown office ten minutes ago. This evening would have been a whole lot more bearable if his ride-or-die pal, Roman, were here to make a dumbass of himself too. He'd also hoped to hang with Roman tonight because he knew his pal was heading off on business until Thanksgiving. And Roman always went to ground in the run-up to Christmas too, because it was a tough time of year for him. Alex shivered. He'd never liked Christmas much himself, not since he was a little kid.

Thanks, Pop.

He shook off the unbidden reminder of his father, Carmine Da Costa. A man who everyone had adored, except for Alex. Because Alex knew the truth of his father's lies and half-truths. The evasion and the subterfuge. The 'other women' Carmine had kept all over the Bronx, while pretending to be a great husband. And a devoted father.

His mom had figured it out eventually, but his siblings not so much.

He squinted down at the party guests, surprised by

the feeling of aching loneliness that he hadn't felt in a long time. Why the heck was he thinking of his old man? The family he never saw any more?

Time to get over yourself, Costa.

But just as he was about to head inside, his eye caught a waitress winding her way through the guests—in a costume the size of a place mat. He rubbed his hand across his mouth, annoyed by the shot of lust racing through his bloodstream as he took in her slender shape and the tumble of chestnut curls piled on top of her head.

What the heck was she supposed to be? Because she looked like an R-rated pixie. Whose dumb idea had it been to dress the wait staff like that at the end of October? She had to be freezing. As he followed her movements through the crowd—his gaze glued to the tempting sway of her butt in the barely there green silk skirt that fluttered around toned thighs displayed in fishnet pantyhose—he got even more pissed about the decision.

When was the last time he'd felt this visceral rush of attraction? Way too long ago.

But there was no way he was hitting on the wait staff—because that was so not a classy move. Which meant Roman was definitely the only one getting lucky tonight.

He chugged the last of the whisky, felt the burn in his throat and walked inside.

Just one more reason to give his pal hell next time he saw him.

'Hey, cutie, you got any more of these witchy martinis?'

Ellie swung round, tottering on the mile-high heels

that had given her blisters the size of Brooklyn hours ago, to see the preppy-looking Frankenstein who had been leering at her all night stumbling back towards her station.

Just kill me now.

'Yes, sir. I'll fetch another.' She lifted the tray onto her aching arm and made to dart round him.

'Hey,' he slurred, his green brows lowering over bloodshot eyes, and blocked her path. 'Don't go running off again, cutie pie.'

Cutie pie? Seriously...?

She stiffened when his palm caught her waist.

'Take your hand off me, sir.' She twisted away from him, her skin crawling and her temper igniting. She was cold, sore, jet-lagged and so over this guy and it wasn't even midnight. If he touched her again, he would regret it.

'Aw, come on. I'm the CEO of Radisson Investments. Costa won't like it if you play hard to get...'

But then his wandering hand cupped her backside. A red mist descended over her vision and the buzz in her ears became turbocharged. She knocked his hand away. 'Touch me again, Frankie, and you're a dead man.'

Frankenstein, though, was not listening, because his offending hand landed back on her bum.

Okay, that did it. Her fingers balled into a fist, and she socked him square in his green jaw.

'Ouch!' she bit out, pain ricocheting through her knuckles as he staggered backwards, knocking her tray of drinks up and drenching her.

Heat charged into her cheeks as the previously oblivious guests nearby turned to stare. Swearing furiously and looking a lot more sober, Frankenstein staggered back towards her, testing his jaw.

'I'm gonna sue you to within an inch of your life. I think you've cracked one of my implants.'

She lifted her fists in front of her. 'Touch me again and I'll do more than crack an implant.'

But as Frankenstein approached, and she went to swing at him, something hard banded around her waist and yanked her back against a solid wall of muscle.

'Chill out, Pixie girl,' a gruff voice whispered in her ear. 'Believe me, he's not worth it.'

She sucked in a breath to protest, shivers streaking down her spine at the feel of the forearm pressed intimately against her literally heaving bosoms. But then the same voice growled at Frankenstein. 'Get out, Brad, and don't come back.'

'But she punched me!' Frankenstein whined.

'You want me to punch you, too?' the voice asked, the calm conversational tone belying the steel beneath— which sent another irritating shiver through Ellie's overwrought body.

Frankenstein held up his hands. 'No, man, I'm good.'

'Before you go, you can apologise to the lady,' the voice added, his warm arm flexing against her midriff. She found herself holding onto him, her legs turning into wet noodles as the adrenaline rush of the fight drained.

A sea of ghoulish, witchy, devilish faces surrounded them—some giggling, some taking photos with their phones and all of them openly enjoying the spectacle.

Frankie's disgruntled gaze dropped to her face.

'Sorry.' He ground out the word, before pushing through the throng of party guests to disappear.

'Show's over, folks,' Mr Forearm announced, which did nothing to dispel the crowd. But then his forearm released its hold on her. As soon as her legs took her weight, they buckled.

'Hey?' Warm palms landed on her waist, preventing her from falling over as he turned her towards him.

She had to look way up to see his face.

Her head swam, the underside of her breasts burning where he'd touched them, as she took in the fierce features, the jet-black hair combed back to reveal a widow's peak, the white silk shirt, severe black cloak, and the blood dripping from one of the fangs peeking out from impossibly sensual lips.

I've just been saved by a six-foot four-inch vampire.

'Dracula?' she murmured.

'At your service,' he said, the sensual lips quirking. The fangs sparkled, and she imagined them sinking into her neck and sucking the last of the blood out of her head.

'Can you stand on your own?' he asked, the concern in his voice belied somewhat by the heat lighting the gold shards in his hazelnut eyes.

No. 'Yes,' she said. But then she shivered.

His searing gaze dipped to the bodice of her costume. 'You're soaking wet.'

'That'd be F-Frankenstein's fault,' she stammered.

His lips curved in a loaded smile that sent the jumping beans in her stomach into overdrive. What was with that?

This situation was catastrophic. Not giddily exciting. People were still staring. She looked an absolute fright—and felt worse. She was probably going to get sued by Frankenstein, and, as she spotted Carly hurtling towards them at speed, about to be unemployed. Would she even get paid for the six hours' work she'd already done?

Even so the warm spot in her stomach swelled as she had to lean into the vampire count's steady hold.

'Why did you belt Brad?' Dracula asked.

The fact he didn't know but had ridden to her rescue anyway made the warm spot throb.

'He put his hand on my bum,' she said.

'That son of a…' Fury flared across his face, vindicating the indignation battling with the jumping beans in her stomach. But then the gold shards gleamed again. 'You're Scottish, right? What part of Scotland are you from? My pal Roman's family are from there originally too.'

She stared at him for a moment, surprised, not just at the mention of the mysterious Roman Fraser of the long-lost sister fame, but that he'd recognised her accent—most New Yorkers she'd met so far seemed to confuse a Scottish accent with an Irish one. But then she suspected Dracula was very observant, his searing gaze doing all sorts of unfortunate things to her thigh muscles. Before she could give him an answer, though, Carly pitched up and broke the spell.

'Mr Costa, I heard what happened, I'm so sorry. Mr Radisson told me one of the waitresses had accosted him. I'll have Ms MacGregor escorted off the premises.'

Costa? She shrugged out of his hold. This guy was no knight in shining armour—or rather no knight with shining blood-drenched fangs—he was the entitled jerk who had forced her to wear this stupid costume in the first place.

'And your name is?' he asked Carly, the easy tone gone.

Her supervisor blushed crimson to match her devil's outfit. 'Carly Jemson, the party planner Marilyn Holsten's staff manager, sir.'

His warm hand folded around Ellie's shoulder. 'I'm taking Ms MacGregor inside so she can change. She's soaked and freezing and she just got assaulted by Radisson, so we'll both be lucky if she doesn't sue us.' The chilling tone froze Carly in place. 'She's taking the rest of the night off. I want her wages doubled.' His searing gaze skimmed back over Ellie's drenched outfit. 'And tell Marilyn *if* I ever hire her again I don't want the wait staff wearing something so damn inappropriate.'

Leaving Carly sputtering apologies in his wake, Costa swept through the crowd with his hand still clamped on Ellie's arm, then headed up a staircase onto the penthouse's top floor, which was off-limits to guests and catering staff alike.

Still feeling hideously exposed, not to mention struggling to control the hot brick now wedged between her thighs, Ellie allowed herself to be led. But as soon as they entered a vast living area, the glass wall on the far end of the space delivering a stunning view of Manhattan at night, she tugged her arm out of Dracula's grasp.

'Thanks,' she muttered, not feeling very thankful.

Maybe he hadn't fired her. And maybe he hadn't known about the costumes the waitresses had been asked to wear. But this was his party. And she could lay money on Carly getting her blacklisted from similar jobs after the way he'd humiliated the woman downstairs. She didn't just feel clueless now, she felt vulnerable. And she hated that feeling. 'If you can show me the way out, I'll be leaving now.'

'Don't be dumb, you're soaking wet. And freezing,' he said, sounding as annoyed as she felt. Which was rich. Who had been assaulted here? 'You're not going anywhere until I know you're okay.'

He snagged her hand, and lifted it, to inspect her bruised knuckles. The tender gesture was so unexpected—and his expression so fierce as he scowled down at the raw skin—it took her several seconds to yank her fingers free.

'Go take a hot shower while I hunt up a first-aid kit,' he said, completely unfazed by her glare. 'We should put some antiseptic on that. There's some dry sweats in the closet and some good Scotch in the cabinet, help yourself.'

'I can't shower here, Mr Costa,' she said.

'The name's Alex,' he said, turning back to her, but then he pulled out the fangs. It didn't make him look any less dangerous. 'Or Count Dracula, whatever works.'

'Do you think this is funny?' she demanded at the wry comment. She was sticky, probably in shock and dead on her feet. All she wanted to do right now was sleep for a week. And ignore the uncomfortable sensation making the jumping beans do back flips every time he looked at her. The last thing she needed was an overbearing billionaire making jokes at her expense.

His gaze only became more intense. 'Nope.'

'I should leave,' she said again. Why did she feel so

drowsy? And so cold—except for the warm spot, which was glowing like a hot coal. He walked towards her, his hands wrapping around her upper arms, as her knees started to give way again and tremors began to wrack her overwrought body.

'Do you have anyone who can come pick you up?' he asked. 'And watch over you tonight?'

She shook her head, her throat drying to parchment. Why did he have to be so handsome? And so over-whelming? And why couldn't she think straight? Or stop shaking?

'I—I j-just arrived in New York…' she said. 'B-but I've been on my own for a while.' She steeled herself against the ripple of grief—and wondered why she'd revealed something so personal to a man she didn't know…

Calling on the last of her strength, she locked her knees and pulled away from him.

This is no time to fall to pieces, Ellie.

'I d-don't need anyone to w-watch over me,' she said, as demonstrably as she could manage while her teeth were chattering like castanets. 'I c-can w-watch over myself.'

'Sure you can,' he said. His thumb—warm, callused and strangely proprietary—skimmed down her cheek. 'Go wash up. If you can say all that again without stam-mering when I get back, I'll have my driver take you wherever you want to go. If not, you're stuck here till morning. Got it?'

'Wh-who made you the b-boss of me?' she said, grit-ting her teeth as she wrapped her aching arms round her damp costume.

'I did,' he said with an arrogance that would have outraged her—if she hadn't reached peak outrage already.

First I get groped by Frankenstein, now Dracula is kidnapping me! Could this night actually become any more of a nightmare?

The fact her reaction to Costa was a lot more disturbing and unpredictable than her reaction to Brad the creep wasn't settling the jumping beans a bit.

'I'm assuming you signed an employment contract tonight,' he added. 'So I am *literally* the boss of you until dawn anyway.'

'I w-was hired to s-serve drinks,' she hissed, her legs shaking again. 'N-not get t-trapped in your penthouse lair, you overbearing…'

'Give it up, Pixie girl,' he said, the amused tone and the sparkle of admiration in his eyes almost as infuriating as his astonishing arrogance.

They didn't celebrate Halloween on Moira, and now she knew why. Because it was fast becoming her least favourite American tradition—right alongside adding taxes you weren't aware of to every purchase and the widespread belief this side of the pond that Scotland was a part of England.

'You're stuck in my penthouse lair until I'm convinced you're okay, so you might as well enjoy it.' He brushed his thumb over her chin. The tiny touch sent another disturbing shiver of sensation straight to the hot spot between her legs. But worse was that strange feeling of safety, and security, and the gut instinct to trust he wouldn't take advantage of her, when she had absolutely no evidence he was any more trustworthy than the blood-sucking count himself.

So not good.

'I'll be back in a half-hour. Make yourself comfortable while I'm gone.'

She wanted to protest some more. But unfortunately she seemed to have lost the ability to speak as he marched across the room and disappeared.

Terrific. So what did she do now? She could still leave. He couldn't actually stop her.

But as she glanced out at the night sky—picking out the ornate splendour of The Plaza across the park—it was hard not to be overwhelmed all over again.

The shivers finally began to subside, making her wonder if they had been a reaction to her fatigue, her fight with Frankenstein, or simply the devastating presence of her billionaire boss.

She slipped the heels off her aching feet, and headed to the drinks cabinet, her bare feet sinking into the exquisitely soft carpeting. She poured herself two fingers of Scottish single malt whisky from a distillery she knew was one of the best in the Highlands.

At least Dracula knows his whisky.

She knocked it back. Fine, she'd take him at his word. She'd have a hot shower, change into some dry clothes and then deliver the line again about not needing anyone to watch over her—*without* stammering. Once she'd passed his asinine test, he would have to release her from his clutches.

And if he thought she wasn't going to bill him for the extra hour she'd been held captive in his lair, he could think again.

Fortified by the whisky and her righteous indignation, she explored the apartment's private suites. So this was how the other half lived? She'd never seen anything so luxurious, she realised, as she wandered into an enormous bedroom with no personal touches—which had to be a guest room. She locked the door to the vast en suite bathroom and dragged off the sticky costume. It took her several attempts to figure out how to switch on the shower, which had a control panel that would put a space shuttle to shame. Propped against the granite wall, she let the hot powerful jets pummel her cold flesh back to life.

Her skin buzzed as she wrapped a fluffy towel around herself. She found a pile of designer sportswear neatly stacked in the bedroom's enormous walk-in wardrobe. The baggy sweat top reached her knees, affording her considerably more modesty than her elf costume. She added a pair of boxer shorts and some white cotton socks—because the sweat pants were way too big for her.

Once she'd passed Costa's silly test, she could get her own clothes from the staff quarters. She returned to the living area and sank into one of the buttery leather sofas. The room's lighting had dimmed automatically. Her eyelids drooped as she stared at the blinking light of a plane, flying over the towering skyscrapers stacked like building blocks on the other side of Central Park. The cosy burn of the whisky in her stomach spread to envelop her whole body.

She dropped her head onto the armrest. But as her eyelids drifted shut, cutting out the stunning view of Manhattan at night, she found herself dragged into a vivid dream featuring a staggeringly hot and pushy vampire, with a pair of fangs that raked over her erect nipples and made the hot spot between her thighs become a volcano of molten need.

CHAPTER TWO

THAT HAD TO be a first, Alex thought ruefully, as he gazed down at the enraged Scottish pixie who was now sound asleep on his couch. When was the last time a woman had fallen asleep in his place without being in his bed?

Then again, he had no plans to hit on her. Not only was she still in his employ, she had just been through an ordeal. First thing tomorrow, he planned to ensure that jerk Bradford Radisson IV and his investment fund were blackballed all over Manhattan.

Brad had been one of the entitled little bastards who had made Alex's life hell when he'd been the scholarship kid at Eldridge Prep in upstate New York. Roman Fraser had been the only boy who hadn't looked down his nose at him because Alex's old man was a construction worker from the Bronx.

He didn't know how Brad had even got an invite to the ball. But he intended to make sure it never happened again.

As he studied Eleanor MacGregor—whose name he'd sourced from his now ex-party planner—snoring softly, something weird happened to his chest. She'd certainly given good old Brad a taste of his own medicine—knocking him flat on his ass with an impressive right hook. And she'd been pretty damn feisty with him too, even though she'd looked cold and miserable and ready to face plant the minute he'd got her to his suite.

That she'd somehow managed to captivate him while staring daggers at him he didn't plan to examine too closely. Chalk it up to Halloween night doing weird things to his libido.

He wasn't usually attracted to women who thought he was an arrogant jerk.

Nor was he the type of guy to want to watch over anyone—making his decision to insist she stay the night even weirder.

He'd killed his white-knight complex a long time ago when trying to protect his family—and especially his mom—from the truth about his old man had blown up in his face.

He frowned, not liking the pulse of guilt at the memory of that miserable Christmas night twenty years ago, and his mom's tear-streaked face.

Why the heck had his white-knight complex come out of hiding when he'd spotted the enraged Scottish pixie knocking Brad on his ass? Sure, he'd immediately figured that Brad had been the one in the wrong—he knew the guy—and he'd wanted to deal with him. But he could have handed Eleanor over to the wait-staff manager with instructions to pay her off, generously, once the altercation was over, rather than spiriting her up here.

He tilted his head, attempting to study her dispassionately, and felt the hot pulse of awareness return—an awareness which had been there right from the moment he'd spotted her earlier.

Damn. What was with that?

Why did she still turn him on? With her pale legs tucked under her butt, her feet clad in a pair of his athletic socks, her wild chestnut curls rioting around her delicate features and his oversized sweatshirt disguising the slender curves he'd noticed earlier, she should not have looked remotely hot.

Unfortunately, his libido hadn't got the memo, the scent of his own shampoo doing nothing to douse the heat. He adjusted the jeans he'd put on after changing out of the vampire costume.

She'd given every impression that she thought he was an arrogant jerk. But he'd seen the arousal in her eyes too. He knew when a woman wanted him. That she'd been as determined to fight it as he was though had added an interesting novelty value.

Even when he'd been starting out, his drive and ambition and his blue-collar origins, coupled with the Bronx accent he'd worked hard to lose, had been a major turn on for high-class women looking to be pulled off their pedestals. He'd happily obliged at first, but once his investment portfolio had taken off, he'd got a whole lot more discerning. But it had been a very long time since he'd enjoyed the thrill of the chase.

Whatever.

She was still way out of bounds. Even if she didn't work for him, and she hadn't had a run-in with Brad the jerk tonight, he could smell the peaty aroma of his best Scotch on her breath. Plus there was that weird white-knight response to her, which he had no plans to encourage.

'How about I carry you to one of the guest bedrooms so you can sleep it off till morning?' he said, at which time he could let her go with a clear conscience. Hopefully putting his white knight back in its box once and for all.

She didn't stir.

'I'll take that as a yes, Eleanor.'

Hooking one arm under her bent knees and the other around her back, he scooped her off the couch and into his arms.

She shifted slightly, then curled into his chest, her furled fingers gliding over his pecs before landing in her lap, the citrus scent of his shampoo mixed with the fresh, clean scent of her skin. He tensed, the surge of heat nowhere near as disturbing as the surge of protectiveness.

'Mmm…' she mumbled, her warm whisky-scented breath nuzzling his neck.

The weight in his pants hardened, and he cursed softly.

He hadn't had this much of a hair trigger since he was a teenager. Around the same time he'd been sent away from everything he cared about for the duration of his adolescence.

He pushed the humiliating thought to one side as he carted her down the corridor. But instead of taking her to one of the guest suites, he entered his own bedroom. The urge to have her sleep in his bed, even if he wasn't going to be in it with her, was somehow undeniable.

Yeah, he'd have to examine that reaction at a later date too.

After yanking back the quilt, he deposited her on the bed. He spotted the pale blue cotton of his shorts covering her lush butt, the waistband tied in a knot to stop them slipping off. The swift shot of arousal was joined by the strange pulse of admiration in his chest—his pixie was nothing if not resourceful.

His pixie? He scrubbed his hands down his face and sighed. He definitely needed to get laid.

But as he left the room, he resigned himself to having to resort to his first hand-job in years when the pulse of heat refused to die.

CHAPTER THREE

ELLIE'S EYELIDS FLUTTERED open to the sound of... Was someone humming?

The husky murmur rippled through her snug body. She pushed up into a sitting position, finally focussing on the unfamiliar surroundings. She certainly wasn't in the hostel dormitory any more.

But where on earth was she?

The luxury bedroom furniture—all sleek lines, muted masculine colours and expensive fabrics—was like something out of a magazine spread, lit by the thin strip of sunlight peeking under the blinds covering a glass wall opposite the bed.

She noted the logo of an exclusive sports brand on the oversized sweatshirt she wore. And what on earth was she wearing?

She brushed her wild hair back, then flopped on the bed, as it all came rushing back. The hours of wielding expensive Halloween-themed cocktails in her freezing outfit. The rub of her too-high heels. Frankenstein grabbing her bum. The agony as she'd punched him, followed by the shocking blast of heat at her first glimpse of her host—six feet four inches of toned muscles, darkly compelling eyes and attitude… With a capital A for arrogance.

Was he the person humming?

She slipped out of the huge bed. At least she didn't feel like a limp dishcloth any more. She glanced at the clothing she remembered putting on after her shower.

His clothing.

She could hear movement from the walk-in wardrobe where she'd located the sweats. The humming stopped. To be replaced by a series of rustles.

Was he getting dressed in there?

She stood dumbly in the middle of the bedroom not sure whether to run, hide or demand to know how the heck she had ended up in his bed. Because this *had* to be his bed—despite the lack of any personal touches in the room.

She stared at the rumpled sheets. Had he slept with her? But then she noticed the lack on an indent in the pillow next to hers.

She pulled her hands back through her hair, and then down to her bare legs, trying to remember how the night had ended. But all she could seem to grasp was the image of his face, with that wry, knowing smile, and the sparkle of appreciation in his hazelnut eyes.

The heady shot of adrenaline and desire blindsided her. The same way it had last night. But this time, it infused her whole body.

He couldn't have slept in here. Because she definitely would have remembered it. After all, she'd never shared a bed with a man before.

But instead of feeling relieved, she felt strangely disappointed. Because all she could feel was the languid heat that had followed her in dreams all through the night... Dreams of him, being forceful, arrogant, and super-hot.

'Hey, you're up... How are you feeling?'

Ellie's head jerked up at the gruff statement. And her gaze became glued to a magnificent male chest. *His* chest. His completely *naked* chest.

Wow.

Her jaw went slack as her gaze devoured each ridge and sinew, each muscular bulge, his tanned skin given a golden glow by the diffused lighting. Curls of hair flared around flat brown nipples, then trailed into a thin line, bisecting washboard abs, before disappearing beneath the sweatpants settled low enough on his lean waist to reveal beautifully defined hip flexors.

The languid heat popped and sizzled, flaring up from her core to explode on her cheeks.

Sweet Lord, the man is a work of art.

'Hey, Eleanor.' Strong fingers clicked in front of his six-pack—no, make that an eight-pack—snapping her out of her fugue state. 'Up here.' The fingers beckoned, and her stunned gaze rose to the devastating face she remembered from last night.

But not.

His deep brown hair was no longer jet-black and no longer ruthlessly slicked back, but fell in damp waves over his brow. The recently showered look should have softened his strong, angular face—the blade-like nose, the full, sensual lips, the chiselled jaw covered in beard scruff, the piercing hazelnut gaze sparkling with rueful amusement—but it didn't. At all.

'How are you?'

Had he asked her that already? Because her mind had gone totally to mush.

'G-good,' she squeaked.

How could he stand there, looking so casual, so confident, while she felt as if she were burning up, from the inside out?

'Are you sure?' he asked, those sensual lips curved in a mocking smile she recognised. But whereas last night that smile had annoyed her, now it just excited her... Which could not be good. 'You're still stammering.'

Of course I'm stammering, I could spontaneously combust at any moment. Duh.

She bit off the comeback. And swallowed, to bring her brain to bear on the problem at hand.

'Really, I'm good,' she said, grateful when she managed to get the words out without squeaking. But seriously? Who wouldn't squeak in the face of such extreme hotness?

She'd grown up on a remote Scottish island where there were about five thousand sheep to every available guy under sixty. And to say her parents had been a wee bit overprotective would have been putting it mildly. She'd never even been in a man's bedroom before, let alone a bedroom as vast and well-appointed as this one. And that was without even factoring in the stunning chest currently commanding all her attention.

'Uh-huh.' He sounded doubtful.

Then to her consternation, he lifted the T-shirt she hadn't realised he was holding and tugged it over his head—covering those glorious pecs, the stunning eight-pack, the delicious happy trail, the breathtaking hip flexors.

Her low groan of protest echoed around the room. 'Ach, no.'

She'd come all the way to New York to find adventure, her mushy brain reasoned. And she couldn't think of anything more adventurous in that moment than gazing at those perfectly formed pecs for the rest of her natural life.

'Is there a problem?' he asked, the tone low with amusement.

The heat spread across her collarbone. He was making fun of her, but, even so, the recklessness that had got her into so much trouble as a teenager had her blurting out the truth. 'Your chest is so beautiful. Can I gaze at it a wee bit longer?'

Beautiful?

Alex had to stifle a laugh. No one had ever called him beautiful before.

'Are you serious?' he said, disconcerted by the vicious swell of heat stirred by the fierce appreciation in her gaze and the artless, forthright comment.

When he'd found her still curled up on his bed, fast asleep, he had planned to get dressed before she woke up, head out for his regular hour-long morning run in Central Park and direct his staff to make sure she was appropriately compensated and gone before he returned.

As much as he'd wanted her last night—hell, as much as he still wanted her—he hadn't changed his mind about hitting on her. She was an employee, even if only a temporary one. And she was way too sweet beneath the snarky attitude. Not his usual type, at all. He preferred his dating life to be simple, and the women he dated to be smart and sophisticated and to know the score. This woman—if you could even class her as a woman, given the air of innocence that clung to her— had vulnerable written all over her.

But then her gaze lifted to his face, and he could see the glazed purpose in it, and the sheen of arousal.

The heat pulsed hard in his groin.

'Aye,' she said, her Scottish accent only making the single word more beguiling.

He didn't take orders from anyone any more, but something about the way she'd asked fascinated and ex-cited him, the shudder of uncertainty behind the fierce determination making him suspect she was as surprised as he was by her request.

To hell with it.

Lifting the hem of the T-shirt, he dragged it off and watched as her hot gaze become glued to his abs again.

He knew he was in good shape. She wasn't the first woman to admire his physique. He'd been skinny as a beanpole as a kid, especially once he'd grown to his full height at fourteen. And he'd worked hard to fill out every inch in the years since. But when her gaze met his again and the passion flared, it occurred to him no one had ever looked at him before with such undis-guised yearning.

'Satisfied?' he asked, both amused and impossibly aroused at the staggered rasp of her breathing.

She nodded.

Flinging the T-shirt away, he stepped towards her, the urge to touch her not something he could deny a moment longer.

He skimmed a knuckle under her chin, ran his thumb

across her bottom lip. Her sharp intake of breath at the light touch electrified him.

Damn, was it possible she wanted him as much as he wanted her?

The enraged pixie had become an artless seductress. Would it really be so wrong to give in to this attraction, if it were mutual? Surely she couldn't be as sweet and vulnerable as she'd appeared if her raw need was anything to go by?

His thumb pressed against the throbbing pulse in her collarbone, and the too-big zip-up sweatshirt fell off her shoulder, revealing the sprinkle of freckles across the upper swell of one breast.

'How old are you?' he asked, aware he was holding his own breath now.

'Twenty-one,' she said.

Thank God. Totally legal, then.

He cruised his thumb across the top swell of her breast. He forced himself to keep his touch light. Or as light as he could manage while the desire was blocking off his air supply.

'Your turn,' he said.

'What?' she asked, her eyes widening.

'To take off your sweatshirt,' he challenged.

Her brows launched up her forehead, and vivid colour mottled her pale skin as a string of emotions rioted across her expressive features—surprise, panic, awareness.

The admiration that had blindsided him the night before returned in a rush.

Either she was an award-worthy actress, or the most

transparent woman he had ever met. But whichever it was, that blush only made him want her more.

'But I'm no wearing anything underneath,' she said.

He grinned, he couldn't help it. 'So?'

The fierce determination flashed into her eyes, and his desire became turbocharged. But still it surprised him when she gripped the sweatshirt and lifted it over her head—the gesture somehow as brave as it was provocative. Why did he get the impression she'd never done this before, when she must have? Surely no woman could be this alluring without practice.

The soft mounds of her breasts bounced as she flung away the top, making the need tighten in his gut. But then she folded a concealing arm over her beautiful rack.

His amusement dried up, as his mouth watered, the desire to capture the ruched peaks all but unbearable.

'Hey,' he said, the protest so husky it was barely audible. 'That's cheating.'

To his astonishment she dropped her arm.

'Can I touch?' he asked, the boulder of need growing to impossible proportions.

Her gaze remained fixed on his, but just when he felt sure she would refuse him, she murmured, 'Aye.'

The rush of relief made him light-headed as he cradled the plump flesh and heard her harsh gasp.

Unable to wait a moment longer to taste her, he leant forward and circled the delicate nipple with his tongue. Reverence and desperation combined to make him moan. Her fingers sank into his hair, her body bowing back, holding him against her as he trapped the tender peak, rejoicing in the erotic feel of it elongating.

Her sobs made the raw need arrow down, as he suckled, and licked, nipped and tormented. But the game they'd been playing became deadly serious as he felt his cast-iron control start to shatter.

Scooping her petite body into his arms, he placed her on his bed, the adrenaline rush joined by the painful throbbing in his groin.

He kicked off his sweats, and the huge erection sprang free. She gave a startled gasp and he hesitated— her gaze as shocked as it was eager.

'Are you okay with this?' he forced himself to ask, even though the urge to plunge inside her was already tearing at his control like a ravening dog. He knew he was a big guy, women had commented on his size before, but usually to flatter him. She looked a lot less sure of herself all of a sudden.

He waited, ready to stop if she asked him to, even though it would probably kill him. But she didn't say anything, simply nodded, as the slight tremor made her high, firm breasts quiver.

His breath gushed out.

Brushing his palms up the outside of her legs, he hooked his thumbs in the waistband of his own shorts and dragged them down her thighs. Her panting sobs spurred him on.

All she wore now were his athletic socks. He'd never seen anything more erotic in his life.

Caging her small body in, he captured the hard nipple in his mouth again, while his fingers found the slick seam of her sex. Carefully, cautiously, he delved, probed. Damn, she was so wet, so ready for him… And so tight.

Her breath hitched in raw heady pants as he found the hard nub, and circled it, mercilessly drawing out her pleasure. She writhed, bucked, her startled cries echoing in his ears.

'You like that?' he murmured, trying to sound amused, in charge of this seduction, even as he could feel his control slipping further.

'Oh… Yes, yes,' she cried, lost in her own passion.

Grasping her thighs, he found himself sinking between her legs, the desire to taste her, to bring her to a mind-numbing orgasm, the only thing keeping him from losing it altogether.

The second his tongue touched the moist heart of her, she bucked, the shocked gasp making the feast all the sweeter. He held her open, ruthlessly teasing the tight nub with his lips. He worked the sodden flesh, glorying in her uninhibited response to him. So open, so wild. She thrashed on the sheets, her hips lifting into his caresses, as he finally captured the swollen bud and suckled hard.

She cried out, the sound hoarse and raw, the fierceness with which she surrendered to her own pleasure only making her more intoxicating.

He licked her through the last throes of her orgasm, felt her body collapse onto the bed. As he drew back, he fumbled for a condom in the bedside cabinet, his hands shaking, his movements clumsy. She lay under him, her body sated, her face relaxed, the wariness gone to be replaced by stunned satisfaction.

Grasping her hips, he angled her pelvis. She pulled him towards her as he settled between her thighs. He couldn't wait a moment longer. Every part of him focussed now on satisfying the driving need to see her surrender again, this time with him.

'Hold on,' he murmured. He'd planned to take it slow, but as she lifted her hands to his shoulders the trust on her face had him burying himself to the hilt in one slow thrust.

Ellie stiffened, the sublime cloud of afterglow torn away by the shockingly full penetration.

Alex paused above her, his face tense as he swore softly. 'Are you okay? You're so tight,' he said, the raw need reverberating through his voice.

She nodded, unable to speak, needing him to move, to ease the tight clasp of her body.

She could feel him everywhere, the wild exhilaration joined by the shocking surge of vulnerability.

Her heart crashed against her ribs. Her lungs worked like organ bellows as she tried to gather enough air to regain a semblance of herself.

She felt conquered, branded, all her emotions too raw, too real.

She'd always assumed losing her virginity would not be that big a deal. But how had he known exactly what to do to drive her wild…? And why had she thrown herself at him with such abandon? A man she hardly knew? If he knew how close to tears she had come when her first climax had hit her like a freight train, and how overwhelmed she felt now, how possessed, she would never recover from the humiliation.

'Are you sure?' he asked, cradling her cheek and forcing her gaze to his.

She swallowed, scared to speak in case he heard the shocked emotion still battering her. She nodded again.

He still hadn't moved, was still lodged deep inside her. Her tender flesh contracted around him instinctively, trying to drag him in still further. Her face flushed as he groaned.

He cursed again, his breathing as ragged as hers. 'I've got to move.'

'Yes,' she managed, her throat dry.

As he drew out, and rocked back, slowly, gently, her tender flesh opened to receive him. And the terrifying intensity of her pleasure ignited again.

She clung to him, his shoulders the only anchor in a new sea of turbulent sensation.

He grunted, the rhythm he established assured, relentless, unyielding. Her body opened further, but this time she couldn't seem to hold back even a small part of herself, as he conquered her by exquisite degrees— sinking deep, drawing out, sinking deeper still.

She began to meet his thrusts, joining the devastating dance, compelled to follow his lead, her total surrender inevitable.

She tried to cling to that scrap of sanity, hold together the pieces he'd shattered once already. But even as she tried, he demanded more of her. Gripping her hips, he rotated to stroke a place deep inside. She jerked, the intense pleasure making her moan.

'That's it, come with me this time,' he murmured.

The furious sweep of release tumbled towards her— harder, faster—on an unstoppable wave.

She sobbed, the pleasure battering her, but he was relentless, working the spot he'd located with unerring focus. She cried out as the wave crashed at last, his shout echoing as she soared over the high wide ledge, and he pulsed heavily inside her, finding his own release.

He collapsed on top of her, pushing her quaking body into the mattress.

She could feel him, still huge, still hard inside her, and the vulnerability, the sense of paradise found, then lost, hit her like a brick wall.

What the hell was that?

Alex buried his face against Eleanor's neck and breathed in the erotic scent of her—sleepy, musty, refreshing—his erection still rigid inside her.

He felt washed out, exhausted, turned inside out by a climax so raw it had taken him to another plane of existence.

He shuddered, the dumb thought almost as nuts as the shattering pleasure that had shredded his control.

Lifting onto his elbows, he gazed at her face. She looked away, but not before he'd caught the stunned look in her eyes.

Snap.

He decided it was some consolation that she looked almost as shocked as he felt.

He eased out of her swollen flesh. She winced, making the guilt from that first deep thrust return. She'd been so tight. He was always careful with women. But had he been careful enough?

Rolling off her, he struggled to even his breathing, and get a grip on the renewed yearning. How could the titanic orgasm have barely taken the edge off?

He'd had good sex before. Hard, hot, sweaty, addictive sex before. But never anything this all-consuming.

He was still trying to figure out what the heck to say to her when she scooted towards the far edge of the bed.

With her back to him, she grabbed the sweatshirt off the floor and yanked it on.

Shame washed over him.

'I should go,' she said, her voice trembling as she scooped his boxers off the floor and wriggled into them.

He frowned, still trying to get his brain in gear.

She glanced over her shoulder. 'Goodbye, Mr Costa.'

What the...?

He lurched across the bed to grab her wrist, before she could shoot off.

'Mr...?' he said, unable to keep the cynicism out of his voice. 'Seriously?'

He still had the damn condom on. He was semi-hard, and the soporific afterglow pulsing through his body was making it hard for him to string a coherent sentence together, and she was running out on him? Without even addressing him by his first name?

It was a long time since he'd felt used. But she'd managed it.

She twisted her wrist. 'I should go.'

'Not so fast,' he said, keeping a firm grip on her wrist and swinging his legs off the bed while keeping the sheet over his lap. Because he'd be damned if he'd let her know how much he still wanted her.

He snagged her other wrist and—sitting on the edge of the mattress—tugged her closer, until she was caught between his knees.

She didn't look happy about it, the vivid blush visible even in the half-light.

She struggled. 'Let me go.'

'Chill out, Eleanor,' he said. 'You're not going anywhere until we talk about what just happened.' Even as he said the words though, the incongruousness of the statement occurred to him.

Since when was he the kind of guy who liked to have meaningful conversations after sex? Not ever.

But he couldn't seem to control the urge this time. Because something told him, if he let her run off, he might never see her again. And that would be bad.

'No one calls me Eleanor, my name's Ellie,' she whispered as she continued to struggle against his hold.

'Okay, Ellie.' He held tight.

'Will you let me go?' she said. 'You big—'

'Not until you promise not to run off,' he interrupted her.

She stopped struggling and glared at him. 'Fine, I promise.'

He wasn't sure if he trusted her, but he was forced to release her.

He dug frustrated fingers through his hair. The prickle of shame was something he hadn't felt in a long time… And didn't like one bit.

'Why don't you grab a shower?' he said, knowing he needed to buy time. And chill out before they had this conversation. Because something wasn't right. About this whole set-up. And he didn't like it.

'I can take a shower later—' she began.

'You need your clothes to leave,' he interrupted her.

'Unless you plan to walk out wearing nothing but my shorts.'

The stubborn tilt of her chin became more pronounced. But so did that beguiling blush. That she wanted to leave was obvious. That he wasn't going to let her only made the situation more weird. When was the last time he'd had to persuade a woman to hang around after sex, instead of trying to shoo them out of the door?

'Okay,' she said. 'But then I have to go,' she added. And marched off to the bathroom.

Why are you in such a hurry?

The questions intensified at the sharp snap of the bathroom lock closing.

He waited until he heard the shower before he headed to the bathroom next door. After getting rid of the condom, he texted his housekeeping staff to locate his guest's clothing and leave it outside his bedroom door. Then he had the fastest shower in living memory. After dragging on jeans and a sweater, he returned to his own bedroom, picking up the neat stack of her clothing on the way.

The shower had stopped, but he could hear her moving around in the bathroom.

Ordering the bedroom shades up—so he could get a much better look at her when she reappeared—he lifted the quilt, planning to sit on the bed and wait.

He tensed, spotting rusty stains on the white sheet.

He stared, struggling to process what he was seeing for a moment.

Was she on her period? But even as the innocuous explanation occurred to him, the memory of her—art-

less, sweet, that beguiling recklessness he'd assumed
was all an act, and then how tight, how tense she'd been
when he'd pushed inside her, slammed back.

The trickle of shame became a flood, but right alongside it was that traitorous desire. Intense, unstoppable,
overwhelming. And the devastating feeling of protectiveness that had confused the hell out of him last night.
But far, far worse was the feeling of responsibility. A
trap that he had spent most of his adult life escaping.

And suddenly he knew exactly what had been off…
Way, *way* off.

Right from the start.

When Eleanor MacGregor got out of the bathroom,
she had a lot of explaining to do. Starting with why she
hadn't told him he was her first lover. And what the hell
she expected to gain from that deception.

CHAPTER FOUR

THE SHARP TAP on the bathroom door made Ellie jump, and her heartbeat ram into her throat.

'I've got your stuff. If you want it, you're going to have to open the door before the next millennium.'

Ellie frowned at her reflection in the mirror, the husky voice—edged with impatience—not helping to calm her down. A radioactive blush spread up her neck to highlight the beard burn she'd been inspecting on her cheeks.

'I've not been in here that long,' she shouted back, even though it had been a good half an hour since she'd fled into his bathroom. Unfortunately, even after a long hot power shower, she wasn't feeling any less shaky.

How could her first time have been so spectacular, so overwhelming? And how did she get out of here now without having the 'talk' he'd mentioned? Because she didn't want to talk about it. She felt disconnected from the sense she'd always had of who she was, and what she wanted. As if she'd given this man a glimpse of the woman she could be, but wasn't sure she wanted to be. It was all so confusing. And having to talk to him, when he was the cause of it all, would only make it worse.

The only saving grace now was he hadn't figured out he was her first.

The knock sounded again. Harder this time. 'Are you still in there or did you jump out the window?'

Very funny. She scowled at her reflection. *The guy's a comedian.*

She sighed. Then headed across the marble tiles, wincing as she became aware of the beard burn in another more intimate part of her anatomy.

She opened the door a fraction and stuck out her hand. 'If you could give them to me, please. I'd prefer to get dressed in private,' she said, with as much frigid politeness as she could muster.

'Sure,' the disembodied voice said as her own clothes were dumped into her outstretched palm. 'Breakfast arrived a while ago and it's starting to fossilise,' he added. 'So when you're dressed, meet me in the living area.'

It was an order, not a request.

Holding her clothing to her chest, she slammed the door shut.

She took her time getting dressed, not just to keep him waiting, but because the thong and lacy bra she donned first rubbed against places she had become a lot more aware of in the last hour.

Once she'd eased on her jeans and socks and her T-shirt and hoodie she felt more human again. More herself.

If only she had some foundation to cover the rough patches where he'd kissed her into oblivion. Or a comb to tame her insane hair.

Ten full minutes later, she ventured out of her hideout having run out of delaying tactics.

The bedroom was empty. Her lungs deflated, the relief tempered by disappointment. Which made not a mite of sense.

She found her boots beside the bed and her backpack on the nearby dresser. Stamping on the boots and slinging her pack over her shoulder, she wondered if she might be able to duck out after all. But as she headed towards the stairway he had brought her up the night before a cool voice echoed down the hallway.

'You're going the wrong way, Eleanor.'

She swung round to see his tall frame leaning against the arch leading into the living area.

Busted.

Her heart lurched back into her throat, her face blazing again. She could probably still make a dash for it, but something about the way he was standing there, waiting for her to run, made her determined not to.

When had she become such a coward? And what could he possibly have to say to her that could be more disturbing than what had already happened?

Lifting her chin, she made her way towards him. He turned and entered the room.

When she walked into the double-height living space, the staggering view of Central Park—the crisp autumn sunshine glinting off the skyscrapers in the distance—was nothing compared to the arresting sight of Alex Costa in a cashmere sweater and black jeans picking up a coffeepot from a table with a lavish breakfast laid out on it.

Her stomach rumbled.

He lifted his head, the nonchalant once-over causing goosebumps to riot over her skin. 'How do you take your coffee?'

The off-hand question had giant knots forming in her already jumpy stomach.

How could she have slept with this man when he didn't even know she didn't drink coffee, that she preferred a strong cup of tea?

Her parents would be so ashamed of her. They'd lived such quiet, practical, steady lives. And they'd always wanted her to do the same. They'd kept her sheltered for so long that the wanderlust, the need to escape, had become all but overwhelming. She'd bucked against their strong moral code, believing it was too restrictive, and boring, and set her sights on getting away from Moira and 'finding herself'... And now here she was, living the dream of being young, free and single in New York City only to discover she wasn't nearly as brilliant or brave as she'd thought.

She swallowed down the grief—and embarrassment. 'Milk, two sugars,' she said, deciding she would need the caffeine hit to survive their 'talk'. She'd thrown herself at this man and now she needed to own it.

He poured her a cup and doctored it accordingly. Then, taking his own cup, stood waiting beside the table. 'You'll have to come closer to drink it.'

He sipped his coffee as she crossed the room, watching her over the rim of his cup.

But as she picked up the coffee he murmured, 'Why didn't you tell me you were a virgin?'

She dropped the cup, the clatter of it hitting the table matched by the discordant kick of her heartbeat. 'How...? How did you know?'

'I figured it out,' he said, and she noticed the edge in his tone for the first time.

She wrapped her arms around her waist. Was he mad about it? Why?

'You haven't answered my question,' he said again, his gaze narrowing, the brittle cynicism in his expression only confusing her more.

She hadn't meant to deceive him. She'd been carried away on a tidal wave of sensation. But she could hardly tell him that, because it would give him more power. And he already had enough.

'I didn't think it was important,' she said, which was true. She'd always considered her lack of experience had no bearing on who she was as a person. Because it didn't. If she'd grown up like most teenagers—who got to socialise in big groups—instead of being home-schooled on Moira and knowing so few eligible boys, surely she would have lost her virginity sooner?

'You should have told me you were innocent,' he said, his jaw rigid. 'I wouldn't have touched you.'

Ellie stiffened, the accusatory glare wrong on so many levels she didn't even know where to start.

Temper burned in her chest, going some way to cover the brutal feeling of vulnerability at his cold expression.

'Well, I'm no innocent any more, so there's no need to worry about it,' she snapped, the last of her cool deserting her. What exactly was he suggesting—that she'd somehow connived to have him take her virginity? To what purpose, for goodness' sake? She was the one with beard burn in some unfortunate places now, not him! 'And if you wanted me to stay so you could insult me, you can go to hell.'

She turned, ready to march out of the apartment.

'Oh, no you don't…' He caught her in two strides. 'You tricked me into becoming more involved than I want to, and I want to know why.'

'Tricked…?' She stared at him, so astonished by the accusation and the barely leashed fury behind it, she was speechless.

'Don't sound so surprised,' he scoffed. 'You wanted me to feel responsible for you. And now I do. So job done. Now I want to know what you expect to get out of that.'

'You're no responsible for me,' she hissed, bracing her forearms against his chest, trying to push him away. But it was like pushing against a brick wall. A very stubborn brick wall. 'My virginity is my business, no yours.'

'Not any more it's not,' he said, but then he grasped her chin and lifted her face to his.

But just as she was about to demand he release her, *again*, the colour drained from his face.

He swore, releasing her so suddenly she stumbled backwards.

'That imperfection in your left eye…' he murmured, staring at her as if she'd grown an extra head. 'You're one of *them.*'

'One of what?'

He didn't look annoyed any more, he looked stunned. But why had the patch of brown in her left iris she had been born with triggered that shocked reaction?

'You want me to introduce you to Roman. That's it, isn't it?' He raked his fingers through his hair, furrowing the waves into haphazard rows. 'You thought if you threw yourself at me, got me to take your virginity, you could trick me—and him—into believing his sister is alive.'

'I don't have the first clue what you're talking about,' she sputtered, her outrage and indignation no longer anaesthetising her against the humiliation and, worse, the hurt. Whatever he was accusing her of now, he despised her for it...

'You think you're the first of them to try and go through me? You're not. But I've got to give you credit, you're the first one I ever fell for. The virginity was a stroke of genius.'

Her mind reeled, struggling to make sense of the brittle accusations.

'How much?'

'What?' She stepped away from him. He had gone mad. That much was obvious.

'How much do you want to leave Roman the hell alone?'

She shook her head, the foolish tears stinging her eyes now, and scouring her throat.

He yanked his wallet out of his back pocket, counted out the bills, thrust them towards her.

'I've got five hundred on me.' His gaze skated over her again, scathing this time, and all the more painful for it. 'I can wire you another five grand. You were more than worth it.'

The humiliation engulfed her. She stared at the wad of bills.

'You bastard,' she whispered, then turned and ran. She had to get away from him, before she let a single tear fall.

'Five and a half grand is my final offer.' The cruel shout chased her down the hallway.

She hated him, but she hated herself more. For caring, even for a moment, what he thought.

CHAPTER FIVE

The day before Thanksgiving

'WHY DON'T YOU close up the bar now and clear out, honey?'

Ellie looked up as the afternoon light hit the countertops of Sully's Bar in Staten Island. Her new boss, Bethany Sullivan, the woman who had saved Ellie's big American adventure after its disastrous start nearly a month ago in Alex Costa's penthouse, smiled at her.

'But it's only three o'clock?' Ellie said, lifting the glasses out of the industrial dishwasher under the bar's counter.

'Ellie, it's Thanksgiving tomorrow and I'm driving to Philly tonight to spend the vacation weekend with my grandbabies.'

Ellie had known Bethany was planning to close the neighbourhood bar over the next four days, but she'd hoped to make at least a few tips tonight to keep her solvent this month.

She'd taken the Staten Island ferry on a whim the day she'd run out of Alex Costa's penthouse in tears. The Help Wanted flyer in Sully's window had been a lifesaver. But the knowledge she couldn't return to Manhattan had limited her considerably.

The residual pulse of heat and longing and hurt whenever she thought about that morning returned, humiliating her all over again.

She never wanted to see Alex Costa again, why couldn't her body get the message?

In many ways that morning still felt like a strange, confusing dream. A dream that had become a nightmare so quickly. She still wasn't quite sure how it had happened. But she knew he was to blame for it.

He'd accused her of things she hadn't done. So why couldn't she forget him?

How could she possibly be another of the gold-diggers who had turned up out of the blue ten years ago claiming to be Roman Fraser's sister?

She understood the search for his missing sister had probably been traumatic for Alex's friend. Nobody liked being scammed. Or given false hope. But what did any of that have to do with her?

What she hated most, though, was how much Alex Costa's paranoid accusations had hurt.

'Hey, honey, you got anywhere to go on Thanksgiving?' Bethany asked, breaking into Ellie's pity party.

'No, but I'll be fine.'

Bethany opened her mouth to protest, when the rumble of a plane passing overhead became deafening. 'What the…?' Bethany murmured, then left to investigate.

Following Bethany out of the back entrance to bar, Ellie was almost bowled over by the gust of wind as a huge black helicopter settled in the empty lot at the back of the building.

A door opened and the roar downgraded as the blades slowed. People gathered on the outskirts of the lot, staring at the new arrival.

Was it a rescue helicopter? Ellie didn't think so. The logo on the side—a shining gold C with a T over it—looked vaguely familiar.

'Whoever he is, he sure fills out that suit nicely,' Bethany announced as an impossibly tall man, dressed in a designer business suit perfectly tailored to his muscular physique, walked down the chopper's steps.

As he strode towards them, pushing his wavy hair back as it got whipped up by the helicopter's blades, recognition streaked through Ellie's body like a lightning strike.

Alex Costa.

She lurched back, hitting the bar door with a dull thud.

'You okay, honey?' Bethany's voice seemed to come from a million miles away. 'You look spooked.'

Ellie shook her head, unable to form words as her gaze remained glued to the approaching figure.

You're dreaming, Ellie. Wake up.

But she couldn't seem to move, her limbs felt like they were encased in treacle, the lightning strike reaching her abdomen as the X-rated memories came flooding into her head. Of that big body shooting her to paradise, the cruel humiliation that had followed as he held out a wad of bills and plunged her self-esteem into the toilet. The hole in her chest cracked open. The same gaping hole she'd spent nearly a month attempting to fill back in, with hard work and determination.

Then his head rose and those hazelnut eyes locked on her face.

The helicopter blades finally stopped, but the powerful humming in her ears remained. Bethany was talking but she couldn't hear her. She couldn't even look at her, all her attention focussed on her worst nightmare as he stopped less than a foot away.

Her rampaging heartbeat slowed to a thundering crawl, the punch of her pulse making her light-headed.

'Hello, Eleanor,' he said, the rough murmur of his voice triggering the sizzle of heat she thought she'd killed.

'What are you doing here?' she managed, still not convinced this wasn't all a horrible dream, which she could snap herself out of—if she tried hard enough.

His eyebrows flattened, his gaze intensifying. 'I'm here to say I'm sorry,' he said, the sparkle of admiration turning the rich hazelnut to a shimmering gold. 'For the crummy way I treated you.'

She tensed, desperate to ignore the jolt of surprise and vindication. He actually sounded sincere. But she didn't believe him, any more than she believed he'd piloted a helicopter to the back lot of Sully's Bar to deliver his apology.

Because every bit of what was happening right now was completely nuts.

The telltale warmth spread into her cheeks regardless.

'And to invite you to my place in the Adirondacks for Thanksgiving weekend,' he added, the note of arrogance finally breaking the spell he seemed to have cast on her with his arrival.

'Uh-huh. Well, how about you shove your apology in a place where the sun doesn't shine?' she said, glad when her voice barely wavered. And pathetically grateful for the fury that had helped to cover up the gaping hole he'd shot through her self-esteem. 'And you can shove your invitation up there too,' she added, spurred on by his visible wince. 'I wouldn't spend Thanksgiving with you if you were a freshly baked pecan pie with whipped cream and a cherry on top.'

His mouth quirked into the seductive half-smile she recognised. And the traitorous jolt of heat streaked back through her system.

'Whipped cream?' he murmured. 'How about I let you lick it off my chest? Would that persuade you?'

'Oh, shut up. You big jerk!' she shouted, then stalked back into the bar—so mad she was surprised she hadn't exploded, annoyed even more by the jolt of heat that had bottomed out in her abdomen.

She hated him. And she did not want to see his naked chest again, not even if it were covered in whipped cream.

Not ever.

She really is glorious when she's mad, Alex acknowledged as the dull ache settled below his belt. An ache he'd thought he'd got used to in the last three weeks.

Not even close, buddy. His gaze roamed over Eleanor's retreating figure before the door slammed shut behind it.

The ache throbbed as he also acknowledged he would

much rather see the mad in her eyes than the sad, confused, hurt look he'd put there three weeks ago.

He didn't blame her one bit for still being mad about the things he'd said and done.

He'd overreacted, treated her like dirt and then insulted her.

And if that weren't bad enough, he'd spent over a week sulking, convinced his dumb behaviour had been perfectly rational and she would come crawling back to accept his money. Then another week determined to forget her.

But he hadn't been able to forget her. And as well as the dull ache that had woken him up every morning far too ready for her, the shame had crept in too as he'd re-examined all the evidence… And finally figured out he was the one in the wrong.

Dead wrong.

At first, he'd tried to blame his crummy behaviour on loyalty to his buddy Roman. But the truth was protecting Roman from another woman claiming to be the sister who'd died long ago had not one thing to do with why he'd flown off the handle with Eleanor MacGregor and been a total jerk. And everything to do with the mind-blowing effect she'd had on him that morning.

She'd thrown him out of whack. A guy who was always smooth and in control with women. Because he'd lost his precious control with her. And so he'd turned on her.

But the ache hadn't died. His fascination with Eleanor MacGregor was all about the sex. He got that.

He'd never had that kind of instant, incendiary connection with anyone before, or a woman who responded to him with such artless enthusiasm. And she'd been a virgin. That had blown his mind too.

The chemistry wouldn't last, but indulging it over the Thanksgiving weekend would kill two birds with one stone—it would rewrite what had happened a month ago, and help him get through a vacation weekend he'd always found a tedious chore, because, unlike the rest of the country, he had no desire to spend it with his family.

So as soon as he'd got an address from the investigator he'd hired, he'd had the company helicopter fuelled and headed out to Staten Island en route to his place in the Adirondacks.

But he clearly had more grovelling to do first. A lot more grovelling.

Fair enough. It served him right for being such a contemptable ass the morning after Halloween.

'You're Alex Costa, aren't you?' The older woman who had been standing with Ellie sent him a curious look. 'I saw your picture in that list of hot eligible bachelors,' she added, and he bit back a groan. 'You and your pal Roman Fraser were vying for the top spot again this year.'

'He won,' he snapped.

He hated that damn list. It made him feel like a piece of prime rib.

Plus, he wasn't an eligible bachelor. He came from a long line of men who had failed at marriage. Dating was great, good sex even better, but commitment? No way. Because unlike his old man, he had no intention of faking it.

The fact his pal Roman had beaten him out to the top spot this year only added to the burn. Because even though he didn't give a damn about that dumb list, he hated to be second place, at anything.

'And you are?' he asked, deliberately changing the subject. Maybe he could enlist her help in his campaign to make amends with Eleanor… And get her to upstate New York for Thanksgiving.

'Bethany Sullivan, Ellie's boss. I own the lot you just landed on.'

'How much do you want—?' he began.

'Save it, buster. I'm not interested in your money.' She looked insulted—he seemed to have that effect on women in Staten Island today. 'Seeing you land on my lot is the most excitement I've had since my Eddie died.'

The comment had him choking out a rough chuckle, his first in a long time. 'Good to know.' He decided he liked Bethany Sullivan. She was a straight talker.

Her eyes narrowed, her expression becoming shrewd. 'So how do you know our Ellie?'

'It's a long story,' he said, and one he did not plan to repeat, because he wasn't exactly the hero. More like the big bad billionaire who'd stolen Ellie's innocence and then treated her like a hooker.

'I wish I had the time to hear it,' Bethany said, the shrewd look becoming razor sharp. 'But I've got to get to Philly before the vacation traffic hits I-95.'

'Are you closing the bar for the whole of Thanksgiving?' he asked.

She nodded. 'Sure am.'

So Eleanor was at a loose end? Surely chilling out with him at his place on Gold Lake had to be a better prospect than hanging out alone in Staten Island?

Especially as he'd seen the desire she couldn't hide in her eyes.

'Ellie deserves a break,' Bethany supplied, because as well as being a straight talker, Eleanor's boss also appeared to be a mind reader. 'She's been working her butt off doing double shifts most days ever since I hired her on November first.'

Alex frowned, the guilt making his chest feel tight—if he'd taken two seconds to think three weeks ago he would have figured out Eleanor was the opposite of a freeloader.

'I'm planning to change that,' he said, more determined than ever now to whisk Eleanor away for the weekend.

Not only did he want her—but he owed her. She deserved to be properly seduced. He'd initiated her into sex with not a lot of his usual finesse. He could do better. A lot better. And show her how good their rare sexual chemistry could be. The fact he would also enjoy it—and her fascinating company—was an added fringe benefit.

'Yeah, I heard your invitation,' she said. 'That's why I'm going to let you try to change Ellie's mind without an audience.'

'Thanks,' he said, but as he went to charge past her Bethany blocked his path.

'Not so fast, fella,' she said, her tone steely sharp. 'I want your word if she says yes, you'll treat her right.'

Alex had given his word before and broken it. He was a ruthless goal-oriented over-achiever who had no qualms about doing whatever was necessary to get what he wanted. But something about Bethany's fierce expression reminded him of the girl inside the bar. The girl he'd hurt three weeks ago without realising he could. And so when he gave Bethany his word, he made a silent vow to keep it this time—and give Eleanor MacGregor a Thanksgiving weekend she would never forgot… If she'd let him.

CHAPTER SIX

ELLIE HEARD THE back door close as she finished wiping down the bar. Or rather scrubbing it so hard she was surprised she hadn't scraped off the veneer.

Of all the arrogant...

She straightened. She hadn't heard Alex Costa's helicopter take off, and until it did she would be on edge. But once he was out of her life again, she'd be okay. Thank goodness she'd stood up to him this time. It would give her closure. Eventually.

'I won't be long, Beth,' she said, when her boss didn't say anything. 'If you want to get away, I can—'

'It's not Beth,' the husky voice cut her off. 'She's heading to Philly.'

Ellie swung round. *'You?'* she exclaimed, the fury roaring back to life.

He stood not two feet away, his backside propped against the counter, his hands sunk into his pockets. Relaxed, in control, as if he owned the place.

She threw down the cloth. 'I'm not interested in you or your—'

'Woah, Eleanor, I get it.' He tugged his hands out of his pockets and lifted his palms. 'You're mad and you have every right to be. I behaved like a total jerk. But would you give me a chance to explain?'

She didn't want to give him a chance to explain, because something about his presence in the bar was giving her goosebumps, and making the heat twist and swell in her abdomen. But the arrogance she remembered had disappeared, his expression convincingly contrite. Or as convincingly contrite as it was possible for a ridiculously hot, six-foot-four-inch billionaire to look.

She picked the cloth up to concentrate on scrubbing off the veneer again, determined to ignore the goosebumps. 'Fine, but you'll have to talk while I finish up,' she said, wearily. Temper always took it out of her and she'd been working double shifts all week.

But as she bent over the counter, he reached around her, his chest flush against her back for a moment—which gave her a disturbing lungful of his delicious scent, bergamot cologne and citrus soap. Before she had a chance to protest though, he'd taken the cloth from her and stepped back.

'How about you let me finish up, while you sit down, relax and listen to what I have to say?'

She scowled, not liking the pushy attitude, or the heat making her goosebumps prickle, but short of wrestling the cloth off him she didn't have much of a choice. 'Are you sure you know how?' she asked, not attempting to hide her disdain.

'Yeah,' he replied as he shrugged off his jacket. 'Bar work got me through MIT.'

'You went to MIT? I can't see you as a tech nerd,' she said.

'That's because you haven't seen me in my spectacles.' He sent her a wry grin as he rolled up the sleeves of his expensive shirt to reveal powerful hair-dusted forearms.

'You wear glasses?' she said, trying hard not to imagine how sexy he would look.

'Only when I'm trying to prove to women how hot tech nerds are,' he shot back.

She choked down the unbidden laugh. And frowned. He was turning on the charm. But the hurt was still real.

She propped herself on a bar stool as he got to work, and forced herself to look away from the sight of his strong shoulders flexing under the tailored shirt.

As he wiped down each of the bar's tables in fast economical strokes, she waited, refusing to prompt him, and determined not to give him an inch. He'd hurt her, more than she would ever let him know. But *she* knew.

He began to lift the chairs, swinging them upside down to stack on the tables before he finally broke the weighty silence.

'When I spotted the segmental heterochromia in your eye, it brought back bad memories that had nothing to do with you,' he said slowly, referring to the harmless genetic mutation he'd noticed that morning in his apartment. 'Ten or so years ago, a lot of people came forward with their eleven-year-old daughters, claiming they could be Roman's kid sister. But only one of them had the same mutation. It was one of the things he remembered about his kid sister because he has the same mutation.' He paused to stretch his back before continuing to stack the chairs, his voice heavy with a mix of controlled anger and sadness. 'He was convinced this kid was Eloise—didn't even want to do a DNA test he was so damn sure, and so overjoyed. I think Roman's always carried a ton of guilt about how she disappeared. He figured he should have saved her, stopped her from disappearing somehow. It killed him he couldn't even remember what had happened because he'd been going in and out of consciousness.'

'But that's preposterous,' Ellie remarked, absorbed in the story, her anger with Alex dying at the tense look on his face. It seemed Roman wasn't the only one who felt guilty the search for his sister had been a dead end. 'He was only ten years old, wasn't he?'

He stopped stacking the chairs and stared at her. 'So you *do* know the details?'

Her temper spiked at the slight edge in his tone. 'Yes, I do. I looked up all the details on the Internet after you made me feel like dirt.'

'Right,' he said, and the suspicious look died.

Ellie relaxed into the seat, glad they'd finally got that straight. She knew how cynical Alex Costa was—but maybe it wasn't that surprising. Alex and Roman had been best friends since their school days. It must have been hard watching his friend go through that.

Alex shrugged as he continued flipping and stacking the chairs with practised ease. 'At that point we didn't know the information about Eloise's eye-colour mutation was being touted on the web. One of the detectives Roman hired leaked it.' He let out a heavy breath. 'Turned out the girl's mom had a contact lens made, got her kid to wear it. I made Roman get a DNA test. When the results came back, he was devastated. But the way I see it he had a lucky escape.' He scrubbed his hands down his face. 'It caused kind of a rift between us for a while—because I finally agreed with everyone else that his kid sister must have died that night. He went off the rails, drinking and partying even harder. Took a while to get him over that hump.'

He finished stacking the chairs and turned towards her.

'I guess it brought the whole sorry episode back, seeing the mutation in your iris. You're about the age she would be, and Scottish. Plus I was already feeling bad about taking your virginity. So I put two and two together and got five hundred. I really am sorry. Do you believe me?'

'Yes.' Her throat closed.

She didn't doubt his sincerity. But she had no real clue what to do with his apology. Or the uncomfortable tightness in her chest at the mention of her virginity. *Again.* Why had that freaked him out so much?

He headed towards the bar. 'You got a mop? So I can swab the floor?'

'Seriously?' A laugh burst out of her mouth, breaking the tension in the room—the pragmatic offer from someone of his power and influence and wealth completely incongruous.

'Yeah, seriously,' he said, the twinkle in his dark eyes making her heartbeat accelerate.

Oh, no, you don't, Ellie. Don't you dare fall for that industrial-strength charm again.

She jumped off her stool, and headed for the utility cupboard, needing something to do.

'I appreciate you coming here, and apologising,' she threw over her shoulder, hoping he would take the hint.

'And I understand now why you freaked out.' Maybe not about the virginity thing, but she certainly wasn't about to mention *that* again. 'But I've got this now.'

Grabbing the bucket, she sprinkled in soap power then turned on the hot tap.

But then his big body was enveloping hers again, his hard chest warm against her back, as he leant past her to switch the tap off and lifted the heavy bucket out of her hands. She took in another tantalising lungful of that delicious scent.

She reached for the bucket. 'Really, I'm good, you should go.'

He hoisted the bucket out of her reach. 'I've got this, Eleanor.'

She shivered, the way her given name—the name no one called her but him—rumbled off his tongue somehow unbearably erotic.

She tried to forget the other skilful things his tongue had done to her before her goosebumps got goosebumps.

'How the hell else am I going to buy enough of your time to talk you into a Thanksgiving booty call?' he added.

Another laugh bubbled out. She slapped her hand over her mouth, but it was already too late, his eyes had taken on that predatory gleam that proved he could see right through her resistance—and was going to enjoy changing her mind.

'You're absolutely incorrigible,' she said, wanting to sound stern, and getting breathless instead, when his gaze slid over her features with a singular purpose that made her heartbeat accelerate and her skin burn... *Everywhere.*

'I've been told it's one of my best features,' he said, that devastating smile warming her from the inside out.

He leaned past her to grab the mop from the corner of the cupboard, but as he pulled back she made the mistake of looking up, and found herself trapped in that piercing hazelnut gaze—rich with appreciation.

The moment seemed suspended in time, heavy with possibilities.

His mouth descended slowly, giving her time to refuse, then slanted across hers. Her breath gushed out, the bold kiss making need spear through her body and ignite the devastating heat all over again.

He drew away moments later, but even so she felt dazed when he winked at her. 'Hold that thought,' he said, then marched out of the cupboard leaving her breathless and shaky and stupidly aroused.

Blast the man.

As she watched him mop the floor for her, she could feel all her perfectly valid objections to spending Thanksgiving weekend with him fade with each erratic heartbeat.

After he'd rinsed out the bucket and put away the mop, he levelled the intense gaze back at her as he rolled his sleeves down, re-buttoned the cuffs and grabbed his jacket.

'Okay, Eleanor,' he said. 'It's make-your-mind-up time. Are you coming with me to my house in the Adirondacks for a do-over Thanksgiving booty call, or are you staying in Staten Island to die of boredom?'

She stared at him, the heat pulsing at her core, but much more disturbing was the tug of yearning in her chest. Because it felt like the same longing that had dogged her throughout her childhood and adolescence on Moira. The longing for adventure, but also the need to belong…

Maybe she could have resisted Alex Costa's arrogant charm, his breathtaking sex appeal, his gorgeous physique and the uber-sexy take-charge confidence. She might even have been able to resist the thought of spending the weekend in his luxury lake house and all the exciting things she could already imagine him doing to her needy, far too inexperienced body… But one thing she couldn't resist was the glimpse of the man she'd seen when he'd spoken of his friend, of protecting him and standing by him. Or the sight of that broad strong body wearing two-thousand-dollar shoes, designer suit trousers and a deluxe shirt that had probably also cost a small fortune, now all liberally splattered with dirty water.

Who knew that watching Alex Costa do barroom chores would be her downfall?

She tried to lock down the stupid pulse of emotion in her chest…

She didn't have a connection with Alex Costa, other than a surprisingly intense sexual one. And she didn't belong in his rarefied world any more than he belonged in hers—despite his surprising willingness to do her chores for her. But what would be so wrong about exploring the connection they did have, for one adventurous weekend?

'I hope I don't regret this,' she said at last. 'But the answer's yes.'

He laughed. Then grasped her round the waist and tugged her flush against his body. The kiss was deep, and illicit and unashamedly possessive this time. Before he was forced to rip his mouth away so they could both come up for air. 'I intend to make sure you regret it in the best possible way,' he said, the devilish grin and the boyish twinkle in his hazelnut eyes hopelessly compelling.

Her heart bobbed into her throat as he grasped her hand and dragged her out of the bar. The helicopter still stood in the lot—the pilot fending off the crowd of onlookers.

'Wait a minute, shouldn't I pack something to wear?' she asked as she tried to control the rush of exhilaration.

Am I actually spending Thanksgiving weekend with one of the hottest bachelors in Manhattan?

'Nah,' he said, tightening his grip as he led her aboard the big black bird. 'I intend to keep you naked the whole weekend.'

CHAPTER SEVEN

The day after Thanksgiving

'HEY, COME BACK HERE. It's the middle of the night...' Alex lurched across the bed to catch his Thanksgiving booty call before she scooted away and ruined all the plans he had for that delectable little body.

They'd spent most of Thanksgiving Day in bed, getting reacquainted with the spectacular chemistry that had got him chasing her all the way to a neighbourhood bar in Staten Island two days ago.

He hadn't regretted the decision one moment since.

Even so, the need still pulsed in his groin as she evaded him and ripped open the drapes on the master bedroom's picture window.

He swore and threw his arm over his eyes, the light gleaming off the new layer of pure white snow enough to blind him.

'It's not the middle of the night, it's nearly noon. And I'm famished,' Eleanor declared.

He lowered his arm as she strutted to the pile of clothes by the open fire, which had burned out during the night. Her slender body, and beautiful breasts gilded by the morning light made his chest ache as well as his groin.

Damn.

He sat up, loving the sight of her—all flushed and indignant, her skin glowing from too much sex. Her wild hair—which he'd washed yesterday in the rainfall shower during one of their brief interludes out of bed—haloed around her head in an untamed cloud of chestnut curls and made her stubborn frown and the sprinkle of freckles across her nose all the more adorable.

'Hey, I fed you yesterday,' he said, with mock outrage, his good humour returning. So what if she'd evaded him? It wouldn't take much to lure her back into bed.

His little Scottish spitfire had turned out to be as insatiable as he was. Throwing herself into everything this long weekend had to offer with a vigour that was nothing short of exhilarating.

'What more do you want?' he added, enjoying her *tsk* of disapproval.

He'd rustled up steak and eggs at some point yesterday to keep up their stamina, and let her roast marshmallows over the firepit, introducing her to the glory of s'mores, so she didn't go stir crazy.

'Well, I need feeding again,' she said, tugging on a pair of his shorts and making his indignation real. As cute as she looked in his shorts, he preferred her out of them.

'And what happened to the turkey dinner I was promised?' she added as she hooked her bra round her waist then conspired to wiggle into it without giving him a flash of the gorgeous breasts he was becoming obsessed with—especially her supremely sensitive nipples. *The spoilsport.*

He adjusted himself, the heat rushing into his groin to tent the quilt.

'I never promised you a turkey supper,' he said. He'd given the five-person staff the weekend off before they'd arrived. He wanted the place to himself, so he and Eleanor could christen every room without fear of interruption. Even in a property with six en-suite bedrooms, a state-of-the art kitchen, a billiard room, a library and a boathouse they were still on target to get it done before they had to head back to civilisation on Sunday night. Cooking anything fancy seemed like a waste of time that could be better spent finding out if he could make her come simply by worshipping her nipples—his latest goal.

'And anyhow, Thanksgiving was yesterday,' he added. 'We missed it.'

She propped her fists on her hips and sent him the indignant glare he'd become addicted to as well.

'That does not mean we can't celebrate it today. I can cook the turkey in the fridge for tonight. And you can make pancakes for breakfast.'

'Oh, can I, now?' He arched an eyebrow, not sure why he found her ballsy attitude as enjoyable as her responsive nipples. But he did. 'And who made you the boss of me?' he said, glad when she choked out a laugh. They'd come a long way from that first night when she'd found his arrogance so aggravating.

'As if!' she said, the appreciative once-over making the heat in his groin pulse.

He had never allowed any woman to make domestic demands on him before, but her pragmatism made it seem like no big deal. Which was good. Because it had occurred to him late last night—her sleepy body snuggled against him, the afterglow making his eyelids droop and the firelight shimmering off her hair— he might have given her the wrong impression about where this was all leading by arriving in a chopper to whisk her away for the weekend.

But she'd made no mention of anything past Sunday. Nor had she asked him any probing personal questions. The conversation had been determinedly light and shallow. Just the way he liked it.

She rummaged in his antique dresser and pulled out one of his shirts, a cashmere sweater and a pair of socks. 'If I'm to cook dinner, I think it's only fair you cook breakfast.'

Damn, she had him there.

'And as you didn't let me bring any clothes, I'm wearing yours,' she announced. 'I want to go exploring.'

'What for? It'll be freezing outside,' he said, but the stubborn tilt of her chin made him chuckle. 'Once we've eaten, I say we go back to bed,' he added, enjoying goading her. Another first.

'You would,' she said, the stern expression somewhat belied by the arousal darkening her gaze as it glided over his naked chest. 'You're completely insatiable.'

'I didn't hear you complaining last night when you were begging me to suck your...'

'Stop,' she said, the fiery blush highlighting her freckles and making the tentpole in his lap hit ninety degrees. What was it about that combination of innocence and awareness that made her so damn adorable?

Initiating her into the joys of sex had been the most erotic experience of his entire life. Go figure?

'No way am I letting you give me another orgasm,' she declared, 'until I've been properly fed and you've given me a tour of this magnificent estate in the snow.'

'We'll see about that,' he said, throwing back the quilt to reveal the erection and then leaping out of the bed naked.

She shrieked and shot out of the room, and into the bathroom. He was laughing so hard, he failed to catch her.

But as he heard the lock click, he smiled. Good thing he was a goal-orientated guy… And he'd discovered all her most easily exploited erogenous zones in the last twenty-four hours. Because it meant her chances of making good on her threat were zero.

He'd feed her, and let her cook him a turkey supper later, but no way did they have time for her to see the whole estate. It was five hundred acres and he had much better—and warmer—things for them to be doing. Plus they still had a ton of rooms to christen and they were running out of time.

But as he pulled on some sweatpants—leaving his chest bare because he knew it was his secret weapon— then padded into the open-plan kitchen to rustle up some pancake batter, it occurred to him he had never smiled this much on Thanksgiving, especially since his father's death.

He watched the snow fall in desultory flakes covering the forest and the boathouse by the lake in a blanket of white. Perhaps he should consider keeping Eleanor MacGregor around for longer than three days? Because

Christmas was one of his least favourite seasons too—thanks to all the bitter memories from his childhood. And Eleanor was turning out to be one hell of a distraction.

'I see beech and fir and pine and that must be aspen over there. You have so many different species here.' Eleanor's breath purred around her pink cheeks in white puffs as she gazed at the forest surrounding the lake as if she'd discovered the rarest treasure.

'They're all just trees to me.' Alex caught her round the waist, captivated all over again by her enthusiasm. Then yanked her back into his arms so he could sink his face into her hair and take in a lungful of her scent—summer flowers and his own citrus-scented shampoo. 'Who knew you were a tree nut?'

'I'm not.' She laughed, the bubbly sound so beguiling it dialled down his frustration that he hadn't managed to coax her back into bed—again—while their turkey supper cooked. 'It's just there are so few trees on Moira, I appreciate a good forest.'

'Moira? Is that where you're from?' he asked, surprised by his curiosity about her. He didn't usually interrogate the women he dated because it encouraged intimacy. But there was something about Eleanor that fascinated him. She dived into every new experience with an energy that was as reckless as it was captivating, and he couldn't help wondering where it came from.

'Yes, it's a remote island in the Outer Hebrides off Scotland's west coast. My parents were crofters—tenant farmers—they moved there not long after I was born. I was their only child so they were very protective of me,' she said absently, settling into his arms with a contented sigh. 'Oh, is that an eagle?' she asked, pointing towards a bird of prey skimming the surface of the lake.

'Probably,' he said, because being a city kid he could just about distinguish a hawk from an emu. 'How long did you live on Moira?' he asked, intrigued now despite himself. It sounded like a secluded, sheltered childhood, very different from his own.

'All my life, until about a month ago,' she said absently. 'It took me two years working in the only pub we have there to earn enough to get my flights and a temporary work visa to come here. Crofters are rubbish tippers.'

'Wait a minute.' He frowned, swinging her around to face him. He forced himself not to get distracted by the delicious flush on her cheeks, or the slender curves disguised by the heavy jacket she'd borrowed. 'You came straight to New York from the middle of nowhere in Scotland?'

She nodded. 'Yes, I hitchhiked down to Glasgow then caught the first plane to New York.'

His frown deepened, as did the strange tug in his abdomen. Was that astonishment, or guilt?

She'd come to America, alone and innocent with no experience whatsoever about life in a big city, let alone a heaving metropolis like New York, and thrown herself into the experience with about as much caution as an NFL line-backer. And then he'd pounced on her. Taken her virginity and treated her like a whore. But she'd fought back.

Somehow the realisation only made her seem braver, and bolder, and made him feel like more of a bastard.

'You hitchhiked?' he said, trying not to freak out as that damn white-knight complex squeezed his ribs again.

'Yes, it was perfectly safe. People in the Highlands look after each other,' she said with a naiveté that would be cute, if it weren't so damn scary.

'Yeah, I'm sure they do, unless they're serial killers.'

She grinned, the sparkle in her eyes making him notice again the imperfection she shared with Roman.

'Luckily I didn't catch a lift with any of those,' she said with a jaunty disregard for her own safety.

'Luckily...' he growled, not sure whether to be horrified or beguiled by her cock-eyed optimism and her faith in human nature. For all her recklessness, and her newfound enthusiasm in discovering the joys of sex, Ellie MacGregor was about as worldly-wise as Bambi. He placed his hands on her neck, stroked the vibrant pulse there and wanted to strangle her, for taking her life into her hands. 'Eleanor, you could have been raped and murdered.'

'It's nice of you to worry,' she said. 'But you mustn't. I'm perfectly capable of taking care of myself. And I don't need any more overprotective people in my life,' she finished, but he spotted the sheen of sadness in her eyes before she swung back around. He wondered who she was talking about. Surely it had to be her parents, who had kept her on that island for the whole of her life.

'Point taken,' he murmured, stifling the renewed surge of concern.

She was right. She was an adult... Something he'd become intimately aware of in the last thirty-six hours.

Plus she wasn't his responsibility. And he didn't want her to be.

But even so he couldn't help asking. 'Exactly how old are you? When's your birthday?'

'June.' She chuckled. 'Why, are you planning to throw me a party?'

He laughed too, because they both knew this fling would be over by the summer, but the sound came out raw and forced.

'No, it's just…' There was something pushing at the back of his mind. Something that didn't make any sense, but he couldn't seem to let go of it. 'You said your parents moved to Moira when you were a baby. Do you know where and when you were born? Exactly?'

She glanced over her shoulder at him, the curious smile making him feel kind of dumb. 'Aye, of course I do. It was a home birth on June twentieth. They were living in a remote area of the Highlands on Scotland's northern tip, my father was working as a forester in Drummorag National Forest. Why so interested?'

It was dumb and he knew it. No way was she Eloise Fraser. She couldn't be, because he was already convinced Roman's kid sister had died in the Highlands over twenty years ago. No baby could have survived that weather for any length of time, and no one could have taken the kid without leaving a trace behind them…

But he couldn't seem to shake the weird feeling that Eleanor was the same age as Eloise, with that same damn heterochromia that Roman remembered his baby sister having… And if no one had witnessed her birth but her parents… It wasn't completely outside the realms of possibility. And he needed it to be.

Because surely this was where the niggle of guilt was coming from.

The nasty possibility, however insane, that he might be sleeping with his best pal's long-lost sister, rather than the even more insane thought that a white-knight complex he had destroyed years ago had suddenly come back to bite him on the butt…

He sucked in a breath, ran his thumb down her cold cheek and murmured, 'How would you feel about taking a DNA test?'

'A DNA test…' Ellie smiled. Surely he had to be joking, but, for the first time since they'd arrived in the Adirondacks, he looked deadly serious.

In the last few days, she'd barely had a chance to breathe, she'd been so overwhelmed by Alex Costa's energy and purpose and the discovery of a playful, provocative side that had driven her insane with lust.

The man was a sex machine. But it turned out so was she. Who knew? And wasn't it glorious to discover that as well as the adrenaline rush of great sex, she felt absolutely no guilt about indulging it. Because Alex was so adept at convincing her their chemistry deserved to be indulged at every available opportunity.

Why should she worry about later? When this adventure was the best she'd ever had. She'd certainly made up for the celibacy of her teenage years in the last thirty-six hours. Big time.

She knew it wouldn't last. In fact, she didn't need it to last. As well as being a sex god, Alex Costa was also the most guarded man she'd ever met. He was completely unavailable, emotionally. Which meant she'd have to be a fool to fall for him. And one thing she'd never been was a fool.

He'd made it clear, with everything he hadn't said, that hot nights and hot lazy days were all he had to offer, for a limited time only. So she had decided to grab it with both hands before she had to let it go.

But let it go she would. Because this adventure wasn't a part of her real life, any more than Alex Costa's insanely beautiful lakeside retreat.

She wasn't sure what she'd expected to find when she'd boarded his helicopter in Staten Island. Probably something glaringly modern and expertly designed like his penthouse apartment. But this log 'cabin'—elegantly built during the 'Great Camp' era of the eighteen-nineties for a railroad baron and his family as they pretended to 'rough it' in the lap of luxury—was the exact opposite of that style-conscious statement property on Central Park West.

Constructed from wood cut from the local National Forest and firestone mined in nearby quarries—the interior designed to complement a bygone era with hand-crafted rugs and quilts and lovingly restored walnut and beechwood furniture—the cabin with its six bedrooms, three sitting rooms, vaulted living room with open fireplaces and a Shaker-style kitchen the size of a football field, was more like a mansion. The perfectly appointed lakeside setting, complete with jetty and boathouse, had taken her breath away that first morning, when she'd woken up after a night of no-holds-barred debauchery to see the snowflakes tumbling down while Alex's rampant erection perked up against her backside.

Really the whole experience so far had been nothing short of a sensory overload.

But it felt as if something fundamental had changed in the last few minutes. The disapproving frown on his face when she'd told him about hitchhiking to Glasgow almost as disturbing as the preposterous request.

'Why on earth would I take a DNA test?' she said, although she had a sneaky suspicion she knew why. She stepped out of his arms, upset. And not wanting to be. 'I told you, Alex. I'm not Eloise, nor am I pretending to be. I hope you're no still…'

'Hey, I know you're not.' He cupped her cheek, his gaze darkening with something that looked disturbingly like regret. 'It's just there's enough about your background that doesn't add up to make me want to be sure.'

'What about my background doesn't add up?' she asked. Was he really that cynical? To believe her perfectly normal upbringing was somehow suspicious?

'You're the age she would be, and you have the same genetic abnormality that Roman—'

'Which is not *that* uncommon,' she interrupted him. Wondering if he realised this whole conversation said so much more about him than her.

'Yeah, I know… But your eyes are a similar shade to his, too. It's almost certainly just a coincidence but… There's also the fact your parents were the only people to witness your birth.'

'For goodness' sake, Alex. That's mad. There was probably a midwife there, they just never talked much about my birth to me. But what's more, you're missing the obvious here…'

'Which is?' he asked, clearly not getting it.

She puffed out a breath that pearled in the frozen air. 'For me to be Eloise, my parents would have had to steal me. And then have lied to me about it my whole life.'

'Yeah, so what—how can you be certain they didn't?' he said. He was playing devil's advocate, she got that. He couldn't really believe she was Roman Fraser's sister.

But still she felt desperately sorry for him, the brittle scepticism making her wonder how anyone could be so cynical, so disillusioned to believe a parent would lie with such impunity to their own child.

'Because they wouldn't do that, they loved me,' she said simply.

He blinked, momentarily confused, and then the seductive smile that had prompted her into bed too many times to count twitched on his lips. But this time there was superiority in it. As if she'd said something impossibly naïve, which he found adorable.

'Okay,' he said slowly, humouring her. 'That's cool, and you're probably right, but where's the harm in doing the DNA test?'

Because then it would seem as if I didn't trust them.

She cut off the thought. Why was she making a big deal about this? Ross and Susan MacGregor were dead. They would never know.

She shrugged. 'Okay. But I still think it's bonkers.'

He laughed, then gripped her round the waist to lift her off her feet.

She grasped his shoulders, a muffled laugh popping out when he spun her around in the frosty air. Then let her body sink down against his. He gripped her cheeks and captured her lips.

Heat speared through her torso, the hot brick pulsing between her thighs, as his hands cupped her backside under the heavy jacket and he pressed the hard ridge in his pants against the place where she ached for him. Always.

By the time he released her they were both panting, and the need had become razor sharp.

How did he do that?

Grasping her hand, he headed back towards the log mansion, the winter sunset throwing red and gold glimmers across the afternoon sky above the snow-laden trees and shimmering off the glassy surface of the lake.

'Come on,' he said. 'We've got time for a quickie before the turkey's done.'

She laughed and scrambled to keep up with him, pushing the wariness down. This was a sex obsession, nothing more.

Alex Costa could never be the man for her in the long term… But in the short term, he was irresistible.

CHAPTER EIGHT

ALEX DRAGGED OFF his headset as the company heli-
coptor settled onto the disused lot behind Sully's Bar.

Eleanor sat across from him, her gaze fixed on the
bar as her boss appeared and waved. She waved back
before Bethany retreated back into the bar.

The noise from the engine faded and she sent Alex
a sweet smile that didn't reach her eyes. And finally he
knew, he couldn't wait any longer.

He wanted her to come to Manhattan with him. He'd
waited to see if the need would die—because he'd never invited any woman to live with him before now. But it hadn't.

The co-pilot appeared to open the door.

'Thank you, Alex, for a wonderful weekend,' Eleanor
said, the fake smile still in place. 'I'll remember it always.'

He frowned. *Really?* She was planning to just walk
away now?

He'd expected her to ask if they would see each other
again. Giving him the opening to tell her to pack a
bag and come with him, so they could enjoy Christmas—his schedule allowing—the way they'd enjoyed
Thanksgiving.

He had to get back to work, but he wanted her waiting for him in the evenings. He'd planned to give her a credit card and put a car and driver at her disposal. She was independent and resourceful and the shopping and sightseeing opportunities alone should keep her from getting bored while he was at work.

But she hadn't said a word about wanting more from him all weekend—unlike all the other women he'd ever dated.

He would have appreciated the irony—that the 'where do we go from here?' conversation he hated had failed to materialise the one time he wanted it to—if he weren't facing the bigger irony of having to bring it up himself.

But as she headed down the helicopter's steps he realised he was all out of alternative options.

Undoing his own belt, he headed after her.

She'd made it across the lot and almost to her boss, before he could catch her. What the hell? She was practically sprinting away from him.

'Hold up, Eleanor.' He caught her elbow.

Just like before, a crowd had gathered. He ignored them. Having an audience was the least of his worries, it seemed, when he spotted the blank look in her eyes.

'That's it? That's all you've got to say?' he asked, then wanted to kick himself.

It almost sounded needy. He didn't do needy. He didn't *need* Eleanor MacGregor in his life, he *wanted* her, until this constant hunger had died. Big difference.

'What more is there to say?' she said, still looking at him with that wide-eyed innocence. He wasn't buying it. She'd had as much fun as he had. 'I have to go back to work now…to my real life,' she said. 'And so do you.'

'What about the DNA test we agreed on?' he asked, inspired. He wasn't about to beg any woman to move in with him. But she'd said she would do the test. And it was a good Trojan Horse to coax her to Manhattan.

She tugged her arm free. 'You're no really serious about that, are you?'

'Deadly.'

She sighed, looking harassed. 'Okay, I guess I could post you a sample, if you really want one.'

'That's not gonna work for me.'

Her brow creased, her expression becoming confused. 'I don't under—'

'I want you to move in with me,' he said, suddenly through with beating about the bush. 'Until after Christmas.'

The frown lifted to be replaced with complete astonishment.

'It'll take a couple of weeks to get the results from the lab at this time of year.' Not true but he could drag it out and make the timing work for him. 'And then it'll be Christmas. I figured we're not through with this... This...' He shrugged. How did he describe the driving need still pulsing through his system, making him ache constantly? The need that hadn't been sated by seventy-two hours of non-stop indulgence. 'Whatever *this* is. But another four weeks should get it out of our systems. And we can have more fun while we're doing it. Manhattan's at its best this time of year. I can show you the town.' Again, not something he knew a damn thing about, because he didn't usually indulge in the festive crap Manhattan laid on for tourists and families and starry-eyed romantics. But he could break another of his golden rules if it got him what he wanted. Namely Eleanor in his bed until New Year. By which time this need would have surely run its course.

But now he thought about it, he would get a kick out of seeing Christmas in the city through her eyes. Roman had texted him to say he was going to be out of town until after Christmas now—something he did every year because Christmas wasn't a happy season for him since he'd lost his whole family at this time of year—so he didn't have anyone else to hang out with. And Eleanor would love all that festive crap, because it was new and so different from the sheltered, unsophisticated upbringing she'd been subjected to by parents who had stifled her wild side, deliberately. He, on the other hand, wanted to help her indulge it. And not just in bed, he realised, surprising himself even more.

'So what do you say?' he asked, aware of her boss coming towards them now, but confident of getting the right answer. She still looked wary and shocked, but then he had shocked himself a little. She wouldn't turn him down, because no woman ever had before. And anyway, he was offering something a great deal more enticing than serving drinks and washing barroom floors in Staten Island. 'Why don't you go pack?' He glanced at his phone. 'I'll meet you back here in a half-hour.'

Surely she couldn't have that much stuff, and anyway he could buy her some new gowns for the kind of high-class parties and events he got invited to. Events he was looking forward to actually attending. With someone as vibrant and outspoken and unpredictable as Eleanor on his arm, those VIP events would be less of a chore. He stroked her cheek, because she was still staring at him. He grinned when he felt her familiar shudder of awareness at the slight touch.

You've got this, Alex. And it hadn't even been that hard to ask.

Ellie jerked back, her heart thundering in her chest, the cruel weight pressing against her ribs doing nothing to alleviate her confusion. And panic.

Alex Costa's offer was the last thing she'd expected. In fact, she'd been determined all weekend not to even think about the possibility of more after Thanksgiving was over.

She'd worked so hard to stave off that feeling of loss, of regret. She'd congratulated herself on managing to smile and bid him goodbye in the same spirit she'd entered into their devil's bargain in the first place. She'd practically raced across the lot, to get into the bar before she let any of those feelings derail her. Feelings she didn't want to have and certainly didn't want to let him see. Because then she'd feel like an insecure fool. The naïve virgin sacrifice he'd once accused her of being.

But now he'd gone and ruined it. Because the minute the offer had left his lips, her heart had begun beating in double time. And for one sweet, blissful moment she'd thought she could say yes. But as he'd continued speaking, and she'd realised what he was really offering—just an extension of their casual fling for another month—she knew she'd be a fool to agree to it. Because she was already way more invested in this fling than she had any right to be.

He'd been her first and only lover. And while she didn't want that to mean something, somehow it did. And not just because he was such an inventive, generous, experienced lover—who seemed to know just how to touch her, to tempt her, to make her beg. But because he had so many secrets. So many facets he wouldn't let her see, which intrigued and excited her. Even though she knew they shouldn't. Because she very much doubted he would *ever* let her see them.

'I canny do it,' she said. 'I canny go with you.'

His dark brows launched up his forehead, shock suffusing his features. 'Why not?'

The unguarded arrogance would have made her laugh, if the pain in her chest weren't making it so hard to breathe.

'Because I have a job here,' she said, going with the practical, for once. Something she'd forgotten while living in his unattainable world for four glorious days and nights.

But she was back in the real world, now. *Her* world. And she couldn't afford to venture into his again. Because it was intoxicating. Not so much the luxury, the indulgence, but Alex Costa himself.

It occurred to her the real draw had always been him. His taciturn charm and all the things she didn't know about him had begun to fascinate her—like where he came from, how he'd earned so much so young, why he was so devoted to his pal Roman, why he didn't have a family to spend Thanksgiving with…

'But that's not…' He looked even more astonished, but then his lips kicked up in the assured smile she had always found so hot. 'You won't need to work, Eleanor,' he said, as if it was the most ridiculous thing he'd ever heard. 'I'd pay for everything, obviously. And when we decide to part ways, I can support you until you find a new job. I own a lot of realty in Manhattan. You can pick out an apartment to live in, free of charge, for as long as you want.'

She stared at him. Did he even realise how insulting his offer was? Apparently not from the confident smile, which she was finding a lot less endearing.

'Well, thanks, but no, thanks,' she said, then turned to stalk into the bar. The tidal wave of indignation was welcomed in to combat the hollow feeling of hurt. Hurt she knew she had no right to. She'd jumped into this relationship on his terms. But she had to end it now on hers.

'Hey, Ellie, you're back.' Her boss, Bethany Sullivan, sent her an easy smile, but her gaze remained fixed on the man behind her. 'Looks like you had an even more eventful Thanksgiving weekend than I did,' she added, the smile now full of undisguised curiosity.

'Yes, but now it's over,' Ellie said. 'And I'm eager to get back to work.'

Alex's gruff voice interrupted them both. 'What the heck do you mean, thanks, but no, thanks?'

She spun round. So he was going to insist on doing this in front of her boss, a woman she respected and whom she hoped respected her.

'What I mean is…' she enunciated the words clearly '… I've no plans to become your kept woman. I have a job here, and commitments which are important to me. Is that clear enough?'

'*Kept woman?* What the…?' His voice rose to match hers. 'What century are you living in?'

'Okay, mistress, then, paid escort, sex worker,' she added, throwing her hands up, as her own temper took hold. 'Whatever you want to call it.'

'Damn it.' He went to grasp her elbow again. She

jerked her arm away from him. She must not let him touch her. He had a hold on her he'd exploited. A hold she'd happily let him exploit. But she needed to break that hold now. Or she'd be even more vulnerable to all the 'what ifs' than she was already.

'Eleanor, this is nuts. All I want is for you to come stay at my place for a month,' he said, sounding genuinely exasperated now. 'So we can get the DNA test done and I can show you New York at Christmas. We can enjoy ourselves the same way we have over the last four days. Why are you turning that into an insult?'

'Just answer me this, would there be sex involved?'

'I sure as hell hope so,' he shot straight back.

'Then there you have it,' she announced. And marched right past Bethany, who was staring at them both open-mouthed.

She didn't care, she thought as she slammed the bar door shut. The two regulars inside both jumped. She greeted them through gritted teeth, saying she hoped they'd had a happy Thanksgiving—then loaded up the dishwasher with enough force to crack a beer glass.

'Okay, calm down, honey, before you break enough glassware to put me out of business.'

She whipped round to find Bethany standing behind her. The concerned smile made the hole in Ellie's chest open up again.

Alex was probably climbing back into the helicopter as they spoke. And then he would be gone. And she would never see him again. She'd never feel that heady adrenaline rush every time he touched her, tasted her, tormented her. But worse than that, she would miss the man himself, the one she'd discovered out of bed—she would miss that guy's charm, his wit, his confidence, even his arrogance, and the way he looked at her. As if all the things about her she had been told needed to be curbed and controlled—her recklessness, her wildness, her desperation to experience everything to its fullest—were actually things to be nurtured and admired.

While she wanted to feel vindicated, and righteous and pleased with herself, for rejecting his insulting offer, all she felt now was deflated. Over the last four days, he'd made her feel as if her flaws, her weaknesses, were also her strengths, and that had been so intoxicating.

She wrapped the broken glass in some newspaper and dumped it in the trash.

'I'm sorry you had to witness that,' she murmured, embarrassed now, as well as sad. She'd overreacted, that much was obvious.

'Don't be, I found it very entertaining,' Bethany said. 'I'd say Alex Costa is a guy who needs to be taken down a peg or two, and you appear to be the woman to do it. I doubt there's been many others.'

She sent Bethany a wistful smile. 'I'm not special. And even if I were, I expect he's sure now I'm not worth the effort.'

'He didn't leave, you know,' Bethany said. 'He's waiting outside. He told me to tell you, you've got thirty minutes to change your mind.'

Ellie's heart gave another giddy leap. She squashed it like a bug.

'Oh, for...' She swore softly. The man was intractable, as well as incorrigible.

She sighed as the conflicting emotions—regret,

guilt, embarrassment, longing—tangled into an enormous knot in her stomach.

'I wish he'd just leave,' she muttered, because she didn't want him to go, but she knew she should.

'Do you?' Bethany asked, the sceptical look making Ellie feel transparent. 'Where's the girl who told me a month ago she had come to New York to live her best life? To have an adventure she could tell her grandbabies? To be bold and brave and unafraid?'

Ellie groaned. Had she really been that naïve? 'To be reckless and self-indulgent, you mean?'

Bethany smiled. 'Just tell me one thing. Did you have a good time with him over Thanksgiving?'

'The best time,' she said, because she couldn't lie about it. 'He's exciting and funny and smart and compelling and so…' She puffed out a breath. 'Well, he's the hottest man I've ever met. He found my G-spot on the first attempt and he knows his way around a clitor—' She clammed up, her face heating about fifty thousand degrees. Had she just been waxing lyrical about Alex's astounding abilities in the sack to her boss?

But Bethany just laughed. 'I can well imagine. So what's the problem with taking him up on his offer? Because it sounds like it would be one hell of an adventure to me.'

'You mean apart from the fact I have a job here?' Ellie supplied, trying to cling to the practical again.

'Honey, as much as I'd love for you to stay working here, I can see that serving beers every night to old farts like Rex over there—'

'Hey, Rex heard that,' Rex said, before going back to his beer.

Bethany laughed off the interruption. 'Isn't going to be a patch on spending four weeks celebrating Christmas with the hottest guy you've ever met.'

Ellie finished loading the dishwasher.

'So why don't you tell me what the real problem is?' Bethany continued. 'And let's see if we can figure it out before that helicopter leaves.'

Ellie huffed. Clearly her boss wasn't going to let this drop. 'Honestly, I just don't think I can spend a whole month with him on his terms. He wants a no-strings-attached fling, and I'm not sure I can do that. He fascinates me and excites me and I know if I went to live with him, I'd want to get to know him better. Which means I'd never be able to stick to his rules.'

'So don't,' Bethany said, as if it was really that simple.

'But…' Ellie began.

'Sweetie, he can make any rules he wants. Doesn't mean you have to follow them. Who made him the boss of this fling anyway?'

'Well…' Ellie frowned. Did Bethany have a point? 'I guess *he* did. But if he's paying for everything, I'd feel powerless.'

'So don't let him pay for everything. You can work in Manhattan just as good as you can here. And if he really wants you with him, he'll have to agree to your terms.'

Excitement surged, but then crashed back to earth.

'I'm not sure I *can* work in Manhattan though. I got bad-mouthed by the event planner after punching one of the guests at Alex's Halloween party and I expect she'll have spread the word.'

Bethany chuckled. 'Where's Costa's penthouse?'

'Central Park West.'

'Okay, I know a classy cocktail bar near Columbus Circle owned by a friend who used to bus tables at Sully's. I can give you his number. Mel's always looking for reliable bartenders, especially in the run-up to Christmas.'

'Really?' Ellie said, stupidly touched, but also unable to deny the wave of excitement starting to build under her breastbone. Could she really make this work? Could she risk moving in with Alex Costa? Risk getting more invested in a relationship that was never supposed to last?

'Yes, really,' Bethany said. 'Now go get packed, you've only got ten minutes left.'

The excitement surged, but with it came the panic. 'But… What if I fall in love with him?' Even as she said it, though, she could hear how cowardly she sounded, and how melodramatic.

Seriously, Ellie, are you a smart, brave, single woman about town, or the too-stupid-to-live heroine in a cheesy romcom?

'Honey, I guess what you've got to ask yourself is, is the ride worth the risk?' Bethany said. 'In my experience you never regret the risks you take. Only the ones you don't. And spending Christmas in Manhattan with a guy like Alex Costa… That promises to be one hell of a ride.'

Ellie slammed the dishwasher closed. 'You're right,' she said as the giddy rush of adrenaline threatened to burst right out of her chest.

'Of course, I am,' Bethany said. 'Now scram, before he leaves without you.'

CHAPTER NINE

Five days later

ALEX SAT IN the muscle car, in the back alley behind Columbus Circle, the heating purring as the sprinkle of snow whirred around the neon sign announcing the exclusive cocktail bar where Eleanor had worked for five nights straight.

It was close to two a.m. And he had an important meeting downtown in under six hours.

Why had he agreed to let her work her butt off into the early hours of the morning?

Because she didn't give you a choice, buddy.

He scowled, willing her to come out of the damn bar so they could go home, as he recalled her stubborn expression when she'd come out of Sully's with her backpack slung over her shoulder, and he'd been sure all his Christmases had come at once.

'*I'll come with you, but only if I can work. That's my final offer.*'

Agreeing to her ultimatum had seemed like the lesser of two evils at the time, because he'd been about to stride into Sully's, chuck her over his shoulder and kidnap her when she'd finally appeared. And while he would have been okay with that, so confident in his ability to keep Eleanor so sexed up she would have had a hard time objecting, his legal team would probably have pitched a fit.

And now here he was, paying for his moment of weakness big time. Not only had they not had sex for the last two nights, because she'd been way too exhausted, she'd even objected to having his car and driver pick her up at the end of her shift.

'Honestly, Alex, you can't make the poor wee man sit outside for hours when I'm perfectly capable of walking four blocks.'

In the middle of the night? In the snow? Four inches had blanketed the city last night but she'd arrived at the penthouse having dismissed his driver six hours before, shivering from the cold and with the dirty New York slush dampening her jeans to the knee. And the 'poor wee man' she was so determined not to inconvenience was a six-foot-two-inch retired Navy SEAL whom he paid a very generous salary to sit in the car at any time of the day or night. He'd been so frustrated he'd wanted to cuss her out for putting herself in danger, but she'd been so cold and tired and miserable he'd been forced to hold onto his temper.

He swore, and switched off the radio, which was playing the type of elevator jazz that could send a hyperactive toddler into a coma.

So here he sat, hanging around waiting to pick her up himself at two in the morning, like a besotted teenager, instead of a thirty-something billionaire who'd never been besotted in his life.

He didn't even recognise himself any more. And he didn't like it.

He checked his phone for the fifteenth time. One minute after two.

Her shift was over. Grabbing his jacket, he got out of the car, put the jacket on and, sinking his fists into the pockets, headed to the front of the building. The door was locked, but he could see Eleanor at the back of the bar, stacking glasses. Her shoulders were slumped. She looked shattered.

The shot of frustration was joined by the ripple of concern.

He banged on the door. A tall black guy, almost as tall as him, answered it.

'Sorry, man, bar's closed.'

'I'm here to pick up my…' He paused. What even was Eleanor? His date? His girlfriend? His mistress? His live-in lover? He'd never got to the stage of labelling the women in his life—because all his relationships had been so casual. 'Eleanor,' he managed at last. He nodded to the back, when the guy sent him a blank stare.

'Oh, you mean Ellie,' the guy said, glancing over his shoulder, where Alex's *whatever* was so absorbed in wiping down the bar she hadn't even noticed his arrival.

'You her guy?' the man asked.

'I guess,' Alex said, kind of surprised he wasn't that bothered to own it.

'She'll be done soon,' he said.

'Why isn't she done already? Her shift's finished.'

The guy frowned. 'Because I pay her to clean up, not that it's any of your damn business.'

Alex lowered his voice—the solution to his problem suddenly obvious. 'How much do you pay her?'

'Twenty-two bucks an hour plus tips—what's it to you?' the man replied.

Alex did a quick calculation—figuring in the fact her tips would go up in the evenings. 'I'll pay you three times that to ensure she never works a night shift or a weekend again, and to bump up her tips in the daytime to whatever she's getting in the evenings,' he said, keeping his voice low.

Eleanor would get her panties in a knot if she knew about the deal with her boss, but that was too bad. He needed to figure out this situation. And not just because he wanted to get laid more often and he didn't want to have to drag himself out of a warm apartment to ensure she got home safely. But because he didn't want her working herself to exhaustion. He didn't want her freezing her gorgeous tush off in sub-zero temperatures either. Nor did he want her to risk getting accosted by some low life while walking home alone in the middle of the night.

Plus he wanted her nights and weekends free, so she could spend the time with him. Instead of serving drinks to strangers. He'd understood why she'd insisted on paying her own way—after he'd got over being pissed about having to agree to her compromise. Eleanor's independence and her pride were important to her. He got that, and in a lot of ways he admired her for it. But her insistence on working was screwing up his plans for their Christmas hook-up.

The bar owner took a moment to consider the offer, then shrugged. 'Okay, man, I guess I can give the extra money to the people taking the shifts in her place.'

'Great.' Alex held out his hand and they shook on it.

His protective instincts had been dormant for so long, it felt weird to worry about someone else's welfare. But the weight of responsibility didn't bother him too much as he watched Eleanor drag off her apron and tuck it under the bar.

The wide smile which split her face as she spotted him had the weight sinking deep into his abdomen. He made the decision to cancel the meeting he had scheduled for tomorrow and take the weekend off. He'd been sent box seats to the opening night of a show at the Winter Garden Theatre, followed by some fancy after-party.

'Alex.' She waved, her slumped shoulders lifting. The genuine pleasure in her expression made his heart thump. He ignored the heady reaction. What they had was still just an extended booty call, which would be ruined if she got a frostbitten butt.

'You didnae need to come get me,' she said as she headed towards him. Her Scottish accent was always more pronounced when she was tired, or angry or about to come. He smiled, the discovery just one more major turn-on.

'No way am I letting you walk home in a snowstorm,' he said.

She laughed, the musical sound making his heart jiggle. Before she got too close, he murmured to her boss. 'By the way, the deal's between us, okay?'

'Not a problem,' the man said, slapping Alex on the shoulder and sending him a knowing smile. 'I get why you'd want to look out for her. She's a keeper.'

Huh?

He hadn't had a chance to process the odd statement, when Eleanor threw tired arms around his shoulders. 'Hello,' she said, looking stupidly pleased to see him.

He sank into the kiss, swallowing her little sob of pleasure and ignoring the ripple of unease. He devoured her mouth in quick, greedy bites.

The bar owner cleared his throat. 'Okay, you two, get a room.'

Eleanor laughed, her face flushed. 'Yes, Mel.'

'I'll see you Tuesday, Ellie,' he added. 'Enjoy your days off. You're on eleven to five all next week,' he finished, winking at Alex before closing the door behind them.

Alex winked back, before slinging his arm over Eleanor's shoulders.

He led her through the snowy night—the swish of cars driving through the slush the only sound—to the back alley where he'd parked the Merc.

He drove back to the penthouse, the falling snow glittering in the streetlamp light.

The next order of business was to get her into the apartment, unwrap her, maybe give her sore feet a massage and then see if he could get lucky before she fell fast asleep.

Finally, Christmas was starting to come together.

'It's time to wake up, Alex. I'm laying on the activities for today,' Ellie said, already dressed and raring to go.

Alex groaned and rolled over. She hummed, getting momentarily fixated on his chest. When would she get over the rush of seeing all those gorgeous muscles bulging and flexing in unison as he moved languidly in bed?

'You're kidding,' he murmured. 'It's like dawn. And we were up past midnight.'

'I know, and it was the most spectacular night of my life,' she said, still grinning like a loon.

After they had spent Saturday morning in bed yesterday, catching up on missed sleep and then a lot of missed sex, a stylist had arrived with a selection of designer gowns for her to choose from for a 'special surprise' that evening. She'd wanted to object to Alex buying a gown for her, but when she'd seen the stunning display—from a range of designers she had heard of but never thought she would have the chance to actually wear—she'd decided it would be churlish and small-minded not to accept his very generous offer. He'd given in when she'd demanded the chance to work, had even got sweetly overprotective about making sure she got home safely by picking her up on Friday night from the bar. So it would be unappreciative not to allow him to buy the spectacular off-the-shoulder emerald velvet creation. Surely?

The surprise night had turned out to be even more stunning than the gown. She'd felt like a queen on Alex's arm, taking her seat in a private box at the Winter Garden, a heritage theatre on Broadway—which had been converted from a horse exchange, of all things, in 1911—for the opening night of a brand-new musical. The singing and dancing had been stirring and exciting, but not as stirring as the smouldering glances from the man by her side, resplendent in a black tux perfectly tailored to his muscular frame, nor as exciting as the incendiary kiss on her bare shoulder as she'd shed a tear, completely engrossed in the show's romantic climax.

They'd ended up at an exclusive after-party in a rooftop bar overlooking the Rockefeller Center's ice rink. The rink's eighty-foot Christmas tree had taken her breath away, as she'd absorbed the blaze of a thousand flickering gold lights glittering in the night just for them, it seemed. She'd shared champagne cocktails, cordon-bleu canapés and small talk with an array of famous people she'd only ever seen before on TV. She'd chatted with an ex-President and his First Lady about the Highlands, a rock icon about her latest album and had congratulated the A-list Hollywood star of the show for his bring-the-house-down performance. All the while, Alex's large hand had rested on the small of her back, possessive and protective, as he'd whispered in her ear about what he'd planned to do to her later… Even more exciting was arriving back at the penthouse to have him strip off her designer gown as soon as they got out of the elevator and make mad, passionate love on the floor of the entrance hall… Because they'd both been too desperate to wait. They'd remedied that oversight later in the en suite shower and then in his bed. Twice.

Heat hit her cheeks at the memory of his thick girth sliding into her from behind as the hot spray from the shower rained down on both of them, his callused palms clasping her breasts to anchor her for the ruthless internal stroking as he rode them both to another epic orgasm.

Bethany had been right. This Christmas was going to be the most amazing adventure she had ever had, and she planned to experience every single second to the full and stay resolutely in the moment. She and Alex didn't have a future or a past, but they had a sizzling, kinetic connection right now, which she intended to explore out of bed today.

While she couldn't possibly match the glitz and glamour of what Alex could afford, she had ideas of her own on how to experience a New York Christmas.

She'd interrogated Mel and her co-workers at The Circle Bar for ideas that were not only within her budget, but which she doubted Alex had ever experienced either. Because he'd told her yesterday on the way to the theatre he didn't 'do Christmas' as a rule.

Whatever that meant, it needed to be remedied.

Christmas was a season that had always seemed pregnant with so many possibilities during the quiet Christmases she'd spent on Moira. She'd always enjoyed the day itself, one of the few her parents hadn't worked non-stop. They'd decorate a plastic tree her father set up in the parlour each year, cook a turkey shipped over from the mainland—and which they would all be thoroughly sick of by the time the leftovers were finished in January—and exchange home-made gifts. But the season had been literally one day, the farm work taking precedence and any snowfall quickly becoming a burden because it meant bringing all the sheep in from far-flung parts of the smallholding. Since Ross and Susan MacGregor had been gone, she'd celebrated Christmas at the pub, while daydreaming about what it would be like to be somewhere where you could anticipate every moment in the run-up to the day itself.

It was already December fifth. They only had twenty days left to make the most of the festive bling New York was famous for, and only two more weekends—with no guarantee she wouldn't have to work. All of which meant, however much she loved spooning with Alex on a Sunday morning while he lazily stroked her to orgasm, they had to get a move on.

Marching over to the room's control panel, she keyed in the code to lift the shades on the glass wall.

Alex swore and covered his eyes. 'What is it with your sadistic use of daylight to wake me up?'

She chuckled. He really was adorable when he was all rugged and rumpled and sleep deprived. And naked. She slapped down the shot of lust and threw a pillow at him.

'Hurry up and take a shower while I fix breakfast,' she said, skipping away from him as she made a dash for the door. 'We need to get to the first stop on Ellie MacGregor's Budget Christmas Tour of Manhattan *early* because I have it on very good authority it gets super-crowded.'

'Hey, how about we do Alex Costa's Budget Christmas Tour of Eleanor MacGregor's Clitoris instead?' he shouted after her. 'Think of all the money we'd save!'

She was still laughing—and trying to control the all-over body-blush at the memory of the in-depth tour of her clitoris he'd taken in the early hours of the morning—as she headed to the penthouse's kitchen.

As she set out the ingredients she'd sourced at a gourmet grocery store, she suspected Alex was going to be complaining even more when he discovered he was getting Scottish porridge for breakfast.

He'd thank her later, she decided. She couldn't think of a better way to keep their stamina up during the day she had planned—highlights of which included ice-skating in Bryant Park, window-shopping along Fifth Avenue, feasting on take-out hot pastrami and rye sandwiches and then heading home through Central Park in the winter twilight.

Once they arrived back at the penthouse, maybe they could get to Alex's alternative tour suggestion. She poured the milk and steel-cut oats into a saucepan as the blush went haywire.

CHAPTER TEN

'Hey, you're freezing. Let's head back to the apartment,' Alex murmured into the spray of chestnut curls
peeping out from under Eleanor's beanie.

He breathed in a lungful of her scent—sweet, spicey
and addictive.

'Can we just watch the sunset?' she asked, relaxing
into his arms. She pointed across the park from their
vantage point on Bow Bridge.

The bow-shaped Victorian arch that connected
Cherry Hill to the Rambles in Central Park had been
featured in a ton of romantic movies—none of which
he'd watched.

He probably should have been more wary when she'd
asked about the bridge, but he was too damn exhausted
and content to be cautious and so here they were snuggled up like a couple of loved-up newly-weds—watching a sunset, of all things.

'I can see your penthouse from here,' she said, with
the exhilaration that hadn't dimmed since too-early
o'clock this morning when she'd woken him up.

She'd lapped up every experience today—checking
out the window displays in Bergdorf Goodman's on

Fifth with exactly the same artless excitement as she'd had when meeting a former US President and his First Lady at last night's party.

He'd found it charming and cute and hot as hell. Watching her tear up during the climax of last night's show had floored him, the sheen in her eyes when he'd kissed her bare shoulder blade—which had been driving him nuts all evening—turning the pale blue of her irises into a rich sapphire. How could she be so open, so connected, so easily stirred by something that wasn't even real? And why the heck did he find it so captivating?

All he'd wanted to do after that was take her back to the apartment and re-establish the only connection between them that *was* real. But he'd forced himself to take her to the after-show party, knowing she'd get a kick out of meeting the cast and the VIP guests. And needing to prove to himself he didn't have to jump her at every opportunity. To prove he wasn't *so* addicted to the endorphin rush, he couldn't control it for a few more hours. But by the time they'd finally got back to his place, he'd been so desperate to hold her, to bury himself inside her, he'd torn the dress he'd paid a fortune for just to get to her soft flesh, to drive into her body and hear those staggered sobs in his ear as she shattered. And then he hadn't been able to stop touching her, stop needing her for hours afterwards.

Despite his protests this morning, he'd been happy to get out of the apartment today. He was becoming obsessed with her.

But teaching her how to ice-skate at the Bryant Park rink—while tons of other couples did the same—strolling down Fifth and watching her freak out over each new window display, seeing her sink her teeth into a pastrami sandwich almost as big as her head and listening to her incessant chatter all day, the Scottish burr getting thicker the more excited she got, had been as captivating as watching her come apart in his arms. Not only that, but she'd somehow managed to open his eyes to the magic of Christmas in Manhattan.

What had once seemed like a dumb festive cliché to him had somehow become enchanting after having Eleanor cling to him as she'd slipped and slid across the ice in the majestic shadow of the New York Public Library. And only got worse as the day went on.

Until here he stood, with his arms wrapped around her, watching the afternoon sun settle over the New York skyline on a bridge which—looking at the other people milling about—was a Mecca for lovers, young and old.

He spread his hands over her tummy, and felt her shudder of response, the curve of her bottom pressing enticingly into his crotch. The familiar surge of lust went some way towards dispelling the soporific feeling that had settled over him during the day, threatening him with emotions that couldn't be real.

Somehow she'd beguiled him, enchanted him, bewitched him into believing in the festive magic of the city... Even though he'd lived here all his life and never seen it before. Or not since he was eight anyway, and his old man had destroyed all his illusions.

She laughed and then sighed. 'It's a good thing you can skate or today would have been a wipe out before we'd even started,' she said. 'I had no idea it would be so tough.'

'It's called balance,' he murmured, glad she hadn't

tried to take the conversation in a romantic direction. 'I'm guessing they didn't have a lot of ice rinks on Moira?'

'Not one!' She spun around in his arms, the sparkle in her eyes as beguiling as everything else about her. Not only did he want her all the damn time, but she was surprisingly good company too—her quick wit and easy smiles challenging the comfortable cynicism he'd always relied on to keep his dates at arm's length.

'Where did you learn to ice-skate so well?' she asked.

He chuckled. 'I'm not *that* great, you're just real bad.'

She laughed, the musical sound weaving around him the way it had done so many times in the last few days. 'Yes, but…' She dropped her head, toyed with a button on his coat. 'You must have done a lot more ice-skating than I did when you were a kid.'

'Nah, there weren't any ice rinks where I grew up in the Bronx. But they did have a roller-skate park. My mom would give me a couple of bucks to take my brothers and sisters there on weekends to wear them out.' He hadn't really intended to give her so much information, but when she looked up her face glowed with pleasure.

'How many brothers and sisters do you have?' she asked, sounding so impressed with the possibility he blurted out the truth again.

'Six—four sisters, two brothers. My folks didn't bother with birth control. There was a new baby almost every year for years.' *Until my old man started going elsewhere for his kicks.* 'Even though there was never enough money to feed the ones they already had,' he finished, only aware of the bitterness that still lingered—years after he thought he'd buried it—when Eleanor's gaze darkened with concern.

'I always dreamed of having siblings, but I guess being from a big family can have its problems too.'

'Yeah.' He pushed down the echo of guilt, the dark feeling of inadequacy that always clung to him when he thought of his family. The brothers and sisters he'd supported, but ghosted for years. The mother who had never been able to look at him without pain and accusation in her eyes. Didn't matter, he didn't need them. His mom had died years ago and he'd paid for the funeral, which he hadn't attended. His brothers and sisters still sent him birthday and Christmas cards every year, but he knew why. There was no love lost there, no real connection. He'd paid a lot of money once he'd made it to make sure of that. But somehow the sadness in Eleanor's eyes—the regret on his behalf—brought the heavy feeling in his chest back that he'd ignored for so long.

'Do they still live in the Bronx?' she asked.

'No, they all live in Brooklyn now—last I heard,' he said evasively. He didn't want to talk about his family. Or that kid, who had been cut loose from the only place, the only people he had ever known. That kid was long gone. The kid who'd bitten his lip until it bled so he didn't cry like a baby in the dorm room at Eldridge Prep. The kid who'd wanted his mom's forgiveness and never got it. The kid who'd yearned to come home. That kid had been a sentimental sap. He liked the loner he'd grown into much better. Driven, smart, successful, rich beyond his wildest dreams, in charge of his own destiny with nothing and no one dragging him down. The guy who didn't need a family any more because he had himself, and his company and five homes now, instead of one.

'You don't speak to them any more?' she asked, look-ing so shocked the band around his chest cinched tight.

He shrugged, but the movement felt stiff. 'We lost touch.' Not entirely true either. He was still more than happy to employ them in his subsidiary companies, to bankroll their kids' college funds through a trust he'd set up and buy a whole city block in Brooklyn eight years ago to move them all out of the old neighbour-hood, which had been going downhill for years. His only stipulation had been that they respect his privacy. 'We have nothing in common any more.'

But the words felt hollow and forced. As if he re-ally were the entitled jerk Eleanor had once accused him of being.

'Doesn't that make you feel lonely?' she said. He could hear the wistful tone and hated it.

Even though it shouldn't matter to him one bit what she thought of him. She was just a distraction—a hot, funny, sweet and surprisingly enchanting distraction. Once Christmas was over, and they'd worn out the chemistry that bound them at the moment, they'd part ways. With no regrets.

He didn't need her approval any more than he needed the approval of his family now.

He sure as hell didn't need her pity.

'I guess it would,' he said, 'if I needed family.' His temper spiked. What was she so sad about anyway? 'But I don't.'

'I see,' she said, but he was pretty sure she didn't, be-cause the sadness still lingered in her eyes. 'That's re-markably self-sufficient of you,' she added, but it wasn't a compliment. Because he could still hear the wistfulness.

He got it, she'd once yearned for a family, for siblings. Living such a secluded life with two older parents in the middle of nowhere must have been really tough for an extrovert like her, a girl who could converse with ex-Presidents and Hollywood stars with a refreshing lack of pretension. For a people person like Eleanor, it would have been agony to grow up in such an isolated place. It made sense.

But not for him.

His mom had sent him away to that damn school on a scholarship, cut him out of her life, and while it had crucified him at first, he could see now she'd done him a favour. She'd made him a stronger person than he would ever have been if he'd stayed in the Bronx. Who was to say he would ever have had the focus, the ambition or determination to make such a spectacular success of the raw talent he'd been given without those lonely years at Eldridge Prep? Families were messy, complicated, and the support his family had offered had always been conditional.

Plus he would never have met his best pal, Roman.

'Yeah, that's me,' he said. 'Self-sufficient to the core. And proud of it.'

Ellie shivered, the words dropping into the pit of her stomach, the flat direct gaze piercing the bubble of exhilaration that had kept her happily cocooned from the chill all day.

She wasn't sure if Alex meant the comment as a warning. Not to get too close. Not to make the mistake of thinking this interlude, this time together, meant more than it did. But she understood it as such.

Today had been magical in so many ways, just like last

night. He'd held her in strong arms this morning while she'd stumbled over the ice and prevented her from falling flat on her bum more than once. He'd chuckled as she'd oohed and ahhed over the magnificent artistry of the window dressings in Saks and Macy's and Bloomingdale's and had been happy to stroll along Fifth Avenue being jostled by tourists and native shopaholics alike. He had suggested the best place to get hot pastrami sandwiches and eaten them with her on the sidewalk. And he'd insisted on treating them both to a hot chocolate at his favourite chocolatier and kissed the milk moustache from her upper lip. He'd even strolled through the park with her before sunset and held her as they watched the sun drop towards the trees in a blaze of red. And for once his hard-bitten cynicism had been softened by the magic of Manhattan all dressed up for the season of goodwill. But it was back with a vengeance now, as she recalled the way he'd talked about his family.

There was a bitterness and anger there, which he was determined not to acknowledge. And she couldn't help wondering what had caused it. Why would anyone want to lose such a close connection? A connection she'd yearned for her entire life. To have people who knew you, who understood you, who had grown up with you and had the same experiences, and who could reminisce with you about the people you'd lost. To have people to share your pain as well as those small domestic joys that had been a part of your childhood, but no one but you could remember now?

Except, not everyone had a good childhood. A happy childhood. Even a functional childhood. Why had it never even occurred to her the things she'd yearned for growing up might have their own challenges, provide their own problems?

She'd been so lonely as a child, had never felt as if she truly belonged. As a result she had always yearned for more. More family, more people she could depend on, more memories, more connections, and parents who didn't live such small, secluded lives and didn't depend on her to give their lives meaning.

And as a result, here she was in New York, living her very best life and falling for a man who couldn't be more emotionally unavailable if he tried.

Falling for? What the hell? You're not falling for Alex Costa, Ellie.

Because that would be insane.

'You're cold,' he said, when she shivered again. But as his tawny gaze searched her face, she was scared it saw more than she wanted it to see. 'Have you had enough of the sunset yet?' he asked, the gruff amusement in his tone, tempered with impatience, somehow another warning.

A warning she knew she didn't need.

She glanced over her shoulder, to see the sun had sunk beneath the trees, leaving the sky with a dull amber glow. She swallowed heavily, forcing herself not to take his detachment and the brief glimpse he'd given her of the man behind the mask personally.

Alex Costa was unattainable for a reason. A reason she couldn't change and had no right to question.

She swung round to find him watching her with the guarded look she'd become used to, realising he already regretted letting his guard down—even a wee bit.

She tucked her arm into his, clamped down on the emotion pushing against her chest. And ignored all the questions filling her head, about the man who had decided he didn't need the connections she had always craved.

You are self-sufficient too, Ellie. And you need to stay that way.

'Yes, I've had enough of Christmas for now.' She gave a theatrical shudder as the cold seeped through her warm clothes.

'Good,' he said, that penetrating gaze flaring with a familiar heat—and the flicker of relief. 'Because I know a great way to warm you up.'

'I bet you do,' she said coquettishly, channelling her inner sex kitten and ignoring the little girl who had always been ready to throw herself into a new adventure—but had never considered the consequences. 'Would it involve taking all my clothes off?'

His chuckle rumbled across her cold skin as his warm palm settled onto her hip and slipped under her jumper to stroke her back. She shivered again, but this time not from the cold.

'You know me too well,' he murmured as he increased the pace.

But as they made their way home through the park, she knew she didn't really know him at all.

Their feet crunched on the frozen snow, and her heart hurt at how easy it would be to romanticise today—and the torrid passion they would share again tonight.

She needed to be sure not to fall any deeper under his spell.

Alex Costa was fascinating and gorgeous and provocative and so hot it hurt, but he wasn't offering her a place to stay for long, or a place where she could belong.

CHAPTER ELEVEN

The day before Christmas Eve

'I'M OUT OF HERE, CHERYL,' Alex said as he strolled past his personal assistant's desk in the executive offices of Costa Tower—an art deco building he'd rescued from demolition and rehabbed as the headquarters of Costa Tech. The place where he had spent all his time, until he and Eleanor had returned from their Thanksgiving vacation—and he'd found it harder and harder to stay away from her.

He ignored the now familiar one-two punch in his heart rate. The fear of missing out had only got worse over the last few weeks, each morning leaving her curled in his bed to do the work that had once defined his life. Or on the afternoons he sat at his desk, the late sunlight shining off the polished wood flooring, watching the vintage gold clock face embedded in the cherrywood panelling and waited an eternity for the hands to edge towards four-thirty. The time he'd pinpointed as respectable enough for him to play hooky for the rest of the day, but which also happened to be the perfect time to ensure he was back at the apartment when Eleanor got in from her shift at The Circle Bar.

Mel had come through on that score, and hadn't booked Eleanor for any evening or weekend shifts. Which had given him even more excuses not to work on weekends too, the way he always had in the past. And that was without counting all the meetings and overseas trips he'd cancelled during the past three weeks.

Don't think about it. It's Christmas in two days and your last chance to make the most of this chemistry while you still can.

Plus there were all the events he never would have attended in the past, which had become enchanting with Eleanor by his side. His marketing team were having orgasms about the media coverage the two of them were generating. The speculation about New York's Hottest Eligible Bachelor—because apparently the media had forgotten Roman had won this year's title!—and the 'mystery Scottish girl' had been gold dust, according to his PR department. Not that he wanted that kind of attention, but Eleanor had taken it in her stride, had even seemed amused by the speculation.

'If they only knew I'm just using you for your abilities as a tour guide of my clitoris,' she'd joked last night.

His heart beat in hard heavy thuds at the thought of the New Year, when their Christmas hook-up was set to end.

Was that why her joke hadn't seemed as funny as he'd wanted it to? Any more than her failure to ask about his plans past New Year had reassured him… Eleanor seemed so adept at staying in the moment, enjoying each new experience as it came, it was actually starting to bug him.

He stalked into the closet to pick up his coat.

Get over yourself, Costa. You're not that desperate to spend time with her...you're just learning to enjoy Christmas in New York with someone who knows how.

It was the season he found captivating, not Eleanor so much. After all, when was the last time he'd had a chance to trash his favourite designer coat so he could teach a date how to make snow angels in the park?

No one would call him a Christmas nut, or even a romantic, because he wasn't. But when they'd been walking back from the bar last night—after he'd decided to make a last-minute detour on the way home so he could walk Eleanor back after her shift—and she'd fessed up about having never made a snow angel before, he'd had no choice but to shove her into the fresh drift on Sheep Meadow. A tussle had ensued and then a snowball fight, before he'd discovered Eleanor had a better throwing arm than the Yankees' current roster of starting pitchers.

The ride on the Central Park carousel had been the only way to distract her from the snowball war before they both froze to death.

The secret smile crept over his face as he shrugged on the coat.

'Yes, Mr Costa,' Cheryl replied, now used to him ducking out early. 'By the way, the Galloway Clinic called half an hour ago. They asked if you could call them back.'

'The Galloway?' he asked, surprised by the news.

He'd finally sent in the DNA sample Eleanor had

given him as planned at the beginning of this week—even though he no longer needed it as an excuse to keep her by his side for the duration of the month. In the end he'd decided not to let Roman know he was doing the test at all. The clinic had a DNA profile for Roman to check the sample against, and his friend had given Alex the authority to use it back when they had tested several of the girls and women who had come forward over the years since the initial search. Why bother Roman with the possibility when he knew the test would be negative…again?

'Yes, I'm sorry I didn't put it through,' Cheryl said. 'But you were on that conference call to Berlin.'

'Not a problem, I'll call them on my way out.'

But even as he strode out of the office and tugged his cell out of his pants, panic started to consume him. Had they found something? Something wrong in Eleanor's DNA sample, some genetic disease or inheritance? What other reason could they have for contacting him direct, instead of just emailing the results?

The clinic picked up on the second ring and put him through to the relevant department.

'Mr Costa,' the technician's voice came over the line bristling with excitement. 'I thought I should call you straight away with the good news. The DNA sample for Eleanor MacGregor shows a one hundred per cent match for a filial relationship with Mr Fraser.'

He stopped dead, his footsteps echoing into silence as he struggled to process the information. *'What?'*

'It's conclusive, Mr Costa—which isn't always the case with siblings. Miss MacGregor and Mr Fraser come from the same genetic ancestry. They match in more than fifty per cent of the markers—which in lay-man's terms means they come from the same parents. They are full brother and sister.'

The technician then proceeded to launch into a load of scientific jargon, none of which Alex could hear, past the thunder of his heart crashing against his chest wall.

Eleanor is Eloise Fraser.

She was the baby girl whom he had assured Roman must have died twenty years ago in the Scottish High-lands. The little girl who had been stolen by two people who she thought had loved her. And who had hidden her on a remote island for nearly all of her life.

Those bastards.

She was the rightful heiress to a billion-dollar for-tune who right now was probably stacking cocktail glasses in a dishwasher.

He thrust his fingers through his hair, the reality still not entirely computing as her eyes—the intense ceru-lean blue with the dark rim around the edge, and the patch of brown Roman had remembered—swirled in his mind's eye. And he now realised they were much more like Roman's eyes than he'd ever wanted to ac-knowledge.

Except they weren't Roman's eyes, or the eyes of a baby lost long ago, they were Eleanor's eyes. *His* El-eanor's eyes. Full of wit and compassion and excite-ment and honesty. Full of the expressive looks he had got drunk on ever since he'd first spotted her hauling drinks around in that joke costume at the Halloween Ball… And he'd wanted her for himself.

He stared out of the large wood-framed window at the Midtown skyline, bathed in the golden glow of a winter twilight, as his heartbeat began to choke him. And the technician continued to talk while he was too distracted to listen.

He'd slept with his best friend's kid sister. Not just slept with her, hell, he'd taken her innocence and then fed off her artless desire, the recklessness and sense of adventure that had only made him want her more.

The same girl Roman had been searching for ever since he was a kid himself. The girl he knew Roman had beaten himself up about for years because he'd failed to save her.

Alex probably ought to feel guilty, ashamed, but all he felt was the fierce sense of possession, of need, that had blindsided him months ago and had never faded no matter how many times he took her.

He placed his palm against the cold glass, watched it tremble as the emotions he didn't want to feel and had no damn clue what to do with rolled around in his gut like a boulder.

He swore viciously.

'I'm sorry, Mr Costa, is there a problem?' The technician's voice broke through the dismal buzzing in his ear.

Yeah, there's a damn problem. You've just given me information that changes everything...

'No,' he said, but the rasp of breath didn't even convince him, let alone the technician.

The guy's voice was a lot less perky when he spoke again. 'I... I have Mr Fraser's cell number on record, should I let him know the good news too?'

'No,' he spat out.

Not yet, he needed time. To tell Eleanor. To tell them both. He'd suggested the damn test, believing it was no more than a dumb hunch that would be disproved by the test. Because he'd convinced himself he'd totally overreacted when the idea had first entered his head.

But had he always known, somehow? Had some sixth sense told him Eleanor was really Eloise? Was that why he'd got so hung up on her? Was that why she had come to mean more to him than any other woman ever had or ever should? Was that why he'd been clock-watching every afternoon like a lovesick jerk for weeks? Why he hadn't been able to concentrate on anything but her? Why he'd been unable to stop wanting her when he was with her? And to stop thinking about her when he wasn't?

Because she was the only living relation of a man he loved like a brother? A man who trusted him. Who mattered to him. The ride-or-die pal who had saved him from the misery of that God-awful school.

But even as the thought came to him, he knew that wasn't it. This churning in his gut, this weird frantic feeling in his heart, this sense of having lost something important he could never get back felt way too real to be based on anything as hokey as a sixth sense. Or a biological connection that still didn't seem real to him.

This reaction wasn't about Eleanor being Eloise, this was much worse than that, this was about feelings he didn't want to feel, and didn't want to acknowledge, but couldn't seem to control. Feelings that had hoodwinked him months ago but had since become much tougher to avoid especially now he'd uncovered a secret which he didn't want to know.

'I'll handle it,' he said. He got the technician's reassurance that no one would be given the details, not even the clinic's clerical staff, before he ended the call.

When the truth got out, it would be headline news. The search for the Fraser Baby had made the papers around the world twenty years ago, even he remembered hearing about it as a kid in the Bronx before he'd ever met Roman. And Roman's search a decade ago when he'd first come into his inheritance had received a lot of column inches too.

Eleanor and Roman would need time to adjust to this new reality before it became a media circus.

But as he shoved the phone into his pocket, he knew they weren't the only ones. Because his hands were shaking, his stomach was churning, and nothing made any sense any more. Nothing except the hollow weight in his gut he remembered feeling for the first time when he'd been eight years old, shivering in his pop's Chevy pickup on a cold Christmas eve obsessing about the second-hand bike at Morty's garage he was hoping Santa might bring him the next day if he prayed hard enough at midnight Mass. The weight that had appeared from nowhere, then grown to impossible proportions as he'd watched his old man come out at last from the house in a neighbourhood Alex had never been to before… And start making out on the porch with a woman who wasn't Alex's mom.

The weight that had twisted and burned in his gut after the brutal box around the ear he'd received when he'd asked Carmine Da Costa who the strange woman was on the drive home.

'None of your business, Sandro. You keep your mouth shut or there'll be more where that came from, you hear?'

That was the night he'd stopped being a little kid,

stopped caring about Santa and Christmas... And discovered that other people's secrets could screw up your life, no matter what you did with them.

He hated keeping secrets, hated even knowing them... They were toxic, especially if they weren't your own.

But how did he tell Roman his kid sister had been alive all this time, that Alex had got it so wrong—along with everyone else—when he'd helped to persuade him she had to be dead?

And how did he tell Eleanor her whole past was a lie, the person she was trying to find had never existed, and the parents she loved had betrayed her? Without making her hate him too?

He gazed at the skyline as night fell over the city. And for the first time in weeks the punch of adrenaline, that desperate desire to race back to the apartment and see the flare of excitement in her eyes when she saw him again, didn't come.

Because the sick feeling in his stomach he remembered from the day he'd first realised what a phoney his old man was had swallowed it whole.

Ellie arranged the last strip of tinsel on the tree, breathed in the magical scent of fresh pine resin, then switched on the lights. The twinkling glow reflected off the penthouse's glass wall, shining into the night.

Her heart bounced into her throat. The tree looked beautiful, softening the stylish furnishings and bringing the magic of the season into the space.

When she'd seen the small fir looking forlorn—the last one left on the Columbus Circle Christmas Market stall she passed on her way home each day—she had made an executive decision. Because she'd always wanted a real Christmas tree, just once. She'd then gone a bit crazy, buying coloured lights, shiny baubles and too much gaudy tinsel, and hefted the lot home through the slush. The cleaning-service maids had helped her set it up. She'd given them both a big tip before they'd left for the evening.

She tilted her head. She really wasn't sure what Alex would make of the chintzy addition to his designer bachelor pad. She knew he wasn't big on Christmas, or so he'd insisted. But he'd seemed to enjoy all the festive fun as much as she had in the last few weeks. She huffed out a laugh, recalling the snowball fight they'd had a few days ago, after he'd insisted on teaching her how to make a snow angel in the park… Which had basically entailed him flinging her backwards into a snow bank then sitting on her. It had been worth getting soaked, though, to see the boyish amusement in his hazelnut eyes and then the mock outrage when she'd ended up besting him in the snow battle that had followed.

The grin that had been lurking all day spread across her face and reflected in the glass.

Alex wouldn't mind, this would be just another great memory they could share of her best Christmas ever before New Year came and they parted… She swallowed, the smile faltering.

Stop it. No silly emotions. No regrets. You promised.

She brushed her hands on her jeans, the grin returning when she heard the ding of the elevator doors opening.

Finally, he was home. She couldn't wait to show him the tree.

She switched off the room's main lights. The spellbinding effect of the colourful tree lit up against the Manhattan skyline made her breath stutter before she shot down the hallway.

'Alex, I have a surprise for you,' she announced as he stepped out of the elevator.

Her smile fell when his head lifted. The fierce appreciation she had become used to whenever he arrived home, or she did, had been replaced with a blank, weary, oddly tight expression.

'Hi, I got hung up on something at the office,' he said, unwrapping the scarf around his neck, and dropping his briefcase on the hall table. But instead of hauling her into his arms and kissing her senseless—their go-to greeting after a day spent apart—he simply stood there.

'What surprise?' he asked.

At exactly the same moment as she said, 'What's wrong?'

The blank expression became remote.

'Nothing's wrong,' he said, but something about the sharp tone made her sure something definitely wasn't right.

She'd been careful not to stress about the fact it was already eight o'clock. She'd waited after getting the tree set up to decorate it with him. They usually arrived home together. Scratch that. They *always* arrived home together, or he was here already. But when he hadn't put in an appearance, she'd stopped herself from texting him to ask him where he was.

She wasn't a wife, or even a proper girlfriend, she didn't want to appear needy or demanding. They simply didn't have that kind of hold on one another. This was a fun, seasonal escapade, nothing more.

After twenty minutes of stressing about not stressing,

she'd got busy decorating the tree on her own. It would make more of an impact that way, she'd told herself. And while it might have been fun to decorate it with Alex, he wasn't particularly domesticated. She didn't want to turn the whole thing into a chore, when it had been her idea. And she'd had such fun doing it alone in the end, it hadn't mattered.

But when he asked again, 'What surprise?' she had to paste the smile back on and make an effort to regain the excitement of moments before as the insecurities she'd kept so carefully at bay crept back.

Had she made a stupid mistake? Crossed a line she hadn't intended to by buying the tree? It hadn't seemed like such a big deal, until this moment.

They'd been living in the penthouse together for three weeks—sharing breakfast each morning or spending lazy weekend mornings in bed. They'd used it as their base for all their festive adventures, and made love pretty much everywhere but the broom closet. He'd cooked a few times and so had she and they had shared takeaway feasts from every local restaurant and eatery, dozed on the couch watching a cheesy weepie one night and a loud action thriller the next. He'd even got hooked on her oatmeal for breakfast, much to her astonishment, and his.

But she felt strangely apprehensive now about showing him the surprise she had been anticipating showing him for hours.

Och, get over yourself, Ellie, and stop messing about. It's a wee Christmas tree, no big deal. It's not as if you've re-wallpapered his penthouse in tartan paper.

'Right,' she said. 'The surprise.' She held out her arm

to direct him down the corridor. 'Come this way, Mr Costa. The Christmas elves have been busy…'

Maybe her joy sounded forced, but she refused to overthink his reaction.

'Ta-dah,' she said as she led him into the room, the tree sparkling like a beacon, the joyful coloured lights so festive her heart began to pound.

For a long time he didn't say anything. She couldn't turn to look at him, her heart shrinking with each second of silence that ticked by.

Is he getting bored with Christmas…? Bored with me?

The thought whispered in her head, insidious, and devastating. Upsetting her more than it should. This relationship had always had a time limit, just like the season itself. When had she stopped believing that in her heart?

'A tree… You got a Christmas tree,' he said, the gruff rumble of his voice filled with a raw edge that only made her more wary, more insecure.

'Yes.' She forced herself to look at him at last. The coloured lights glittered in his dark eyes. A muscle twitched in his jaw as he stared at the tree. His face was an implacable mask, a cover for some deep emotion he wouldn't let her see. It was the same expression she remembered from that day in the park, several weekends ago now, when she'd asked him about his siblings, and he'd shut her down.

'You don't like it?' she said dumbly, feeling hurt, even though she knew she shouldn't be.

It's just a wee tree. Don't overreact.

He blinked, as if waking from a trance, his gaze focussing on her at last. What she saw wasn't boredom though, or indifference, whatever it was it was fierce and passionate and all-consuming.

He grasped her wrist and tugged her into his arms. 'Come here,' he growled.

She went to him, her heart getting lodged in her throat as he framed her face and slanted his mouth across hers.

His tongue thrust deep, turning the kiss from desperate to demanding in a heartbeat. As his hands roamed down to cup her bottom—triggering the instant hunger—and the thick length of his arousal prodded her belly, she couldn't help but respond. She opened her lips to let him take more, to meet his demand with demands of her own.

She didn't know what was happening, why he was so tense, his emotions more volatile than she had ever seen them, but whatever it was it felt better than indifference.

He yanked off her top, unhooked her bra with clumsy fingers, and pressed his face into her breasts, capturing each nipple in turn and suckling hard, making them harden and the desire swell and pulse at her core.

'I need you,' he said.

'Yes,' she said, the desperation in his voice spurring her own passion. She drove her fingers into his hair, but was forced to release him as he stripped off her clothing. Lifting her naked body, he placed her on the couch. The coloured lights shone off his hair as he stood over her to tear off his own clothing, his urgency as arousing as his desperation.

Finding his wallet in the pile of discarded clothes, he took out a condom, ripped it open and rolled it on the huge erection with trembling fingers.

The dark desire on his face had turned to something more, something brutal and overwhelming as he grasped her hips, angled her body and thrust in to the hilt.

Her sodden flesh struggled to adjust to the thick intrusion—so powerful, so overwhelming—but as he began to move, digging ruthlessly at the spot he had found months ago and exploited so many times since, she felt taken, devoured. Whatever he was hiding from her, he needed her, and for the first time ever he had let her know.

The pleasure swelled, like a wave, battering her, brutal in its intensity.

'Come for me,' he growled, his hips pistoning now, forcing her to the pinnacle too fast, too soon.

She clung on, as if perched on the edge of a precipice, scared to fall, as she struggled to control the firestorm of need and the brutal swelling in her heart, wanting to understand the pain in his eyes.

But as the vicious climax gripped her, flinging her over the edge, she found herself falling into a bottomless abyss.

She cried out, bucking against his hold, the pleasure shattering her.

He shouted out as his own orgasm hit, his big body collapsing on top of her.

Their rasping breathing filled the quiet night, but as she gazed at the tree lights, which had seemed so sweet only minutes ago, she felt dazed, and disorientated, and scared. Because she knew she had just lost the battle she hadn't even realised she'd been waging for weeks, to keep her heart safe. From him.

CHAPTER TWELVE

Christmas Eve

ALEX EASED OUT of bed and headed into the shower. He turned on the jets, forcing his body to wake up. Not easy after the night he'd put in.

He'd taken her, too many times to count. They'd ended up eating cold takeout off their laps, the tree lights twinkling in the background and mocking him.

Because the more times he sank into her, the more times he saw the compassion in her eyes, the more desperate he felt.

He'd been looking forward to doing dumb, Christmassy things with her today for over a week. Had planned to take the day off work, maybe build a snowman in the park, hire a chef to cook them a fancy dinner on the terrace. He'd even bought her a gift. The first gift he'd ever got a woman he was dating that he'd picked out and ordered himself instead of delegating the job to Cheryl. He had even ensured Eleanor didn't have a bar shift today, thanks to his trusty inside man, Mel.

But as he walked back into the bedroom, and saw

her curled up on the bed, still asleep, the tightness in his chest made it hard for him to breathe.

He couldn't stay with her today, doing Christmas stuff, without thinking about all the things he had to tell her. About Roman, about the people she'd trusted.

All the things he couldn't bear to tell her yet.

Perhaps he'd harboured some dumb notion he could extend this arrangement past New Year. But he'd decided during the night he had to make a clean break. Stop living in some fantasy where he got to keep her.

Because that would mean a commitment he couldn't give her. He'd seen the emotion in her eyes, the first time he'd taken her last night, after taking a direct hit from that damn tree. She was so transparent…he had no doubt at all she had convinced herself she was falling in love with him. But she didn't know him, not who he really was. Because he hadn't let her see that guy. The guy who had lied to his own mom for years, who had pushed away his family, who couldn't form a commitment to anyone without screwing it up. Even his best pal Roman, it now transpired—by sleeping with his kid sister.

He'd used her, just as he'd used everyone in his life before her, everyone who got too close.

He padded to the adjoining closet. Getting dressed in silence, he ignored the sharp tug of regret at the loss of the Christmas Eve he'd had planned. The loss of the hopes he hadn't even admitted to himself he had been harbouring for something more. Back before he'd discovered not just who she really was, but who he was too.

He wasn't the guy who made snow angels in the park or who got emotional over a gaudily decorated Christ-

mas tree. He was the guy who was going to keep her
true identity from her, for a couple of days more, until
he was able to let her go.

Once she figured that out, they'd be history. It might
hurt for a little while, because beneath that veneer of
practicality and pragmatism Eleanor was a hopeless romantic. A reckless adventuress who had put her faith
in all the wrong people.

He left the bedroom without looking back and headed
for the elevator. It was early yet, the brittle morning
light struggling to seep through the snow flurries.

When he reached the parking garage beneath the
building, he drew out his cell and sent her a brief text.
The last thing he wanted was to be alone with her in
the apartment tonight.

But as he drove out of the garage, the hollow ache in
his chest only got heavier. And the thought of spending
the day alone in his office, instead of with her, made
him feel as if he were leaving a part of himself behind…
Which he might never get back again.

Got to work today, see u for supper @ seven.
Car will pick u up.

Ellie read the text a second time, which she'd found
on her phone after waking up. The pragmatic, busi-
nesslike, oddly detached tone of the text reminded her
of the man who had arrived home last night with that
blank look on his face.

But it's Christmas Eve.

How could he work on Christmas Eve? She blinked,

the tender spots on her body not nearly as tender as her far too easily bruised heart.

They'd made love so many times. And each time he'd held her, each time he'd taken her as if she was the only woman he would ever need, more of the lies she'd been telling herself for weeks had gone up in flames, until all that was left was the terrifying truth.

She had fallen hopelessly in love with Alex Costa, one of New York's hottest bachelors… And the most emotionally unavailable man on the planet.

This wasn't just the magic of the season, or all the spectacular sex—which had seemed more than a little desperate last night. This was a deep, visceral connection she was afraid she would never be able to break. Even though it was obvious Alex Costa didn't love her back. And probably never would.

Because he'd always held a crucial part of himself back.

Should she tell him how she felt? How could she do that, when he wasn't even here? And why was he working the day before Christmas? Had he realised how she felt somehow and decided to avoid any messy scenes today?

And what was she going to do on Christmas Eve on her own?

Snow was still falling outside, as it had been most of the morning. After seeing Alex's text she'd rung Mel to see if he needed any extra cover for today, especially as he'd been so understanding giving her all the easy shifts since her first week. But the bar owner had told her to take a load off, chill out and enjoy her Christmas break.

Easier said than done, with my heart ready to implode.

The last thing she needed was more time to think about things.

She needed something to distract her.

She'd always been so good at making her own entertainment as a kid, because she'd had to be. How had she lost that in the last three weeks?

Perhaps it was time she got it back.

Heading down to the screening room in the penthouse's lavish entertainment suite, she made herself popcorn, poured a glass of vintage champagne, doctored it with orange juice—it was barely noon, after all—then grabbed the best seat in the house, and searched the massive inventory of movies at her disposal with the word 'Christmas'.

Lovesick she might be, and about to be ceremonially dumped, but she refused to allow her wayward heart or Alex Costa's taciturn behaviour to ruin the best Christmas ever.

Ellie jerked awake at the sound of the phone ringing. Yawning, she switched off the adorable old-school Christmas romcom about a girl and a guy and a meeting on the Empire State Building at midnight—most of which she'd missed—and grabbed the phone. Perhaps Alex had changed his mind about avoiding her all day?

'Ms MacGregor, I have a lady on the line says she's related to Mr Costa,' Ed, the penthouse's service manager, said, sounding harassed as Ellie's heart sank back into her chest. 'She's very persistent, says it's an emergency.'

Related to Alex? Ellie's curiosity peaked, alongside her concern. Even if Alex wasn't speaking to his family, surely he'd want to know if something had happened to one of them.

'I'll take it,' she said, willing to give this woman Alex's number if she checked out.

'Hello,' she said, when the line clicked through.

'Hi, my name's Mia Da Costa, I'm Sandro's youngest sister, is he there? I don't trust the goon I just spoke to,' the woman demanded in a sharp Brooklyn accent.

'Sandro?' Ellie asked, confused as well as impressed by the woman's determination. Ed tended to scare off most people.

'Sandro, my brother. Alessandro Da Costa,' the woman replied. She sighed heavily. 'You probably know him as Alex Costa. We knew him as Sandro, until he started ghosting us.'

'Oh, right.' Ellie understood the young woman's frustration. She'd got an inkling today of how it felt to be ghosted by Alex. 'I'm sorry, he's not here, he's at his office. But Ed said something about an emergency?' she prompted, convinced the woman was genuine. She sounded almost as forceful and dynamic as Alex.

'Your accent...' the girl said, her tone softening. 'You're her. The Scottish mystery girl? Right. The one he's so into from all the pictures we've seen of you two on the Internet.'

'Um...yes.' Ellie's felt her face heat, knowing Mia Da Costa's brother wasn't quite as into her any more, in anything other than a sexual sense. Why did that make her feel so compromised, when it really hadn't before?

'It's so cool to speak to you,' Mia said, the enthusiasm in her voice surprising Ellie even more. 'We've all been so excited. It's about time Sandro got hooked

by the love bug. Even my sister Arianna…' She hesitated, but only for a nanosecond. 'That's my oldest sister. She's ten months younger than Sandro, three kids,
divorced, not the romantic type since her rat of an ex
started boning his secretary.' She took a breath, giving
Ellie a crucial moment to correlate the stream of information. 'Anyhow, even Ari thinks he's smitten. He
looked so happy—and possessive—in those photos, like
he would never let you go. Even I was swooning and
he's my brother.' The woman let out an infectious laugh.
'So you're living at his penthouse? That's awesome,' she
added, sounding increasingly excited. 'Matty—that's
Matteo, my second-oldest brother, twenty-six, a rookie
firefighter, thinks he's the boss of everyone 'cos he can
scale a hundred-foot ladder in ten seconds—he calls
Sandro's penthouse the Fortress of Bachelorhood, so
Sandro must really adore you.'

'That's nice of you to say,' Ellie said, feeling stupidly devastated by the woman's misreading of the situation, but also enchanted by her candour. Alex had
said he'd lost touch with his family, but apparently his
family hadn't lost touch with him. Was the truth more
one-sided? *Had* he ghosted them, as Mia said? And if
so, why? 'But I'm only staying here until after Christmas, this is just a wee holiday fling, for both of us,' she
added. 'No' a big deal at all.'

'Uh-huh, I'll bet,' Mia said, not sounding at all convinced.

'So, about that emergency?' Ellie continued, trying
to redirect the conversation. Again.

'It's not an emergency. Specifically,' Mia said, sheep-
ishly. 'It's just…' Her voice took on a wistful quality,

tempered with regret. 'Every year we invite Sandro to Thanksgiving, and then Christmas in Brooklyn. And he never comes. I figured this year I'd be more proactive. I haven't seen him since I was a little kid. None of us have. He's got a ton of nieces and nephews he's never even met. And we never got to thank him for all he's done for us, as a family. It just seems dumb. I know he's got issues with what happened when he was a kid. According to Ari and Isabella—that's another of my older sisters,' she supplied helpfully, 'Mom was always super tough on him. But she was a broken woman after Pop's death. And Sandro looked so like him, maybe that had something to do with it?' Mia sighed. 'But she's been dead for ten years now. And it just seems wrong somehow, that we'll all be getting together on Christmas Day, and he'll be missing again. I know Ari and Bella, especially, would love to see him, because they remember him better than I do.'

'That sounds heartbreaking, for all of you,' Ellie said, not sure what else to say.

'I know, right,' Mia said. 'You're very nice to listen to all that,' she added, making Ellie feel like a bit of a fraud.

'Well, I—' Ellie began.

'Could you at least tell him I called?' Mia interrupted, the plea in her voice making the empty space in Ellie's chest grow again. 'Tell him how much we'd all love to see him tomorrow,' Mia continued before Ellie could formulate a reply. 'And you should totally come too, we'd love to meet you. And it might make it a bit easier for him. We can be pretty overwhelming all in one go.'

Ellie couldn't imagine Alex being overwhelmed by anything, but there was something about this whole situation that just seemed so wrong, and so sad to her. She drew in an unsteady breath. This really was none of her business.

But what harm could it do telling him Mia had called?

'I canny promise anything...' she began. 'But I don't see any harm in at least asking him.'

'Oh, thank you,' Mia gushed, sounding so excited, Ellie felt guilty.

'Really, I doubt it'll do any good,' she added, trying not to get the girl's hopes up. 'We really don't have that kind of—'

'Yeah, I know, just a vacation fling,' Mia shot back, still sounding delighted. 'Tell him we're meeting at Aldo's house. That's my youngest older brother. Him and his girlfriend, Sammy, have a newborn. Their first. Luca Alessandro Carmine Da Costa. Eight pounds three ounces of unbelievable cuteness born two weeks ago. That's the emergency I was talking about,' she said, laughing. 'The address is 1543 West Acacia Avenue. We'll be gathering there after Mass from noon onwards. Sandro knows where it is, because he paid for the remodelling of our whole block. See you tomorrow.'

Before Ellie had a chance to interrupt the flow of details, the line had gone dead.

She stared at the phone, stunned. What had she just agreed to? Because it felt like a lot more than she was capable of delivering on.

One thing was for certain, she thought as she dropped the phone back into its cradle. There was absolutely no question there was a genetic bond between Alex Costa and Mia Da Costa, because the woman had the same ability to make Ellie feel as if she'd just been run over by a bus.

Ellie's breath caught as she walked down the black marble staircase into the upscale Madison Avenue restaurant at seven-twenty. The white and gold Christmas décor complemented the starkly modern space, adding an enchanted glow to the marble cornices and double-height ceiling that had been adapted from an old nineteen-thirties bank building. Once a cathedral to commerce, the interior was now a cathedral to everything America's best modern cuisine had to offer— with eye-watering prices to match. She'd checked out the menu online once Dax, Alex's driver, had told her their destination, and was still in shock.

The maître d' directed her to a private booth at the back. She spotted Alex, busy typing something with both thumbs on his phone as she approached. As soon as he spotted her, he stood to greet her. Her breath got trapped somewhere around her solar plexus.

Tall and muscular in his business suit, the jacket undone, the tie gone, he looked both powerful and commanding and yet so familiar now. His gaze skimmed down her figure, his eyes blazing when they fixed back on her face.

'You look stunning, Eleanor,' he murmured, the raw edge to his voice making her feel as if they were suddenly alone. Unfortunately, though, knowing he desired her didn't have the power it once had to paper over the cracks in her heart.

She forced a smile, flattered and wary as she slipped into the booth opposite him.

'Thanks,' she said. 'I'm glad I made the effort,' she added, having opted for a vintage red velvet designer dress—one of the many the stylist had supplied for her to choose from in the last three weeks. It had occurred to her as she had donned it half an hour ago that she would have to leave the stunning wardrobe behind when she left. She had no use for the gowns and accessories once this was over, and she didn't want Alex too much out of pocket. 'You could have warned me you'd booked one of the most exclusive restaurants in the country,' she continued, sending him what she hoped was a quelling look. 'What if I had decided to turn up in jeans and a T-shirt?'

He gave a low chuckle, the sound oddly strained. 'I'd still want to strip you naked on sight.' The arousal in his eyes told her he was only half joking.

Awareness pulsed over her skin, but only made her heart jump and jiggle more.

'You're such a guy,' she said, trying to keep the longing out of her voice and maintain the light-hearted humour that had always been so much a part of their relationship. And had protected her from the depth of her own feelings for so long.

Unfortunately, she couldn't seem to get the lightness back now, when she needed it most.

'Guilty as charged,' he said, but as his gaze searched her face she couldn't see the teasing wit she'd become so used to. In its place was a guarded watchfulness that only made her feel more insecure.

'Eleanor, there's something I need to tell you...' he began, all traces of humour wiped from his expression.

And suddenly she knew, he was going to tell her their Christmas fling was over.

But I'm not ready to lose him yet.

Her panicked thoughts were interrupted by the waiter, who came to take their drinks order. But as soon as the man left, Alex's gaze fixed back on her face—intense, wary, determined, as if he had a bitter truth to deliver and didn't want it blowing up in his face. His sensual lips opened, and the panic exploded in her chest.

Don't let him say it.

'Yes, we do need to talk. Because I met your family today.' She threw the words out before he could say anything more.

His eyebrows shot up his forehead and his mouth closed with a snap. His expression went completely blank for a moment, then a muscle in his jaw started twitching.

'What did you say?' he croaked.

He didn't sound angry, she realised, he sounded stunned.

She'd meant to stop him dumping her. She hadn't expected it to be quite so effective though. In all the time she'd known Alex, she'd never seen him as rattled as he was now. Even when he'd been apologising to her all those weeks ago in Staten Island.

'Well, I didnae actually meet them,' she admitted. 'I had a long chat with your youngest sister, Mia, over the phone.' She began to babble, desperate to fill the charged silence and ease the turmoil on his face. Whatever had happened to Alex to make him want to ghost his family, it was still a source of pain. 'She introduced me, sort of, to your other siblings. Arianna, aka Ari, the divorcee with three kids. And Isabella, who misses you a lot too. And Matteo, who is training to be a fire-fighter and is very bossy. And Aldo, who's just had his first child with his girlfriend, Sammy. They named him Luca Alessandro, after you. I guess there's one other, though, she must have missed, because I make that only five siblings and you said you had six.' She finally wound to a stop.

'Lucia,' he whispered, the name raw with emotion.

He looked away, the muscle still twitching, as he dragged his fingers through his hair, sending the stylish waves into haphazard rows. Then he swore viciously, the force and fury behind the expletive making her tense.

'I'm sorry, I know it's not my business,' she said softly, covering his hand, which was bunched into a fist on the white tablecloth.

His fist jerked as soon as she touched him. He drew his hand away, rejecting her comfort. His gaze locked back on her face, probing, searching, but where she'd expected to see anger, all she saw was strained tension. As if he were holding onto his emotions by a thread.

She didn't want to snap the thread. She knew she had no right, so she said nothing. The silence stretched tight as he stared at her. But she wasn't even sure if he could see her any more. He looked shell-shocked.

The waiter arrived with their drinks, a Scotch for him, a dry martini for her. He downed the liquor in one gulp.

The tumbler hit the table with a sharp crack.

'Are you ready to order, folks?' the waiter asked, apparently oblivious to the tension.

'No,' Alex snapped, with enough force to make the man jump. 'We'll let you know when we're ready,' he said, his gaze still locked on Ellie's now burning face.

The waiter disappeared.

'How?' he said. 'How did you find Mia's number?' She heard it then, the snap of accusation. And temper.

'I didnae call her,' she said. 'She called the penthouse to speak to you.'

The frown on his face darkened. 'What did she want?' he asked, his tone tight with suspicion.

'To ask you to come to their Christmas gathering tomorrow in Brooklyn,' she said, unable to keep the sadness out of her voice. 'I think you should go,' she added, before he could respond. 'It's been ten years since your mother died…' She pushed the words out, ignoring his incredulous expression. She hadn't just crossed a line now—she'd leapt over it with both feet. But there would be no going back now, and maybe that wasn't a bad thing. 'Why punish your brothers and sisters if the issue is to do with your mum?'

Whatever Alex's reasons for avoiding his family, it was clear his brothers and sisters had no idea what they were. Didn't he at least owe them an explanation?

The frown became catastrophic, but right behind it she could see the shadow of guilt… Which made no sense. If he felt bad about this situation, why hadn't he corrected it? He'd had ten years to build bridges with his family. Why hadn't he gone to see them? He'd always struck her as a man who took what he wanted, who got the job done. Alex was a doer, not a bystander.

He didn't second-guess his decisions. It was how he'd become such a success in his business, but also one of the things she found so attractive about him.

She'd been told so many times by her parents that going after what you wanted was reckless, dangerous, and that not accepting the status quo was one of her greatest faults. Alex was living proof the opposite was true. That going after what you wanted could be a good thing, despite the risks. He'd encouraged her in the last few weeks to grab the moment with both hands, to indulge every whim, enjoy every sensation. And it would be one of the things she would miss the most when she lost him. His vitality, his energy, his take-charge attitude.

But it didn't diminish her love for him to see he could struggle too. That he had vulnerabilities he wanted to hide. That sometimes he wasn't as sure or certain as he appeared.

She covered his hand again, her heart jolting when his gaze met hers. The tortured expression was quickly masked, but this time, instead of withdrawing his hand, he turned it over, to link his fingers with hers.

The gesture had her heart lurching in her chest, her love expanding.

'I could come with you, if you want,' she said gently, her heart breaking for him… And in many ways for herself. If she could help him heal this rift, maybe she could leave something behind her, other than a few Christmas memories. 'I'd love to meet them. Mia sounded like a lot of fun. And she invited me, just in case you needed an ally. She said they can be quite overwhelming.'

'You have no idea…' Alex murmured.

Easing back in the booth, he let his fingers slip from

hers, but he could still feel her touch—the burn of her compassion, her tenderness, right down to his soul.

She had no idea what a bastard he was. How he'd used her.

He'd spent the whole damn day thinking about her and the secret he should have revealed yesterday, but hadn't had the guts to tell her.

And now she'd jumped in on his big confession and given him the perfect excuse to avoid telling her about Roman for another day.

He shouldn't take it. A part of him didn't even want to take it. He had no desire whatsoever to see his brothers and sisters again after all this time.

But Mia—from what he could remember of his kid sister—had always been a firecracker, the kind of kid who couldn't resist stirring up trouble and had the persistence of a steamroller.

As he searched Eleanor's face and saw, not just compassion for the boy he'd once been, but also the spark of curiosity, he knew Mia had handed him the perfect opportunity to finally show Eleanor what he was and was not capable of.

She'd always yearned for siblings, a big, chaotic, in-your-face family like his, because she'd thought that would give her a place to belong. When the truth was she'd only ever lacked those things because she had never truly belonged with the people who had stolen her. He wanted to hate Ross and Susan MacGregor for what they'd done to that defenceless baby, but how could he, when he'd done the same damn thing to the girl she'd become? He'd taken her innocence and her naiveté, her vulnerability and her compassion, her optimism and honesty and all her energy and wild enthusiasm for life and fed off it like a vampire.

He might have tried to deny it, but he'd known when he'd made her come so many times the night before that she was falling in love with him. He could see it in her eyes, the glow of infatuation. Because on top of everything else she was so easy to read. And he'd fed off that too.

Was that the real reason he'd run out on her today? Not just because of the secret he didn't want to reveal, but because of the guilty knowledge that had become lodged in his chest like an unexploded bomb.

'Okay, let's go to Brooklyn tomorrow,' he said, not making much of an effort to disguise his reluctance. Better she knew that he was doing this under duress, so she didn't get her hopes up.

'Are you sure?' Her eyebrows launched up her forehead, drawing his gaze to the dusting of glitter she'd applied to her eyelids—which only made her look more delicious.

The familiar heat pounded in his abdomen. He concentrated on it, realising the heat was pretty much the only thing about this situation he understood any more. She'd changed him in some fundamental way, which would be funny if it weren't so damn disturbing. Changed him enough to make him decide that going to see the family he'd distanced himself from for close to two decades was better than spending Christmas alone with her and the confusing emotions churning in his gut.

'Yeah, I'm sure,' he said, resigned to the inevitable.

'On one condition,' he added, the tightness in his chest easing at the realisation he'd won himself a reprieve.

'Which is?' she asked.

'We don't have to talk about it,' he said. 'Or anything else that doesn't involve either food, or how much I want to get you out of that dress.'

'We have a deal, Mr Insatiable,' she said, the bright, instant smile making the heat climb up his torso to wrap around his heart.

CHAPTER THIRTEEN

Christmas Day

'WE'RE HERE. I guess Aldo's place is the house on the left.'

Ellie watched Alex's jaw clench as his gaze roamed over the row of houses in the up-and-coming Brooklyn neighbourhood. Fairy lights hung from the porches of the wood-framed buildings that stood in an orderly line on top of sloping snow-covered lawns. Three storeys high, Aldo's house was painted in dark green with white trim, had a wraparound porch and a peaked roof with dormer windows. To add to the building's vintage charm, a couple of crooked snowmen stood in the front yard.

Alex looked so uncomfortable Ellie still couldn't quite believe he'd agreed to accept Mia's invitation yesterday evening. Or that he'd followed through on that decision this morning.

So far the day had been everything she could have hoped for. Fun and magical but also unbearably poignant.

She'd woken up, groggy and a little emotional, surprised to find the bed empty beside her. But also glad. They'd made fast frantic love last night when they'd returned from the restaurant, after a meal she'd barely been able to swallow. Basking in the afterglow, she'd almost blurted out the truth about how she felt to Alex.

But luckily, she'd managed to hold back. She wanted above all to end this affair with dignity. Which meant she needed to get her emotions under control. She'd almost blown it completely when—after a breakfast of fat pancakes and fresh berries—Alex had handed her a slim black velvet box in front of the Christmas tree. The beautifully designed silver lattice necklace inside, studded with what she was very much afraid might be real sapphires, had taken her breath away.

And made her eyes sting with unshed tears.

Her first instinct had been to refuse the lavish gift. Where on earth would she ever be able to wear it? Plus it had probably cost him about five thousand times what she had spent on the knitted beanie cap she'd found to replace the ones of his she'd managed to trash in the last few weeks.

But when he'd lifted the stunning necklace out of the box and hooked it around her neck, then pressed his lips to her nape—making the familiar fire sparkle and leap over her skin—she hadn't been able to find the words to refuse the gift. They'd made love again, with her wearing only the necklace, but she could still feel the distance growing between them—his detachment, the air of wary tension as real and vivid as the way he could command her surrender with the strong overwhelming thrust of his body into hers.

And so as they'd showered and got dressed for the

trip to Brooklyn she'd said nothing about the stupidly over-the-top gift, because it seemed to fit perfectly with the nature of their whole relationship. Beautiful and giddily exciting but ultimately a fantasy.

She would keep the necklace with her always—even if she would never wear it again—as a memento of the first man she had ever loved. And a reminder not to beat herself up too much for making such a fundamental mistake. Alex Costa was an overwhelming man, in so many ways, so was it really any surprise she'd let her reckless heart get the better of her? Despite all her best intentions.

The good news was, she wouldn't have had it any other way. He'd given her so much in the short time they'd been together and she refused to regret it. After all, anything this good was always bound to hurt when it was gone.

'Looks like he did a good job of the remodelling,' Alex said absently.

'Mia said you bought all the houses on this block for your family?' she said. 'That was incredibly generous of you,' she added, thinking it wasn't the actions of a man who didn't care.

Alex frowned. 'Not really, I bought the block at a knock-down price eight years ago, because it was earmarked for demolition. Seemed a shame as a lot of these buildings are historic. They just needed some care. The family were still living in the Bronx, wouldn't have looked good for my corporate image if the press had got hold of the story. So I gave them a budget to do their own building works—they came in well below budget. Costa Tech has a share in the equity. So it's a win-win financially and my PR team was in heaven. Believe me, it wasn't a gift, it was a smart business decision. I didn't do it out of the goodness of my heart.'

'Okay,' Ellie murmured, wondering why he found it so hard to admit he cared about his family. The siblings now all lived together in a beautiful area of Brooklyn, something they couldn't possibly have financed on their own, but he'd also found a way to preserve their pride by letting them contribute their labour.

'Unfortunately, they refuse to see it that way,' he murmured, turning back to stare at the row of beautifully preserved houses. He gave a heavy sigh. 'They'll be back from Mass by now, let's get this over with,' he said.

'We don't have to go in there, if you don't want to,' she said.

He shrugged. 'It's not that big a deal,' he said, and she wondered if he was trying to persuade her or himself. 'And we don't have to stay too long.'

But after they got out of the car, and she retrieved the bottle of wine and the bunch of winter blooms they'd bought as a hostess gift, she could tell it *was* a big deal. He took hold of her hand and squeezed her fingers as he led her up the path to the porch, then tensed at the sound of laughter and conversation from inside the house.

She could see him struggling to relax as he pressed the bell.

Seconds later a woman flung open the door, wearing jeans and a Christmas sweater covered by an apron, and with a tinsel crown perched on a tumble of dark curls. Tall and statuesque with the same lavish good looks as and similar colouring to Alex, the woman had to be one of his sisters.

Her chocolate-coloured eyes widened, her cheeks flushing with colour as she gasped.

'Hey, Arianna,' Alex said, his voice gruff and deceptively casual.

The woman, who Ellie now realised was Alex's oldest sister, pressed a hand to her mouth, the raw emotion in her eyes making them shine.

'Sandro,' she whispered. A brilliant smile split her features, turning stunned emotion to fierce joy. 'I can't believe you're here.'

'Me either,' he replied, still tense, still wary, but his tone rough with emotion now too. And suddenly Ellie knew what he had told her all those weeks ago in Central Park wasn't true. Maybe he wanted to believe he didn't need this connection, didn't want to be a part of this family, but this reunion meant as much to Alex as it did to his sister.

Arianna shrieked and threw her arms around his neck. He caught her, his hands holding her steady, as tons more people began crowding into the doorway—men and women all with the same stunning bone structure and dark good looks shouted greetings, slapped Alex on the back and introduced themselves to Ellie while a gaggle of children ranging in age from early teens to the newborn in their host Aldo's arms made as much noise as possible.

As they were led into the house surrounded by so many people of all ages the smells of roasting meat and garlic, herbs and spices infused the bright airy space filled with conversation and laughter. The love these people had for Alex was so real and all-consuming and the welcome they gave her too—for 'finally getting Sandro to take his head out of his ass and come see us', as his brother Matteo had put it—so warm and generous, she found herself blinking back tears herself.

A huge tree stood in one corner of the living area, the hardwood floors were polished to a high gleam and the kitchen packed with people and what looked like a feast of antipasto and lasagne and other delicacies for the meal ahead. Christmas decorations—some clearly home-made by the gang of children, whose names Ellie was struggling to remember—adorned every surface, while more lights had been strung from the ceiling.

As they had their coats taken, wine was poured, and the flowers placed in pride of place on the huge makeshift table that stretched from the kitchen into the living room. Everyone talked at once, asking questions, introducing yet more children, offering around plates of cold cuts and warm nibbles. Ellie had never felt more overwhelmed in her life, but for the first time ever she felt like a part of something more than herself.

Alex stood beside her throughout, and while the tension didn't leave his body—a body she had become so attuned to she could feel every ripple, every jolt—she could also feel the emotion she knew he was trying so hard to hide. Her heart pounded against her ribs as she watched him react to the outpouring of love, of laughter, of joy and emotion, and sensed how hard it was for him to remain aloof, and untouched. He responded with wit, with charm, but beneath it was that brutal whisper of cynicism that told her, while these people loved him, he didn't feel comfortable in their midst.

Alex reluctantly took a toddler thrust into his arms by his sister Lucia's girlfriend, Ava, then stared at it as if it were an alien being.

Alex didn't know how to be loved, she realised. Was that it?

Would it be wrong to try and fix that? Surely not, especially if she didn't make the mistake of thinking she could make him love her too.

'Hey, Uncle Sandro, you wanna go shoot some hoops with me and Jacie?'

Alex stared at the gangly kid of about twelve who had offered the invitation—Ari's son Leonardo, if he remembered correctly. The boy reminded him of himself as a pre-teen, all elbows and knees and not a lot of coordination. But unlike him, the boy's winning smile was as instant and beguiling as the confidence that oozed from him. He looked so comfortable in the melee of a Da Costa family Christmas, his place assured and understood. Unlike Alex at his age.

By the time he was eight, Alex had lost all that confidence, had stopped feeling like a part of his own family.

The prickle of resentment, and anger for that lost kid twisted in his gut now, along with the meal he had struggled to digest over the last two hours, while his family fired good-natured questions at him and Eleanor and regaled her with stories about him as a boy.

She'd lapped it up, as he'd known she would—and his family had adored her. She'd remembered all the kids' names, cooed over the baby until his brother Aldo's head had grown to twice its usual size, and helped with the meal prep like a pro. Once they were all seated, she'd dived into the platters of cold cuts, enthused over his brother Matty's famous lasagne, and still found room for the roast beef joint and a very alcoholic tiramisu. And all the time, he'd sat there struggling to swallow a single bite.

The Da Costas were a boisterous, welcoming bunch who knew how to cook, and they'd lavished Eleanor with the uncomplicated affection he remembered from his siblings as a kid. Because they didn't know the ugly truth of what really lay beneath all those big family get-togethers from their past. And he had no plans to ever tell them. It was the least he owed all of them, not to destroy their memories of their childhood the way his childhood had been destroyed. And why he had avoided them for years. He wished to hell he'd done the same thing today, because every attempt to include him in the conversation, to show him the uncomplicated love and affection they obviously felt for the boy they re-membered only made the guilt heavier in his gut. He hadn't been that boy in twenty years.

'Isn't it kind of cold to shoot hoops?' he said, even though he could do with getting out of the house. He couldn't give these people what they needed from him. Because he was a coward and he always had been. But the struggle to hold back the truth was starting to give him indigestion.

The boy slung a protective arm around his kid sister—a petite dark-eyed girl dressed in overalls and a Yankees sweatshirt who clearly idolised her older brother.

'Nah,' the boy said. 'Uncle Aldo always keeps the court clear so we can come shoot hoops with him, cos our dad doesn't come around much any more,' the boy added with a maturity beyond his years. Alex remembered the boy's father had run out on his kids and Arianna a couple of years back, according to the very talkative Mia, who had cornered him earlier.

'Okay, good enough for me, let's go,' Alex said, hauling himself out of the chair, grateful for the chance to escape. Arianna's kids clearly craved male attention, he'd seen his brothers Matteo and Aldo making a fuss of them earlier, and he could do that much at least.

'For real, Uncle Sandro?' the little girl asked, clearly astonished her sulky new uncle would agree to hang out with them.

'Yeah, for real,' he murmured, patting her soft curls, and struggling to dismiss the renewed pang of guilt when she stared at him with the same hero worship he remembered from when his siblings had once looked up to him.

Don't get too attached, kid. I'm not gonna be any better at being an uncle than I was at being a big brother.

'By the way, my name's Alex now,' he added, correcting them automatically, surprised when the pang throbbed at the thought that Sandro no longer existed, and hadn't for a long time.

'Yes, sir, Uncle Alex,' the boy said, that uncomplicated smile beaming back at him.

He followed the children out of the back door, before anyone could jump in to stop them. But the weight he had hoped to lift off his shoulders as he shot hoops with his niece and nephew while the light faded failed to budge an inch.

Ellie picked up the framed photograph from the sideboard picture gallery she had noticed earlier while being given a tour of the house by Aldo.

It showed a young family—a heavily pregnant woman with a slightly worried smile on her face, with two little girls and a smaller boy holding onto her skirts. An older boy of about eight or nine, who had to be Alex, stood to one side, and a strikingly handsome man, who looked exactly like Alex, was throwing a chuckling toddler up in the air.

Ellie studied the photograph. They should have looked like a happy family, because they were all smiling in varying degrees, except for Alex. But something wasn't right with the photo, just as something hadn't been right with Alex all day.

She recognised his expression in the photo. Watchful, wary, cautious, and so guarded. It was the same one he had been trying to hide behind today, a bland smile and the easy confidence he had worn like a mask all afternoon—which hadn't fooled anyone.

'That's our pop two years before he died,' Isabella, Alex's second oldest sister, murmured from behind her. 'Sandro always looked so much like him, and that hasn't changed.'

'He's very handsome,' Ellie said, her fingers tensing on the frame. She could hear the note of grief in Isabella's voice and her heart went out to her. 'It must have been very hard for you, losing your dad when you were all so young.'

'Yeah.' Isabella sighed. 'He was such a huge part of our family, charming, charismatic, the kind of guy every woman in the neighbourhood threw themselves at. There were a lot of broken hearts when he died suddenly—not just my mom's and ours. But it was hardest on Sandro,' she said, with a simple compassion Ellie had to admire, but which made her feel strangely guilty at the same time.

The visit hadn't been a success. Alex's brothers and sisters had been so kind, so sweet, so welcoming, so happy to see him, but he hadn't reciprocated. Not really. Deflecting their stories, eating very little of the incredible feast they'd laid out. And she couldn't understand it.

Gone was the witty, charming, exciting man she had met two months ago, gone too was the confident, arrogant, overwhelming man. In his place was a strained, tense shadow of that man.

'I'm so sorry about today,' Ellie said, deciding there wasn't much point in avoiding the obvious. 'I thought if he came, he would be...' She shrugged. Good God, what did she really know about the inner workings of a family like theirs, when hers had been so small and constricted? 'More open.'

Isabella smiled, her expression kind and thoughtful, which made Ellie feel like more of a fraud. She had no right to be here, witnessing their pain.

'It's not your fault,' the other woman said. 'We're still incredibly glad you got him here,' she added. 'It's a big step in the right direction.'

'Do you really think so?' Ellie asked, wanting to believe her, but not convinced Alex would ever return.

'I'm sure it is.' Isabella turned to gaze out of the window, where Alex was still playing basketball with Arianna's two oldest children even though night had fallen. His other siblings were washing up, putting younger children to bed, or watching the rerun of a baseball game in the rec room. But Ellie had felt the energy in the house drop as soon as Alex had gone outside, and she knew, just as his siblings knew, the decision to go shoot hoops with the children was another avoidance tactic.

'We don't want to pressure him,' she added, the sadness in her eyes unmistakable when her gaze returned to Ellie. 'Something happened to Sandro a long time ago, before Pop died.' She took the framed photo from Ellie. 'You can see it in his face here. I think Ari tried to talk to him about it, when Mom died. Matty too. But he blew them off. And he's been avoiding us ever since…' Isabella shrugged. 'Sandro was only eleven when Pop died, but it was like Mom blamed him somehow, like she couldn't look at him,' she said, echoing what Mia had said two days ago. 'She packed him off to that boarding school when he got a scholarship, and wouldn't even let him come home for vacations after the first couple of years. We all knew how much that hurt him, even though he wouldn't admit it. I'm sure that's why he doesn't want to see us now. If only he would talk to us about it. But we can't force that, he has to decide he can trust us again.' She placed the photo on the sideboard, then smiled at Ellie, the gesture so generous, so open, Ellie's heart contracted in her chest. 'You got him to come, Ellie, and we can't thank you enough for that.' She laughed, the smoky sound full of hope. 'Seeing the way he looks at you, me and my sisters are totally convinced, anything is possible now.'

'Why?' Ellie asked, confused. 'I don't have any influence over him.'

Isabella grinned. 'Of course you do,' she said. 'When you're the first woman he's ever fallen in love with.'

He doesn't love me—that's just nuts. Isabella is clearly even more of a cock-eyed optimist than I am.

Ellie repeated the mantra in her head, to try and dispel the bubble of hope that had been sitting under her breastbone ever since she and Alex had left the Da Costa's Christmas gathering to drive back to Manhattan ten minutes ago.

Alex sat silent and rigid beside her as the car headed across the Brooklyn Bridge. The string of white lights attached to the iconic bridge's suspension cables glowed through the scatter of new snowfall, guiding their way through the night back home.

Except his apartment is not your home.

She pushed the thought down, past the bubble of hope, to concentrate on something she had decided was more important while she had watched Alex say stilted goodbyes to his family.

What made it so hard for him to be a part of his own family? Was it rooted in the experiences of that wary child, the mysterious thing that Isabella had referred to that had changed him so fundamentally but that he couldn't talk about even now?

Would it be so wrong to try and help him heal? Because whatever it was that was holding him back, it seemed so wrong to her not to embrace people—kind, good, generous people—who wanted so much to be a part of his life.

The silence continued as they drove through the Lower East Side, the streets mostly empty, the swish of the snow against the tyres the only sound.

A part of her knew she didn't have the right to probe into his past. But if she didn't, who would? She couldn't bear the thought of Alex sealing himself off again, when his family had so much to offer him. After all, she knew what he was rejecting with his silence, his stubbornness, because she had yearned for so long for the one thing he seemed determined to throw away.

He reached to turn on the radio, but she stilled his hand before he could touch the dial.

'Can I ask you something?' she said. 'Something personal.'

His gaze flicked to hers, the frown making her certain he could guess what she was going to ask, but then to her surprise he replied, 'Sure, I guess you've earned the right.'

It was a strange thing to say. But she swallowed the foolish leap of hope. This wasn't about her, about them.

'Did something happen to you as a little boy, that alienated you from your siblings?'

'How the hell did you know about—?' He stopped dead, but she could hear the defensiveness, and she'd heard enough to realise Isabella had been spot on.

'Isabella told me,' she said carefully as his knuckles whitened on the steering wheel. 'They know something happened, something devastating, because you changed and they think that's why it's so painful for you to spend time with them,' she rambled on, scared of making things worse, but much more scared of not doing what she could to fix this rift. 'She says Ari and Matty tried to talk to you before about it, when your mother died, but you brushed them off. But they don't understand why you can't talk about it now.'

'It's not important,' he said, his gaze fixed on the road ahead as they drove through the park.

It was a ridiculous thing to say, even he had to know that.

'How can it not be important,' she said gently, 'when

it's stopped you from being with people who love you so much?'

He said nothing for a long time, the muscle in his jaw clenching and releasing, as he drove the car into the underground garage. She waited, patient but determined. This was incredibly hard for him, she got that, but maybe if he could talk about it to her, whatever it was would release him from its clutches.

He switched off the ignition and sat with his head bowed, his breathing ragged. At last he turned to her, but what she saw in his eyes made no sense. Not sadness, not fear, not even the guarded tension she had become used to today, but guilt and shame, naked and unguarded for once. 'They wouldn't love me quite so much if they knew the truth,' he said. 'And neither would you.'

The words rammed into her chest, destroying her defences in one fell swoop.

He knew how she felt about him? *How* did he know? But, worse, was that why he felt guilty? Because he didn't feel the same?

'How did you know that I've fallen in love with you?' she asked, the words forced out through the crushing weight on her chest.

He let out a harsh laugh, then touched a thumb to her cheek, slid it down to cup her chin. His touch was electric as always, the shudder of response she couldn't control only making the ache worse.

'You're so damn transparent, Eleanor. It's been obvious for a while.'

She tugged her head free, determined to hold back

the tears scouring the backs of her eyes. The apologetic look on his face somehow worse than the guilt.

'What did you mean, I wouldn't love you if I knew?' she asked, trying desperately to shore up her defences again, to get through this and do at least some good.

You knew he didn't love you. Don't make a scene.

He swore softly, dropped his head back, the sinews tightening in his neck as he struggled with demons she couldn't see. But at last he spoke. 'Damn, I guess I owe you this much before I tell you the truth.'

What truth? What was he talking about?

But before the questions had even registered he launched into a strained monologue, the tone brittle with anger and frustration, but also a grim self-loathing. But as he talked, she began to understand what had been done to that little boy all those years ago, to make him so scared to love. And so scared to rely on anyone but himself.

'I was eight, nearly nine, the first time my father used me as cover to go screw one of his mistresses…'

Alex said the words he'd held inside for so long. Weird, then, that saying them now, to her, a woman whose respect he wanted but knew he could never deserve, felt like tearing a plaster from a fresh wound. He couldn't look at her, though, with those wide blue eyes with the genetic mutation full of compassion he didn't deserve. So instead he stared at the concrete wall of the parking garage as the car chilled around them, not unlike his heart.

'That first time he made me sit in the truck. Even though it was winter. I didn't understand what was going on. He'd told me he was taking me to meet up with some of his friends. I'd been excited. I loved Pop's pals, they always treated me like one of the guys. But instead of going to the pool hall where he hung out when he was busy avoiding his paternal responsibilities, he drove out of the neighbourhood to a house I didn't know. I was sitting in that truck for what felt like hours, but could only have been about twenty minutes. He came out and started making out with her on the porch. I asked him who she was when he got back into the truck, and he socked me.'

He breathed in, still feeling the pain of that back-handed slap even now, because it had signalled the end of his childhood.

'It was the first time he ever hit me. But it wasn't the last.'

'Alex, I'm so sorry,' she said, but he couldn't look at her still. Because he knew she would feel sympathy for that kid. But he knew he couldn't trade on her pity any longer. 'He sounds like a cruel and selfish man,' she added.

'Yeah, that's one way of putting it.' He let out a hollow chuckle—hell, she still had no idea she was sitting beside a man who had exactly the same weaknesses. Maybe he didn't screw around, but he'd lied to her, for days, had kept a secret he had no right to keep so he could continue to use her. And how was that any different?

'He used women, then discarded them,' he continued, the bitterness tempered now by the brutal echo of self-disgust. 'And I kept that secret for him, always. He got into the habit of taking me with him, made me sit in the parlour while he was banging them upstairs. I could hear them. Going at it. And that somehow made it so much worse. I'd much rather be outside in the truck, freezing my butt off, than have to listen to it, but he got mad when I asked.' He let out another brittle laugh. 'You know what he said to me?'

She shook her head, her eyes so wide with concern now he only felt more ashamed.

'"How am I gonna explain you getting pneumonia to your bitch of a mom?"'

He sighed, the horror of that bitter, brutal comment still too fresh.

'They all thought he was a great guy. A great dad. That he loved them. That he loved her. But it was all just an act. She found out the truth though, when he died of a heart attack in another woman's bed.'

He shivered, not from the chill in the car, but from the memory of his mother's face when she'd arrived just after the paramedics, holding Mia in her arms. Frantic, scared, devastated. And then the truth had dawned on her.

'She saw me standing in the parlour with the woman he'd been screwing, who was in hysterics. She looked right through me…' He huffed out a breath, rolled his fist against the knot in his chest, that was still there after all these years. 'And I knew then she would never forgive me.'

Eleanor touched his hand, and he turned to see the tears in her eyes, for that lost boy who was long gone. 'How old were you when he died, Alex?'

'Eleven,' he said, but he'd been so much older than his years even then.

'She had no right to blame you,' she said with such passion the guilt only increased. 'And had nothing to forgive you for.'

She still doesn't get it. But she will.

'Maybe,' he said, because he wanted to bask in that misguided adoration, just for a little while longer. How pathetic was that?

'It's cold, let's get up to the apartment,' he said.

She looked exhausted as she nodded. He knew how she felt as he stepped out of the car, walked around to her door to help her out, because he felt about a thousand years old too.

He wanted to touch her, wanted to hold her, wanted to drive into that tight wet warmth once more, hear her sobs of pleasure, smell that glorious scent, which he was very much afraid would haunt him for the rest of his life, and let her love him—or rather let her love the man she thought he was—just one more time. But as they travelled up to the penthouse in silence, he could feel her compassion, her need to heal him, pressing on his conscience like a concrete block and he knew he couldn't use sex to avoid the truth any longer.

As they took off their coats she said softly, 'You have to tell them, Alex. They deserve to know the truth. And you don't deserve to suffer a moment longer.'

The stubborn set of her chin, her honesty and certainty and reckless determination to make things right were so like her, he felt humbled, even as he knew how misguided she was.

She stepped closer to him, pressed her palm to his cheek. He grasped her wrist, tugged the consoling hand away from his face.

'Don't…' he said. She flinched, and he knew he'd hurt her, because she couldn't disguise it.

But he couldn't take it any more. Couldn't lie to her any longer.

He swallowed heavily, determined for once to live up to his word, to be the man he might once have been, if only he'd been able to believe in love and family, and the essential goodness of people, the way she did. But he knew how deluded she was, not just about him, but about all of it.

'You don't know me,' he said. 'You think I'm some kind of victim, some kind of good guy, but I'm not,' he continued, because he could still see the sheen of compassion in her eyes. 'And I never was, even as a little kid. I do what I have to do to look out for number one. Always. And to get what I want. Just like my old man. And just like your so-called parents.'

'My… What are you talking about?' she whispered, the blank confusion on her face making his ribs contract. And his heart lurch painfully in his chest.

He hated himself for destroying her innocence. For taking that sweet, tender compassion and the delusions about the people who had pretended to care for her away for ever. But it was way past time she woke up to what they had done to her. He pushed the anger, with them, with his old man, with himself, to the fore to get the words out.

'They stole you—and gave you a life you should never have had,' he said flatly. 'Hiding you on some tiny island, keeping you to themselves when you should have had so much more. I got the DNA test back two days ago. You're not Eleanor MacGregor and you never were. You're Eloise Fraser, Roman's sister.'

'That's not true…it canny be,' she whispered. The stunned emotion in her eyes had his heart splintering, but he couldn't stop. Couldn't hold onto the secret any longer.

'They wouldn't do that to me,' she said, but he could see she knew the truth now, from her horrified expression. 'They loved me.'

She would hate him, he got that. But wasn't that what he had always deserved?

He grasped her arms as she braced against his hold. 'They didn't love you. How could they, when they robbed you of everything?'

She broke away from him, her face a picture of so much pain, he could feel it ripping him apart. He hadn't meant to tell her like this. He had meant to soften the blow. But this was for the best, he decided. Or how else would she ever realise he was no different from the people who had kidnapped her, who'd lied to her, her whole life?

The tears rushed down her cheeks, but instead of dissolving as he had expected, instead of collapsing, she straightened. Her eyes narrowed, but, instead of pain or confusion, all he saw now was bravery.

It made the empty space in his heart open even further.

She was beautiful, even now. Valiant, courageous, and so fierce.

'I'll no believe it,' she said, the Scottish accent thickening, as it always did when she was upset.

'A DNA test doesn't lie,' he said, suddenly unbearably tired.

'It's not that I don't believe the truth of the test,' she said, the hurt replaced with anger. 'It's their motives. They *did* love me. In their own way. They showed me that every day. If they took me from that wreck, they must have believed it was the right thing to do.'

He swore viciously, angry too, now, that she couldn't see what was right in front of her eyes. 'The right thing for them, you mean, not you. Can't you see, they kept you there all those years to protect themselves, not you? There's no excuse.' Any more than there was any excuse for what he had done, to destroy his mother, his family, all to placate a man who had never deserved his loyalty. 'Are you really so naïve you'll forgive them? Even now?'

He went to take her arm again, suddenly desperate to hold her, to show her, to force her to see the truth.

She pushed him away, her voice steely and so cold it chilled his heart. 'Don't touch me… *You knew.* For two days. And you didn't tell me? Why didn't you?'

He raked his fingers through his hair. 'Isn't it obvious? Because I still wanted to sleep with you,' he said, knowing it was the only explanation that made any sense. 'And I figured once you knew you weren't a pauper anymore, you might not be so amenable.'

She flinched, her hand covering her mouth. 'You bastard.'

She shook her head, and then she fled into the bedroom. He could hear her packing. He stood waiting, his heart shattering all over again.

Perhaps he could stop her, perhaps he could explain, perhaps he could beg her forgiveness. But what would be the point? He would still be the same man.

When she appeared, holding her backpack, he stood

rigid, unfeeling, refusing to let her see the emotions churning like acid in his gut.

'You had no right,' she said, her cheeks red with tears already shed, her eyes empty, 'to keep that from me.'

'Ya think?' he said, imbuing the words with every ounce of cynicism he had ever felt, ever been taught to feel. By a man who had taken his innocence.

Carmine Da Costa had destroyed that kid, but he couldn't escape the fact any more he was entirely responsible for the man that broken boy had become.

She left him standing there in the hallway. The swish of the elevator doors closing behind her jolted him out of his trance. He walked into the bedroom in a daze, to see the necklace he had given her. The one he had chosen, like a lovesick fool, lying on the bed. He picked it up, brushed his thumb against the precious stones, still warm from her skin.

And he cursed again, the words broken this time. Just like him.

Damn, had he really believed he could buy her affection? That a lavish gift, lots of mind-blowing sex, could make him worthy of her?

What an ass.

He sat down on the edge of the bed, his hands shaking as he pulled out his cell, and dialled Roman's private line.

CHAPTER FOURTEEN

December 26th, morning

'HEY, MACGREGOR, YOU need to vacate the room. Hostel's closing for the day in ten.'

Ellie jolted awake in the narrow single bed at the sharp rap on the door. She groaned, her whole body aching from too many tears and too little sleep.

'Okay, thanks,' she murmured back, her voice as raw as her stomach, which hurt from the roller coaster it had been riding all night—as her emotions veered crazily between panic and confusion, shame and devastation. She attempted to sit up, her brain already rerunning the events of last night in Alex's penthouse—in painful detail.

All the things he'd told her—about Roman Fraser, the MacGregors, the childhood that had always been a lie—had been bad enough. But so much worse somehow was the cold dismissive look in his eyes, when he'd thrown her love for him back in her face.

She raked shaky hands through her hair.

Why couldn't she hate him? For using her. For lying to him. Why couldn't she believe him when he'd told her he'd only ever wanted to sleep with her, that he'd used her, that he didn't love her? Why couldn't she turn off her feelings for him? Now she knew the truth.

'Hey, by the way...' the voice came back through the door '... Jess says there's some rich dude in Reception asking for you. Says you won't want to miss him, he's super-hot.'

Alex? It has to be.

Ellie's battered heart careered into her throat. And her stomach climbed back aboard the roller coaster.

Had he come to apologise? To explain? And did she even want him to? Hadn't she been hurt enough? But still her foolish heart refused to stop punching her ribs at the thought of seeing him again.

'Thanks,' she shouted back, her voice firmer now and at least a little less broken. 'Tell Jess to ask him to wait. I'll be right down.'

After dressing and packing her bag to stick in the hostel's lockers, Ellie headed downstairs, her heart still thumping her solar plexus. But when she walked into the hostel's lobby area, having stowed her bag, she knew instantly the man standing at the desk with his back to her—in a black coat that probably cost more than the whole building—wasn't Alex. This man was tall too, and broad-shouldered, but not quite as tall as Alex and he didn't have Alex's wavy hair, his was even darker, and more curly.

Her heart dived into her stomach, the foolish bubble of hope popping like a party balloon. He turned, almost as if he'd sensed her arrival, and she found herself trapped in his dark blue gaze.

He has my eyes.

The thought struck out of left field. Her staggered heartbeat rose back into her throat. Her lungs worked like bellows as she saw the same shock of recognition in his expression.

Her mind cleared enough to identify him from the photos she'd found on the Internet weeks before.

Roman Fraser. His classic good looks, the chiselled cheeks, the dent in his chin, those intense blue eyes with the same imperfection as hers.

He walked towards her as she stood rooted to the spot. Her mind reeled, her pulse accelerating to warp speed.

Had she sensed, somehow, that they were related when she'd first seen his picture? Was that why Roman Fraser's striking features had never attracted her, the way Alex's had?

Stop thinking about Alex. He doesn't want you any more.

Fraser stopped in front of her, his expression as stunned as her see-sawing emotions.

'Eloise…' he murmured, his voice hoarse. 'You look just like Grandma Joan.'

'I'm Ellie,' she corrected him. She had no idea who Grandma Joan was. 'Eleanor MacGregor,' she added, hearing the desperation in her own voice—to be the person she had always believed she was. But as he continued to stare at her, so intently, as if she were a phantom who might vanish at any moment, she knew that Ellie MacGregor was gone. Or at least altered beyond all recognition.

She could never have that naïve, hopeful, innocent,

reckless girl back, not entirely. And it hurt so much to know people she had loved, she had relied on, had never been who they'd said they were.

It felt like losing Ross and Susan all over again. It felt as if layers of skin were being torn off, to reveal a complete stranger—someone she didn't know and wasn't sure she wanted to know.

Alex with his stupid DNA test had changed all their lives irrevocably. She'd always had this empty space inside her, this yearning for something more, something different. She had always known *somehow* she didn't belong on Moira. But she had never for a moment believed finding her true self would cause so much pain.

'Of course.' Fraser nodded, the sadness in his eyes unmistakable. 'I'm Roman.'

'I know, I recognised you.' Her voice broke on the words. Something flashed in his eyes that might have been hope. 'I saw your picture. On the Internet,' she clarified quickly, and the flash flickered out.

'Right.' His gaze finally detached from her face to glance around the hostel's shabby entrance lobby. A frown of displeasure flattened his brows. 'Grab your stuff and I'll take you to my hotel uptown.' The laser-sharp gaze landed back on her face, his tone firm, commanding. 'You can stay in a suite there for now.' He paused. 'Or you can move into the Fraser Mansion on the Upper East Side. I keep it fully staffed but I'm not there much myself so that will give you your own space. We'll meet with the legal team tomorrow to settle the inheritance. Then you can take your pick of the other properties owned by Fraser Holdings.' He hesitated again, as Ellie tried to figure out what the heck was happening. This was too much, way too much. 'Or simply buy your own place,' he added. 'Whatever works for you. But I don't want—'

'Whoa, wait,' she interrupted the flow of information, or rather instructions, her head starting to hurt, along with everything else. 'I'm no' going anywhere today,' she managed. 'And I don't want to speak to any legal team tomorrow.'

His brows lowered even further, as if she'd just said something incomprehensible. Clearly he was not a man who was used to having his instructions ignored. Or countermanded. Not unlike his best friend.

The sudden thought of Alex, in full-on He Who Shall Be Obeyed mode the first night she'd met him, had her stomach flipping over. It didn't help to quell the nausea that had been lying in wait since last night.

'Why not?' he asked, as if her desire to control her own destiny made no sense whatsoever.

Ach, terrific. Just what I need—another overbearing man in my life.

'Because I live here, this is what I can afford,' she said as firmly as she could manage while her hands were trembling and the nausea was rolling around in her stomach like a dislodged oil tanker. 'And I have shifts working in a bar in Columbus Circle today and tomorrow.'

'Eloise, I don't think you understand...' he began calmly, the tinge of condescension making her stiffen.

'Ellie,' she corrected him. *Again.*

He blinked. 'Right, Ellie.' He took a deep breath, as if he were struggling to understand. *Really? Why was it so hard to understand she needed her indepen-*

dence? 'You're now worth upwards of five billion dollars in real-estate dividends, share options and a trust fund set up in your name twenty-one years ago,' he said with strained patience. 'You can afford to live wherever you want. And there's no charge to live at the hotel, or at the Fraser Mansion. Because those places belong to you too. You're my sister.'

She flinched and saw him tense too as he said the word. It was the first time their sibling relationship had been acknowledged aloud—apparently, they were both still struggling with the information.

She couldn't move out of here, not yet, and she certainly did not want to see any lawyers, but maybe she should give him a break. She opened her mouth, trying to figure out a possible compromise when he added:

'And no way am I letting you continue to work in a bar.'

'Excuse me?' The spurt of outrage at his high-handedness felt strangely cathartic. But then she blew it. 'Who made you the boss of me?' Repeating the exact phrase she had once said to Alex torpedoed the outrage, reopening the great gaping wound from last night.

Alex... Who didn't want her any more, had never really wanted her. And had sicced his best friend on her—because surely he must have found out where she was staying and told Roman Fraser somehow. Because he was done with her now, and he'd made her Roman's responsibility. Passing her over to his best friend like a parcel he didn't want to open.

'I don't think you understand. I don't want the money.' She sniffed, horrified to realise she was close to tears. 'I don't want any of this,' she added, barely able to catch her breath, the misery pressing on her chest like a barbell. 'I'm not ready, to meet you, to deal with all the lies they told me—' She stopped abruptly. She was rambling, making a spectacle of herself. But worse was the gut-wrenching realisation that the thing that hurt most was knowing she would have to adjust to this new life without Alex.

She missed him, so much. Why had he abandoned her?

She blinked furiously, determined to hold onto the tears. Breaking down in front of this man, this stranger, felt somehow so much worse than breaking down alone in her hostel room.

But instead of looking shocked, or embarrassed, or even annoyed, Roman Fraser simply nodded again and said very slowly, 'I'm sorry, you're right.' He hesitated again, the silence stretching as they both struggled to come to terms with the enormity of this situation. 'How about we start over?' he said at last. 'Find somewhere private to talk? We have a lot to discuss.'

She sniffed again, scrubbed away a tear that had escaped. 'Really?' she said, the foolish feeling of gratitude making her knees shake now as well as her hands.

'Sure, I've got my car parked out front,' he murmured. 'We can sit in there, if it hasn't been towed already.'

A strained laugh popped out of her mouth, the rueful offhand remark reminding her again—stupidly—of Alex, and all the sparring matches they'd had. But the recollection didn't hurt quite so much this time. She could understand why Alex and Roman had become friends—they shared the same wry sense of humour.

Roman. My brother.

She gave a shaky sigh, finally able to acknowledge that fact without wanting to puke.

Progress. Of a sort.

'Would it be okay if we went for a wee walk instead?' She didn't want to sit in his car. No doubt it was as deluxe as he was and her stomach did not feel one hundred per cent reliable—she did not want to risk throwing up in his fancy motor. 'Central Park is only a block away.'

She'd avoided walking through the park yesterday evening after leaving Alex's apartment, because it had been far too painful after their break-up, with all the memories they had shared there. But that was just another thing she needed to get over.

Roman hesitated, obviously wanting to object. Perhaps he was concerned he might be recognised—he was Manhattan's Hottest Eligible Bachelor after all. But then he nodded.

'Sure, if that's what you want.'

As he arranged to have his car picked up before it really did get towed, she found herself relaxing a bit, unable to shake the thought Roman Fraser had just made a major concession by agreeing to a walk in the park. And not pressing the point about moving out of the hostel today. Or seeing his lawyers tomorrow.

She still felt nervous, her heart as jumpy as her stomach. But when they headed down the road towards the park, the nausea had downgraded another notch.

Maybe getting to know him didn't have to be so awful. After all, she'd always wanted siblings... She just hadn't envisioned her big brother being a billionaire with movie-star good looks and enough money to purchase Edinburgh Castle several times over.

You can adapt, Ellie, and it will be one hell of an adventure.

Surely they could find a way to connect despite everything? Plus there were so many things she could ask Roman. About the people who had sired them both. She couldn't think of William and Edith Fraser as her parents yet. But maybe if she could at least talk about them, about the accident, and find out a lot more about Roman himself—what he loved, what he hated, his dreams, his disappointments, that sort of thing—this would all feel a little less overwhelming. A lot less terrifying.

And then there was the fact Roman Fraser was also Alex Costa's best friend. She knew she shouldn't want to ask him about Alex, shouldn't need to know more about the man who had dumped her—hadn't she found out enough already after what he'd said about his childhood last night, the brutal cynicism that had been baked into him at such an early age?

But how else was she going to stop blaming herself for completely misconstruing everything that had happened between them? And get the closure she needed.

'Sure you don't want a waffle to go with that?' Roman asked as he handed Ellie the hot tea he'd bought for her at a waffle cart on Central Drive.

'No, thanks,' she replied, although after almost an hour of walking and talking with her new big brother, she had to admit her stomach was a lot more reliable.

While her heartache—about Alex—and her confusion and panic about becoming a billionairess overnight were both still very much there, it had been illuminating and fascinating to talk to Roman. Not just because of all the things he'd told her, and all the things he'd wanted to know about her, but all the things she could sense he had held back.

She hadn't been wrong, he was an extremely guarded man. There was a sadness, a solitariness about him, which she suspected came from the years he had spent on his own. And from a misplaced guilt about the accident.

Alex had been dead right about that, she'd realised, when Roman had offered her an apology at the beginning of their walk. Once she'd finally realised that he was apologising for his inability to prevent her from being kidnapped, while he was in shock, gravely injured, his leg trapped under the wreckage, and he was going in and out of consciousness, she'd told him he was crazy. That he couldn't possibly blame himself for what had happened that night.

He had said no more about it, but she could see he didn't really accept that. They'd changed the subject, but as she'd quizzed him further—about his life now, his childhood and adolescence, their parents—she had soon realised that there were some things he was happy to divulge and others he was not.

He'd given her an in-depth account of all the Fraser businesses, for example—which included a luxury train line set up by their grandfather Ken, a property portfolio to die for and a number of other lucrative ventures, which she had no interest in whatsoever—but had said very little about his hopes and dreams, his plans for the future. And his own past. She'd had to tease that out of him gradually, but she had managed to uncover a few interesting nuggets. It seemed he had hated Eldridge Prep as much as Alex had until they'd become friends, and there was definitely something going on in his love life—because he'd clammed up completely when she'd asked him about it.

She had also discovered to her dismay that he had lost everyone who mattered in his life twenty-one years ago, not just her and their parents that Christmas, but also his grandparents—*their* grandparents—Joan and Ken, who had died earlier the same year. He'd spoken about them both with more affection than he had about his parents, which seemed significant somehow, although she wasn't sure why. Because he'd been quite guarded about that too, only pointing out that William and Edith had struggled to have a second child for close to a decade, and because of that they had loved her very much. Even though he hadn't said so, Ellie had suspected the quest to have a second child might have put a huge strain on the marriage and their relationship with their son.

One thing was certain, she couldn't even imagine having to deal with so much grief as a ten-year-old and had decided that had to explain why he was such a cautious man now… And maybe also why he was a tad overprotective. Because he'd mentioned a few times already how he really wasn't happy about her working in Mel's bar.

Add persistent to the mix.

She took a fortifying sip of her tea. They'd talked about everything now, but the one subject still burning at the back of her brain.

Alex.

'So, you said you and Alex got friendly at the prep school,' she ventured. 'What was he like back then?' she asked, as casually as she could manage.

But not casually enough, she realised, when Roman frowned. 'Why are you so interested in Alex Costa?'

Her heart plummeted into her stomach at the puzzled look in his eyes. The devastation she had kept at bay for over an hour, as she got to know her brother, twisted in her gut.

'He didn't tell you?' she whispered. 'About us?'

She shouldn't be surprised, she realised, that he hadn't spoken about their relationship to Roman. As far as Alex was concerned it was over. But even so, it hurt to realise just how quickly she had been forgotten. Had she really meant so little to him?

'What do you mean *us*?' Roman's tone sharpened, something fierce and volatile flashing in his eyes. 'Did Alex seduce you?'

Colour leapt into her cheeks. Awkward much?

'No,' she said, not sure what he was so upset about. 'We seduced each other. Not that it's any of your—'

'That son of a…' He swore, the fierce flash turning to fury. 'What the hell was he thinking? I'm going to murder him. How dare he take advantage of my kid sister?'

'Wait a minute.' She grasped his arm, before he could march off to do heaven knew what. Was this some kind of weird big brother thing? Because his protective instincts had just jumped off a cliff. 'Alex didnae know I was your sister when we first slept together.'

Roman stopped dead, his brows rising up his forehead.

'What do you mean, *first* slept together? How many times did it happen?' he demanded.

'Again, not your business,' she said, just to be absolutely clear. She had no idea what the etiquette was when it came to having a big brother, but she was pretty sure it did not involve her divulging intimate details about her sex life. 'But we've been living together since he took me to his mansion in the Adirondacks for Thanksgiving weekend.'

The outrage on Roman's face dropped away to be replaced with complete and utter shock. 'Living together? *You* and Alex?' he said, as if the words simply would not compute.

'Yes, me and Alex. Why are you so surprised?' Maybe she had loved Alex and he hadn't loved her, but was it really so hard to believe Alex Costa had wanted her, at least for a while?

'It's just… Alex is a player. He doesn't do relationships,' Roman said. 'Not for as long as I've known him.'

The information had Ellie's heart expanding, right alongside the foolish bubble of hope she'd tried so hard to crush.

'And even if he did,' Roman continued, a dash of colour marking his chiselled cheeks, 'you're not his usual type. At all.'

'So what *is* his usual type?' Because suddenly she wanted to know. Why hadn't she been enough? Why had he pushed her away so callously, when she needed him the most?

'I'm really not sure I want to be having this conversation with my sister,' Roman said, as if he had a choice.

'Well, tough,' she shot back, feeling her confidence returning at last. 'You started it.'

'Okay, fair point,' Roman huffed. He did not look happy. 'You said yourself you came straight from Moira to New York. I'm guessing there weren't a lot of eligible men there.'

She nodded, because he seemed to need an affirmation.

'All I'm saying is, Alex usually dates women with…' He cleared his throat, his colour—and extreme discomfort—heightening. 'Women with a lot of experience.'

It was Ellie's turn to frown. Her heart sinking again. 'I see.' Of course, she already knew that, because he'd freaked out so much when he'd discovered she was a virgin. 'To be fair,' she said, musing out loud, 'he didnae know I was a virgin when we first slept together at Halloween.'

'You were a…? Oh, hell. I seriously did not need to know that.' Roman swore again and collapsed onto the nearest park bench, running his fingers through his hair. 'Now I don't know whether to kill him or torture him first,' he murmured, but he didn't look mad any more, he looked shell-shocked.

Ellie sat down beside him and patted his knee as a wave of tenderness for him washed over her. Clearly there were complexities to this brother-sister thing that they would both have to learn to negotiate. But it was good to know he was as clueless about it as she was. And his desire to protect her felt more sweet now than overbearing.

But as they sat together on the bench, silently considering this new phase in their relationship, Ellie re-examined everything he had just told her about Alex and his dating habits.

And the bubble of hope became a balloon.

Because suddenly none of what had happened the night before made quite so much sense.

Had she given up on them too easily? Why had she allowed Alex to dump her without ever questioning his motives? And why hadn't she wondered about that little boy—who had kept such a devastating secret for so long? And then blamed himself when the secret was revealed? Was that the real reason he hadn't told her sooner about Roman? Was it all mixed up together somehow?

Or was she just being delusional? Wanting to believe Alex felt more for her than he did, because she felt so much for him?

She and Roman talked a bit more, about everything *but* Alex—and Roman told her again there was no need for her to go to work, ever again.

But this time she didn't get mad with him, she simply smiled—having a brother was hard work, but oddly rewarding too.

'Let's talk some more, soon,' she said. Going with instinct when he nodded, she stretched up on tiptoe and gave him a quick peck on the cheek. He tensed, but didn't draw back.

She considered that a major win before saying goodbye. Then she headed off to Mel's through the park, feeling lighter than she had in over twelve hours.

She had a lot of thinking to do—and maybe she was dead wrong about her and Alex, maybe there was nothing to salvage, no reason to hope—but she felt so much stronger than she had when she'd woken up.

One thing was certain, she wasn't going to let Alex call all the shots any more.

CHAPTER FIFTEEN

December 26th, evening

ALEX STARED AT the Christmas tree in the corner of his living space. With the lights off, the branches starting to droop under the weight of way too much tinsel and a scatter of fallen needles on the floor, the damn thing seemed to be mocking him by projecting his own feelings back at him.

The tree—which had seemed so enchanting less than three days ago—now seemed hopelessly out of place in the impersonal designer space that had once represented his success so perfectly.

Why hadn't he called the cleaning crew and asked them to take it away?

Because it's all you have left of her.

He tensed as another wave of crippling sadness hit him, the way they'd been doing all day. Ever since he'd woken up alone, inhaled a lungful of the rich spicy scent that clung to the sheets and the empty space inside him had become a chasm.

It was a chasm he recognised from the night his

father had died. But this time, the chasm felt deeper, darker and much harder to see the bottom of.

You miss her. You'll get over it.

This desperate yearning would end, eventually. It had only been one day. But why then did it seem to touch every aspect of his life? He hadn't been able to sleep last night, hadn't been able to eat this morning, had barely picked at his lunch and hadn't even been able to lose himself in work today. Nor did he have the luxury of picking up the phone and shooting the breeze with Roman, who had texted him earlier after meeting Eleanor for the first time.

Met Ellie today. Thanks for finding her. But you should have told me about the two of you. WTH?

'You have no idea, buddy,' he murmured into the Scotch he'd poured for himself as soon as he'd arrived home but had struggled to drink—because it reminded him of her.

But then every damn thing reminded him of Eleanor, and the devastated look on her face when he'd told her the truth about who she was, and about himself, about them.

He heard the ding of the elevator arriving.

Slamming the glass down, he headed towards the lobby, the spurt of frustration still doing nothing to fill the empty space inside him.

Whoever the hell that was, they could leave. He wasn't in the mood for company.

But he stopped dead in the hallway as the elevator doors closed again.

He stared, the empty chasm, the crippling sadness consumed by the fierce rush of longing.

'Eleanor?' he whispered, his heart expanding so fast it made his throat hurt.

She looked so beautiful, the skinny jeans and sweater combo clinging to her lithe curves. Her wild hair tumbled around her shoulders, her soft skin flushed pink from the cold. He jammed his fists into his pockets to resist the urge to grab her and carry her straight to the bedroom, so he could show her how much she meant to him the only way he knew how... Scared that if he touched her, she might vanish.

'I met Roman,' she replied. Then let out a heavy sigh. 'I met my brother, this morning.'

'Yeah, I know, he texted me,' he said, still struggling to talk. He just wanted to drink her in, every aspect of her. All the things he would miss for the rest of his life. Her smarts, her wit, her precious face and the soft Scottish brogue that wrapped around him now—if only for a little while.

'Why didn't you tell him about us?'

He registered the edge in her tone—hurt and confusion... And something else, something that sounded an awful lot like accusation. He frowned. *Huh?*

'How do you know that?' he asked.

'Because we talked, and he told me, you idiot.'

She strode towards him—fierce, provocative, magnificent. He dragged in a lungful of her scent and the regret flooded back in.

He stepped back, snapping out of the strange dreamlike state he'd been in.

She was here and all he wanted to do was beg her to come back, to forgive him.

'Now answer my question, why didn't you tell him about us, Alex?' Colour flared up her neck, highlighting the freckles on her face, the hurt in her eyes crucified him, but where there had been tears before, and devastation, now there was only determination... 'Was it because I meant so little to you? Why didn't you tell your best friend we'd been living together for a month?'

The words struck like body blows. Maybe he could have lied to her, but he couldn't hurt her again, not even to protect her, from him.

'That's not...' He swallowed around the raw spot in his throat—which had always been there, even since he was a little kid, but seemed bigger now, more jagged, more destructive. 'Don't ask me that.'

'You knew I loved you and yet you threw it back in my face. *Why?*' she asked again.

'You know why. I told you why,' he said, trying desperately to deflect and deny, to do anything that would take the guilt away. 'I didn't want to hurt you.'

'Oh, really?' Her eyes flashed with blue fire, only making her look even more magnificent. 'Well, it's a wee bit late for that, because you devastated me. But now I want a proper answer. No some rubbish about the sex,' she said, the Scottish accent getting more pronounced. 'This was never just about sex, not for either one of us. If you can't see that you're an idiot. Were you ashamed of me, was that it? Why did you have to make me feel like nothing?'

He swore viciously, turning away from her, unable to face her, unable to face himself. He slapped his hands down on the hall table, braced his arms, but he couldn't stop the shaking. He sank his chin into his chest. His whole body trembled, the waves of regret and sadness, nothing compared to the deep lancing pain arrowing into his ribs. He'd seen the vulnerability, the deep hurt he'd caused, and all he wanted to do now was take it away.

The way he'd wanted to do with his mom, but never could.

He felt broken inside, unworthy, unwanted, all the pieces of himself he'd spent so long rebuilding, replacing, so he would never be vulnerable again, ripped apart by one ferocious Scottish girl, who had somehow snuck under his guard and seen through all his defences to the lost, lonely, frightened boy beneath—in the space of one holiday season.

She'd given him a glimpse of what he could have, of what he could be—with her in his life—and he hadn't taken it, because he'd been so terrified it would all disappear if she found out the truth.

'I was never ashamed of you,' he murmured, the words torn from his chest. 'I was ashamed of myself. Because I wanted you to love me, but I was terrified of loving you back.'

Ellie stroked away the tears from her cheeks as she stared at the man with his back to her, his head bent, his body trembling, the pain inside him so harsh he was struggling to remain upright. The tall, indomitable, overwhelming man, who had been humbled now, as she had been, by emotions that scared the living daylights out of him.

A tentative smile broke through her tears, spreading sunshine into her belly, across her chest.

And I thought he couldn't break my heart a second time?

She let out a shaky breath.

But this was a good break, a clean break, a necessary break, so they could get past the darkness—of his stolen childhood, and hers—and finally walk into the light.

She crossed the last of the distance between them, and wrapped her arms around his waist, and pressed her cheek into the rigid muscles of his spine.

She held onto him as he tensed, tight enough for him to feel her heart beating against his back. Close enough so that he could feel how much she loved him. And know that however scary this was, he could love her back and she wouldn't hurt him.

Slowly, surely, each tight, tense muscle in his body began to relax, the trembling stopped and his staggered breathing evened out.

'What he did was never your fault, Alex,' she said softly. 'He made you keep a secret that was never yours to keep.'

His shuddering sigh passed through his body into hers. 'I guess I know that now.'

At last, he turned in her arms, and cradled her cheeks in his hands. 'I don't know what I ever did to deserve you,' he said, those hazelnut eyes searching her face. 'But there's no way in hell I'm going to let you go a second time.'

She grinned, and reached up to circle his neck. 'That's good,' she said, tugging his mouth down to hers. 'Because you couldn't get rid of me now if you tried.'

And then his lips captured hers.

The kiss was deep, drugging, possessive, full of relief but also full of the driving hunger that had consumed them both right from the start. But when he boosted her into his arms, and she wrapped her legs around his waist, she forced herself to drag her mouth free.

'Just a minute,' she said, breathless, giddy, euphoric, but still determined. 'You need to say it too.'

'Say what?' His brows arched, but she could see the mischievous twinkle she'd missed so much.

They had survived the pain, now the only thing to do was indulge in the pleasure… And start building a new life, where there was trust, and compassion and openness… And hope.

'Say you love me,' she said.

'I don't just love you. I adore you,' he said, pressing his face into her cleavage and making her nipples tighten.

'And promise me you're going to fix things with your family and tell them everything.'

He glanced up, narrowed his eyes, but then he nodded. 'Okay, if you insist.'

'I do,' she said, the power intoxicating.

'Anything else?' he asked, marching down the hallway towards the bedroom.

'Yes,' she said, laughing as he chucked her into the middle of the bed and stripped off his shirt. 'Promise me that you're going to devote the rest of your life to giving me unlimited orgasms whenever I request them.'

'Done!' He kicked off his shoes and ripped open his flies. 'Now get naked, Eleanor,' he added as he tugged off his trousers and boxer shorts and the strident erection leapt free. 'Before I tear off all your clothing.'

Then he pounced on her, to start making good on all his promises.

EPILOGUE

New Year's Eve

Dear Mr Costa,
As per our phone conversation and my previous
email, here is an interim report on my investiga-
tion so far into the Eloise Fraser/Eleanor Mac-
Gregor disappearance.

The birth certificate Ms Fraser has in her pos-
session for an Eleanor Fitzgerald MacGregor
born on June 20th, is not a forged document, as
I originally assumed, but the actual birth regis-
ter of a baby girl born to Ross and Susan Mac-
Gregor that summer.

I managed to track down the midwife, Cathe-
rine Wilson, who attended the birth in the remote
forestry cottage where the couple were living at
the time in Drummorag National Forest in the
Highlands. Ms Wilson said it was a difficult birth
and the child was born two weeks early.

I now suspect the child must have died sud-
denly that winter. After checking phone records
and the weather reports in the region around the

time of the Fraser car accident, it seems the couple were essentially snowbound and unable to contact anyone for a week prior to the crash.

With the help of the local forestry commission, I discovered a small grave in a glade approximately a quarter of a mile from the MacGregor cottage, marked by a home-made cross with the name Ellie, a heart, and a date three days before the accident inscribed on it. Apparently, the forester had always assumed it was for a pet of some description.

I now surmise the couple might well have been travelling to Inverness to report the death of their daughter when they came across the wreck and took the Fraser baby—i.e. Ms Eloise Joan Fraser—from the site of the accident. They relocated soon afterwards to the remote island of Moira in the Outer Hebrides, thus avoiding scrutiny from the extensive police investigation that ensued the following year.

If you would like to have the grave in the Drummorag Forest exhumed, to check the remains are those of the MacGregor child, ascertain the cause of death, etc., I can go about getting the necessary permissions from the local authorities involved.

I have sent the findings of my investigation so far to the local constabulary.
Regards,
Ian McKenzie, PI

Ellie sniffed and wiped a tear from her cheek as she folded the written report from the private detective Alex had hired in Scotland and placed it carefully on the desk in Alex's study.

'I canny believe he found all that out so quickly,' she said, her heart throbbing in her chest, her breath hitching.

No wonder Ross and Susan had always referred to her as their miracle baby. They must have been grief-stricken and traumatised, unable to get help for their child that winter, then forced to bury it alone. And then they'd found her on that bleak empty stretch of road, and probably saved her life. She was sure from Alex's conversations with Roman about what he remembered about the crash that they must not have seen Roman, or realised he was alive, or they would surely have helped him.

'I guess it's easier when you know where to look,' Alex murmured, his arms banding around her from behind. He tugged her gently into his body, enveloping her in his strength, and his unconditional support. She held onto him, the love she felt for him in that moment overwhelming.

Alex accepted her for who she really was. He loved her for her weaknesses as well as her strengths. In fact, he saw her flaws and thought they *were* her strengths. He understood her, in a way Ross and Susan MacGregor had never truly been able to, because they'd convinced themselves she was someone she wasn't… The baby girl they'd lost.

'Weird to discover after all this time the solution to the mystery was so damn simple,' he added, the whisper of his breath on her nape as comforting as it was exciting.

'And so heartbreaking,' Ellie replied, letting out an unsteady breath.

Even as her heart shattered for what the MacGregors had gone through before they'd found her that night, she felt a wave of relief washing through her. As if a huge concrete slab she hadn't even realised she had been carrying had been lifted from her shoulders. A concrete slab that carried within it the burden of all those expectations Ross and Susan had always had of her—why wasn't she quieter, less reckless, more content, happy with the life they'd given her? She understood now why she had never been able to fulfil those expectations, because the life Ross and Susan had wanted her to settle into wasn't hers.

'You want me to ask him to get the grave exhumed? So we can confirm everything?' Alex asked.

His arms tightened as he waited for her answer. How did he know instinctively when she needed his support the most?

She shook her head. 'No.' She sighed, and turned in his arms, needing to see his face, needing to feel that heady connection. 'Little Ellie MacGregor deserves to rest in peace,' she said, knowing she wasn't just talking about Ross and Susan MacGregor's dead baby, but also the reckless, free-spirited girl who didn't need to try and replace that lost child any more.

She touched his face, felt his hard cheek soften against her palm. 'And thank you, Alex, for giving me this closure. It means a lot to know that, however deluded they were, they did love me in their own way. Just not *me* exactly,' she added with a watery smile.

He covered her hand with his, drew it away from his

face and then placed a gentle kiss in her palm. 'Damn, Eleanor, you're something else,' he said, his gaze full of that rich appreciation she intended to bask in for the rest of her days. 'How can you be so forgiving? How can you not hate them, for what they stole from you?'

'Because I know, in my heart of hearts, they never meant to hurt me,' she said, but he looked unconvinced.

'Yeah, right,' he said.

She huffed out a breath. But she couldn't help smiling at Alex's disgruntled expression, knowing this time his cynicism, his reluctance to forgive the MacGregors, stemmed from his fierce desire to protect her from anyone who would ever hurt her.

'And now I have everything I need,' she added simply. 'Most especially, I have you and Roman, and your wonderful, totally overwhelming family.'

'You mean my way too big, don't-know-how-the-heck-to-mind-their-own-business family?' he cut in, but she could hear the lightness in his tone.

His family had texted him en masse after their Christmas Day visit, until he'd finally agreed—with a lot of additional prompting from her—to host another family gathering at his estate in the Adirondacks in the new year. At which point she would be by his side, while he told them the truth about their father.

She'd also started repairing her family drama too, by messaging Roman, and arranging a meeting with him and his legal team next week.

She still wasn't sure why settling the inheritance was so important to Roman, but she would find out everything about her new brother. Eventually. Once she and

Roman both got to know each other better. Something she was now determined to do.

She even planned to solve the mystery of what the heck was going on in her brother's love life, which Alex had begun to pick up on too when he had been forced to admit Roman was being even more guarded than usual.

But she was glad that at least Roman and Alex seemed to have settled any issues they had about Roman's best friend dating his kid sister.

'Not to mention more money than I could ever spend in my lifetime,' she added, cheekily. 'And more orgasms than I know what to do with.'

Alex laughed, but then his hands drifted down to slide under the sweater she wore and touch bare skin. 'About that…' he said, his rough palms making sensation zip and zing over her back and sink deep into her abdomen. 'How do you feel about skipping the bash at the High Line tonight and ringing in the New Year here? Alone? Just you, me and lots of extra-curricular orgasms?'

She let out a delighted chuckle as his hands finally cupped her backside and tugged her against the definite ridge forming in his pants. Grasping his shoulders, she leapt into his arms, knowing he would catch her, and wrapped her legs around his waist.

'Why, Mr Costa!' She laughed, going the full sex kitten, as he lifted her out of the study and down the hallway towards their bedroom, his lips already doing dastardly things to her neck. 'I thought you'd never ask.'

Three exhausting hours later, Alex held the woman he adored naked in his arms, his body still humming as they watched the fireworks burst into the night sky from the different displays across the city.

Could life ever get any better than this? *Doubtful*.

'Alex?' Her voice beckoned from the darkness. He looked down to see her watching him intently, her head tilted back against his shoulder, her serious expression lit by the explosions of coloured light outside.

'Yes, Eleanor?' he teased, even as his arms tightened around her, loving the feel of her, the smell of her, the weight of her snuggled against his chest—and the knowledge that she would always be his.

He'd fallen in love with his best bud's kid sister. What the hell?

'I think maybe you should call me Eloise from now on,' she said.

His breathing slowed, and the sensual smile on his lips died as his heart thumped his ribs, and he realised the enormous significance of the name change. 'You sure?'

'Yes, Eleanor is dead now…she's been dead for a long time. Just like Sandro.'

He brushed his thumb across her lips, letting his gaze roam over her, staggered again by her bravery, her fearlessness, her compassion.

'Everyone else can still call me Ellie,' she added. 'Because the nickname kind of fits with both names. But you've always seen me for who I really am. So it feels right to change my name back to Eloise Fraser and have you call me that.'

He nodded, his heart swelling in his chest and making it tough to breathe.

'Roman will be overjoyed,' he said, because he knew

how much his friend had always needed to have Eloise back. And this would be an important step on that journey.

'What about you?' she said, and he heard it then— the tiny note of doubt, of caution, of insecurity, which he'd helped put there, and which he intended to undo, even if he had to spend the rest of his life showing her exactly how much she was worth. 'Do you think it's the right thing to do?' she asked.

Sinking down in the bed, his leg sliding deliciously between her naked thighs as he pulled her closer still. 'Honestly, Eloise,' he murmured, cradling her chin to lift her mouth to his. 'You could ask me to call you Quasimodo Fraser and I'd think it was the right thing to do.'

'For Pete's sake!' She slapped him playfully on the shoulder with mock outrage, but she was still laughing as she surrendered to his fierce, ferocious kiss.

As he explored her mouth, drinking in her passion, revelling in their shared happiness, he vowed to offer her another new name soon, to add to the other two.

Eloise Fraser Costa sounded even more right to him, now he knew he didn't have to be afraid of his father's legacy any longer.

Because Eleanor—or rather Eloise, he corrected himself—saw him for who he really was too. And if he was good enough for a woman like her to love, he couldn't possibly be that bad a guy after all.

* * * * *

NINE MONTHS
AFTER THAT NIGHT

MELANIE MILBURNE

MILLS & BOON

To my beautiful grandchildren
Willow Esme and Torrance Theodore.

You have blessed my life in so many ways
and brought such joy and laughter.

It will be a long time before you can read Nanny's
books, but this one is dedicated to you all the same.
xxxxxx

CHAPTER ONE

HARPER LAY ON the hospital gurney in a sweat-soaked panic. Was she going to die? The niggling pain in her back that had started three days ago was getting worse. It was spreading to her abdomen—tight, rigid bands that made it hard for her to breathe. Was it endometriosis? Or…or *cancer*? She was only twenty-seven—how could she die of cancer? She had so much left to do. Her career was taking off. She had a book deal featuring her photographs—photographs she had yet to take in Paris in six weeks' time. This was definitely the wrong time to contract a terminal illness.

The pain gradually subsided like a retreating tide and Harper flopped back on the pillow and let out a shuddering breath. But she knew it would be back. The time intervals between the spasms were shrinking.

Only a junior doctor had examined her so far and he had seemed a little baffled by Harper's symptoms. The doctor took a blood sample for Pathology and told Harper the more senior emergency doctor would be back with the results, as soon as they came through.

Harper closed her eyes and tried to meditate while she waited for the results of the test. Not that meditation had ever been her forte. Her one and only visit to a health spa retreat had made her feel antsy and agitated the whole time, while everyone else was chanting and cleansing and rebalancing their chakras. Her chakras were obviously beyond repair. As for her mind? It was hardly ever still, which she put down to her turbulent childhood. All that time in foster care had made her hypervigilant. Every noise, every sound, every footfall and she was wide awake and alert.

A and E was busy with the usual dramas of a Saturday night. Harper could hear the noise of someone coughing a couple of cubicles away. Not a simple virus cough but one that hinted at some sort of hideous lung disease like emphysema or cancer.

Cancer.

Why could she not stop thinking about the C word?

A man was shouting in another cubicle about wanting more morphine. Harper wondered if he was suffering from the same disease. Maybe the Swan women weren't destined to live beyond thirty. Her mother had died young, so too her grandmother.

Another band of pain tightened around her abdomen like an iron cable. Sweat poured like tears from her hairline, her teeth were gritted together so hard she was sure she was going to crack every one of her molars. But hey, if she was going to die, what would it matter if every tooth fell out?

I don't want to die!

It was a scream inside her brain, as if a panic button had been pressed in her head, a piercing siren of distress only she could hear.

The curtain was swished aside and a more senior

emergency doctor came in. She placed a hand on Harper's wrist, her expression grave. 'Is your partner waiting outside?'

'I don't have a partner.'

'Oh, well, your next of kin? Your mother?'

'My mother died when I was eight.' Harper could say it without any trace of emotion but it had taken years of practice. Years of concealing her true feelings behind a mask of indifference. Years of blocking the vision of finding her mother lying lifeless on the floor of their cramped bedsit when she came home from school on that fateful day. Later than she should have come home. If she hadn't stopped on the walk home to play with a stray kitten…

'A sibling?'

'I'm an only child.' Which, strictly speaking wasn't quite true. Harper had several half-siblings she had never met because her father hadn't wanted his dirty little secret—*her*, his secret love child—to be revealed to his wife and family. 'Love child' was a bit of a stretch. Her father hadn't loved Harper's mother. He had used her to break his marital boredom and then left her when she got pregnant.

'Harper…' The female doctor's voice was gentle, as if she was preparing to deliver shocking news.

'It's okay, Dr Praneesh,' Harper said with a grim smile. 'You can be straight with me. It's cancer, isn't it?'

Dr Praneesh frowned. 'No, you don't have cancer.' She moistened her lips and continued, 'It's a different type of growth—you're pregnant.'

Harper rapid-blinked. Her heart knocked against her ribcage with the force of a punch. 'I—I can't possibly be pregnant.' Was she having some sort of hallucination? A bad dream? How could she be pregnant and not know? And more to the point—*not show*? Sure, she wasn't the slimmest woman on the planet but she could distinguish a baby bump.

'When was the last time you had intercourse?'

'Erm…months ago.'

'Nine months?'

Harper did the mental arithmetic, a worm of worry wriggling through her mind. Her stomach swooped and dipped and dived. Her one-night stand with Jack Livingstone. How could she be pregnant to a playboy? It was her worst nightmare. How could she tell him? How could she rock up to him carrying a full-term baby in her arms? How could she be having Jack's baby? Anyone's baby? She hadn't planned on having kids. She wasn't the maternal type. She was a career woman. She had no room in her life for a baby. She hadn't even held a baby since she was a kid. 'Yes, but that's ridiculous. I—I've had a period every month since.' She looked down at her slightly rounded abdomen just as the pain began again. 'Oh, God, here it comes again.' She gripped the doctor's hand so hard Dr Praneesh winced.

'You're in labour, Harper. It seems you've had a cryptic pregnancy. It's not as rare as you'd think. One in two thousand five hundred pregnancies in the UK, which is about three hundred a year. You can still have a light period each month and not have any other symptoms of pregnancy, or at least none that you notice, especially if the placenta is in the front of the abdomen, as it lessens the sensations of the foetus kicking and moving. I'll have to examine you to see how close you are to delivering.'

'Delivering…' Harper swallowed a lump of dread. 'You mean, I'm having a baby? *Now?*' Her panicked shriek rivalled the volume of Morphine Man in cubicle six.

'Your contractions are ten minutes apart, so it won't be long now. From what you told the triage nurse, you've been in non-active labour a couple of days. I'll do an ultrasound to check the baby's development, and the sex if you'd like to know, and then do an internal examination. Would you like to call a friend or the baby's father to be with you?'

Harper gulped. Her two best friends and business partners were out of town—Ruby had only days ago got engaged to Lucas Rothwell and was spending the weekend with him in the Lake District. And Aerin was visiting her parents in Buckinghamshire for their thirty-sixth wedding anniversary. God only knew where Jack Livingstone would be—no doubt in bed with his latest hook-up in one of his plush hotels. But she had to tell him, right? He was the father and he had to be given the choice to be present at the baby's birth, not to mention the choice to be a part of his child's life.

Like her own father, he could always say no.

Jack was poring over some bookwork in his London penthouse at his boutique flagship hotel when his phone buzzed on his desk. He glanced at it and gave a slow smile when he saw who was calling him at this late hour on a Saturday night. Maybe the elusive Harper Swan had changed her mind and decided to see him again and collect the earring he still had in his possession. 'Hello there.'

He could hear her heavy breathing on the end of the line. 'Jack, there's no easy way to tell you this…but I'm in hospital and—'

Jack sat bolt upright in his chair, something in his chest flapping like a wind-whipped sail. 'Are you all right? What's wrong? Have you had an accident?'

'Kind of…' Harper gave an audible swallow. 'I'd like to explain in person…if that's okay? Are you in London right now?'

'I am.' He pushed back his chair and reached for his jacket and sports car keys. 'Which hospital are you in?'

'St Agnes's. I'm still in A and E but—'

'I'll be there in a few minutes.' Jack ended the call and then opened the second drawer in his desk. He took out the earring she had left behind after their one-night stand and slipped it into his pocket. At least now he would be able to give it to her in person.

Jack wasn't a fan of hospitals but something about Harper's call had set his nerves on edge. She had mentioned some sort of accident. A minor prang? A bump on the head? She must have a concussion if she'd changed her mind about seeing him. She had ignored his calls for months and, while he'd been disappointed, he hadn't let it get to him. He wasn't the type of man to get hung up on a woman. He had enjoyed their one night together and had hoped for a fling with her but she hadn't seemed interested in a follow-up. Harper had been so adamant about not seeing him again she had refused to collect her earring. He knew he could have posted it or dropped it off at her office but he had kept it. He couldn't explain why other than every time he looked at it, it reminded him of their explosive night of bed-wrecking, spine-tingling, mind-scrambling sex.

Jack also couldn't explain why he hadn't had a hook-up with anyone since. It was out of character for him to leave it so long but he'd been busy acquiring another property for development in Yorkshire. He hadn't wanted any distractions while he secured the Rothwell Park deal. Turning the ancient estate into one of his boutique hotels was a dream he had harboured for months and now it was coming to fruition. Not that reliving every second of that night of passion with Harper wasn't a distraction in itself. He had found it near impossible to get her out of his mind. Was it because she had walked away without begging for a follow-up date like every other woman he'd met? The challenge of winning Harper over was like a background thrum in his blood. He tried to ignore the niggling sense of failing at a goal he had set himself. A box that hadn't been ticked to his satisfaction. Not that he viewed any woman as a prize or trophy he could win, but because something about Harper got to him in a way no other woman ever had.

Once he arrived at the hospital, Jack was led by a nurse to the A and E cubicle Harper was in. 'Here she is.' The nurse gave a briskly efficient smile. 'We're waiting on an orderly to collect her. He shouldn't be too long now.'

Harper was lying on the hospital gurney on her side, her features pinched and white and racked with pain. Sweat poured down her face and in one of her hands she had a blue stress ball that she was squeezing so hard it was bulging in between her fingers like a squashed plum. But then a flood of colour entered her cheeks. 'Jack…' Her voice was a strangled whisper, her grey-green eyes not quite willing to meet his. 'I'm *so* sorry…'

Jack took her other hand and gave it a gentle squeeze. 'Hey, you. What's going on?'

'I don't know how to tell you this…' She bit her lip so hard he was worried it would split and bleed. 'I thought it was backache. I had no idea. I truly didn't. I didn't think it was possible to not know, to not recognise the signs. I didn't even *have* any signs that I can remember.'

'Signs? What are you talking about?'

'I thought it was cancer. Can you believe that?' She bit off a self-deprecating laugh and pulled her hand out of his and pushed her sweat-soaked hair back off her face. 'I thought the doctor was going to tell me I had inoperable cancer. That I was dying at the ripe old age of twenty-seven.'

A fist of fear clutched at Jack's guts. 'You don't have cancer…do you?'

'No…' She bit her lip again and squeezed the stress ball hard, her features contorting in pain. 'I feel so stupid. How am I going to explain this to everyone? To Aerin and Ruby? We have weddings booked solidly for the next two months, including Ruby's and Lucas's. Summer is our busiest time of year. I mean, it's like a bad dream or something. I can't believe this has happened to me of all people.'

The cubicle curtain was twitched aside and the nurse reappeared. 'The orderly is on his way now to take you to the maternity ward.'

Maternity ward? The words were like a bomb going

off in Jack's head. *Ba-boom.* His thoughts flying everywhere like shrapnel. He whipped around so quickly to face the nurse he almost knocked over the portable blood pressure machine. He reached out to steady it with a shaking hand. 'Maternity?' His voice came out hoarse, his heart thumping as if he needed to be admitted himself. To the cardiac unit.

'I was trying to tell you…' Harper said, with a frustrated eye-roll.

'Tell me what?'

'I'm having a baby.'

Harper was pregnant?

Jack let the words sink into his brain. She was having a baby. A sharp prick of disappointment stabbed him in the gut. Harper was having someone else's baby. Not that he was keen on having a family or anything himself, but still. She had moved on and found someone else and got pregnant. But what did that news have to do with him? She didn't look as if she was very far along. Was she in the early stages? He knew that pregnancy could trigger appalling nausea in some women that required hospital admission. Why, then, had she called him? He wasn't her next of kin, he wasn't her partner—he wasn't strictly speaking even a friend. It didn't make sense. She had friends and family, surely? And what about her partner, the father of her baby? That was who was supposed to be by her side right now. Not him. A casual lover she had cast off without a backward glance.

'Are you the proud father?' the nurse asked Jack with a beaming smile.

'No, I—'

'Yes,' Harper said. 'He's the father.'

Jack stared at Harper in a gobsmacked silence. How could he be the father? He hadn't seen Harper in months. Nine months. He had counted every one of them. He gave his head a shake, wondering if he was caught in some weird time warp. Nothing was making any sense. 'I'm the father? How?'

But there was no time for clarification or explanation, for the orderly came in with energetic efficiency and released the brake on the gurney.

'First baby?' the orderly said with a cheery smile.

'Yes…*oh*—' Harper's voice was cut off by a spasm of pain that flashed over her features.

Jack glanced at the nurse, who was collecting Harper's purse and phone from the table next to the gurney. 'Can't you give her something for the pain?'

'I don't want anything,' Harper said before the nurse could respond. 'I want a natural birth.'

Jack wasn't exactly up to date on what was de rigueur around pregnancy and motherhood these days but he had heard the term 'natural birth' bandied about and it sounded as if it could be extremely painful. 'This is the twenty-first century, Harper,' Jack said, following alongside her as the orderly wheeled the gurney towards the lift situated outside A and E. 'There's no need to suffer unnecessarily.'

'I know, but I figure the only way I'll accept this is really happening to me is if I feel everything now.'

'You're not making a lot of sense. You've had nine months to prepare yourself.' Jack had had only minutes. It wasn't enough. His head was reeling, he was light-headed, his pulse was racing, his heart thumping with a host of emotions—panic, dread, fear. He was about to become a father. It didn't seem real. It didn't seem possible. They had used protection. He had never had a yearning desire to have children. He enjoyed his freedom too much. Why hadn't Harper told him before now? Why hadn't she given him the heads-up months ago? Or had she been worried he would pressure her to have a termination? He would not have done any such thing, but he would have liked to know he was to become a father well before the day of its freaking birth.

Never had he felt so out of control.

So blindsided.

It was like finding himself as a fully signed up member of a club he had never expected to join—the Fatherhood Club. Once in, you couldn't leave.

'I haven't had nine months to prepare,' Harper flashed back. 'I only just found out half an hour ago.'

'Cryptic pregnancy,' the orderly explained. 'It's not common but it happens. I've seen one before. Teenage girl had no idea she was pregnant until she got to A and E with severe abdominal pain. She thought it was appendicitis. You should have seen her mother's face when she was told she was about to become a grandmother.'

A cryptic pregnancy. So Harper hadn't known? How could she *not* have known? Surely there had been a hint or two? Or had she been so determined to put everything to do with him out of her mind she hadn't noticed the subtle changes in her body? But then, denial was a powerful mental tool. It could make normally rational and sensible people ignore things they didn't want to face. Issues they didn't want to deal with, truths they didn't want to confront.

There was an issue Jack had to face and fast. He was

going to be a father and he wanted his child to have his name. Marrying had not been part of his life plan but he was going to have to rethink that, otherwise his child would grow up without the protection and shelter of being a Livingstone. Marriage was a monumental step for any couple but for him and Harper, who had only met once before—the night they conceived their baby—it was off-the-charts madness to be thinking about tying the knot. But marrying Harper and raising their child together was the only option. He couldn't see any other way forward. He had not had the happiest childhood himself due to his father's long and painful decline in health but that didn't mean Jack couldn't give his child a wonderful childhood. But he couldn't do it from a distance. He wanted to be a hands-on dad, involved from the get-go. Marrying Harper and providing a safe and secure home for their baby was the only thing he could control in this out-of-control situation.

The lift doors swished open. They all bundled inside and the doors closed again. Jack glanced at the sign reading Maternity Wing on the third floor and his guts turned to gravy. He glanced at Harper but she was in the middle of another savage contraction. Her face was screwed up, her panting breaths sounding as primal as those of a cavewoman. He took one of her hands and she gripped it until he thought his bones would snap like twigs. He figured now was probably not the best time to propose marriage.

'Are you sure you don't want some pain relief?' he asked with a concerned frown.

'If you can't stomach seeing me in pain, don't come

to the birth,' Harper said, through gritted teeth. 'No one's forcing you.'

'You want me to be there?'

'Only if you *want* to be there.' Her emphasis on the word 'want' didn't escape his notice.

Jack scraped his free hand through his hair. 'It's not something I've ever thought about before.' Like marriage, like commitment, like settling down with one person for the rest of his life. But he had a child to consider, a baby who was about to be born in the next few minutes. A baby he was not prepared for in any way.

The lift doors swished open on the maternity floor and his heart gave another almighty lurch.

'Better hurry and make up your mind, then,' Harper said on an expelled breath as strong as a wind gust. 'I have a feeling this baby isn't going to wait.'

CHAPTER TWO

HARPER WAS WHEELED into the delivery suite and she
mentally prepared herself for Jack abandoning her at
the door. But to her surprise he didn't. It was obvious
he was way out of his depth suddenly finding himself
smack bang in a maternity unit, but then, so was she.
His features were white with shock, his stance stiff and
guarded as if preparing himself for an event he had
never expected to experience.

The birth of a child.

His child.

Her child.

Their child.

Harper was still having trouble getting her head
around the fact she was about to deliver a baby. A
baby her body had harboured in secret for close to nine
months. A baby she had done nothing to prepare for—
no clothes, no toys, no accessories, no pastel-painted
nursery, no pram or baby seat or changing table. She
had done no emotional preparation, either. No sense of
excitement or anticipation, so sense of joy or wonder. No
connection with the baby at all. Surely that was bad for

the baby? Would her baby sense her lack of preparation? Her lack of anticipation and joy? Her lack of emotion?

Harper's decision to refuse pain relief was her way of finally coming to terms with the reality of what was happening. Otherwise, she was worried she wouldn't properly bond with the baby. She might not know much about babies but she did know bonding was everything. Some of the kids she had grown up with in foster care had not experienced secure bonding with their parents. Although on one level she knew her mother had loved her, she still had reason to question her mother's overall commitment to her. Her mother had always seemed a little overwhelmed by being a single parent—it hadn't been what she had been expecting, having loved Harper's father and dreamed of them living happily ever after together. Harper had put her mother's distant parenting style down to the fact that her father had left her mother holding the baby, so to speak, not supporting her at all, either financially or emotionally. That lack of support had led to her mother ending her life, the burden of bringing up a child alone too much for her to handle.

Harper was determined not to repeat the cycle. She would do everything in her power to bond with her baby, to provide love and support no matter what.

Her baby.

The words were so foreign to her, like those of another language. The language of motherhood she hadn't planned on learning. Not for her talking to friends about sleep times and feeding schedules and babies' milestones. Not for her the endless hours of self-sacrifice and sleepless nights her mother had spoken of in one of her many down periods. Not for her the interruption of her much-loved career.

But those things were destined to be Harper's to experience now. She had no choice in the matter. Would she be a good mother? How would she juggle her career with an infant? There was so much to think about, to organise, and yet here she was, minutes away from holding her baby for the first time. But how was she supposed to bond with a baby she'd had no idea was coming? She hadn't stroked her abdomen for the last nine months, talking to her baby bump the way first-time mothers were encouraged to do. What if her lack of engagement with the baby so far caused irreparable damage? Panic swept through her in a flood as she suddenly realised she didn't have a name picked out. It wasn't something she had ever thought about—naming a child. She hadn't even named a pet, much less a child. The responsibility terrified her. What if her baby grew up hating the name she'd given her? What if it didn't suit the baby's personality? She tried to think of some names but her brain was sluggish with tiredness and pain, her thoughts as jumbled as clothes in a dryer that had overrun its cycle.

Harper glanced up at Jack, her heart thumping. 'We have to think of a name.'

'What, now?'

'We should have some names ready. One for a boy, one for a girl.'

'You don't know the sex?'

'No, when the doctor in A and E gave me an ultrasound, while I was waiting for you, I chose not to find out. I want it to be a surprise.'

His look was ironic, his tone dry. 'Haven't there been enough surprises already?'

'Good point.'

The midwife came in and introduced herself. 'My name is Meg. I'll be looking after you during the delivery. I need to examine you, if that's okay?'

'Do you want me to go out?' Jack asked.

'No,' Harper said, surprising herself. The thought of being so exposed and vulnerable with him watching should have embarrassed her, but she wanted his support. Needed it. It was too late to call anyone else…besides, she wanted her baby to meet its father. For him to be one of the first people to welcome the baby into the world.

The midwife examined her while Jack held Harper's hand. He mopped the sweat from her brow with a soft cloth the midwife had handed him. Harper prepared herself for another contraction, breathing into it, quietly amazed at the power of her body as it laboured to bring the baby further down the birth canal.

'You're just about fully dilated,' the midwife said, pulling the cover back over Harper's bent legs. 'Not long now.'

'Good, because this is getting pretty intense…' Harper clenched her teeth and squeezed Jack's hand.

'I'm going to check on a patient next door,' Meg said. 'Press the buzzer if anything changes.'

'Will do.'

'You're doing so well, Harper,' Jack said, once the midwife had gone.

'Names…' Harper said between panting breaths. 'We have to decide on a name…'

'Maybe we should wait until we meet the baby.'

'I want to have a name for my baby. I haven't got anything else ready, the least I can do is choose a name.' Tears formed in her eyes and she choked back a sob. What sort of mother was she going to be if she couldn't even think of a name for her baby?

Jack stroked the damp hair back from her forehead. 'Okay. Do you have any favourites?'

It was impossible to think clearly when her body was in the throes of another contraction. 'Not really, do you?'

He frowned in thought. 'I guess it would have to go with my name.'

Harper narrowed her gaze. 'Why's that?'

'I want the baby to have my surname.'

'Why?'

'Because we'll have to get married, that's why.'

Harper gaped at him. *'Married?'* She choked back a laugh of disbelief. 'You're surely not serious?'

'Of course I'm serious. I want to provide for my child and the best way to do that is for us to marry.'

Harper didn't get the chance to argue the point, for another contraction took hold as well as the overwhelming desire to push. 'Quick—press the buzzer for the midwife. I think the baby's coming.'

Jack reached for the buzzer and the midwife and her assistant came in soon after. He knew his job was to support Harper, so he concentrated on mopping her brow and holding her hand so she could ride out the final contractions. But it was agony to watch her, knowing it was his fault she was pregnant. How on earth had it happened? He was always so careful. He never had sex without protection. But somehow they had made a baby together and it was about to come into the world. He hadn't seen a birth before, only an acted one in a movie or television show. Nothing could have prepared him for the reality of childbirth. What a woman had to go through—the torturous pain, the indignity of having her body so open and exposed, the sheer vulnerability of giving birth astounded him. A flicker of fear lit in his gut and spread like a forest fire. What if things went wrong? Women still occasionally died from complications in childbirth and sometimes so did the baby. What if there was nothing he could do to save either of them? He was totally useless with his field of knowledge of hotel development. He knew little of medicine other than basic first aid. The sense of powerlessness sent his heart rate soaring and a trickle of sweat to drip down his spine.

'Time to push,' Meg the midwife said, coaching Harper in the final stages. 'Strip off your gown so we can put baby skin on skin. You too, Jack. Open your shirt so the baby can feel your skin and get to know your smell.'

Jack swallowed a boulder of emotion as he helped Harper pull her gown down off her shoulders, before he undid his own shirt buttons. He wasn't the sort of guy to cry. He hadn't even cried at his father's funeral. But right then, a wave of unexpected emotion swept through him like a tsunami. His chest tightening as if his heart was looking for room to expand but held back by the cage of his ribs.

Harper gave a primal cry and bore down, her hand gripping his with pulverising force.

'You can do it, sweetie. Almost there,' he said, glancing at the business end of things where he could see a tiny dark-haired head crowning. It didn't seem real, it didn't seem possible he was glimpsing his own flesh and blood. His chest swelled, his heart thumped, his breath stalled at the raw and earthy beauty of seeing his baby come into the world.

Harper gave another cavewoman scream and the baby was expelled from her body. The midwife scooped the little wizened bundle up and laid it on Harper's naked chest, umbilical cord still attached. 'You have a beautiful daughter. Congratulations.'

He had a daughter. The baby gave a loud cry that to Jack was like the sweetest music he had ever heard. He blinked against the sting of tears, his throat so tight he couldn't speak. The rush of emotion at seeing his daughter for the first time blindsided him as much as Harper's cryptic pregnancy. The tiny body curled up like a comma on Harper's chest was *his* little girl.

His mother would be overjoyed. She had dropped hints for years about grandchildren but he'd always shut her down, telling her not to get her hopes up. Like him, his mother hadn't had time to prepare for such a momentous event but he knew she would relish every moment now. He whipped out his phone and took a few photos, knowing his mother would never believe what had just happened without photographic evidence. He was having enough trouble believing it himself. A baby girl. *His* baby girl.

'Would you like to cut the cord?' the midwife asked.

'I… Yes,' Jack found himself saying in a trance-like daze. He put his phone down and he did as the midwife instructed and watched as she put a clamp on the cord next to the baby's little tummy.

Harper was sobbing with relief and joy as she cradled the tiny baby against her breasts. 'Oh, Jack, isn't she beautiful?' The note of wonder in her tone sent another wave of emotion through him. Call him biased, but surely not *all* babies were as beautiful as his little baby?

'She is indeed.' He stroked a soft finger over the baby's downy head. 'She's so tiny. Like a doll.'

Harper gave him a speaking glance. 'She didn't feel too tiny a few minutes ago.'

Jack leaned down to press a kiss to Harper's forehead. 'You were amazing. So brave. I'm in awe of what you just did.'

Harper looked up at him with shining eyes. 'Thanks for being here. I would've hated to be alone.' She looked down at the baby again, her voice softening to a soothing coo as she said, 'Hey, little one. Sorry we haven't got a name for you yet.' The baby began nuzzling against Harper's chest, her tiny, mewling cries making Jack's heart squeeze as if it were in a vice.

'You can offer her the breast,' Meg said. 'Were you planning on breastfeeding?'

'I guess so…' Harper said. 'It's best for the baby, isn't it?'

'We like to encourage mums to try and breastfeed, but if it's too hard, don't beat yourself up about using formula,' the midwife assured her.

Harper helped the baby latch onto her breast and Jack wondered if he'd ever seen such a beautiful sight.

A mother and her newborn baby. *His* baby. His little daughter. It was like a miracle to see her perfectly formed, tiny body. The little starfish hands, her feet smaller than the length of his thumb, her downy head covered in jet-black hair, the same as his. He blinked and blinked again, fully expecting he would find himself back at his hotel penthouse, waking up from a weird dream. But no, he was in the delivery suite, watching his newborn daughter having her first feed. Emotions he had never felt before flooded through his body. Emotions he had resisted feeling for most of his adult life. Emotions that tugged on his chest as if strings were attached to his heart, pulling at the shield of armour he had built around it.

He was a father.

A dad.

His little girl needed him in her life. He had responsibilities now that were so important they surpassed everything he had achieved in his career so far. He would not—could not—allow anyone else to rear his child. It was his responsibility to see she had everything she needed to thrive. He had heard someone say that every childhood lasted a lifetime and it had resonated a little too well with him. There were aspects of his childhood he would do anything to prevent happening to his daughter.

The midwife finished cleaning up, and once the baby had finished feeding, she wrapped her in a soft blanket, and left them to continue to bond with her. Jack took some more photos with his phone, still finding it surreal to be a father. Had his own father felt this sense of awe and wonder at his birth? Jack had a handful of good memories of his father as a younger man but the slow and painful progression of his father's Parkinson's Disease had tainted many others. Jack had been sent to boarding school to spare him the worst of it. And he had been sent away for holiday camps as well because his father refused to travel. Home had ceased to be a home and was more of a hospice. A place of gloom and doom and disappointment. His father's death when Jack was eighteen had not devastated him, as it had his mother. His emotional response had been relief instead of grief. But now he was a father himself, he couldn't imagine wanting anything but the best for his daughter. He wanted to be fully present in raising her. He wanted to be there for her for as long as he lived. She would be seen and she would be heard.

The baby soon fell asleep and Harper glanced up at Jack again. 'Would you like to hold her?'

Jack couldn't remember ever holding a baby before, certainly not one so young. What if he didn't hold her correctly? Wasn't there something about their necks being fragile and needing proper support? What if the baby began to cry? What if she didn't recognise him as her father? 'I don't want to wake her. She looks so peaceful.'

Disappointment flickered briefly over Harper's face but then she covered it with bitterness. 'Would you prefer to have a paternity test done first?' Her tone was sharp as a scalpel, her grey-green eyes hard.

Jack had not even thought of asking for a paternity test. He knew most men in his position would do so and would be completely justified in asking for one, except he didn't for a moment doubt the baby was his.

He couldn't explain why, it wasn't rational at all, just a feeling. And he wasn't normally the type of man to rely on feelings. But…that screwed-up little face topped with its liberal dusting of black hair did resemble him as a baby. And he felt connected to her in a way he couldn't explain. A connection that was almost spiritual. 'Is there any reason I should have one done?' he asked.

She shrugged one shoulder. 'I just thought you'd want one. I might have had numerous partners since you.'

'Have you?'

'No.' Her shoulders went down on a little sigh and she traced a gentle finger across the baby's tiny forehead.

Her confession surprised him and secretly delighted him. He had been celibate for the whole time too, but what were her reasons for not dating anyone since? 'Why?'

Another shrug, her gaze shifting from his. 'I'm not going to feed your already overblown ego by telling you I didn't fancy sleeping with anyone else after that night of…of amazing sex.' Her cheeks flushed a delicate shade of pink and she sank her teeth into her lower lip as if she wished she hadn't revealed quite so much.

Jack gave a lazy smile. 'Then I won't feed your ego either and tell you the same.'

Harper's gaze flicked back to his, her eyes as wide as dishes. Satellite dishes. 'Are you serious? You haven't slept with anyone since?' Her incredulous tone made him wonder if his reputation as a playboy had been a tad over-exaggerated. Sure, he didn't stay in a fling long, but he often had breaks between lovers. Long breaks. Not as long as nine months, but still. When he was working on a new hotel development he liked to focus. He put his private life on hold in the early stages of a project so he could concentrate his whole attention on the job at hand. And it paid off. He had brokered numerous deals and invested millions in spectacular hotel developments, which had built the Livingstone Hotel chain to a luxury brand that rivalled some of his biggest competitors. 'I've been busy securing a deal in Yorkshire.'

Another glimmer of bitterness shone in her eyes. 'Yes, I heard about that. You bought Rothwell Park.' Her resentful tone seemed to suggest she thought he had bought it deliberately to spite her.

'You know it?'

'My business partner, Ruby Pennington, grew up there with her grandmother. I visited once when I was about twelve. We had a wedding there recently—I did the photos. You probably saw it in the press or heard about it from Lucas Rothwell. Delphine Rainbird, the American actress.' She straightened her shoulders and added, 'Was it a coincidence or did you know I had a connection to the place?'

It was Jack's turn to shrug. 'Mere coincidence.'

The baby gave a tiny yawn and turned her head in Jack's direction, her dark eyes gazing at him like a baby owl.

'I think she wants you to hold her,' Harper said. 'She's starting to recognise your voice.'

Jack came closer and gently took the baby from Harper. He couldn't stop staring at her tiny features—the button nose, the rosebud mouth, the squinty little eyes that opened again as soon as he touched her and stared up at him without blinking, as if she didn't dare let him out of her sight. 'Hey, little one...' His voice caught on something rough at the back of his throat and he had to swallow to clear it. 'You've created quite a stir, young lady, turning up unannounced. You'll have to forgive us for being a little unprepared.'

Thing was, Jack was *never* unprepared. He was a planner, a box ticker, a details man who left nothing to chance. He never allowed himself to be surprised by anything. Meticulous planning removed the surprise element—mostly. But nothing was more surprising than to suddenly find himself the father of a baby girl.

She opened her little mouth and yawned again, and something in his chest flipped open like a faulty latch on a locked door. He was ambushed by unfamiliar feelings. Emotions he had never allowed free rein before. Emotions that had the potential to tilt his neat and controlled world on its axis. He fought those emotions, pushed and shoved them back where he could look at them from a safe distance, knowing they were there but still under his control. He could provide for his child and provide well. And he would provide for and support Harper too.

'Jack?' Harper's voice was tentative. 'I know you must think I'm an idiot for not knowing I was pregnant. If I had known, I would've told you straight away.'

'Why didn't you want to see me again?'

She chewed at one side of her mouth. 'I was ashamed of how I let you distract me from my work at the Tenterbury wedding. It was so unprofessional of me to be sneaking off upstairs with the best man. I have never done anything like that before or since. I'd made a pact with myself to never mix business with pleasure and you made me break it.'

'I seem to recall there was quite a lot of pleasure that night.' Jack still got shivers thinking about it. The fiery heat of attraction, the flirty banter that went on for hours until they dashed upstairs and engaged in the most mind-blowing sex of his life. Truth be told, he had avoided hooking up with anyone since because he wanted to linger over the memory of that night. To relive the tingling sensations, to revisit the incredible kisses and caresses that had stirred him so deeply.

And that episode of passionate lovemaking had produced this tiny infant—his daughter.

Harper's gaze avoided his and stared at the baby in his arms as if she too couldn't quite get her head around the fact they had made a baby. A worried look came over her face and she glanced up at him again. 'Parents usually have months and months to prepare for this. I didn't address a single word to her while I was carrying her. What if that damages her in some way? I didn't even eat properly most of the time.' She blew out a whoosh of air and added, 'But thankfully, I'm teetotal and a non-smoker.'

Jack looked down at the tiny bundle in his arms. 'She looks perfect in every way, so don't worry too much.' The baby opened her tiny mouth and gave a yawn and then opened her dark blue eyes and stared at him again. The tugging sensation in his chest was stronger this time and he took a deep breath to settle it. He took one of the baby's miniscule hands and marvelled at the tiny fingernails on the ends of fingers so small it didn't seem possible there was room for bones and ligaments and tendons inside. 'Hey, little one. What are we going to call you, hmm?'

'I don't want any way-out names,' Harper said. 'She'll be an adult a lot longer than she'll be a baby, so it should be a name that won't embarrass her as she gets older. But I don't want it to be too old-fashioned either.'

'I agree,' Jack said. 'Do you want to name her after someone? Your mother? Your grandmother?'

The flash of horror that flicked across Harper's face made him realise he hardly knew anything about her. But then, what did she know about him other than what she might have read in the gossip pages or online?

'No, there aren't any family names I'd want to inflict on my child.'

'Okay. My mother's name is Elizabeth, although she gets called Liz most of the time. Susannah is her middle name.'

Harper shifted her mouth from side to side. 'I like both but more as middle names.' She glanced at the baby thoughtfully and added, 'We could give her two middle names, I guess.'

'Why not? I have three.'

Harper turned to look at him again. 'Really? Isn't that a bit excessive?'

'A little, but apparently there were a lot of people to please when I was born,' Jack said.

'So what is your full name?'

'Jackson Sebastien Miles Rochester Livingstone.'

Her eyebrows lifted. 'Rochester? Seriously?'

Jack grinned. 'As in *Jane Eyre*? Yep, it was my paternal grandmother's maiden name.'

Harper looked back at the baby. 'What about Marli

with an I? It's not too out there and it's not old-fashioned.'

Jack nodded. 'I like it too.' He looked down at the baby, who was now clutching one of his fingers in her tiny hand. A warm feeling spread through his chest and he smiled. 'Hello, Marli Elizabeth Susannah Livingstone.'

'Swan.' Harper's tone was adamant, her gaze as hard as stone.

'You do realise what the acronym of her name will be if you don't marry me? MESS.' It was a heck of a tactic to convince Harper to marry him, but he was prepared to use whatever was at his disposal.

Harper held her arms out for Marli, her expression faltering as if she could see the sense in his point but was too proud to admit it right there and then. 'I want to hold her now.'

Jack passed the baby back to her, his arms feeling strangely empty without the tiny bundle cradled there. He straightened and stood next to the bed. 'She belongs to both of us, Harper, so she should have both our names. We can hyphenate them after we get married.'

Her chin came up at a defiant height. 'I am not marrying you.'

'I probably need to work on my proposal but I want Marli to live with me. I don't want to be a part-time parent.'

'But you travel all over the world for your work.'

'You do too.'

'Not as much as you.' She looked back down at Marli and frowned. 'Although I have to go to Paris in six weeks.'

'For a wedding?'

'No, for a photo shoot for a book I've been asked to contribute to.' She stroked a gentle finger across the baby's forehead again, the action one of wonder, as if she couldn't quite believe she was holding a live baby. Her baby. His baby. *Their* baby. 'I have no idea how I'm going to be able to juggle work and the Paris trip now I've got a baby...' Her teeth began to savage her lip again and her small, neat chin began to tremble.

Jack placed his hand on the top of her right shoulder. 'We'll figure out how to do it together. She's both our responsibility and I am not going to let you do this alone, okay?'

She flicked him an upwards glance. 'I can only imagine what the press is going to make of this. We're practically strangers and now we've got a baby.'

'It doesn't mean we can't be great parents or a well-functioning couple,' Jack said, and, reaching into his trouser pocket, took out Harper's earring. 'By the way, I have something of yours you left behind last time we met.'

Harper looked at the earring for a brief moment, then took it from his open palm and put it next to her phone and purse on the table next to the hospital bed. 'Yes, well, I have something of yours too.' She passed the baby back to him with a wry twist of her mouth. 'Your baby.'

CHAPTER THREE

JACK SAT ON the chair beside the bed holding Marli while Harper had a shower. The nurse had brought in a portable crib for the baby but he hadn't yet transferred her to it. He didn't want to risk waking her—especially while her mother was out of the room. But neither did he want to miss out on these precious early moments of her life. He balanced Marli in one arm and took out his phone and called his mother. 'Are you sitting down?' he said when she answered.

'Oh, darling, don't tell me you're finally madly in love?' The excitement in his mother's tone was unmistakable. And annoying because he had no intention of ever falling in love.

'No, but I am going to get married.'

'You can't possibly marry someone you don't love.'

'I can because she's the mother of my baby,' Jack said.

The silence was short but intense, like the ticking of a time bomb. *Tick. Tick. Tick...*

'Your...*what*?' His mother's voice was a screech of shock.

'I have a baby daughter just a few minutes old.'

'Oh, my God, but why didn't you tell me before now? I didn't even know you were dating anyone long-term. When can I see the baby? What did you call her? Oh, I'm so excited I can barely stand it. I have to go shopping and get her a present. Lots of presents and toys and dolls and a proper teddy bear. Oh, I can't believe I'm finally a granny. But you haven't even told me your fiancée's name. Do I know her? Have I met her?' The questions were like bullets fired out of an automatic weapon. 'When can I see the baby? Can I come now? Where are you? In London? Oh, I can't wait to hold her. I never thought this day would come. I think I'm going to faint with shock.'

'Mum, calm down.'

'Don't tell me to calm down on the most exciting day of my life since I had you,' his mother said. 'If I wasn't so excited, I'd be furious with you for not telling me you were expecting a child. How could you have robbed me of the joy of anticipating becoming a grandmother? Did you do it deliberately? I never thought you could be so mean.'

'I only found out half an hour before she was born.'

'What?'

'My...fiancée—' Jack decided to refer to Harper as his bride-to-be because he was not going to take no for an answer '—had what's called a cryptic pregnancy. She only found out herself just before she delivered.'

'Oh, my goodness! I've heard about that sort of thing but I never believed it was possible. How could she not know? You nearly kicked your way out of my abdomen when I carried you. And my stomach still has the stretch marks to prove it.' His mother paused to draw breath and then continued, 'But surely you would have noticed the changes in her body, especially if you were…you know…intimate with her all this time.'

'I wasn't with her over the last nine months,' Jack said, already hating how this was going to sound to his conservative mother, married for years to one man. 'We had a one-night stand and—'

'Oh, Jack, is this young woman a gold-digger? I mean, this is an old trick but a good one. You're a handsome billionaire. Who wouldn't want to trap you into a shotgun marriage?'

Jack pinched the bridge of his nose and hoped his daughter was too young to understand the words her grandmother was saying about her mother. 'Mum, I want to marry Harper. No one's forcing me to do anything. In fact, I have to convince her to agree to it. She's not exactly been too keen so far on the idea.'

'What? But you're a prize catch!'

'I don't think Harper quite sees me that way.'

The bathroom door opened and Harper came out in a fresh hospital gown and her hair wrapped turban-like in a towel.

'That's another trick—playing hard to get.' His mother's voice was loud enough to wake the dead in the morgue downstairs. 'Have you asked for a paternity test? You must insist on one, Jack. Don't get too attached to the baby until you're sure it's yours. And for God's sake, don't marry that girl unless you're absolutely sure she's being straight with you.'

Jack clenched his jaw and gave Harper an apologetic glance. 'Mum, I have to go. I'll arrange a time for you to meet Marli Elizabeth Susannah in the next day or two.'

'You named her after me?' His mother's tone softened. 'Oh, how sweet of you.'

'It was Harper's idea, actually.'

Another short, tight silence.

'Well, I'll look forward to meeting her too,' his mother said. 'Send me some photos? I won't believe I'm a grandmother until I see proof.'

'Sending them now. Bye.' Jack ended the call and deftly sent some photos of the baby to his mother. 'Sorry you had to hear that.' He put his phone back down and looked at Harper, who was now sitting on the bed with a pinched look on her face.

'See? I told you. A paternity test is necessary.'

'And I told you I don't need one,' Jack said.

Harper bounced off the bed and then winced as if she'd forgotten she had given birth less than an hour ago. 'I'm going to have one done no matter what you say. I don't want people speculating or calling me a flipping gold-digger.' She came over and took the baby from him to cradle her close and protectively against her chest. 'That's why marriage is out of the question. Who's ever going to believe we're in love?'

'What's love got to do with anything? We can have a perfectly satisfying relationship without being in love with each other. That one night together nine months ago proved that.'

Harper's mouth dropped open. 'What? You don't believe in love in marriage? Is that what you're truly saying?'

'I'm saying it's not as necessary as you might think,' Jack said. 'Obviously it's the ideal, but plenty of relationships survive on much less than that.'

'Survive, yes, but do they thrive?' Harper placed the baby gently in the crib and covered her with the pink blanket, tucking in the edges tenderly. 'I want the best environment for Marli. I want her surrounded by love. I don't want her to be around people who can't bear the sight of each other.'

Jack came over to stand behind her, placing his hands on her shoulders. 'What's this talk of us not liking each other, hmm?'

She turned to face him, her expression guarded. 'We don't know each other, Jack.'

He trailed a lazy finger down the curve of her cheek. 'I know what turns you on.' He lowered his voice to a husky drawl. 'And you know what turns me on.' He sent his finger over the plump cushion of her lower lip. 'I couldn't get you out of my mind. It's why I wanted to see you again. I wanted to make sure I hadn't imagined how good it was between us.'

She cast him a wary look from beneath her lowered lashes. 'Did you really not hook up with anyone since me?'

Jack gently squeezed both her shoulders. 'Not a single person. Nine months is a bit of a record for me. But as I said, I was busy negotiating the deal on Rockwell Park and trying to convince you to see me again.'

'Because of my earring?'

'It looks like a valuable one.'

'Sentimental value, mostly. I bought those earrings with my first paycheck as a photographer.' She dipped out from under his light hold and gave a movement of her lips that wasn't anywhere near a smile and more of a grimace. 'Can I see the photos you took?'

'Sure.' Jack took out his phone but, rather than hand it to her, held it up so they could stand shoulder to shoulder to scroll through the shots. 'I can't say I'm as good a photographer as you, but our baby girl is pretty photogenic, wouldn't you say?'

'I can't believe I just had a baby…' Harper's voice cracked over the words. 'And what sort of photographer am I if I haven't taken a single shot of her? My phone is flat and my camera is at the office.'

Jack handed her his phone. 'Use mine.'

She took the phone from him and moved closer to the crib. She aimed the lens at various angles, taking snap after snap of Marli. She straightened and looked at him again. 'What if I take some of you with her?'

'Good idea,' Jack said. He carefully scooped Marli out of the crib and congratulated himself on not disturbing her sleep. In spite of his lack of preparation, maybe he wouldn't do such a bad job of being a father after all.

'Stand over there where the light is better,' Harper said. 'Now look down at her as if she is the most wonderful thing you've ever seen.'

'She is the most wonderful thing I've ever seen.' Jack held his baby girl against his chest, amazed at how peaceful she looked. 'Looks as if she's got your nose and mouth.'

'You think?'

'Definitely.'

Harper stopped snapping photos to come over to stand next to him to gaze down at the baby in his arms. She was so close he could smell the fruity fragrance of the shampoo she had used in the shower. He slipped an arm around her waist in order to draw her closer, but she jerked back from him as if his touch burnt her.

Her grey-green eyes glittered like those of a cornered cat. 'I know what you're doing.'

'What am I doing?'

She folded her arms across her middle in a keep-away-from-me gesture. 'You're trying to charm me into marrying you, but it won't work. I know it's a hack-neyed phrase, but you're the last man on earth I would ever consider marrying. The point is, I don't want to marry anyone.'

Jack raised one of his eyebrows. 'That's kind of ironic given your line of work—wedding photography.'

'Yes, well, I like photographing weddings but it doesn't mean I want the fairy tale for myself.'

'See? We're perfectly suited for each other. We're both cynical about love.'

'I didn't say I was cynical about love.'

'Marriage, then?'

'I accept some marriages last years. Whether both parties are happy or not is another question.'

'What about your parents? Were they happily married?'

'No.'

'How long were they together?'

Harper turned away to straighten the bed linen as if she were the nurse on duty instead of a new mother who should be resting. 'Long enough for my father to get my mother pregnant.' She turned and faced him with a stony expression. 'When he found out she was carry-ing me and she refused to have an abortion, he dumped her and went back to his wife and family. The wife and family he had told her for months he was going to leave for her, but it was a pack of lies.'

'That must've been tough on your mother.'

'It was.'

'And tough on you too, once you were old enough to understand.'

'Yes, knowing your biological father wanted to get rid of you before you were born doesn't exactly build one's self-esteem.' The bitterness in her tone was raw, shadows of deep hurt in her eyes.

'Shouldn't you call your mother to tell her about the baby?'

Harper gave a hollow laugh that wasn't quite a laugh and sat back on the edge of the bed. 'No can do. She's been dead since I was eight.'

Jack could only imagine how devastating such a loss could have been to a young child. 'I'm sorry to hear that. How did she die?'

'Suicide.' Harper expelled a ragged breath and added, 'I found her.'

'God, Harper, that's awful.' He came over to sit beside her on the hospital bed, taking one of her hands in his. 'So who brought you up? Did your father step in?'

She pulled her hand away and rose from the bed, her arms going around her body once more. It was as if she didn't want to be comforted or supported. Or maybe it was because no one had ever been there for her before. It explained a lot about her feisty nature and independent streak. She didn't allow people too close in case they let her down or deserted her.

'He was contacted by the authorities and he promised to come and get me from emergency foster care but he always cancelled at the last minute or had some paltry excuse for why I couldn't come and live with him. I spent years of my life languishing in foster care, moving from home to home, waiting for him, stupidly believing his empty promises until I finally realised I was on my own.'

'It sounds like you were better off without him,' Jack said. He looked at his sleeping daughter and wondered how any man could walk away from his own flesh and blood. While he might not have planned to be a father, there was no way he could ever turn his back on his own child. He would always be there for her, to provide and protect and encourage her to thrive and reach her potential. And he figured the best way to do it was to marry Harper so they could be a family. Clearly she had not had a happy and fulfilling childhood—all the more reason for him to step in and help her raise their child. 'I can't imagine how disappointing that must have been for you. Do you have any other relatives? Aunts, uncles? Grandparents?'

'No one wanted me.' Her tone was devoid of emotion and yet he sensed an undercurrent of lingering pain and disillusionment.

Jack watched her hover over Marli's crib, her fierce expression reminding him of a mother lion protecting her cub. She stroked her hand over the baby's head and Marli made a soft sound as if she recognised her mother's gentle touch. 'I know my mother loved me in her way. But she struggled badly with her mental health. She drank to self-medicate and misused prescription drugs. It's why I don't drink alcohol and I rarely take anything, not even paracetamol.'

'I'm in awe of your pain threshold, both physical and emotional,' Jack said, coming to stand next to her by the crib.

There was a silence broken only by the baby's soft snuffling sounds.

'Jack?' Harper's voice was quiet and tentative, her gaze still focused on the baby. 'Promise me you won't abandon her? Please? No matter what our relationship is, don't ever abandon Marli.'

Jack placed his hands on her hips and gently turned her to face him. Her features were cast in lines of worry. He brushed a slow-moving finger down the curve of her cheek, his eyes holding hers. 'I will never abandon her. I'll do everything in my power to give her a happy and fulfilling life.'

Her gaze lowered to his mouth and the tip of her tongue came out and swept over her own lips. 'Thank you.'

Jack bent down and placed his mouth on hers in a barely touching kiss. A soft press down that should have ended there but somehow didn't. Harper moved closer, his arms tightened around her and his mouth came down again to hers, moving against hers in a kiss that was gentle and yet throbbed with banked-down passion. He could feel it pulsing in his body in response to her taste and touch. The sweet taste and sensual touch he had craved and dreamed of for the last nine months. Her mouth was an exotic fruit and he wanted to feast on its sweetness until he was drunk from it. She responded to his kiss with a breathless sound that sent a shiver down his spine, her arms snaking around his neck to link behind his head.

But then Harper suddenly pulled back from his embrace and rapid-blinked, as if shocked at what had just occurred. 'I'm sorry. I didn't mean that to happen.' She raised a flustered hand to her face and pushed back her still damp hair. 'It must be hormones or something.' Her cheeks were bright pink, her gaze quickly averted.

'Don't apologise.'

She moved to the other side of the bed as if she wanted a boundary line to stand behind. 'I don't want you to get the wrong idea...to lead you on or anything.'

Jack ran a hand through his hair, trying to get his own hormones to settle down. 'It's been a pretty crazy couple of hours. You probably need to get some sleep.'

'Yes... I am a little tired...'

That would have to be the biggest understatement he had ever heard. Her eyes had dark circles beneath them, her face was drawn and her shoulders were drooping with fatigue. He wanted to hug her, to hold her, to reassure her, but her expression and posture warned him to keep his distance. 'Is there anything I can get you before I go? A drink? Food?'

She chewed one side of her mouth and glanced at the baby, a frown pulling at her brow. 'I have nothing for her. No clothes to take her home in. No baby equipment or—'

'I'll take care of it first thing tomorrow,' Jack said with far more confidence than he felt. He knew zilch about what babies needed but surely his mother or a shop assistant would help.

'I didn't come in my car to the hospital. I caught a cab, so you'll need to get a baby seat for your car.'

'Right…' Jack wasn't sure a baby seat would even fit in his top-model sports car.

'You don't happen to have a phone charger on you, do you? I need to call my friends.'

'I'll get you one from one of the doctors or nurses.'

'Thank you.'

Jack found a phone charger within a few minutes and came back to find Harper curled up on the bed, facing the crib but fast asleep. He plugged in her phone and left it on the bedside table. He stood looking down at her for a long moment, still trying to come to terms with what had happened in the last couple of hours. He had had some pretty eventful days in his life but this one surely topped the lot.

CHAPTER FOUR

'YOU'VE HAD A *WHAT*?' Ruby and Aerin gasped in unison when Harper called them later that night on a video call.

'It wasn't backache, I mean, I did have backache, but it was actually labour,' Harper explained about her cryptic pregnancy, still finding it hard to believe herself. And she wouldn't have believed it if her baby wasn't lying in the crib next to her bed, fast asleep after her last feed.

'But you didn't even *look* pregnant,' Ruby said in a stunned tone.

'You did have a certain glow about you, though,' Aerin put in. 'And you were eating for two. Remember that night when you cleared the platter Ruby prepared? You seemed unusually hungry, especially since you're nearly always dieting.'

Harper didn't have a slim build like her business partners. She had struggled with accepting her more statuesque form for years. But now she had produced a baby, she had a new respect for her body. She was amazed at what her body had done in nurturing and growing a baby and then delivering it. She angled the camera so the girls could see Marli. 'Here's my baby girl. What do you think of her?'

'Oh, she's just divine,' Aerin said with wondrous awe in her voice.

'What a sweet little face,' Ruby said with equal adoration. 'She's like a doll.'

'That's what her father said.'

'Who *is* her father?' Ruby asked. 'Or can I take a wild guess and say it's Jack Livingstone?'

'Was he there for the birth?' Aerin chipped in.

Harper took a breath and released it in a not quite steady stream. 'Jack is Marli's father. And yes, he managed to get here in time for the birth.' Another point in his favour. He had mopped her brow, held her hand and had his practically crushed in return, but had he flinched? Had he complained? Had he walked away and denied parenthood?

No.

He was all in.

And insisting on marrying her, no less.

Harper's mother had birthed her all alone, all the while knowing her baby's father hadn't wanted to meet his child. Hadn't wanted anything to do with his baby girl or her mother. Now that she had given birth herself, Harper realised how awfully lonely and terrifying it must have been for her poor mother.

'Was he…surprised? Shocked?' Aerin asked.

'Probably about the same as me,' Harper said. 'I'm glad he was here, though. With you two out of town, I didn't know who else to call.' It wasn't as if she had a mother of her own to call. Jack had turned up at her request and got there in time to see his baby come into the world. Harper recalled the way he had supported her and his gentle handling of their daughter and fought against the feelings the vision stirred in her chest.

But she was not in love with her baby's father. Jack Livingstone was practically a stranger. He might be devilishly attractive and utterly charming, but she was *not* going to fall in love with him.

And hot damn, she would not think about *that* kiss.

'So, how's it going to go with you two bringing up a baby?' Ruby asked. 'I take it he wants to be involved?'

'He wants to marry me.'

'Marry you?' Aerin gasped again in shock. 'What did you say?'

'No, of course,' Harper said. 'Why would I marry him just because he's the father of my baby?'

'What if he's in love with you?' Ruby said. 'I mean, he wanted to see you again but you always refused.'

Harper gave a clipped laugh of cynicism. 'Jack isn't used to women saying no to him. I was a challenge he couldn't resist.'

'At least he offered to support you,' Aerin said. 'That's definitely a point in his favour.'

Harper could think of dozens of points in his favour—his strong and capable take-charge attitude, his work ethic, his unflappable temperament, his drive for success. And then there was his tall and athletic build, his too-handsome features, the blue eyes that were as dark as a mountain tarn, his lean and chiselled jaw, his swept-back jet-black hair, his long, straight nose and his sensually carved mouth...

Argh. She must *not* think about his mouth and how it felt against her lips. Sensual and seductive, soft and yet commanding. A mouth that could distract her from all of her carefully constructed goals. A mouth that could beguile and bewitch and befuddle her until she couldn't control herself.

But doubts about Jack supporting his child for the long haul circled around her head. Babies were cute, but toddlers could be a handful. And what about the roller-coaster time of puberty and adolescence? What if the novelty of being a father wore off sooner rather than later? What if he abandoned Marli the way Harper had been abandoned by her own father? She couldn't allow that to happen to her little girl. The marriage Jack was proposing seemed a clinical sort of arrangement. What exactly would it entail? And how could she agree to spend her life with a man who openly admitted to not loving her? Or even believing in love? He said he had been celibate for the last nine months but she couldn't see him being celibate for the duration of their marriage. Or would he expect they would sleep together, raise their child together but not fall in love? She had slept with him once and her heart had almost been his. Almost. Sleeping with him again would be asking for the sort of trouble she had spent her life avoiding.

Love trouble.

Deep trouble.

Inescapable trouble.

Marli woke and gave a mewling cry, her little arms waving about her head.

'I'd better see to her,' Harper said. 'Come and meet her as soon as you get back to London.'

'I'll organise a baby shower for you,' Aerin said. 'I

know it's meant to be before the birth, but under these circumstances, what does it matter?'

'That would be nice,' Harper said. 'I have nothing for her, although Jack promised to get me some stuff before we take her home tomorrow.' But where would home be? His place or hers?

'We'll do everything we can to help you, Harper,' Ruby said. 'It'll be a juggle with the bookings we've got coming up but you can take maternity leave if you want. We can get a stand-in photographer for a few weeks. You'll need time to bond with Marli.'

'But I still have to go to Paris in six weeks,' Harper said. 'No one can go in my place. It's my work they want to feature. It's a dream come true for me and I can't back out at the last minute.'

'Then concentrate on that and leave the weddings to us,' Ruby said. 'And give that gorgeous little munchkin a cuddle from me. Tell her Aunty Ruby already loves her to bits and her Uncle Lucas will be besotted as soon as he sees her.'

Harper smiled in spite of her worries for the future. Ruby was like a sister to her and so was Aerin. Through thick and thin, flood and drought and confidence and doubt, they stood by her and she stood by them. What did she need a husband for?

Especially one as dangerously distracting as Jack Livingstone.

Jack had never been in a baby goods store in his life. He stood surrounded by pastel colours, soft, fluffy toys, numerous clothes in a variety of sizes, cots and prams and pushers and baby carriers and bassinets and car seats and change tables and nappies and sippy cups and bottles and even breast pump machines. How could one tiny infant need all this stuff? Where was he supposed to start? He picked up a pink and white unicorn with a gold horn on its head and inadvertently pressed the start button on its stomach and a soothing lullaby started to play. The song from his own childhood stirred deeply buried memories of being surrounded by parents and two sets of grandparents who loved and nurtured him. Relatives who one by one had disappeared through death and disease, leaving only his mother and him still standing.

Love came with a price—loss.

Terrible, heartbreaking, unavoidable loss.

His mother had lost his father by degrees, the man she adored becoming frail and more and more difficult as the ravages of his Parkinson's set in. And Jack had lost his father too, watching as his strong and capable body and sharp mind deteriorated, leaving him the shell of a man who had fought every inch of the way to hide his vulnerability.

And because of his father's determination to conceal his increasing disability, the family hotel business had been all but destroyed by his father's mismanagement, leaving Jack to pick up the pieces to rebuild the Livingstone Hotel brand to make it even better than before. But not before watching as precious heirloom after precious heirloom and property after property were sold to meet the eyewatering debts. Losses that to this day he hated thinking about. Which was why he was always on the hunt for a new property to develop, to make up for those he had lost.

Jack figured the only way to avoid such devastating losses in his own life was not to love in the first place. To keep his emotions in check. In control. Under lock and key.

Safe.

A middle-aged woman came over with a smile on her face. 'May I help you with anything?'

Jack put the unicorn down, packing his memories away like old clothes that were no longer his size. 'My fiancée and I have just had a baby girl and I need to get some gear.' Call him stubborn but he was determined to keep calling Harper his fiancée.

The woman's eyes lit up. 'Congratulations. What things did you have in mind?'

Jack picked up a pink onesie that looked about the right size for Marli. 'Let's start with this and go from there.'

Harper was putting Marli back in her crib after a feed the next morning, when Jack came in carrying bulging bags from a well-known brand of babywear. 'Looks like you've been busy.'

'Just a little.' Jack put the bags on the bed and came over to gaze down at the baby. 'How did she sleep?'

'Like a baby.'

He flashed a grin at her that shot an arrow straight to her heart. She had to be careful not to fall for his disarming charm. She had to keep her emotions out of their relationship...whatever their relationship was now. They were parents of a tiny baby. They were former lovers but, since it had only been a one-night stand, did that even count as a fling? It was a passing moment in time that had brought about the birth of their child.

'You want to have a look at the things I got? The rest is back at my hotel.'

Harper leaned on her hands and pulled her shoulders back. 'Is that where you live? In one of your hotels?'

He gave a loose shrug of one impossibly broad shoulder. 'It makes sense to base myself in the flagship hotel in London so I can keep an eye on things.'

Harper pushed herself off the bed and moved around the other side, folding her arms across the middle of her body. 'I hope you're not expecting our child to live in a hotel?' She had lived in temporary accommodation throughout her childhood—bedsits, caravan parks, shelters and then foster care. None of which were permanent homes. None of which felt like *her* home.

'I expect my child to live with me and her mother.' There was a chord of determination in his tone. 'How can I be a fully present and involved father if I only see Marli every second weekend?'

Harper sent him a look that was so frosty it could have frozen the water in the jug on her tray table. 'I told you I'm not marrying you.'

'Where do you live?'

'I live in a flat in South Kensington.' 'Flat' was too generous a term for the tiny one-bedroom place she paid an exorbitant rent for and Harper wondered how long it would take him to realise it.

'How many bedrooms?'

Mmm...not long, apparently. She couldn't hold his steely gaze and blew out her breath on a sigh. 'One.'

'Hardly big enough to raise a family.' His voice was just shy of condescending.

Harper raised her gaze back to his. 'It will be fine for now, and besides, it's just Marli and me. I can move to a bigger place when she's a bit older.' *When I've had time to adjust to becoming a mother*, she could have added but didn't. But would she *ever* adjust? She was still reeling from the shock of finding herself the mother of a baby. She had spent the night staring at her tiny daughter, chastising herself for not having recognised she was pregnant. Torturing herself with all the what-ifs…what if she had been a drinker? What if she had been a six-coffees-a-day person? What if she had been the sort of person to pop pills whenever she got the tee-niest ache or pain? What if she had eaten some of those listeria-contaminated foods you weren't supposed to eat while pregnant? She could have inadvertently harmed her baby, causing her child irreparable damage, ruining Marli's potential all because she had not for a moment suspected she was pregnant.

'I'll buy a house for us to live in,' Jack said. 'Problem solved.'

Harper gave a startled laugh. 'Nice to be able to just go and buy oneself a house, especially in London, where the price of real estate is out of most people's reach.'

'I'm not most people. I own a chain of luxury hotels and can afford to buy my child and my fiancée a nice home.'

'Which you seem to think I'll meekly agree to live in with you.'

Jack gave her a sardonic look. 'There's not too much

about you that's meek but I'm hoping you'll see the practical advantages of our living with each other.'

Harper upped her chin, shooting him a blistering glare. 'Practicalities meaning you expect me to dive head first into your bed?'

His dark blue eyes glinted as if he was thinking about how she'd done exactly that nine months ago. Trouble was, once she'd got into his bed that night, she hadn't wanted to get out. And that was something she wasn't prepared to risk happening again. He was too attractive, too addictive, too everything. She had no willpower around him. He only had to look at her a certain way and her body would betray her. No one had ever made love to her the way Jack Livingstone had. He had made her pleasure a priority. He had made her feel things she had never felt before. He had touched every inch of her body and celebrated it, worshipped and revered it as if it was the most beautiful and sexy body he had ever encountered. She might have given birth only the day before, but even *thinking* about what he had made her feel on that night nine months ago gave her shivers all over again.

'Isn't that part of the marriage deal?' he asked. 'The couple agree to worship each other's bodies for the rest of their lives?'

Harper snorted. 'As if you would agree to be faithful to one person for the rest of your life. You're a playboy, for pity's sake.'

His expression became grave. 'You have my word, Harper. I will remain faithful but I insist it be a real marriage. And it goes without saying, I expect you to be faithful to me.'

The baby made a sound and Harper went to her crib to check on her. But Jack had moved too, and they stood side by side, looking down at their daughter, who had settled back to sleep with a soft little sigh. Harper was conscious of how his shirt sleeve was brushing the bare skin of her arm. Conscious of the citrus and spice of his aftershave that teased her senses like a stupefying elixir. Conscious of his every breath and the hectic racing of her own pulse.

Jack suddenly turned to look at her and her heart slipped like a stiletto on black ice. His arresting blue eyes had been the first thing she had noticed about him nine months ago. Breath-snatching eyes, fringed with enviably long and thick ink-black lashes, his eyebrows twin dark slashes above an intelligent brow. But there were twin smudges beneath his eyes, too, as if he hadn't slept well the night before. It made her realise with a jolt she hadn't talked to him about how he felt about becoming a father. She had been too consumed by her own shock and surprise to take a moment to reflect on his reaction.

'Jack?' Her voice came out whisper-soft. 'Are you… happy to be a father?'

He gave a slow blink and then let out a serrated sigh. 'If anyone had asked me even a week ago if I'd be happy to be a father, I would have flatly said no. It isn't something I have ever aspired to being. But now Marli's here…' He glanced at their child sleeping in the crib and added in a tone rough around the edges, 'I'm happy, proud, gobsmacked and overwhelmed with the desire to protect her no matter what.'

Harper was well aware that she was one of the 'no

matter what's. Her refusal to marry him was an obstacle he was determined to remove. But how could she marry him without love? She point blank refused to examine her feelings for him. She had buried them as soon as she had left his hotel room that night. What sort of sex-dazzled fool fell in love with a man after a one-night stand? She had confused fabulous sex with full-on love. The feel-good hormone oxytocin released after multiple orgasms had bewitched her into thinking he was The One and Only.

He wasn't.

He couldn't be.

She wouldn't *let* him be. That was why she had got the hell out of his hotel room before it could happen. But he was the father of her baby. And, while Harper's feelings could be ignored and denied or filed away, their baby could not be so easily dismissed. Marli was a living, breathing entity—a little human they had created together.

'What about you?' Jack asked. 'Are you happy to be a mother?'

Harper nibbled at her lower lip for a moment. 'I guess I'm a bit like you. I didn't plan to be a parent. I didn't yearn for it like my friends do. I've always been career-focused.' Her shoulders slumped on another sigh. 'What if I'm not a good mother? What if I mess up her life or something? It's not like I had the best role models for parents. My father didn't want me at all and my mother checked out when it all got too much for her. When *I* got too much for her.'

Jack's warm, strong hands came down on her shoulders, anchoring her. 'You blame yourself? You were only a child. It wasn't your fault she died the way she did.'

Harper lowered her gaze to the open neck of his shirt, where she could see the sprinkling of dark hair that covered his broad chest. 'It was my fault. I didn't get home from school at the usual time.' She released a ragged breath and continued, 'I found a stray kitten on my way home. I stopped to play with it. I lost track of time. I got home and…and, well, I found her on the sofa with an empty bottle of pills and an empty bottle of wine next to her. I called an ambulance but she couldn't be resuscitated.'

'Oh, Harper…' His arms wrapped around her and he brought her closer to his chest in a hug. 'You mustn't blame yourself. It sounds like your mother had some pretty complex issues that had nothing to do with you.'

'But they *were* to do with me,' Harper insisted, wishing it was otherwise, but in her heart, she knew she was to blame for everything. She pushed out of his embrace to look up at him through the glitter of sudden tears. 'If I hadn't been conceived, my mother might have realised in time the mistake it was to get involved with a married man. If I hadn't been born, my mother might have had the life of happiness and fulfilment she had envisaged as a romantic young girl. She might have found someone who would love her the way she deserved to be loved, someone who had wanted to raise a family and grow old with her. Someone who wouldn't lie and make promises he had no intention of keeping. But instead, she died a lonely death in a run-down flat at the wrong end of town. How is that not my fault?' She brushed at her eyes with an impatient hand, her chest tight with

barely suppressed emotion. Emotion she normally controlled so well. Emotion she normally didn't allow herself to feel. 'Sorry. It's not like me to get so emotional.'

'Harper, you've just had a baby,' Jack said, taking her
by the hands in a gentle but supportive hold. 'Your emotions, let alone your hormones, are all over the place.'

Harper looked into his concerned midnight-blue gaze
and wondered if his emotions were in anything like the
turmoil hers were. Like her, he had become a parent
without warning, without preparation, without planning. 'We come from two different worlds, Jack. You
come from a life of privilege. I've come from poverty.
How can we possibly raise a child together?'

'We both love our little girl. That's the most important thing right now. Becoming a family for Marli's
sake.'

It sounded so tempting. So very dangerously tempting. Her daughter would have everything Harper had
not. Marli would not grow up wanting things she could
not have, dreaming of adventures she would never get
to experience. She would have everything money could
buy. She would have two parents who loved her. Two
parents who wanted the best for her.

But what would Harper have?

A husband who had only married her because he
wanted to help raise his child. Not because he loved
Harper for herself. A convenient marriage was not in
her game plan. Any marriage, for that matter. Any relationship that would compromise her ability to make
her creative mark on the world was out of the question.

Except…there was Marli to consider now…

Her daughter already had more love and commitment

from her father in the first day of her life than Harper had ever received from hers in her whole lifetime. Although Marli's arrival had been a shock to Jack—as it had been to Harper—he hadn't shirked from his responsibilities. He hadn't even insisted on a paternity test. He had been all in from the moment he heard she was about to have his child. If Harper refused to marry him, it would certainly make it harder for him to be fully present in Marli's life. Did she want her little girl to have a part-time dad? Better than no dad at all, but still...

Harper slipped her hands out of his hold and gave him a wry look. 'You don't give up without a heck of a fight, do you?'

His flash of a grin did mortal damage to her determination to resist his outrageous proposal. 'When I want something, I do everything in my power to get it.'

And wasn't that the heart of Harper's problem in a crinkly, uncrackable nutshell? Jack Livingstone had way more power than she did. Way, way more.

And he was ruthless enough to use it.

CHAPTER FIVE

HARPER MOVED TO the bed where Jack had left the shopping bags. She began to take the items out and laid them out, but her forehead was creased in a frown as if none of what she was seeing pleased her.

'What? You don't like what I got?' Jack asked. 'The shop assistant helped me with the sizing. And Marli will grow into anything that's a bit big.'

Harper held up the little pink onesie, the first thing he had selected in the shop. 'You bought a lot of pink things.'

'Yes, well, isn't that what you dress baby girls in?'

She glanced at him over her shoulder, then turned back to pick up yet another pink outfit. 'Girls can wear other colours, even blue. It would look good with her skin tone and her eyes.' Which he was ridiculously proud to note were his skin tone and eye colour.

'But won't people think she's a boy?'

Harper turned to face him, her expression now unreadable except for a hard glitter in her eyes. 'Would you have preferred a boy?'

Jack whooshed out a breath, not sure where this was leading. 'It's not something I've ever thought about, to be honest. I never saw myself becoming a father. But to have a healthy child of either sex is surely something to be grateful for? And even if she wasn't healthy, I would still want to be there for her.'

Harper turned back and folded the velour outfit and placed it on the bed next to the pink beribboned teddy bear he'd bought. 'I think we should press pause on the marriage conversation until I get my head around being a mother. There's a lot to get used to…and with my hormones all over the place, I don't think this is a good time to make such a momentous decision.'

On one level, Jack could see the sense in what she was saying. Emotionally driven decisions were often the ones people regretted in the long run. That was why he never made them. Never got emotionally invested. He kept his emotions out of all business decisions, but he was determined to marry the mother of his child. He could not countenance any other option. 'Okay, we'll leave it for now. But I want your answer after we come back from Paris.'

Harper swung back to stare at him. 'You'll come with me?'

'But of course. How else will you look after Marli if I'm not there to help?' Jack had no clue how to look after a baby for hours on end, but he was on a crash course to learn. He wasn't sure how he was going to juggle his busy diary, but he had a good team of staff who would step up in his absence.

'I could engage a nanny… Lots of working women do.' Something about Harper's tone suggested it wasn't something she was completely convinced was the right choice for her. But then, there was so much she hadn't had time to think through about becoming a mother. Jack was conscious that the implications of parenthood, particularly in the early weeks and months, were likely to impact more on Harper than him, especially if she wanted to continue breastfeeding.

'You could but I would prefer to be as involved as I can, especially in these early months. They're meant to be important for proper emotional attachment.'

Harper's expression was cynical. 'I thought you didn't believe in emotional attachment?'

'Not in a romantic sense, but bringing up a child is different. They need secure emotional attachment to their parents and caregivers.'

'Yes, well, I know that more than most.' Harper picked up the lullaby-playing unicorn and pressed the button on its tummy. The sweet strains of the lullaby filled the silence and her expression became wistful. 'I used to have a teddy bear that played this song but I lost it between foster homes.' She put the unicorn down and her expression became masked, as if revisiting that childhood memory had been more painful than she wanted to admit.

'It must have been hard moving from place to place.'

'I survived.'

But at what cost? There was a hard shell to her personality that reminded Jack of his own emotional armour. Was that why he had felt so drawn to her all those months ago? Seeing in Harper Swan a mirror image of himself? A person who knew what they wanted out of life and was determined to let no one and nothing get in their way. Who would let no one get close enough to hurt them. Who would let no one take advantage of them or disappoint them. Who was ruthlessly determined to keep themselves safe at all costs.

And right now he needed his own ruthless determination more than ever, for he was not going to rest until he had made Harper his bride.

Harper was discharged from hospital the following morning. She was privately impressed with how she had convinced the nursing staff at how well she was coping with sudden motherhood. But she had always been good at acting. Pretending she was fine when she was really struggling. Masking her true feelings so others didn't suspect she was feeling vulnerable and alone. Adopting a confident I've-got-this manner when she had no clue what she was doing.

Jack came at the agreed time to collect her and Marli. Harper had to push her feelings even further out of sight, squashing them so deep inside her chest she could feel them fluttering under her ribcage like a flock of frantic finches. What if she couldn't feed Marli properly? What if Marli lost weight and cried all night? What if she couldn't juggle work and caring for her child? A nanny was out of the question. It brought back too many memories of being looked after by strangers in foster care. People who came and went in her life, some of them caring, others not so much. How could she leave her child in the care of someone she didn't know or trust?

You trust Jack.

Did she, though? She hardly knew him, and yet there was something strong and dependable about Jack Livingstone. Something that had drawn her to him in the

first place. Yes, he was a suave and charming playboy but he was also a man who had firm principles
he lived by. His insistence on doing the right thing by
Marli was a case in point. He hadn't bolted as soon as
he'd known he was to become a father. He had stood
by Harper's side and helped her deliver their baby girl.
And he had offered to marry her and provide a secure
home for their child.

But, as tempting as it was to accept such lifelong security for her child, how could she agree to a loveless
marriage? But on the other hand, how could she deny
her daughter the full-time presence of a loving and devoted father? Harper wanted her daughter to have everything she hadn't had growing up, and high on that
list was a loving father.

But what about what *she* wanted?

Was it wrong to want love for herself? Or was she to
be denied it in both childhood and adulthood?

Jack carried Marli in his arms and led Harper out to
the hospital car park. Harper glanced at the shiny dark
blue luxury model sedan complete with a baby seat in
the back. 'This is your car? What happened to the red
sports car you had at the Tenterbury wedding?'

'It's back at the hotel. This is what we'll use when
taking Marli out and about. It's the safest model on the
market.'

Harper had many clients who could afford luxury
weddings in exotic locations, but Jack's wealth was on
another level. He owned a chain of high-end boutique
hotels across the globe. He could buy a brand-new car
without flinching at the cost. Harper's business was
doing well but she still counted her pennies, every sin-

gle one of them. A childhood living in poverty made it hard for her to take anything for granted.

'I thought we'd go to the hotel until the house is ready,' Jack said, pressing the remote control that unlocked the car with a musical beep.

'What house?'

'The house I'm in the process of finding for us.'

Harper frowned. 'But I'd like to go back to my flat.'

A steely glint of determination lit his gaze. 'You need support in these early days. And I want to be around Marli as much as possible.'

But that would mean Jack would be around her as well. Hadn't she already betrayed herself by responding to his kiss in the hospital within minutes of giving birth? She had so little immunity to him, especially now with her hormones and emotions all over the place. 'I don't want to live with you, Jack. We're not a couple and—'

'But we are Marli's parents and I don't want my child living in a tiny flat that looks like it could be a fire risk.'

Harper wouldn't admit it to him but she had her own concerns about her flat. The landlord had been lax about some of the repairs that needed doing and some of the other tenants weren't exactly the nicest neighbours to be around. But she had lived in worse dwellings as a child. Far worse. The thought of spending a few days or weeks in a luxury hotel was rather tempting. More than tempting. It would give her time to adjust to being a mother, to get herself in some sort of routine with Marli. But the pay-off was she would be in close contact with Jack Livingstone, the father of her child. Six feet four of arrant masculinity. Oh, joy.

Jack placed Marli in the baby seat with such meticulous care that Harper found it hard to summon up the cynical dislike of him she had taught herself to feel. He wasn't acting like a worldly playboy now, he was acting like a devoted father of a newborn baby girl. But would he revert back to his playboy ways if Harper didn't agree to marry him? Or even if she did marry him? How could she trust a man she didn't really know?

Jack helped Harper into the passenger seat and then pulled down the seat belt for her to clip across her body. 'Are you comfortable?' His blue eyes were shadowed with concern.

'I'm fine.'

He brushed a lazy finger along the curve of her cheek. 'You probably wouldn't admit it if you weren't, would you?'

Harper gave him a self-deprecating glance. 'I'm not used to having people fuss over me.'

'Maybe it's time you had someone do exactly that.' He closed the door and then came around to the driver's side, checking Marli in the back seat first. He opened the driver's door, slid into the seat and, closing the door with a soft snick, sent Harper a probing glance. 'So, what's it to be? Your place or mine?'

Harper raised her eyebrows and sent him a pointed look. 'You're actually giving me a choice?'

He gave a lopsided smile that made something in her belly swoop. 'Kidnapping isn't my modus operandi.'

No, but lethal charm was and she would have to be on her guard to keep herself from falling for it. And falling hard.

They arrived at the flagship Livingstone Hotel a short time later. The uniformed staff at the rear and more private entrance stepped into action. 'Good morning, Mr Livingstone,' one of them greeted Jack with a deferential smile.

'Morning, Ben,' Jack said. 'This is my fiancée, Harper Swan, and this is our daughter, Marli. Please ensure that only my private staff attend to their needs in my suite. And keep the press away. We'll be making a press announcement in a day or two.'

'Certainly, Mr Livingstone.'

Harper waited until Ben was taking her bag out of the boot of the car to speak to Jack. 'Press announcement?'

'I'd like to formally announce Marli's arrival as well as our engagement,' Jack said. 'It's better to be on the front foot rather than having the press chase us for a scoop. That way we control what's said about us.'

The thought of paparazzi chasing her for an exclusive on her relationship with Jack was nothing less than terrifying. She didn't know even know how to describe their relationship. He kept referring to her as his fiancée but she hadn't accepted his proposal…yet. She was starting to waver on it and it scared her because she had always been so adamant about keeping herself free from emotional entanglements that might get in the way of her career. But she hated the thought of robbing Marli of a close relationship with her father. For now, it was easier to run with Jack's plan in order to get through these early weeks of their baby's life. Would the press announce their 'engagement'? What would everyone make of their relationship? She was hardly his normal model-type. She was used to being behind the camera, not in front of it. Her job was to take photos, not to be the subject of them. And she didn't want her baby girl to be hounded by the press, either. But how could she protect her baby when Jack Livingstone was her father? Everyone would want to know about the woman who had given birth to his child. It would be front-page news for sure.

How on earth could she protect her privacy?

A short time later, Jack opened the door of his penthouse suite and Harper stepped inside, trying her best not to be too impressed by the luxury surroundings. The entrance was bigger than her kitchen, the sitting room that came off it bigger than her entire flat. The plush carpet threatened to swallow her up to the knees but the furniture was minimalist and masculine in design, reminding her she had entered Jack's territory. A place where she did not and could not belong.

Marli gave a tiny squawk from the capsule he was carrying and Harper turned to check on her. 'I think she might need changing.'

'I'll do it.' Jack put the capsule down and unclipped Marli from the fastenings. He took her out and cradled her against his broad chest. 'Where's the changing bag I bought?'

'Here.' Harper handed the bag to him, torn between wanting to watch him with their daughter and needing to keep her distance. He was taking to fatherhood so smoothly, a little more smoothly than she was taking to motherhood—not that she would admit that to anyone. She just needed more time to get used to having a baby. It was all such a shock, an almost traumatic shock in some ways. There was so much responsibility with having a baby. A child was a lifetime's commitment. Harper hadn't even thought about such a commitment, so to suddenly have a baby was profound and emotionally unsettling.

Harper found herself following Jack to his bedroom, where he laid Marli on the king-sized bed. He began to undo the press buttons on her little onesie, softly talking to her in his deep, baritone voice. 'I'm going to change your nappy, okay?' He unpeeled the sticky tabs on the nappy and grimaced. 'Hmm… I think I might need some baby wipes.'

Harper stepped forward and handed them to him. 'Apparently breastfed babies poop a lot.'

'Good to know.' Jack cleaned Marli up and put on a fresh nappy, and then did the onesie back up. He lifted the baby to his chest again, one of his hands stroking her tiny back. His eyes met Harper's and something in her chest flipped open. 'How are you doing?' There was a gentle note of concern in his voice that was as disarming as his steady, deep blue gaze.

Harper gave a shrug and shifted her gaze from his. 'I'm a bit tired…' She glanced at the bed and then wished she hadn't as a rush of heat flowed through her cheeks. 'Erm, where will I be sleeping?'

'In my bed.'

Harper met his look with a flash of fire in hers. 'Do you really think that's wise?'

His expression was inscrutable. 'There's a fold-out sofa in the sitting room. I'll sleep on that.'

'Oh…' Harper wasn't sure why she should be feeling a pang of disappointment. She didn't want to sleep with him…*did she*? She couldn't sleep with him anyway, not so soon after delivering a baby. It was usual to wait at least four to six weeks before resuming sexual activity. Was there something wrong with her that she desired him even now? That he only had to look at her and her insides would flutter and tighten and coil with lust? That every nerve in her body was acutely, achingly aware of him? That her mouth could still taste the sexy, salty tang of his lips and craved it like a potent drug?

The doorbell of the penthouse suite rang and Harper's gaze flew to Jack's. 'Are you expecting anyone?'

'My mother wants to meet Marli. She's dropping off some presents as well as a bespoke bassinet she insisted on buying for her.'

Harper steeled her gaze and her spine. 'But I don't feel like meeting anyone now, especially someone who's already decided I'm a gold-digger.'

'My mother will adore you once she gets to know you.' Jack went to the door and opened it with Marli still cradled against his chest.

A tall and elegantly dressed woman in her late fifties swept into the room carrying loaded bags. There was a luggage trolley outside the door with a staff member in attendance, and an array of things were stacked on it, including a gorgeous pink and white bassinet. 'Oh, Jack, isn't she just divine?' Liz Livingstone placed the bags on the floor and took the baby from him. 'Oh, look at you, my little darling. You're exactly like your daddy with those big blue eyes. And look at all that hair.' She smothered Marli with kisses, her eyes moist with tears. 'I've waited so long for this moment. I still can't believe it's true. I'm finally a grandmother.'

Jack placed his hand on his mother's shoulder to turn her to face Harper. 'Mum, this is my fiancée, Harper Swan. Harper, this is my mother, Liz.'

Harper met the older woman's gaze without smiling or speaking. She knew it was rude of her but she was not going to forgive being called a gold-digger in a hurry.

Liz swept her coolly assessing gaze over Harper. 'Well, you're not exactly what I was expecting.'

Harper raised her eyebrows in an imperious manner. 'As you can see, I'm not your son's usual blonde supermodel-type.'

'But you're beautiful for all that.' The compliment was given in a grudging manner by the older woman but Harper refused to be mollified by it. She did not want to get close to Jack or his mother. Jack's mother turning up with a bundle of presents only served to remind Harper of her own mother's absence. Her baby girl had only one grandmother when she should have had two. Liz Livingstone was a protective mother and clearly only wanted what was best for her son. It drove it home even more painfully that Harper had no one looking out for her.

But wasn't that the story of her life?

Marli began to whimper, giving Harper the perfect excuse to take her from Liz's arms. 'Excuse me, I need to feed her.'

It looked for a moment as if Liz wasn't going to hand the baby over. But then she pursed her lips and passed Marli to Harper. 'You're feeding her yourself?'

'Yes.'

'You'll have to weigh her regularly to make sure she's

not losing weight,' Liz said. 'It wouldn't hurt to give her a bottle or two. That way Jack or I can feed her.'

Harper held Marli close to her chest, sending the older woman a challenging glare. 'I don't want anyone else to feed her but me. And I don't want her handled by too many strangers.'

'But I'm her grandmother,' Liz said, clearly affronted.

'Mum.' Jack's tone had a note of caution in it. 'We're both still getting over the surprise of having a baby. Take it easy, eh?'

Liz let out a huffy sigh, spun on her heels and started rummaging in the bags she had brought in. 'All the clothes in here are organic cotton. It's best for the baby's skin. And I've only bought safety standard approved toys. You have to be so careful with small beads and batteries and other tiny things with infants.' She held up a frilly pink outfit. 'Isn't this so cute? I can't wait to dress her in it.'

'We already have enough pink outfits,' Harper said. 'I want Marli to wear other colours.'

'What? Like black?' Liz said with a scornful roll of her eyes.

The battle lines were drawn, the tension in the air palpable.

'Mum, let's leave Harper to feed Marli in peace,' Jack said on a sigh, taking his mother by the elbow. 'We'll go and have a gin and tonic in the bar downstairs. I'm sure Harper will be happy to see you in a day or two once she's got over the birth.'

'But I want to spend more time with my granddaughter,' Liz insisted. 'I want her to properly bond with me.'

'You'll get plenty of time with her,' Jack said. 'But now's not a good moment.'

'You're damn right it's not,' Harper said under her breath and closed Jack's bedroom door on them both with a resounding click.

CHAPTER SIX

JACK CAME BACK upstairs an hour later once he had seen his mother off. It had taken every one of his negotiating skills and then some to bring his mother around to promising to go slowly with Harper. The last thing he wanted was any animosity between them. He wanted his relationship with Harper to work from the get-go, and any bad feeling on his mother's or Harper's part was not going to do him any favours, nor would it help Marli.

Harper was kneeling in front of the capsule on the floor of the sitting room, rocking it back and forth in a gentle manner. She glanced up at him but went back to staring at their child, her shoulders hunching forward. 'Your mother hates me.'

'Well, you didn't exactly lay on the charm.'

'Why should I? She thinks I'm after your money.'

He scraped a hand through his hair and came over to where she was kneeling. 'You're a mother now, so you'll understand how protective mothers are over their offspring. She just wants what's best for me.'

Harper made a snorting noise. 'Well, clearly that's not me.' She rose to her feet and stood in front of him with a defiant look on her face. 'I can imagine the type of woman she wants you to marry. Someone who comes from an aristocratic background, someone who can move in the circles you move in without embarrassing you.'

'You don't embarrass me,' Jack said, frowning.

She moved past him with a proud toss of her head. 'Yeah? Well, I'm not so sure you won't be embarrassed if the press goes snooping into my background.'

Jack let out a long breath. 'You have no reason to feel ashamed of your background. I know it was tough on you growing up in foster care but look at you now. You're a successful businesswoman.'

Harper picked up a baby blanket and folded it into a neat square, then held it against her body. A flicker of uncertainty passed over her face. 'I'm not sure I can be as successful as I want to be with a baby to look after.'

Jack moved closer and took the blanket from her, placing it on the arm of the nearest sofa. He took her hands in his and was secretly delighted she didn't resist his touch. 'I guess it's a tricky balance for any parent, be they a mother or a father. How do you provide for your family and model a good work ethic while being available and present for your child's needs? It seems almost impossible to get it right.'

Harper lifted her gaze to his. 'Did your mother work or stay at home with you?'

'She stayed at home but sometimes I wish she hadn't.'

'Why?'

Jack released her hands and stepped back. 'My father became ill during my childhood with Parkinson's Disease. She didn't get the chance to resume her career as an architect because my father needed a lot of care, particularly towards the end.'

'Did she want to resume her career?'

'She says not, but she didn't have an easy time with my father,' Jack said. 'He wasn't always difficult, but as the disease progressed he became so. It was tough on her, tougher than she would ever admit, even now. If she'd still had her career, it might have given her an outlet. But my father refused to have anyone but her look after him.'

'I'm sorry to hear that.'

Jack didn't like thinking of just how difficult things had been at times. The sacrifices he and his mother had had to make. The years of hard work to bring things back in the black after his father's mismanagement. 'I was away at boarding school by then, so I didn't always see how difficult things were for her or I might have been able to convince my father to engage the services of a professional carer. The business began to struggle and my mother blamed herself for not keeping a closer eye on things, but it wasn't her area of expertise, plus my father didn't delegate well. He refused to accept his limitations.'

'I read somewhere you built the business back up to what it is today,' Harper said. 'But was it your choice of career?'

No one had ever asked him that question before. Not even his mother. Everyone had assumed he would gladly follow in his father's footsteps and take over the hotel business as his father had done with his own father, Jack's grandfather. The Livingstone luxury brand was an institution that could not fail, certainly not on

Jack's watch. So, upon his father's death, Jack had bludgeoned his own creative dreams into oblivion, determined to rebuild the family business to honour the legacy of his grandfather and father. He could not remember the last time he had picked up a paintbrush and a set of watercolours. It was a part of his life he had cordoned off like a locked room in a castle that no longer had a key. 'I would never have made the money I make today doing anything but what I'm doing.'

'But what did *you* want to do?'

Jack gave an on-off smile to signal the subject was closed and picked up the room service menu. 'I'm going to order some dinner for us. What would you like?'

A short time later, Harper sat at the dining table with Jack. But for once in her life her mind wasn't on food. She kept mulling over the things he had told her about his background. She had always been envious of people who grew up with enormous wealth. They hadn't had to struggle to put food on the table and keep a roof over their head. They hadn't slept under an old coat instead of fine wool blankets or feather and down quilts. But Jack's refusal to discuss his own career aspirations made her wonder if he, like his mother, hadn't been able to pursue his own choice of career due to the responsibilities that fell to his shoulders on his father's illness and then death. Jack had certainly turned the Livingstone Hotel brand into an eye-popping success. There were boutique hotels all over the globe that paid testament to his hard work. The company was one of the most profitable brands in the world and only the rich and famous could afford to stay in a Livingstone Hotel.

Which made it highly ironic that she was now living in one with Jack. She wasn't exactly on the poverty line any more but she didn't move in the circles Jack did. If he continued to insist she marry him for the sake of their baby, how would she navigate his world of high-end luxury, of liveried staff and private jets?

'You're not eating,' Jack said. 'Would you like something else? A dessert, perhaps?'

Harper pushed her plate away. 'How do you do it?'

'How do I do what?'

She waved her hand to encompass the luxury suite. 'Live like this? In a hotel, I mean. Don't you feel…a little claustrophobic?'

Jack put his wine glass down on the table. 'I travel so much that I'm only in one place for a night or two.'

Harper picked up her water glass for something to do with her hands. 'Is that why you only have one-night stands?'

His mouth twisted in a rueful manner. 'It suited me to keep things casual.'

'But now?'

His gaze met hers with a directness that was a little unnerving. 'We have a child to raise. We can't be casual about that.'

Harper looked down at the ice cubes in her water glass. They were slowly melting, becoming one with the mineral water. Was that what was going to happen to her? Her resolve to resist Jack would melt until she couldn't keep herself separate, couldn't live without him? Needing someone was not something she ever wanted to do. Of course, she needed her friends and loved them dearly. But loving a man in a romantic sense had never been on her radar. That was why that night with Jack had been so out of character for her. She had never been so captivated by a man before. She had never been so distracted by a man's charm and banter that she had walked away from her work responsibilities to indulge in a stolen hour or two of toe-curling passion.

Harper looked up from her water glass to meet his gaze once more. 'But you didn't grow up in a hotel, did you?'

'No, we had a home in Buckinghamshire.' He picked up his wine glass again but didn't bring it to his lips. He tilted the glass from side to side, watching as the blood-red wine swirled against the bowl of the glass. 'It was one of the first things we had to sell after my father died. It broke my mother's heart to leave.' He lifted the glass to his lips and took a sip, before putting it down on the table again. His expression gave nothing away but Harper sensed he too had bitter regrets about losing his family home.

'You haven't tried to buy it back, I mean since?'

Jack's mouth took on a cynical curve. 'No, once I say goodbye to something, that's it. I don't look back.'

'Does that apply to people as well?'

His eyes locked on hers, sending a shiver down her spine. 'I didn't get the chance to say goodbye to you. You slipped out of my hotel room before I woke up. Why was that, hmm?'

Harper could feel a rush of heat flowing into her cheeks at how she had behaved that night. It had been as if she had turned into someone else—a sensual woman who didn't think twice about having casual sex with a stranger. It still shocked her that Jack had distracted her from her work, turning her into a wanton woman who could think of nothing but being in his bed having spine-tingling sex. The sort of sex she had never had before. Sex that was exciting beyond measure. Her body had flown into the stratosphere, trembling, quaking, shuddering with waves of delight she had never experienced with a partner before. Before Jack Livingstone, her pleasure had never been a priority. She had lost count of the number of times she had faked an orgasm to get an encounter over with. But Jack's touch had awakened her in an almost frightening way. She wanted more of him but knew she shouldn't. He was like a forbidden drug she must resist before she became completely addicted. Her mother had fallen for a man she could never have, who had promised but failed to deliver. Jack was promising Harper everything but love. How could she settle for riches and not the most valuable thing of all—love? She lowered her gaze from his probing one and stared at the starched white tablecloth in front of her. 'I wasn't interested in repeating our… hook-up.'

'Because?'

She swallowed tightly, trying not to think of how hard it had been to leave his room when all she had wanted was to stay wrapped in his arms and experience his mind-blowing passion all over again. It had taken an enormous amount of willpower to leave. And it *still* took an enormous amount of willpower to keep her distance from him. Not so easy now she had his baby. They were bound together for the next eighteen years or so whether she liked it or not. She couldn't stop him seeing their child, he wanted to be an involved and loving father, and from all she had seen so far that was exactly what he would be. How could she deny her baby that special relationship? The father-daughter relationship she herself had longed for all her childhood? 'Because I wasn't interested in you.'

'Liar.'

Harper forced her gaze back to his, masking her features into cool impassivity. 'You find it impossible to believe any woman can say no to you, don't you?'

His dark blue eyes kindled with sensual heat. 'You didn't say no. You wanted me as much as I wanted you that night.'

A traitorous drumbeat of lust thrummed in her lower body. Had she no resistance? No immunity to his potent charm? 'That night was a mistake on my part. An aberration.'

Jack glanced to where their baby girl was sleeping in her capsule. 'Is that how you want our daughter to see herself? As a mistake?'

Harper frowned. 'No, of course not. I didn't mean it like that.'

There was a pulsing silence.

'If you had found out about the pregnancy earlier, what would you have done?' Jack asked.

Harper chewed at her lower lip, not quite able to meet his gaze. 'I'm not sure what you're asking…'

'Would you have told me? Or simply had a termination?'

She brought her gaze back to his. 'I don't think there are too many women who consider having a termination a simple solution. It's a big decision to make, and not one I would have liked to make, although I respect other people's reasons for doing so.' She paused for a beat and continued, 'I would have told you, though. I would have given you the choice to be involved or not.'

Jack's gaze drifted back to their sleeping baby, his expression cast in lines of awe that tugged on Harper's heart strings. He loved his child; did that mean he might one day fall in love with her? 'I can't imagine not being involved now she's here.' Marli opened her tiny mouth and yawned, one of her little starburst hands stretching above her head. Jack shifted his gaze back to Harper's, his expression turning serious. 'I wouldn't have pressured you into having a termination. I firmly believe it's a woman's choice what happens to her body.'

Harper gave him a pointed look. 'But here you are, pressuring me into marrying you.'

His mouth went into a tight line. 'It's the best possible solution to our situation. It will provide security and stability for Marli and you going forward.'

Security and stability were the two words that were foremost in Harper's mind at the best of times, even more so now she had a baby to consider. But would marrying a man she barely knew be the best possible solution? A man she had suppressed her feelings for out of a sense of imminent danger. A man who only had to touch her and she erupted into flames of rabid lust. Marrying Jack Livingstone might provide her daughter with a loving and present father but it would provide Harper with a temptation she wasn't sure she could resist.

And she suspected Jack knew it.

A couple of days later, Ruby and Aerin arranged to call in to meet Marli. As it turned out, Jack had to see to a work issue at one of his hotels in Edinburgh, so was away from early in the morning to catch a flight to Scotland.

'Oh, look at her, isn't she gorgeous?' Aerin said, melting at the sight of Marli dressed in a duckling-yellow outfit Jack had brought back home the day before.

'You're making me seriously clucky,' Ruby said, with a smile. She turned to look at Harper. 'How are you managing? It must be such a huge change.'

Harper gave a shrug. Should she tell her friends how uncertain she was about everything? Should she admit to the fears that stalked her? Fears about not succeeding with her career. Fears about not being a good enough mother. Fears about never being truly loved by her baby's father. How could she admit to such insecurities without worrying her friends? New motherhood was supposed to be a happy, if not euphoric, time. Instead, she was struggling with a host of conflicting emotions. She loved her baby, of course she did. But she was worried she might become overwhelmed the way her mother had become, the burden of motherhood too much, especially without a man who loved her by her side. 'I'm coping.'

Ruby leaned closer and placed a gentle hand on Harper's arm, her expression etched with concern. 'Only just coping?'

Harper let out a ragged sigh. 'I haven't been out of the hotel since I got here. Yesterday, I didn't have a shower until three in the afternoon. I used to be so organised and now I'm not sure what I'm doing or even if I'm doing it correctly. I worry Marli isn't getting enough milk, then I worry she isn't sleeping or sleeping too much. I didn't realise there was so much to worry about.'

'Oh, you poor darling,' Aerin said, making a sympathetic moue with her mouth. 'You haven't had time to prepare for motherhood. Most pregnant women spend the entire nine months planning and preparing and reading up on it. You were suddenly thrust into all this without notice. No wonder you're feeling a little out of your depth. Anyone would feel the same.'

'Isn't Jack helping you?' Ruby asked.

'Yes, he's been great, but he had to fly to Edinburgh to one of his hotels today. I'm not sure what time he'll be back. He didn't say.' Which kind of summed up their relationship. A come-and-go, fly-in, fly-out arrangement. Jack might insist on marrying her for Marli's sake, but it wasn't a true partnership.

Aerin was still cuddling Marli, moving from side to side in a rocking motion to soothe her back to sleep. 'Why don't you have a shower now and we'll head out for a walk in the sunshine? It's a gorgeous day and the fresh air will be good for Marli. We can grab some lunch and we can mind Marli while you get your hair or nails done. You'll feel like a new woman in no time.'

Within an hour, Harper was sitting at an outdoor café with her three friends, enjoying a late lunch. It was almost like being back to normal, except the responsibility of her baby made her conscious of the change in the dynamic with her friends. How could she fulfil her commitments as a wedding photographer when she was nursing a baby? She didn't want to compromise her bonding with Marli but neither did she want to inconvenience her friends. They had solid bookings for weddings and finding a fill-in photographer was not as easy as it sounded, especially finding one with the high creative standards that matched their business model.

It was amazing how many people coming in and out of the café—mostly women but even occasionally a man who was a new father himself—stopped to comment on Marli. The gushing comments on how cute she was, how adorable her outfit, how tiny she was, couldn't help but make Harper feel proud. Her body had produced this perfect little being, a gorgeous little baby who had come into the world in the most surprising and unexpected way, and yet Harper's love for her was automatic and complete. If only Jack's love for *her* was as automatic and complete as it was for their child.

But just as Harper was packing up to leave with her friends, another person came rushing over and Harper looked up to see none other than Clara Tenterbury, the bride from the society wedding where Harper had spent the night with Jack. Her stomach dropped, her mouth fell open, her mind went totally blank.

'Oh, my God!' Clara squealed. 'What a little poppet. How old is she? She is a she, right?'

Harper was not used to being struck dumb, but trying to explain her circumstances to Clara Tenterbury was beyond her capabilities right then. Maybe there was such a thing as baby brain, for her brain did feel a little scrambled. What twist of fate had led Clara to be at the same café as Harper and her friends? 'Erm…' Harper began but couldn't get her voice to complete the sentence, couldn't get her mind to even form a sentence to say.

'This is Marli Elizabeth Susannah Swan-Livingstone,' Aerin said, with a proud aunty-like smile. 'Isn't she absolutely gorgeous?'

Clara's eyes bulged like oversized marbles. 'Did you say... *Livingstone*? As in Jack Livingstone?'

Aerin bit her lip and glanced at Harper with a worried oops-I-think-I made-a-boo-boo look on her face. Harper was thinking of how many followers Clara had on social media. Thousands, possibly millions by now. It had been a positive thing for her and her business partners when Clara had gushed about how wonderfully they had done her wedding to Hugh Tenterbury. But now? It was a potential nightmare.

Harper fixed a stiff smile on her face. 'How are you, Clara? Enjoying married life?' What else could she do but deflect? There was no way she was going into the details of Marli's conception. No freaking way.

Clara's eyes danced. 'Wonderful.' She placed a hand on her own abdomen. 'I have my own exciting news to share. Hugh and I are expecting a baby. A boy. Hugh is so ridiculously proud. I bet Jack is too.'

After the appropriate congratulations were given, Ruby came to the rescue and diverted the conversation away from Harper by chatting about where Clara and Hugh had gone for their honeymoon, telling her of her own plans for her wedding to Lucas Rothwell. And within a few minutes Clara was gone, giving them all a fingertip wave on the way out.

Harper blew out a ragged breath and passed Marli to Ruby to hold, so she could pack up her things. 'Thanks, Ruby, for rescuing me. I thought she would never leave.'

'That's okay,' Ruby said. 'I could see you were a bit stuck for words.'

'I'm so sorry,' Aerin said, still looking worried about her gaffe.

'Don't worry about it,' Harper reassured her. 'I couldn't think how to explain about my cryptic pregnancy without looking like a complete idiot.' It was hard not to feel a little envious of Clara, who was clearly enjoying every moment of her pregnancy. How had she not known her own body was undergoing the same changes? It still didn't make sense...or did it? Had her mind switched into a pattern of denial so strong it had prevented her from seeing what was right in front of her?

Ruby looked down at the baby in her arms with a wistful expression on her face. 'Marli's like a little angel. I still can't believe none of us suspected you were pregnant.' She glanced up at Harper. 'Did you even for a moment think you might be?'

Harper was about to say 'no' but then realised it wasn't strictly true. There had been odd moments when the thought had crossed her mind but not for long enough to take a firm hold. 'I've been thinking about that... I was late the first month but only by a few days. Then I had sore breasts for a week or two, but then I sometimes do before a period. And I had a lighter than normal period a few times.' She frowned and continued, 'I think I might have been in denial, so couldn't allow the thought any traction in my head. I feel such a fool now, though. How could I not have realised on some level?'

'Denial is a powerful tool when we don't want to face

stuff we need to face,' Ruby said. 'But it all turned out in the end. Marli is perfect and you and Jack are going to be wonderful parents. You're lucky he wants to be involved. Just like for you, it must have been an incredible shock for him.'

'But what if the novelty wears off?' Harper asked. 'Marli is cute now but babies grow bigger and get noisy and messy and hard to control. He might not feel so committed to her once she's a defiant toddler or a moody teenager.'

'But even some mothers can feel ambivalent towards their kids,' Ruby said with a rueful twist to her mouth. 'My mother being a case in point. Jack might prove to be the best father you could ask for your little girl. You have to give him a chance to prove himself.'

'By marrying him?' Harper asked. 'How can I marry a man who doesn't love me? Who doesn't even believe in the concept of long-lasting love?'

'Playboys always say that until they fall in love themselves,' Ruby said with a dreamy smile. 'Just ask Lucas.'

'And my father,' Aerin said with a grin. 'You should have heard his soppy speech about Mum at their wedding anniversary weekend. There wasn't a dry eye in the house, not even his.'

But Harper wasn't so sure she could hold on to the hope that Jack might fall in love with her one day. What if he didn't? What if their marriage became a cold and clinical arrangement that left them both unsatisfied and their child had to grow up witnessing it?

CHAPTER SEVEN

JACK RETURNED TO his penthouse later that day to find Harper and Marli were not there. He went from room to room, trying to quell the panic rising like a toxic tide in his chest. Surely she wouldn't have left without informing him? But her absence brought back the memory of that night nine months ago, waking to find her gone, only the indentation of her head on the pillow next to his. The frustration he had felt shocked him then as it shocked him now. He hadn't been expecting her to do a runner. He was offering her much more now than a simple fling. He was offering marriage and a secure future for her and their child. Why would she leave without at least telling him where she was going? Marli was his child too, so he had a right to know where she was and if she was safe.

The door opened behind him and he swung around to see Harper coming in carrying Marli in a front pouch strapped to her chest. 'You're back,' she said, closing the door behind her with the kick of her left foot.

'Where the hell have you been?' Jack asked. 'I was worried about you. You didn't tell me you were going out.'

Harper's dark eyebrows rose ever so slightly over

her eyes in an unmistakably haughty manner. 'Am I supposed to check in and out with you on my every movement?'

Jack let out a rough-edged breath. 'No, I was just expecting you to be here when I got back. You didn't call or even send a text.'

She slipped the straps of the carrier from her shoulders, her other hand cupping the baby's bottom to hold her steady against her. 'I went out with Aerin and Ruby. We had lunch and they looked after Marli while I got my hair and nails done. Not that I should have to explain myself to you. Last time I looked I was a free agent.'

Jack had to stop himself from pacing the floor in frustration. He couldn't get his panic back in its box. His worries over her and Marli's safety were new things to deal with, new concerns to add to his list of responsibilities. Responsibilities he took seriously. 'But what if the press saw you?'

Harper's gaze hardened to steel but there was a hint of pink in her cheeks, suggesting she might have already thought of the possibility of being exposed. 'So that's what worried you? That I might leak something to the press about us?'

'Don't be ridiculous, that's not what I meant at all. I want to make an announcement about us on my terms. It's important our relationship is seen as the real deal for Marli's sake.' He rubbed the back of his neck, where a knot of tension had built since he left that morning. The hotel management meeting hadn't gone as well as he would have liked. He had tried to focus to problem-solve the issues but he had been completely distracted, wanting to be back with Harper and the baby. It was so out of character for him not to put work first. To narrow his focus so nothing else existed. He had even pressed a pause button on the meeting so he could go out and buy an engagement ring at an exclusive jewellery store he had heard about from a colleague.

Harper laid the baby down in the bassinet and tucked the bunny blanket around her. She turned and glanced at him, her eyes still glittering with ire. 'I've been stuck in this hotel room for days. I needed to get out for some fresh air. Sorry if that doesn't meet with your approval but I can't stay hidden up here like a dirty little secret.'

Jack released another long-winded sigh and came over to her, taking her hands in his. 'You surely don't see yourself as that?'

Her gaze slipped out of reach of his, one of her slim shoulders rising and falling in a shrug. 'I can only imagine what the press will make of me once they hear about us. Your mother already thinks I'm a gold-digger, so I can only assume others will too.'

Jack tipped up her chin with his finger, locking her gaze on his. 'Not once we formalise our relationship.' He released her hands to take the jewellery box out of his trouser pocket. He handed it to her. 'I hope it fits. I had to guess your ring size.'

She hesitated for a moment, then took the square velvet box from his open palm as if it contained something dangerous. She gingerly prised open the lid and gasped at the princess cut diamond. 'Jack…it's too much. It must've cost a fortune.' She frowned up at him. 'It's such a beautiful ring for a loveless commitment such as ours.'

He took the ring out of the box and slid it along her

ring finger, immensely relieved it fitted her perfectly. Was that an omen or what? But so much about Harper fitted him perfectly. Her sensuality was unmatched. He could not remember a lover who had thrilled him the way she had. 'We love our baby, that's all that matters for now.' He took her hand and brought it up to his mouth, pressing his lips against the ring and then each of her fingertips in turn.

Her gaze drifted to his mouth and her slim throat rose and fell over a swallow. Uncertainty shadowed her grey-green gaze. 'Marriage is such a big step...'

Jack placed one of his hands against the curve of her cheek, his thumb stroking the smooth skin of her face in a slow-motion caress. 'We'll be good together.'

She ran the tip of her tongue over her pillowy lips and a drumbeat of lust thrummed in his groin. Was it his imagination or had she leaned closer to him? He placed his other hand on her right hip, easing her closer, his body on fire as soon as her pelvis came into contact with his. She snatched in an audible breath and her gaze focused back on his mouth. 'Jack...' Her voice was little more than a whisper, a husky, sexy whisper that sent a frisson down his spine.

Jack lowered his mouth to hers, taking his time, allowing her the chance to pull back if she didn't want to go any further. But instead of pulling away, she moved forward as if drawn to him by an invisible force—the same invisible force that was driving him towards her. Their lips met in a feather-light touchdown, once, twice, three times. But instead of quelling the need for sensual contact, it fuelled it.

Fervently. Fiercely. Ferociously.

Her mouth came back to his in a kiss that was as hot as fire, the pressure of her lips sending his senses reeling. She opened her mouth beneath the increasingly urgent pressure of his, their tongues tangling in a dance as old as time. Jack knew it was too soon to take things any further, but somehow, knowing they could only kiss and caress for now intensified the contact. It brought something new and exciting to each movement of their lips against each other's. A sweet poignancy that plucked at something deep in his chest, something he had never felt with anyone else. Her mouth was sweet and soft and yet exotic, her tongue playful and yet determined. Her arms wound around his neck, holding him closer, her full breasts crushed against his chest.

Jack lifted his mouth from hers to blaze a pathway of hot kisses down from below her ear to the scaffolding of her collarbone. Her soft, breathless sounds of encouragement and pleasure sent shivers of delight through him. The chemistry between them on their first encounter nine months ago had stunned him then and it stunned him now. How could a simple kiss, a caress, a breathless murmur of pleasure send his pulse skyrocketing?

Jack shifted his mouth to the delicate shell of her ear, breathing in the scent of her freshly washed hair, which tickled his face. He swept it back over her shoulder, placing his mouth on the side of her neck, his tongue teasing the soft, creamy skin. 'You taste so damn delicious, I think I'm getting addicted to you,' he growled deep in his throat.

Harper gave a delicate shudder and lifted one of her hands to his face, sliding it down the rough, late-in-the-day stubble. 'We shouldn't be doing this…' Her voice was still whisper-soft, her eyes dark and lustrous as wet paint.

'We're only kissing,' Jack said. 'It's too soon for anything else.'

A faint blush pooled in her cheeks and she lowered her gaze to his mouth. Her fingertip traced the outline of his lips and every nerve reacted to her sensual touch, making him hot and tight and hard as stone. He recalled how she used those clever little fingertips on his body, tiptoeing all over him, teasing him all those months ago, pleasuring him with her lips and tongue and taking him to heaven and beyond.

Jack brought his mouth back down to hers and she sighed against his lips, her arms going around his neck again. Her fingers played with the hair brushing his collar, sending shivers of reaction down the length of his spine. She eased back from his mouth to glance up at him with a slightly dazed expression on her face. 'I don't think I've ever been kissed like that before.' She circled his mouth with her finger again, slowly, tantalisingly.

Jack captured her hand and pressed a warm kiss to her open palm, teasing the skin with a poke of his tongue, watching as her pupils flared in desire. 'Nor have I,' he said and kissed her again.

Harper knew it was dangerous to kiss Jack. Dangerous and addictive, but how could she help herself? He triggered a need in her that was so strong it overrode every other thought in her brain. All she wanted was the taste and texture of his mouth on hers, the sweep and glide and sexy thrust of his tongue in her mouth that made her blood sing and tap dance in her veins. It didn't seem possible that she could feel such a powerful rush of desire so soon after having a baby. But that was Jack Livingstone's power over her. He was able to undo her physically like no one else.

Jack finally released her with a rueful sigh. 'I'd better stop before I get carried away. Besides, you need your rest. Why don't you put your feet up while I check on Marli?'

'Okay.' It piqued Harper that it was Jack who was the first to break the sensual interlude. Why hadn't she stepped back first? Why hadn't she shown him she could resist him? Why hadn't she had the willpower to keep him at arm's length?

Because she didn't have the willpower. She never had.

Would she ever?

A couple of days later, Harper was having breakfast with Jack before he left for the office, when one of Jack's staff informed him via the intercom his mother was asking to come up.

Harper frowned and put down her cup of tea with a clatter against the saucer. 'But it's seven-thirty in the morning. Why can't she come at a reasonable hour?'

Jack put his napkin on the table and pushed back his chair. 'She hasn't seen Marli since we first brought her home from hospital. She's waited years to be a grandmother. Indulge her. Being a grandmother will make up for all the things she had to sacrifice for my father. It will give her a purpose again.'

Harper understood Jack wanted his mother involved

in his daughter's life. She knew the value of grandparents even though she hadn't experienced it for herself. Ruby, for instance, had been reared by her grandmother and spoke lovingly of the memories of growing up at Rothwell Park, where her grandmother was the housekeeper to Lucas's family. Aerin still had both sets of grandparents and also spoke positively about the joy of being indulged and thoroughly spoilt by the older generation. Harper glanced down at her nightgown and wrap. She had been up a lot during the night, feeding Marli and feeling like a zombie. Jack had got up each time with her, but despite the interrupted sleep he looked disgustingly fresh after a shower and a shave. 'But I'm not dressed for visitors.'

'Why don't you make use of her while she's here?' He flicked his shirt sleeve back to check his designer watch. 'I have to get to an early meeting in a few minutes. Mum can mind Marli while you have a shower or even go back to bed for a bit.'

Jack went to let his mother into the penthouse and Harper sat fuming. The last thing she wanted to do was entertain Jack's mother, even if she was a devoted grandmother.

Liz came into the dining room with a newspaper tucked under her arm, her expression etched in lines of disapproval. 'I suppose we have you to thank for this.' She tossed the tabloid newspaper on the table in front of Harper.

Harper looked down at the photo of her holding Marli at the café with Aerin and Ruby the other day. Her heart came to a jerky standstill, a cold shiver crawling over her scalp like the march of ice-footed ants. The headline read: *Wedding Photographer and Former Foster Child Harper Swan Has Secret Love-Child with Billionaire Hotelier Jack Livingstone.* Her eyes ran over the rest of the article detailing snippets of information about Jack and herself, most of which were fabricated. Surely Clara Tenterbury hadn't fed the press such sensationalist rubbish? Harper glanced up at Jack, whose expression was as frozen as a marble statue. 'Jack, you can't possibly think *I* was behind this?'

His dark blue gaze was hard and cynical. 'Can't I?'

'I warned you, Jack,' Liz Livingstone said. 'This is exactly what I was saying about—'

'Mum, please leave this to me,' Jack said in a clipped tone. 'Go and check on Marli. She's in the bedroom.'

His mother pursed her lips, pulled back her shoulders, turned on her heels and stalked out.

Harper pushed the paper away, nauseated by the thought of millions of people speculating about her. She stood from the table, wrapping her arms around her middle, her pulse thudding in panic and distress. 'I didn't do this, Jack. I would never speak to the press.'

'Clearly someone did. One of your friends?'

'No, Aerin and Ruby would never betray me like that.' She moistened her dry-as-toast lips and continued, 'When we had lunch the other day we ran into Clara Tenterbury. I know she and Hugh are your friends but she's the only one who could have done this. She was fascinated to see me holding a baby. I couldn't think of a thing to say. I didn't know how to explain our situation. But Aerin told her Marli's full name, which of course included your surname hyphenated with mine. Clara then jumped on that and, well, I guess that's what led to this.' She jerked her head towards the newspaper on the table as if it were a poisonous spider.

Jack snatched up the paper, screwed it up and then tossed it in the nearest bin. His expression was thunderous, stark lines of tension running either side of his mouth. 'I wanted to control what was said about us in the press. I planned to make an announcement as soon as we agreed on a wedding date.' He scraped a hand down his face, momentarily distorting his handsome features. He lowered his hand and let out a harsh-sounding breath. 'God, what a freaking mess.'

'Do you believe me?' Harper tried not to sound too desperate for his trust but she needed him to believe her. She of all people knew what it was to be lied to or about, which was why she had a reputation for being honest to the point of bluntness. The only person she ever lied to was herself. But that was something she didn't want to think about right now. Her feelings for Jack, the feelings she tried so hard to squash, were still throbbing away inside her, aching to find a way out of the prison she had locked them in.

Jack came over to her and took her left hand, running his thumb over the diamond he had put there the day she had met with her friends. His eyes meshed with hers, his mouth tilted in a grim smile. 'If you say you didn't do it, then of course I believe you. Anyone could have taken that photo or overheard you talking with Clara and your friends. I'll release my own announcement today.'

Sudden moisture prickled at the backs of her eyes, two tears escaping in spite of her best efforts to hold them back. Jack reached up with his other hand and blotted them with his fingertip, his expression softened with concern. 'Do you want me to send my mother away? I don't like leaving you alone when you're upset but I have an important meeting I can't cancel at short notice. I'll explain what's happened to her. I'm sure she'll understand.'

Harper stepped out of his embrace and painted a stiff smile on her face. 'I'm fine. No, don't send her away. She's the only grandmother Marli has, and it's only right she gets to spend time with her.'

Jack touched her gently on the back of her hand, a light grazing of his fingertips that sent a frisson through her body. 'How does September 1st sound for a wedding day?'

Harper had never pictured herself as a bride. She wasn't like her friends and clients who had dreamed since childhood of finding true love and riding off into the sunset with their soulmate. She was far too practical, too committed to her career to hanker after the happy-ever-after so many others longed to find. But she had a baby to consider now, a child who had the right to be involved with her father. A father who promised to love and provide for Marli. How could Harper deny her little girl the security she herself had longed for but never experienced growing up? 'That's only two months away,' she said.

'Will that be a problem?'

The only problem was the fact Jack would be marrying her without being in love with her. And didn't most brides long for that more than anything else?

'Lucas and Ruby's wedding is in late October. I don't want to disrupt their plans by squeezing in our wedding before theirs. A wedding takes weeks if not months to plan. I don't want to take the attention off them and put it on us. Can't we wait until I get back from Paris to decide on a date?'

Jack let out a sigh of resignation. 'Okay, but I don't believe in long engagements.'

He didn't believe in love either and that was Harper's biggest problem of all.

Jack left after speaking to his mother, and a few minutes later Harper went in to where Liz was seated in the bedroom, holding Marli in her arms. The baby was looking up at her grandmother and Liz was cooing to her in a sing-song voice that made Harper realise how much she had missed out on by not having had a grandmother herself. Liz Livingstone might not approve of her son's choice of bride but no one could question her adoration of her infant granddaughter.

Liz looked up as Harper stood framed in the door. 'I hope Jack isn't making a big mistake in marrying you. I've always wanted him to marry for love.'

Harper adopted a don't-mess-with-me expression, curling her top lip for good measure. 'How do you know he doesn't love me?'

Liz's chin went up to an imperious height. 'He told me so.'

Harper had to work hard not to show how much the older woman's words wounded her. It was like being struck in the face with a blunt object, the pain travelling to every part of her body in stinging, pulsating waves. Surely Jack could have at least *pretended* to love her for the sake of appearances? Was she to suffer the shame and indignity of always being seen as not good enough?

Not worthy enough?

Unlovable? But hadn't she always believed that about herself?

Harper pushed herself away from where she was leaning indolently against the door jamb. 'He might not love me but look at the size of the ring he gave me. Pretty awesome, huh?' She knew she was acting exactly like the trashy little gold-digger Jack's mother thought her to be, but right then she didn't care.

The older woman's mouth tightened like the strings of an old-fashioned purse, her eyes flashing with loathing. 'I don't believe for a moment you didn't set Jack up by deliberately falling pregnant. You saw him as a meal ticket and went for it with both greedy hands. Cryptic pregnancy be damned. You might have convinced everyone else but you haven't convinced me.'

'If you have an issue with me falling pregnant, you'd best speak to your son,' Harper shot back with venom. 'They were his condoms, not mine.'

Liz's cheeks burned a deep shade of pink as if the intimate topic was way outside of her normal experience. 'I only hope you turn out to be a better mother to Marli than you'll be a wife to my son.'

Harper locked gazes with Jack's mother as if she was in a boxing tournament and determined at all costs to win. 'I damn well will be.'

CHAPTER EIGHT

Four weeks later...

JACK CAME IN from a long day, after being in Rome for an important meeting, to find Harper asleep on the sofa in front of the television. The volume was so low he didn't see the point of having it on at all but he guessed she was trying not to disturb Marli, who was usually asleep at this time in the bedroom.

He hunkered down in front of Harper, gently stroking his fingers through her hair. He found it increasingly hard to keep himself from touching her. The magnetic pull had only intensified over the last month. The sensual energy between them was at times palpable. If ever she touched him even incidentally—such as when she was passing him Marli—a lightning-fast zap of energy shot through his blood. And it was obvious she felt the same, for she often pulled her hand back, or blushed, or turned away as if to disguise her reaction.

'Hey, sleepyhead. Wouldn't you be more comfortable in bed?'

Harper opened her eyes and blinked owlishly at him.

'What time is it?' Her voice was soft and slurry from sleep.

'Half one in the morning.'

She groaned and pulled herself up to a sitting position, her long, sleep-tousled hair tumbling about her shoulders. 'How was your trip to…where did you go again?' She scrunched up her face as if trying to recall their conversation earlier that morning.

Jack sat beside her, resting one of his arms along the back of the sofa. 'Rome.'

'Oh, that's right. Sorry, my memory is all over the place.'

He threaded his fingers through her hair again, loving the silky feel of it against his skin, the fruity fragrance of it filling his senses and making him want to bury his face against her neck and breathe in more of her. She didn't move away from his touch, but instead leaned into it, her eyes closing momentarily, like a cat that was blissfully enjoying being stroked.

'It's because you don't get enough sleep.'

She opened her eyes and turned her head to meet his gaze. 'Nor do you. Do you normally work such long hours? And travel so much?'

Jack had actively sought time away to process what was happening between them. What was happening to him. Feelings he refused to acknowledge, feelings he didn't want to name or examine in any detail were burgeoning inside him. Spending day after day with Harper made it near impossible to keep his heart off limits. He wasn't sure what it was about her that chipped away at his emotional armour so relentlessly. But strangely, time away from her didn't help at all. It only made him miss her and Marli all the more. He threw himself into his work with a passion he didn't feel. The only passion he had was for Harper.

Jack let out a long sigh and reached for one of her hands, holding it between both of his. 'There are a few new developments I'm juggling right now. Plus, the house I'm in the process of buying needs some work. I want everything perfect before we move in with Marli.'

'You sound like Aerin. She's such a perfectionist, which is what makes her such a brilliant wedding planner.'

'How are your friends managing without you?'

Her slim shoulders went up and down in a shrug. 'Okay, I guess… They've found a photographer but she can only cover the next couple of months. It's so hard on Aerin and Ruby without me there. We're a team and we complement each other so well. I feel like I've created a logistical nightmare for them.'

He stroked the back of her hand with a lazy finger. 'You really miss work, don't you?'

She gave him a worried look. 'Does that make me a bad mother?'

'Of course not.' He brought her hand up to his mouth, pressing a kiss to her bent knuckles, his gaze meshed with hers. 'You're good at what you do and you're not used to having a break this long from doing it. But we'll be in Paris soon for your photo shoot, so hopefully that will make you feel more in touch with your work. And we can look at engaging a nanny if you—'

Harper pulled her hand out of his and frowned. 'I don't want a nanny.'

'But you were the one who first suggested it.'

She lowered her gaze, her frown still visible on her forehead. 'Like foster parents, nannies come and go. I don't want that for Marli. I want her to experience stability and security. I don't want her passed around like a parcel no one really wants.'

Jack knew Harper carried a lot of emotional scars from her childhood. Even the most normal and loving childhoods still left wounds that often took a lifetime to heal. How much harder must it have been for her, never having a father invested in her and losing her mother so young. It was amazing she had made such a success of her life to date. Many people did not.

'But we're going to have to do something because we both have big careers. What about asking my mother? I'm sure she'd be happy to help.'

Harper bounced off the sofa as if propelled by an ejector button. Her arms went around her middle, her expression stormy. 'I don't feel comfortable around your mother. She's always on her best behaviour when you're around, but she can be so annoying when you're not. She hasn't shut up about that stupid press release.'

Jack rose from the sofa and came over to her, placing his hands on her shoulders. 'I dealt with the press release by officially announcing our engagement.'

Her gaze met his with a diamond-hard glitter. 'But we're not in love and that upsets your mother. She can't bear the thought of her only son marrying someone he knocked up after a one-night stand.'

His hands fell away from her shoulders and he let out a jagged sigh. 'My mother comes from a different generation, in some ways even older and more traditional than the one she was born into. The thought of sleeping with someone just for sex is foreign to her. My father was her only lover and she remained faithful to him for life.'

'Did your father stay faithful to her?'

The question blindsided Jack for a moment. There was so much he didn't know about his father due to how his illness had ravaged him over the years. And because he had been away at boarding school for a lot of that time, there hadn't been too many father-son bonding sessions to be had, even had his father been into that sort of thing.

'That's something I can't answer because I didn't ask and he didn't say,' Jack said. 'We didn't have a particularly close relationship. If we had, he might have told me of the difficulties he was having keeping our finances in order.'

Harper's expression softened into shades of compassion. 'It must have been a terrible shock to find things weren't as in order as you expected.'

Jack gave a grunt of agreement. 'Yeah, it was. I had to do a business degree and Masters in record time to turn things around. It hit my mother hard too. She had to adjust to not only life without my father but also the lifestyle she was accustomed to. And, of course, she had no career to fall back on, having given up so much to look after him.' His mouth twisted in a rueful grimace. 'I think that's why she can be so pedantic and controlling now. She doesn't want to get caught out again.'

Harper stepped closer to him and placed a hand on his forearm. His skin tingled and tightened at her touch and a wave of smouldering heat flowed through his body. 'I'll try and be a little more accommodating to-

wards her, for Marli's sake, as well as yours.' Her voice
had a husky edge that sent a shiver along his nerve
endings.

Jack placed his hands on her hips and held her just
apart from his body. The desire to bring her flush
against him was almost uncontrollable. Her gaze went
to his mouth, stayed there for a beat or two, then she
glanced up at him again.

'Jack…?' This time her voice was barely audible, a
soft, breathless whisper that seemed to contain a be-
seeching plea.

He tilted up her chin to keep her gaze locked on his.
'What else is troubling you?'

She gave a lopsided smile and lifted her hand to his
face, gliding it down the length of his jaw. 'You trouble
me, more than I care to admit.'

'In what way?'

'This way,' she said, and, stepping on tiptoe, planted
a soft-as-a-puff-of-air kiss to his lips. But, for all its
lightness, her kiss still sent a shockwave of fiery lust
through him.

Jack brought her closer to his body, close enough
to feel every sweet curve of her against his hardening
flesh. He brought his mouth down to hers in a kiss that
set off fireworks in his blood. She opened her lips to
welcome the stroke and glide of his tongue and a hot
shiver rolled down his spine. She tasted of milk and
honey and something that was uniquely her. The taste
he had craved for months like a drug he couldn't resist. His tongue duelled with hers in an erotic game that
made the hairs on his head lift away from his scalp. Her
soft little moans of pleasure and encouragement thrilled

him, excited him, fuelled him to kiss her deeper, harder,
more insistently.

He raised his mouth from hers, his breathing already
ragged. 'Isn't it too soon to be doing this?'

Her arms snaked around his neck, her full breasts
crushed against his chest. 'I had my postnatal check-up
today. I've been given the go-ahead to do whatever I like.'

Jack framed her face in his hands, looking deeply
into her eyes. 'Are you sure this is what you want? It's
late, you're lacking sleep. You might see it differently
in the morning.'

She lifted her hand to his mouth, tracing its outline
with a teasing stroke of her finger. 'It *is* already morning. Don't you want to see if what we experienced all
those months ago was just a fluke or…something else?'

It had certainly been something else—something
outside of Jack's not inconsiderable wealth of experience. The sensual energy between them had thrown him
into nine months of self-imposed celibacy. He hadn't
wanted to wipe out the memory of her touch with someone else's. He couldn't understand why she was the one
woman to have such an effect on him. He had slept
with plenty of beautiful women but none had left a lingering need in him to see them again and again and
again. Harper had put a roadblock up, which he had to
accede had only intensified his determination to have
her in the end. He was used to women chasing him. It
was a refreshing change to be the pursuer rather than
the pursued.

Jack's hands tightened on her hips, his need for her
building to the point of pain. 'Yes, I do, but I don't think
it was a fluke. You turn me on like no one else.'

But then a tiny squawking cry sounded from the bedroom. 'Waa-waa-waa.'

Harper sagged against him wearily with a sigh. 'I'd better go to her. She's due for a feed in half an hour anyway.'

Jack gave her one quick kiss before he released her. He suppressed his disappointment because he knew their little baby had to come first. He wouldn't have it any other way—Marli was his top priority, which was why it was so frustrating Harper was still so adamant about waiting until after Ruby and Lucas's wedding to decide on a wedding date. He considered making her wait to resume a sexual relationship with him until after that, but that would mean another two months of torture. Never had he wanted someone as much as he wanted her. It didn't mean he was falling in love. He would never allow his heart to get involved to that degree. He admired her, liked her, respected her and desired her.

And he couldn't see that changing anytime soon, if ever.

Harper fed and changed Marli and settled her back to sleep. She returned to the sitting room to find Jack in the same position he had found her in an hour before. He was lying on his side, his head resting on the same scatter cushion she had used. He was still dressed in his business shirt and trousers but he had taken off his shoes and socks. His black hair was sexily tousled and there was a generous sprinkling of dark stubble on his jaw. She went over to him and perched on the edge of the sofa next to his hip. Every cell in her body ached to touch him, to lean down and press a hot kiss to his mouth, to stir him into wakefulness and arousal.

But something stopped her.

Was she making a mistake by wanting to make love to him again? By wanting to revisit the mind-blowing passion they had shared that had resulted in the conception of their tiny baby? Jack wanted to marry her but not for the reasons most people got married. He desired her—she was in no doubt of that—but was it enough to last a lifetime together? Or even last enough years for them to successfully raise their child?

As if by its own volition, her hand reached out and lightly touched his lean jaw. The prickle of his stubble tickled her fingers but apart from a sleepy murmur, he didn't wake. He had been in and out of the country several times since Marli's birth, always flying back the same day, juggling work and fatherhood with his many other commitments. Like hers, his life had changed in a blink. One day he was a billionaire playboy hotelier who flew around the globe to maintain the success of his hotel brand, the next he was a devoted father, trying to be present and engaged in every aspect of Marli's care. It could have been so different. He might not have wanted anything to do with their baby. He could have left Harper to deal with everything on her own but he hadn't. He had promised to marry her, to provide for and protect her and their child. He loved Marli, there was doubt in her mind about that. But the one thing he hadn't promised to do was to love *her*.

Harper rose from the sofa. ''Night, Jack,' she whispered, and then quietly left the room.

They arrived in Paris two days later by private jet. Harper was touched that Jack had gone to such expense to protect Marli from being exposed to other travellers in case she picked up a cold. She wasn't old enough for all her vaccinations and his care and concern for her only made it harder for Harper to keep her feelings for him in check. Jack had had to fly back to Rome the morning after the night they'd kissed, which meant there hadn't been time or an opportunity to make love. The anticipation of being intimate with him again sent shivers up and down her spine. Was it her crazy hormones or was it simply because Jack was the only lover to connect with her on such an earth-shattering level?

They were staying at a Livingstone Hotel in Paris which had stunning views of the Eiffel Tower. Jack had organised the delivery of her camera equipment to the hotel and all the baby paraphernalia they needed for Marli. His attention to detail was a comfort to Harper, who was still struggling with see-sawing hormones and lack of sleep—not to mention the experience of being a new mother without the preparation other mothers had.

Harper stood in the penthouse suite in front of the expansive windows, drinking in the view outside. 'I think Paris is one of my favourite destinations. It's virtually impossible to take a bad photo here. There's something about the light and the architecture. It gets to me every time.'

Jack came up behind her and placed his hands on her shoulders. She could feel the strong wall of his body within an inch of hers, the thrill of his touch sending shockwaves of electricity through her body. She could smell the citrus and woody notes of his aftershave and she could feel her pulse reacting to his proximity with strong, pulsing beats like that of a tribal drum. Beats that reverberated deep in her core.

Jack leaned closer and placed his mouth against the side of her neck, close to her ear. Her skin erupted in shivering sensations and her heartbeat skyrocketed. 'Are you nervous about tomorrow?' he asked in a low, deep burr.

She leaned her head to one side, unable to resist the feel of his lips teasing and tantalising her skin. 'A little, I guess.'

He turned her to face him, his eyes as dark as a midnight sky. 'You'll be brilliant. And I'll take care of Marli, so you don't need to worry about her unless she needs a feed.'

Harper placed a hand on his chest, her gaze dipping briefly to his mouth then back to his gaze. 'I don't know what I would have done if you hadn't wanted to be involved in raising her. I love seeing you with her. But it kind of makes me realise what I missed out on by not having a father.'

Jack stroked a gentle hand down the back of her head, his touch soothing and yet sensual too. 'It's his loss, not yours.' His expression became rueful and he continued, 'I can't believe I would've missed out on the joy of being a dad if we hadn't got pregnant the way we did. I told myself I never wanted children, never wanted the responsibility of keeping them safe and guiding them through life. But now Marli's here, I couldn't be happier. I wish I didn't have to work so hard so I could be with her more. I don't want to miss a thing.'

'You're everything a girl could ask for in a father.'

'You're doing a pretty fine job of being a mum too.'

There was a long moment of silence. A silence where Jack's gaze moved to her mouth and lingered there for a heart-stopping period. A silence where Harper waited with bated breath for him to close the distance between their mouths, the need in her rising with every passing second.

And then finally, the touchdown. But it was hard to know who had moved first. Harper sighed against the firm press of his lips, opening her mouth to welcome the erotic command of his tongue. Shivers skittered down her spine, and as his tongue played and danced and duelled with hers a pool of molten heat formed in her core. Desire leapt like wildfire in her veins, a throbbing, burning, impatient desire that was threatening to rage out of control.

Jack's mouth shifted position, his kiss deepening, sending another scorching wave of longing through her body. He groaned against her mouth as if he couldn't get enough of her taste. She groaned back, pushing herself closer to the hard frame of his body. One of his hands went to the small of her back, pressing her towards the jut of his erection. A frisson of delight shot through her flesh in anticipation of his intimate possession.

'I want you so badly,' Jack groaned.

'Then have me.'

His eyes glittered with desire. 'Are you sure?'

Harper stepped up on tiptoe and swept her tongue across his lower lip. 'I want you to make love to me.'

He gave a whole-body shudder as if the anticipation was getting to him too. 'God, I love it that you're so hot for me. That was what was so great about our first time together. You almost blew the top of my head off.'

Harper smiled a sultry smile. 'Yes, well, you were pretty hot for me too, if I recall.'

He pushed her closer against his arousal, his dark eyes smouldering. 'I couldn't bring myself to make love with anyone else until I saw you again. I was desperate to experience it again. The passion, the energy, the sheer alchemy of being with you.'

His confession thrilled her beyond words. Her intimate encounter with him had tilted her world on its axis. It had terrified her to be so attracted to someone that he had distracted her from the work she loved. But it wasn't just her physical attraction to him that was so terrifying. It was the love she had for him. The love she had pretended she didn't feel. The love she had packed away in a box inside her head marked *Do Not Open*. It had struck her like lightning the first time he kissed her. And each kiss since had only poured accelerant on the flames of her feelings. They whooshed through her every time he looked at her a certain way—the way he was looking at her now, with eyes lustrous with want.

'No one has ever made me feel the way you do,' Harper said. 'Sexually, I mean.' She didn't feel ready to confess her feelings for him. Would she ever? He wouldn't welcome them in the context of their relationship. He had made it abundantly clear he wasn't offering her forever love. He was too cynical and jaded to open his heart to romantic love. And the ironic thing was she had been exactly the same until she met him.

'Ditto,' Jack said, surprising her beyond measure. 'You totally rocked me.'

Harper chewed at the edge of her lower lip, a moment of self-doubt coursing through her. 'But what if it's different now? What if we're not as in tune as we were back then?'

His mouth hovered above hers. 'Let's go for it and see, shall we?'

CHAPTER NINE

JACK'S MOUTH MOVED against Harper's with increasing passion, his tongue mating with hers in an erotic dance that left her breathless with want. One of his hands was still in the small of her back, the other came up to cradle one side of her face. No one had ever kissed her like that before. No one but Jack had held her in such a tender and yet passionate way, as if on some level he cared deeply for her. Was it too much to hope he did? That, like her, he was denying his feelings to keep himself safe from hurt? How could someone kiss her with such finesse and not feel something for her? Or was it just plain and simple rip-roaring lust?

Harper returned his kiss with equal passion, her heartbeat accelerating as her body encountered the rock-hard ridge of his erection. The primal need in her flesh responded with fervent heat, the ache to get even closer driving her wild. She whimpered her longing against his lips, urging him on with the flicker and dart of her tongue against his.

Jack's mouth left hers to blaze a trail of fire along her collarbone and then to just above her breasts. Even though she was still fully clothed, the closeness of his mouth to her breasts made her ache to feel his lips and tongue on them. He pushed her top off her right shoulder, moving his mouth over her uncovered skin. How could a shoulder feel so on fire? A shoulder! But that was the magic of Jack. The wild and wanton magic of his touch that spoke to every cell in her body. Igniting her flesh into an inferno of lust.

Jack moved his mouth to her generous cleavage, his tongue diving between her breasts, sending a shockwave of delight through her body. 'You like that?' he asked in a throaty, raspy voice.

'I love anything you do. You seem to automatically know where all my erogenous zones are.'

He gave a sexily crooked smile. 'I bet I can find a few more if you give me time.'

Harper didn't doubt it for one second. She began to undo the buttons on his casual shirt, desperate to get her hands on his skin. 'We're both wearing too many clothes.'

'Let me help you with that.' He shrugged off his shirt and then peeled her top off her. The rest of their clothes came off until they were both standing naked. His eyes roved over every inch of her body and she fought against the desire to cover her floppy belly and full breasts.

'You're so damn beautiful,' he said with a hitch in his voice. He stroked a gentle hand over the flesh of her belly almost reverently. 'Even more beautiful than before.'

'I don't know about that…'

'I do.' His mouth came down and kissed the upper curve of her left breast, sending a tingle of delight to her toes and back. He circled her tight nipple with his tongue and then moved his mouth to caress the underside of her breast. He moved to her other breast, taking his time exploring the subtle changes in her body. Sensations rippled through her in electrifying waves, heat pooling like lava in her feminine tissues.

Harper stroked her hands down his hair-roughened chest, his muscles as toned and hard as if he were carved from marble. But unlike marble, he was warm to touch. 'You've been seriously working out,' she said, circling one firm pectoral muscle with her index finger.

'It was a good way to work off my sexual frustration.' There was a wry note to his tone and a glint in his eyes. 'Hitting the gym with a vengeance.'

'Instead of hitting on strangers at a wedding?' Her tone was gently teasing.

He gave another sexily slanted smile. 'I noticed you from the first time you aimed your camera at me. I was determined to have you from that moment.'

Harper raised her eyebrows in a mock-haughty manner. 'So I was just a conquest to you? Another notch to mark in your playboy pocketbook?'

His expression became more serious. 'You weren't a trophy to collect. I was genuinely intrigued by you. You were so cool and stand-offish and yet you kept looking at me as if you couldn't help yourself.' He brought his mouth closer to hers once more. 'But then, to be fair, I couldn't stop looking at you either.'

'I noticed that.' She stroked her hand further down his body, her fingers closing around his erection. His expression contorted with pleasure and he gave a deep, guttural groan.

'Let's take this to somewhere more comfortable.'

Jack led her to the bedroom, then he joined her on the bed, his limbs tangling with hers as if they had been making love for years. He stroked a lazy hand up and down the flank of her thigh, sending a host of shivers coursing over her flesh. 'I brought condoms.'

'I hope you've switched brands since the last time.'

Another frown settled between his brows and his stroking movements on her thigh stilled. 'That night really changed both our lives in a big way, but I can't find it in myself to regret the birth of our baby, can you?'

Harper couldn't have loved him more than at that moment. 'No, of course not. She's perfect in every way. It's just…' She lowered her gaze to his stubble-covered chin and continued, 'I hope my lack of preparation during the pregnancy hasn't hurt her in some way. Emotionally, I mean.'

He tipped up her chin to bring her gaze back to his. 'Anyone can see how much you love her. She can sense it, I'm sure. I don't think you need to worry on that score.'

Harper gave a rueful smile. 'I think worrying comes with the parenting territory.'

He smiled in return and resumed stroking her thigh. 'But at least you don't have to worry alone. I'll be with you every step of the way.' His mouth came back down on hers in a long, drugging kiss that drove every doubt and fear out of her mind.

Harper moved against him, urging him to take it to the next level. 'You're taking way too long. I need you right now.'

'I have to put on a condom first.'

She watched him apply a condom and held her breath

in anticipation. He came back to her, looking at her with such fervent desire burning in his eyes it ramped up her excitement to fever pitch. He kissed his way down from her breasts to her belly, dipping the tip of his tongue into the shallow cave of her belly button. Shivers coursed through her flesh at his caresses, her heart racing as she anticipated his next move. He moved to her feminine mound, using his lips and tongue to separate her folds. His movements were gentle and slow but no less arousing for that. Tingling sensations turned into ripples and then crashing waves of pleasure. She snatched in a breath and went with it, unable to stop it even if she had wanted to. She couldn't hold back her panting cries of ecstasy and she clutched at his broad shoulders to anchor herself from the tumultuous storm racking her body.

'You certainly haven't lost your technique,' she said, struggling to catch her breath.

Jack moved back up to kiss the side of her neck, his strong, muscular legs tangling with hers. 'I want to be inside you.' His husky groan delighted her senses as much as his mouth teasing the sensitive skin of her neck.

'I want you.' Harper had never said those three little words to any other lover. Or at least said them and truly meant them. But with Jack, the need pummelling through her was so desperately intense, she thought she would die without him bringing her to completion.

Jack positioned himself at her entrance, then with an earthy groan entered her with a slow thrust that lifted every hair on her head. Her body wrapped around him, welcoming him, and darts of pleasure shot through her flesh. He began to move within her, slow but steady, then gradually building his pace as she breathlessly urged him on. He slipped a hand beneath her bottom to tilt her pelvis to increase the friction where she needed it. She wrapped her legs around him, raising her hips to meet each downward thrust, enjoying the thickness of his body in the slickness of hers.

Jack brought his other hand between their bodies and caressed her most sensitive flesh of all. The tight bud of her clitoris that was connected to an orchid-like network of nerves spread throughout her womanhood. She lifted off within seconds of his expert touch, the sensations ricocheting through her body like an earthquake.

His own release followed hers, the deep, thrusting movements of his body only heightening the delight growing through hers. He tensed for an infinitesimal moment and then pitched forward with a primal-sounding growl of pleasure, his body shaking and shuddering and shivering.

Jack stayed connected to her for a long moment, his breathing rate still hectic, his face buried in her neck. 'So it wasn't a fluke, then.' His lips as he spoke tickled her skin, then he raised himself on his elbows to look down at her. 'You sounded like you had a good time.'

Harper smiled. 'So did you.'

His eyes twinkled. 'It was definitely worth the wait.' He rolled off her to remove the condom but came back to gather her close, tucking her into his side, one of his hands stroking up and down her arm.

'Jack?'

'Mmm?'

Harper turned her head to look at him. 'I hope you're not going to wait another nine months to make love to me again. Actually, it's ten months because Marli is almost five weeks old.'

Jack rolled her over onto her back once more, caging her in with his arms. He gave a slanted smile that sent her heartrate soaring and her blood simmering in her veins. 'Not a chance, sweetheart.' And his mouth came down and set fire to hers.

Jack watched on the sidelines as Harper worked on the photo shoot over the next couple of days. She had been given several sites in Paris to photograph and it meant each full day was a juggle of feeds for Marli and setting up equipment in each location. Then taking the shots, reviewing them and working with the support team in deciding on the ones they wanted to feature. It was exciting to be back doing what she did best, but she was conscious of Marli the whole time. Worrying about her, needing to check on her, wanting to hold her longer than for a quick feed but unable to because of the time pressure she was under. It was a revelation to her of the dilemma most working mothers faced each day. There were so many conflicting needs and tasks to see to and it was nothing short of emotionally and physically exhausting. But it also gave her a sense of gratitude that Jack had put a pause button on his own work commitments to be with her. To support her and take care of Marli so she could concentrate on her work.

The last place to photograph was Jardin du Luxembourg in the Sixth Arrondissement of Paris. The gardens had been started in 1612 by Marie de' Medici, the widow of King Henry IV, for the residence she built—the Luxembourg Palace.

Harper was halfway through the shoot when she caught sight of Jack sitting under a tree with Marli propped up against his bent knees. He was playing with her tiny feet and smiling down at her with such love and devotion in his expression it brought a lump to Harper's throat. She aimed her camera at him and took a round of shots from different angles. He hadn't noticed her, so it gave her a perfect opportunity—the one most photographers loved and aimed for—the natural in the wild shot.

But as she was taking the last photo, Jack turned his head and smiled at her. 'How's it going?'

'Nearly done.' She came closer and knelt down to stroke her finger down Marli's chubby little cheek. 'I caught her smiling up at you.'

'She's got a knockout smile like her mother.'

'I think they might be the best photos I've taken today, perhaps for the entire shoot.'

Jack gathered Marli against his broad chest, stretching out his long legs on the grass. 'I can't wait to see them.' He flashed a glinting smile up at her. 'And I can't wait to get you alone tonight.'

Harper suppressed a tiny shiver of anticipation. She placed a hand on his broad shoulder. 'Thank you for making this as seamless as possible under the circumstances. I would've hated to have forfeited this opportunity to showcase my work.'

He balanced the now sleeping Marli along one arm and placed his other hand on top of Harper's. 'We're in this together, sweetheart. We're a team now.'

Harper looked down at Marli so safe and secure against his body. Was it greedy of her to ask for more

than he was prepared to give? He clearly loved his baby
girl and he had proved himself to be a steady back-up
to Harper, not resenting her career commitments or insisting she put them aside for his. He was supportive,
encouraging, and was prepared to provide a home and
haven for their little family. And he desired her as much
as she desired him. Surely that was enough for now?

Later that night, once Marli was bathed and put down to
sleep, Jack came out to where Harper was sitting going
through her photos on her digital camera.

'Can I see what you took today?' he asked, sitting
beside her and stretching an arm along the back of the
sofa next to her shoulders.

'I still have to edit a few but some are all right.' She
held the camera so he could see the screen and began
to click through the hundreds of photos taken that day.

'You've really captured some interesting angles in
those shots,' Jack said, leaning closer, the fragrance of
her hair teasing his nostrils.

'This is my favourite.' She clicked through until she
came to one of him sitting with Marli.

Even Jack was surprised at the candid shot of himself cradling Marli. The love the image captured in that
seemingly unobserved moment was enough to melt any
hardened heart. He wondered if his own father had felt
the same level of devotion towards him when he was
a young baby. Or had the pressure of work and then
the slow but steady creep of his father's illness stolen
the early joy and turned it into bitter disappointment
instead?

'Why are you frowning?' Harper suddenly asked.

Jack quickly rearranged his features into a relaxed smile but he could feel the tug of uneasiness deep inside, a question that needed answering. A problem that needed to be addressed. He had never really questioned whether his father loved him, but neither had he ever felt particularly close to him. The early memories of his childhood were overshadowed by the way his father had changed with his illness, becoming more and more distant and difficult and demanding.

'Sorry. I was just thinking about my own relationship with my father.' He let out a long sigh. 'I'm not sure he was as attached to me as I am to Marli, but then it was a different generation. Men were certainly encouraged to be more involved with their kids but my father was not the sort of man who enjoyed being around little kids all that much. And then, by the time I was a little older, he became unwell. Plus, I went to boarding school pretty young.'

Harper placed a gentle hand on his arm, her touch sending instant warmth through his body. 'How old were you?'

'Six.'

A frown pulled at her forehead, a look of shock in her gaze. 'Six?'

Jack shrugged one shoulder in a dismissive, it-didn't-do-me-any-harm manner. 'I coped.'

'But you were so terribly young. Were you homesick? Lonely? Did you find it hard settling in and making friends?'

Jack had more or less blocked out those early memories. He was a put-it-behind-you-and-move-on-with-your-life sort of person. He didn't ruminate over things that couldn't be changed. But Harper's concerned questions tapped at the locked and bolted door he had stored those memories behind. Memories of acute sadness, despair and loneliness. A sense of having to grow up way too fast but doing it anyway. A gnawing sense that he was a disappointment to his father, that he wasn't loveable, that he had been sent away so his father could get on with work without the distraction of his presence. He suspected his mother had agreed to it to keep him safe from his father's occasional outbursts of temper. Jack had suppressed his emotions so deep down inside himself he was uncertain he could access them now even if he wanted to. As for feeling them…well, he refused to feel them. Feeling them made them real again, painfully real.

'I settled in relatively quickly,' Jack said. 'I made friends, some of whom are still friends to this day.'

Harper studied him for a long moment, her expression still showing shadows of concern. 'But it must have affected you, being away from home for so long. Didn't you miss your mum?'

Jack gave a lopsided smile. 'I did for a bit but I didn't let her know it. She would have told my father and it wouldn't have gone down well with him. He had gone to the same boarding school, and so had his father, my grandfather.' He gave her shoulder a gentle squeeze with his hand that was resting near her along the back of the sofa. 'Now, enough about my childhood. Show me some more of your photos.'

Harper lifted her camera back up and clicked through some more shots, but every time he glanced at her she was still frowning. Was she thinking of her own childhood? How different and even more difficult than his? At least he had had a father. Harper's had refused to have anything to do with her. Was she worried he would abandon Marli in a similar way? He could not think of a single set of circumstances that would ever see him walk away from his baby girl. He was even finding it difficult to think of walking away from Harper. In the past, he was the one who'd *always* walked away. He never looked back, only forward. But he knew in his bones if he walked away from Harper or she walked away from him, something in him would die, or if not die, be stunted.

But why would she walk away? He had given her everything money could buy and he had promised to protect her and their child going forward. The love thing was something she kept referring to but love hadn't been what they started with, only lust. They both loved their little girl, so what else did they need? Nothing he was prepared to give in any case.

Jack took the camera from her and set it aside. He took one of her hands in his, the other he lifted to her face to smooth away the frown between her eyes. 'Stop worrying about my privileged childhood. It hardly compares to what you've been through.'

'I guess...' Her eyes fell away from his to look at her hand encased in his. Then she lifted her gaze once more. 'We've had such different upbringings. How are we going to be the best parents we can possibly be when there are so many things we don't know about each other?'

'We'll get to know each other once we're married,' Jack said. 'Which reminds me, now that your photo shoot is over, let's decide on a wedding date. That was the deal, remember?'

Harper pulled her hands out of his and stood, her expression clouding over like a brooding sky. 'I need more time before I make such an important decision.'

Jack rose from the sofa, a sense of things slipping out of his control tightening something in his stomach. 'There isn't a whole lot of time. Marli is already five weeks old. Before we know it she'll be a toddler and—'

'And what if you can't handle being around a toddler?'

He frowned. 'What do you mean?'

'Kids are hard work.'

'I know that, but we'll have the resources to get help if we need it.'

'I told you, I don't want a nanny.'

Jack scraped a hand through his hair. 'My mother is willing and able to help out and would get a lot of joy out of doing it.'

'And we both know how well your mother and I get on,' Harper snapped back. 'Marli is going to see it and wonder. And then one day she'll be old enough to ask her own questions, like why doesn't her father love her mother like other parents love each other?'

'Not all parents love each other,' Jack pointed out. 'Especially a few years down the track when careers and kids and other stresses kill the joy of the honeymoon phase. But because we're not starting at the same place, we can be realistic about how our relationship will work. We both admire each other and desire each other. That's a solid and stable platform to build a workable marriage on.'

'It all sounds good on paper, but we'd have to draw up a prenuptial agreement. I don't want anyone saying I only married you for your money.'

'Fine. We'll get a prenup drawn up. We'll go to the best in London if that will ease your mind,' Jack said. 'Drake Cawthorn is a specialist in them.'

She gave him a searching look. 'You know him personally?'

'Only in passing. Why, do you?'

'He's a friend of Aerin's older brother,' Harper said. 'We've sent a few clients his way. I haven't met him in person but I've heard he's pretty ruthless in making sure his clients get protected if things turn sour.'

Jack knew he should be relieved Harper wanted a prenup drawn up but somehow it suggested she didn't give their marriage much hope for the long-term. *You are hardly a long-term guy*, his conscience reminded him but he pushed the thought aside. He had a baby girl, of course he was committed to her in the long-term, and by default committed to her mother.

Not in love, but one hundred per cent committed.

'I'll give him a call and set up an appointment for when we get back to London,' Jack said.

'Okay.'

Jack suddenly realised how much he wished they weren't going straight back to London. He needed more time with her without the distractions of work. He hated the thought of going back to the hard grind of running his company and not seeing either Harper or Marli for hours on end. He was successful enough to step back a little, not too far but a little. He was too driven and goal-oriented to hand the reins over to someone else.

He liked to be in control but that didn't mean he had to be at the helm eighteen hours a day.

Jack came over to her and took her hands once more. He looked into her grey-green eyes and smiled. 'Hey, you. Did I tell you how proud I am of your work? I've watched you over the last couple of days, juggling Marli and your shoot. I can't wait to see the final product. Will there be a book launch?'

'Yes, but it will be a few months down the track.'

He tilted up her chin to keep her gaze meshed with his. 'I have a proposal for you.'

Her eyebrows lifted in a wry manner. 'Not another one?'

He grinned and planted a quick kiss on her mouth. 'How about we stay on a couple of extra days in Paris? I can reshuffle my diary and I'm sure Aerin and Ruby will manage without you.'

'It sounds nice...' Her gaze was focused on his mouth, her voice soft and husky. 'I've been so keyed up about the shoot that I haven't had time to properly enjoy our time here.'

He brought her close against his hardening body. 'You've enjoyed *some* of our time here, haven't you?'

A light blush tinged her cheeks pink and her eyes shone with desire. 'Now that you mention it...' She stepped up on tiptoe and placed her lips against his, lighting a fire in his body that threatened to engulf him. He took control of the kiss, his tongue mating with hers in a dance that sent shivers coursing down his spine. He literally could not get enough of this woman. She turned him on like no other. And her desire for him was equally fervent, thrilling him to the core of his being.

If that wasn't a recipe for a good, strong, workable relationship, he didn't know what was. Love was for the romantics and fairy-tale believers. For the hopefuls and the naïve.

Not for him.

CHAPTER TEN

A COUPLE OF days later, Harper walked arm in arm with Jack along the Champs-élysées. Marli was asleep in the pram, the sun was shining and the birds were singing, and, while the busy Paris traffic with its mix of sirens and horns was noisy, it didn't spoil the atmosphere for Harper. Her body was still tingling from Jack's superlative lovemaking over the last couple of nights. Jack had been an attentive and surprisingly tender lover but now he was even more so. It was as if something had changed in their relationship, a subtle shift that gave her hope that he was developing feelings for her, even though he had ruled out falling in love with her or anyone. But the love he showed towards Marli was unmistakably solid. He was involved with every aspect of her care apart from feeding. It fuelled Harper's hope that he could open his heart to her too.

They were walking past an art gallery when Jack stopped to look at the artwork displayed in the window. It was a beautiful watercolour with the softest brushstrokes of exquisite pastel colours depicting a cruise boat heading towards one of the River Seine bridges. The brushstroke style was loose and free and yet still managed to capture so much of the essence and light and energy of Paris.

'Shall we go in?' Harper suggested.

'I thought you wanted to go to the eighteenth-century tea salon further down?'

Harper's stomach gave a loud rumble of hunger. Reading about the delicious patisserie with its world-renowned pastries had whetted her appetite, but something about Jack's wistful expression as he stood in front of the gallery window made her curious. 'I do but I'd like to look at the artwork first.' She peered at the French name on a placard next to the painting. 'Etienne Aubuchon. I think I read something about him a while ago. He's very good, isn't he?'

Jack made a grunting sound of agreement and began pushing the pram again. 'We'd better get that cup of tea before Marli wakes for her next feed.'

Harper continued on by his side, wondering why he hadn't wanted to browse through the gallery. It wasn't as if he couldn't afford any of the artworks inside. Perhaps he was one of those people who didn't get the subtlety of modern art, although that painting style leaned more towards Impressionism than modern. They finally came to the quaint tea salon with its array of delectable goodies on show. They were soon seated at a table inside with their orders taken, and Harper had another chance to observe Jack as they waited for their tea and pastries to arrive. Well, *her* pastries, that was.

'Don't you have a sweet tooth, Jack?'

'No.' His lips curved in a teasing and yet indulgent smile. 'But apparently you do.'

Harper rolled her eyes. 'I have a whole mouth full

of them, more's the pity.' She gave him a self-deprecating smile and continued, 'I spent years eating my feelings. It took me a long time to realise that no amount of yummy food was going to satisfy the emotional hunger I was feeling. I had to address the source of that hunger.'

A frown pulled at his brow. 'And were you successful?'

She shrugged one shoulder. 'Yes and no. I guess there will always be a part of me that hungers for things I can't have.'

There was a loaded silence.

'You're not the only one who hungers for things they can't have,' Jack said at last, his mouth twisted in a rueful manner.

'What do you still hunger for?'

'Apart from you, you mean?' His playful tone didn't match the shadows in his dark blue eyes, the same shadows she had seen as they stood outside the gallery window earlier.

Harper gave him a mock-scolding look. 'Be serious for a moment.'

There was another silence.

Jack picked up a teaspoon from beside his china cup and saucer even though their tea had yet to arrive. He toyed with the teaspoon like a baton between two of his long, tanned fingers, then he put it down again with a tinkle against the saucer that sounded eerily definitive. His eyes met hers. 'For as long as I can remember I've wanted to be an artist. It was a yearning desire I had to suppress once my father became ill. I knew it was up to me and only me to keep the family business going.'

'Oh, Jack, that must have been so hard.'

'It was at first but, like most things, the pain goes away after a time.'

'But does it really? I mean, you looked so wistful when we were looking at Etienne Aubuchon's work. Is that what you wanted? To be a successful watercolour artist?'

'Finding success is a bit of a lottery in the arts world,' he said. 'I had some talent, but it didn't get the chance to grow and mature. But that's okay. Not everyone achieves their childhood dream.'

'Do you still paint? I mean, in your spare time, as a hobby?'

His lips curved in a wry smile. 'Hasn't anyone told you a workaholic has no spare time?'

Harper frowned. 'And yet you've given up so much of your time to be with us.' She glanced at their sleeping baby in the pram beside their table. 'I can't thank you enough for being so good about everything. It's not been an easy few weeks.'

Jack reached for her hand across the table, his fingers warm and strong around hers. 'Harder for you than for me, I think. You're a wonderful mother, sweetie. I love seeing you with Marli. No one would ever guess you hadn't prepared for her arrival like other mothers. You're a natural.'

'I don't know about that...' Harper looked down at their joined hands. Her engagement ring winked at her as brightly as the sun outside, reminding her of the purpose of this extra time in Paris. Jack wanted a final commitment from her. He wanted a date to be set for their wedding. But how could she agree to a wedding date when he wasn't in love with her? Wouldn't she be setting herself up for more agonising emotional hunger?

'You're too hard on yourself,' Jack said.

'Maybe.'

Their tea and pastries arrived at that moment but Harper had lost her appetite for anything sweet. Her appetite was ravenous for love—Jack's love. Not just his physical lovemaking but to hear him say the words that no one had ever said to her apart from her friends. Her mother hadn't been the I-love-you type, although Harper knew her mother had loved her. Poor Ruby did not have the same assurance from her mother but at least she had won the heart of Lucas Rothwell. No one could ever question his love for Ruby. It shone from his eyes, it vibrated in the air, it charged the atmosphere whenever he and Ruby were together.

Harper wanted the same from Jack, but was her dream too impossible, too far out of reach?

Jack woke during the night to find Harper wasn't beside him in the bed. His heart gave a stutter but then he remembered she was probably up feeding Marli. But in that second or two of panic, it was like reliving the moment all those months ago, finding his bed empty with only the indentation of her head on the pillow to show she had even been there. He flung off the covers and padded out of the bedroom to find Harper gently putting Marli back in the pram in the sitting room.

'I'm sorry I slept through her waking for a feed,' Jack said in a whisper so as not to wake the baby.

Harper turned and smiled at him. 'It's okay. You looked pretty done in.'

He rubbed a hand over his stubble. 'Yes, well, who knew being a tourist was so exhausting?'

She came over to him and placed a hand on his naked chest, and a lightning bolt of lust zigzagged through his body. 'Was it sightseeing or making love until the wee hours?'

Jack shuddered as he recalled the passion they had shared. It never got any less exciting, any less thrilling and mind-blowing. Even juggling the needs of their baby girl didn't seem to kill or even dampen their desire for each other. Didn't that prove they had what it took for a great marriage going forward?

He placed his hands on her waist and brought her towards his body, another shudder going through him as her soft curves met his harder planes and angles. 'I never get tired of making love with you.'

She looked up into his eyes, her lower body pressed closely to his, her hands snaking around his neck. 'What's the longest period you've made love to the same person?' Her question was casually delivered and yet he sensed in her tone a deeper probe of interest.

'Two weeks,' Jack said. 'But that was years and years ago.'

Harper's brows lifted. 'Why so long?'

For some strange reason he didn't want to smile at her dry humour. For he suddenly realised he had never really ventured out of the shallow waters of casual dating. Not until he'd met Harper. Now he was in deep, so deep his feet couldn't touch the bottom. He didn't even know where the bottom was. All he knew was he was not going to swim away from his baby girl. He was not going to abandon Harper, either.

'I had a fling with a woman I met when I was in New York,' Jack said. 'I'm not proud of it, looking back. I didn't know she was married. She conveniently forgot to mention it.'

'Were you in love with her?'

'No, but it rankled that she hadn't been honest with me.'

Harper lowered her gaze to his mouth for a moment. 'So, telling the truth is a standard you uphold at all times?' Her eyes came back to meet his in an almost defiant manner. 'And one you expect in return?'

'There are probably times when a little white lie is okay in order to keep from hurting someone unnecessarily, but I try to be straight with people. I don't promise things I can't deliver. I don't say words I don't mean.'

Harper gave a crooked smile that didn't meet her eyes. 'Good to know. I would hate for you to pretend to feel things you don't feel.'

Jack placed his hand along the side of her face, gently tilting her head up so her mouth was within reach. 'What I feel right now is almost indescribable.'

'But you don't love me.' Her tone had a sound of resignation about it that plucked at his conscience like a plectrum.

His hand fell away from her face and she stepped back only slightly, but the gap suddenly felt like the width of the River Seine that ran outside their suite below. How could he close it without compromising himself? Without falling in the deep end without any way of getting out? 'You know I care about you, Harper. That's all I can offer you. Care and support and security. You'll want for nothing in life. I'll make sure of it.'

Her eyes misted over, and an invisible hand clutched at his guts. Her expression heralded a warning that he wasn't ready to hear. 'Yes, you'll give me everything but the one thing I want most of all. The thing I've wanted all my life and never got.'

Jack moved a little distance away, determined to stay cool and calm, but it took more self-control than he realised. Fear clawed at his insides, prickly, cold fear that Harper was not going to fall in with his plans for their future. How could he convince her? He had promised her everything he was capable of giving.

He rubbed a hand down his face and released a ragged sigh. 'I don't want to lie to you.'

'It's not me you're lying to, Jack. It's yourself. You're capable of loving and loving deeply. Look at the way you've bonded with Marli. But you don't want to step beyond your comfort zone with me. I get it. I know I'm hardly what anyone would call in your circles a prize catch. But I want to be loved and I can't marry you or anyone without it.'

'I wish you wouldn't run yourself down like that,' Jack said, fighting anger and frustration and fear. 'You're everything a man could want in a partner.'

'But you don't really want a partner. You want a mother for your baby and a lover for your bed. And those roles are not necessarily mutually exclusive. You don't want a soulmate, someone who shares everything with you and you with them. Someone with whom you can be yourself, your *true* self. The person you could be if you would only allow it.'

'You know, you're really losing me with all this psychobabble crap,' Jack said. 'I am who I am. I've been honest with you from the get-go.'

'Yes, you have, and I'm now being totally honest with you.' Harper pulled the ring off her finger and handed it to him. 'I can't marry you, Jack. I'm sorry.' There was a light of determination in her eyes that struck a chord of disquiet in him. She was the only woman to say no to him and it hurt. It hurt in places he had never hurt before. A pain that travelled through his body like a search-and-destroy missile, looking for all the vulnerable corners and crevices he normally kept hidden.

Jack ignored the engagement ring sitting in the middle of her palm. 'Do you need more time? We've only had just over a month together and, what with taking care of Marli and your shoot and—'

'And how much more time would I waste waiting for you to feel something you have decided you can't or won't feel? Weeks? Months? Years of my life?' Harper said. 'I want the fairy tale, Jack. I didn't think I did until…until I met you.'

'But you refused to see me again.'

She gave a gust of a sigh and placed the engagement ring on the coffee table near the sofa. 'Yes, well, you're the only one who is good at lying to yourself. I told myself I disliked you but really it was the opposite I was feeling. You threatened to distract me from my goals and it terrified me. I think that is also why I didn't recognise I was pregnant, even though my symptoms were a little ambiguous. I just couldn't go there in my mind.'

Jack was frowning so hard it was giving him a headache. A band of pain wrapped itself around his forehead, around his neck, around his chest, squeezing, compressing, crushing so he could barely take a breath. He didn't want to hurt her, but how could he promise something he didn't feel? It would only hurt her more in the end. 'Are you saying you love me?'

Harper met his gaze with a level stare. 'I know you don't want to hear it, not from me or from anybody for that matter. But I do love you. I can't say I wanted to fall in love with you but it happened anyway. But I can't be with you if you don't feel the same. I saw what happened to my mother when she loved a man with all of her being but he didn't return those feelings. It destroyed her.'

Jack wasn't sure how to handle what she had told him. Love was a four-letter word he avoided. He avoided it like a deadly contagion that threatened his very existence. He wore an emotion-resistant mask, he wore a suit of armour that was impenetrable. And yet…and yet…he was feeling such agonising pain now. Pain that Harper was not going to marry him. She was not going to live with him and bring up Marli with him in the family life he had envisaged.

'So, this is your final decision?' His brusque tone gave no clue what he was actually feeling. But then, he wasn't sure what exactly he was feeling other than anger, despair, fear and something else that lurked in the background shadows of his mind.

'Yes, Jack, it's my final decision,' Harper said. 'When we return to London tomorrow, I'm moving back to my flat until I find somewhere a little more suitable to live.'

He swallowed a tight stricture in his throat. 'But the

house I bought will be available soon. It just needs some more work before it's ready.'

She gave a sad smile that cast her features into shadows like a dimmer switch on a once bright light. 'It's very generous of you but I can find my own accommodation.' She paused for a moment and then continued, 'I find it so odd you're prepared to commit to buying a house and yet you can't commit yourself emotionally. Why is that?'

Jack knew exactly why he was unable to commit. He had never talked about it with anyone before. It was too deeply personal and painful. But he had already shared with Harper his lost dreams of being an artist. Why not share this too? 'I saw what loving my father did to my mother. I know you don't like her that much but she is a good person at heart. She loved my father dearly and was one hundred per cent committed to him in sickness and in health. Unfortunately, my father's illness meant she spent a lot more time dealing with sickness than with health. She gave up all her own aspirations to be by his side, but I'm not sure he ever appreciated her the way she deserved to be appreciated.'

'But he loved her, didn't he? Or did he ask her to have a loveless marriage the way you proposed to me?'

Jack was uncomfortable being compared to his father, especially now he was a father himself. 'I'm not sure if he loved her the way she loved him. Their relationship always seemed a little one-sided. He wasn't a particularly demonstrative man and I don't recall him ever telling her he loved her. He may have done so in private.'

'Did he tell you he loved you?'

'No, but I didn't feel unloved, or at least not in the early days. After he became ill, he changed. He became hard to be around. Only my mother could handle his moods.' And Jack hadn't even bothered trying. Had he missed an opportunity to build a better relationship with his ailing father? It was too late now.

Way too late.

'When will I see Marli?' Jack was aware of his gut tightening into knots. Aware of a sense of dread filling his chest, a creeping fear that he was going to fail as a father because he couldn't be with his daughter the way he wanted to be. He had never planned to be a father but, now that he was, the last thing he wanted to be was a part-time one. But how could he be anything but part-time when Harper wouldn't marry him?

'You can see her whenever you want. I won't stop you. I'll have to think about some day care for her. I need to get back to work at some point.'

'I can do a four-day week or even a three-day one,' Jack said, wondering if he was turning into someone he couldn't recognise. Where was the man who rarely took a weekend off? Where was the man who worked eighteen-hour days? 'And my mother will be happy to help out.'

'I'll think about it.'

There was a silence so intense Jack was sure she would be able to hear each and every one of his hammering heartbeats.

'Of course, it goes without saying that I won't be sharing that bed with you again tonight or ever,' Harper said. 'It's almost morning anyway.'

It hit him then like a punch. The knockout blow of

reality that he would no longer hold Harper in his arms. No longer feel her electrifying touch gliding along his skin. No longer feel the soft but passionate press of her lips against his own. She was drawing a line underneath their relationship. A boundary line that he would not be able to cross. Or at least not without compromising himself in a way he had sworn never to do.

'This…decision of yours seems rather sudden,' Jack said, unable or unwilling to take the bite out of his tone. 'Or did you want to have the extra time in Paris first?'

A hard light came into her eyes. 'It was your idea to extend our stay, for what reason I'm not sure. Did you think it would charm me into agreeing to marry you?'

'It clearly didn't work if it was.'

Harper let out another heavy sigh. 'I don't want any animosity between us, Jack. We have to put our daughter first, and getting on with each other is important.'

He didn't want to *get on* with her. He didn't want some formal, hands-off type of friendship. He wanted *her*. But how could he have her without pretending to feel things he didn't feel?

Jack walked over to the windows but for the first time ever the view did nothing for him. It was just another river winding through yet another city. Paris, the city of love, the most romantic city in the world, was tarnished by his break-up with Harper.

'Jack?'

Jack turned around to face her but he kept his expression masked. 'Let's not drag this out any more. You've made your decision and I've accepted it.' He hadn't but he would force himself to. He was not going to beg her to stay with him. He already had acted out of character by waiting for nine long months for her to contact him again.

'I just wanted to say thank you again for being so supportive. Not many men would have coped as well as you did with the news of a baby arriving so suddenly. You're a wonderful father to Marli. I wouldn't want any of our baggage to get in the way of your relationship with her.'

Jack went over to the pram where Marli was still sleeping soundly. He stroked a barely touching finger over the peachy skin of her tiny cheek and his heart contracted at the thought of not seeing her every day. How would he bear it? How could he have gone from worldly playboy to devoted dad so seamlessly? One thing he knew for sure—he couldn't go back to his old style of living. The footloose and fancy-free lifestyle that had a stream of nameless women coming and going in his life. But neither could he have Harper, the only woman he wanted right now. He was stuck between the two worlds and, unlike along the silvery river outside, there were no bridges.

No safe passage could get him across.

CHAPTER ELEVEN

HARPER FOUND IT sadly fitting that Marli cried on and off for most of the journey back to London. It seemed as if her baby girl was crying the tears she herself was unwilling to shed—or at least not in front of Jack. She had bared her soul to him last night and it had not produced the results she had hoped for. He remained mostly silent on the flight. He helped soothe Marli, which was a blessing because Harper found it difficult to manage those piteous cries when her own heart was breaking.

Finally, the hellish journey was over and Marli was asleep in her capsule as Jack brought it inside Harper's flat. He had arranged for his staff to transport all the baby paraphernalia from his hotel suite to her flat before they got home. He had even organised fresh food to be delivered so she didn't have to negotiate the shops with a young baby. It was another reminder of the power and efficiency at Jack's fingertips—he could get things done in half a day that would take other people a week, if not more.

That he was angry at her final decision was unmistakable. He masked it well with well-bred solicitousness and cool politeness but she could sense it all the same. A brooding frown had barely left his features, his mouth was tight and his eyes had lost their glinting spark. It was his male pride that was hurt but he would have to suck it up. He was used to getting his own way, but this time she couldn't agree to a loveless marriage. Not without compromising or losing part of herself. The part of herself that had craved love all her life. She had finally come to a place where she realised she had to put herself first in order to guarantee Marli's happiness. How could she be the mother she wanted to be if she was in a loveless relationship with her baby's father? Marli deserved better, Harper deserved better…and didn't Jack? How could he be the man he had the potential to be if she fell in with his emotion-free marriage?

Harper watched as Jack glanced around her flat with a critical eye. Was it her imagination or had those paint cracks grown bigger in the past few weeks? And was the leaking tap in the kitchen even louder than before? The carpet was almost bald in one spot. How had she not noticed that before? But work had always been her top priority. She spent more time at her office than at home, so the flat was somewhere to sleep at night, and because it was only a rental she hadn't bothered freshening it up.

'I know what you're thinking,' Harper said, sinking her teeth into her lower lip.

Jack turned from inspecting the room. 'You have no freaking idea of what I'm thinking.' His tone was bitter, his expression as hard as stone.

She put up her chin, refusing to be drawn into all-out war with him. 'I'm not going to fight with you. We need to be friends.'

His top lip curled. 'You want me to kiss you on the cheek or shake hands whenever we meet? Seriously? After what we had together?' His dark blue eyes flashed like vivid lightning.

Harper could feel a hot blush stealing over her cheeks. She could feel the magnetic pull of him even now, but she knew she had to resist. She had to suppress her desire for him no matter what. She didn't want to be his casual lover. She didn't want to be anything but the love of his life. 'We don't have to kiss or touch at all. We just need to be civil and polite—especially in front of Marli.'

He raked a hand through his hair, leaving it all tousled so that one thick lock fell over his forehead. 'I can't see you without...' He let out a barely audible curse and clamped his lips tightly together.

'Without what?'

His eyes met hers and something tingled in her lower body as if he had sent an electric current across the room. 'You know what.' His voice had a deep and husky edge that unravelled her self-control like a ball of string flung down a steep flight of stairs.

But Harper was made of sterner stuff now she had become a mother. She had made her decision and she was sticking with it. There was no going back. 'I'm sorry, Jack. But that's not going to happen. I can't regret our time together because we have Marli. But I know I will regret continuing a relationship with you that is based on lust, not love.'

He gave a cynical smile that didn't reach his eyes. His eyes, those beautiful, sapphire-blue eyes, were as hard as diamonds. 'I'll see myself out. Call me if you need anything. We'll arrange a visiting schedule once I sort out my diary. It might take a day or two.'

'That's fine. Take all the time you need.'

Jack went over to Marli still sleeping in her capsule. He looked down at her for a long moment, his jaw working, his throat moving up and down. Then he bent and kissed her downy head before straightening again. 'Sleep tight, little one.'

Harper steeled herself against the stranglehold of emotion filling her chest. He loved his baby girl so much. Why couldn't he love *her*?

Aerin and Ruby came over the very same day bearing prepared meals for Harper and more gifts for Marli. Harper had sent both a text informing them of her situation with Jack. She needed the support of her friends right now, it wasn't as if she had a mother or father to go to for emotional support and nurture. But she was also aware of how much extra work she had thrown at her friends by her cryptic pregnancy. Ruby's own wedding was only a few weeks away and Harper had always planned to be the one to do the photographs. How could she support her friend and be a good mother too? It seemed an impossible juggling act, one she had yet to solve.

Aerin swept Harper up in a hug as soon as she came through the door. 'I'm so sorry things didn't work out between you and Jack. You must be so devastated.'

'And then some,' Harper sighed. 'But I have to be strong. I have Marli to consider now. I can't settle for anything less than love.'

'Did you tell him you love him?' Ruby asked.

'Yes, because I remember saying to you that you did the right thing in not telling Lucas you loved him when you broke up with him. But when you got back together, I realised I was wrong. I had to tell Jack. I didn't see the point in holding it in any more. I had to tell him in order to move forward.'

'Are you sure he doesn't love you?' Ruby asked. 'I mean, Lucas pushed me away too until he worked through his issues. Maybe Jack needs a bit of time to process things.'

'But how much time?' Harper said. 'I don't want to waste my life waiting for him to fall in love with me. What if he can't love like that? He can love Marli but he doesn't seem open to the idea of romantic love.'

'I think you're doing the right thing,' Aerin said. 'I wouldn't want to be with a man who didn't love me, who wasn't the perfect match for me.'

'Jack is hardly perfect but he comes pretty close,' Harper said. 'And he's taken to fatherhood so well.'

'Does he tell Marli he loves her?' Ruby asked.

Harper frowned as she thought about it. 'I don't think I've heard him say the words but you'd only have to see him with her to see he does. Look—I'll show you the photos I took of him with her.' She got her camera out of its bag and quickly scrolled through the shots until she got to the one in the Luxembourg Gardens. Seeing that photo sent a wave of sadness through her that threatened to overwhelm her. Jack was such a doting father. Why couldn't he be a doting husband as well?

'Oh, how gorgeous is that?' Aerin said with feeling. 'He looks absolutely smitten.'

'He certainly does,' Ruby said with a thoughtful look on her face.

Harper closed her camera and put in back in the bag and zipped it shut. If only she could pack away her feelings as easily. Out of sight, out of mind, out of reach.

If only.

Jack had planned to take some more time off work so he could be with Marli but, as luck would have it, things went awry with a hotel development in Brussels. There was no one else he could send in his place at such short notice. Packing a bag and travelling from week to week had never been a problem before. He had always enjoyed the change of scene and the kick of excitement at the thought of new casual dating experiences. But now it sickened him to his gut to think of sleeping with anyone but Harper. He couldn't imagine feeling desire for anyone else ever again. Had fatherhood changed him so much?

Had Harper changed him so much?

His hotel suite in London had never felt less like a home. He was almost glad to be leaving it to go to Brussels, but he knew he would have to come back eventually and face the emptiness of the penthouse. It was full of luxury furniture and top-quality furnishings, it had commanding views over London, and he had staff to wait on his every whim. But oh, what he would have given for the sound of his baby daughter stirring in her sleep. Damn it, he would even welcome a full-on crying jag like the one on the journey home.

His staff had followed his instructions to the letter. There was no trace of Harper or Marli in his suite now—no rattles, or pink-beribboned teddy bears or unicorns that played lullabies. Nothing to remind him how much his life had changed.

Jack's phone rang just as he was closing his travel bag. He glanced at the screen and saw it was his mother. He hadn't yet told her of Harper's decision not to marry him. He hadn't wanted to say the words out loud because it hurt too damn much. 'Hi, Mum, I'm just dashing off to the airport. The Brussels development has a few issues to iron out. What's up?'

'Nothing, darling, I just wondered if I could come by and see Marli.'

'You'll have to ask Harper.'

'Can you put her on for me?'

Savage pain seized him in the gut. 'Not at the moment.' He let out a rough-edged sigh. 'She's moved back to her flat.'

'Why?'

'She's decided she doesn't want to marry me.'

'That girl has rocks in her head turning down a marriage proposal from you.' The indignation in his mother's tone would have amused him on any other day, but not today. 'Do you want me to talk to her?' she added.

'I don't think it would help.'

'I hope she's not going to make it difficult for me to see Marli.' His mother's voice was less indignant now and more despairing. A despair he could relate to. But it wasn't just Marli he wanted to see each day. It was also Harper.

Jack propped his phone against his shoulder and jaw as he zipped up his travel bag. 'I don't think she'll do that. She wants what's best for Marli.'

'But if she wants what's best for Marli, why isn't she marrying you?'

'Because she wants me to be in love with her and I can't do that.'

There was an odd little silence. Odd because his mother rarely if ever left room for a silence.

'Can't or won't?'

Jack removed his phone from its propped position against his shoulder. 'I've never been in love and I don't intend to start now. It seems to me to be a loser's game. You only get hurt in the end.'

'And you're not hurting now?'

'Not particularly.' It was a blatant lie but he didn't want his mother to worry about him. Or interfere and make things worse.

'Jack… I know you found things difficult with your father,' his mother began in a tone he had never heard her use before. 'But he was a good man, a decent man who loved his family. You probably don't remember the good times, you were too young. His diagnosis completely shattered him. The prospect of being disabled terrified him and it locked him down inside himself. He literally changed overnight. I kept trying to reconnect with the man I fell in love with all those years ago.'

A lump had come to Jack's throat that made speaking difficult. 'And did you reconnect with him?'

His mother gave a lengthy sigh. 'Sadly no. But I lived in hope until his very last breath, because that's what true love does. It never gives up hope.'

Jack put his phone down a few minutes later and frowned as he thought about what his mother had told him. She had given up her career and the best years of her life to nurse a grumpy and difficult man who had once loved her but never shown it in any meaningful way since, up to the day he died.

If anything, it only confirmed his stance on resisting falling in love. Feeling true love for someone seemed to him a pretty painful way to live.

And right now, he could do without any more pain.

A week later, Harper was in her office sitting at her computer trying to edit photos from the Paris shoot, but Marli was fussing in the pram even though she had been fed and changed. So this was the juggle working mothers talked about. The ceaseless demands of a small infant and the pressing demands of deadlines. Jack was still away in Brussels to deal with some sort of development issue at one of his hotels. They had spoken a couple of times on the phone and he had seemed polite but distant in his manner. But when she'd put on the video function for him to see Marli, his face lit up, reminding her of why she had fallen for him in the first place. Who could resist that killer smile? Those midnight-blue eyes? That sensual touch—?

But no, she was *not* to think of his touch. Not now. Not again. He had probably hooked up with someone else by now. Maybe more than one person. Her stomach churned at the thought, jealousy streaking through her like a poisoned arrow.

'Waa-waa-waa!' Marli bleated from the pram, obviously deciding she wasn't going to settle anytime soon.

Aerin popped her head through the door. 'Can I help? Does she need a cuddle from her Aunty Aerin?'

Harper stood and stretched her stiff back. 'Do you mind? I just need half an hour to work on these photos.'

Aerin came into the room and swept Marli up in her arms. 'I can think of nothing I would like better.' She smiled down at the baby. 'How is the cutest little munchkin in London?'

Marli waved her tiny hands in the air and Aerin captured one and kissed each of her little fingers. 'Gosh, I can't wait to have kids one day.' She gave a heartfelt sigh and glanced at Harper. 'Can I talk to you about something? I know you're busy but…'

Harper pushed her chair back from the desk. She had lost her enthusiasm for the project anyway. She had lost her enthusiasm for a lot of things since she had ended things with Jack. 'Of course you can. What's up?'

Aerin sat on one of the velvet chairs opposite Harper's desk and cradled Marli against her chest. 'You know how I always meet up with the girls I went to school with each year just before Christmas? Well, one of the girls is moving to Australia with her husband, so we're bringing forward our catch-up to next month instead.'

'Yes, I remember, but didn't you say you haven't enjoyed going the last couple of years?'

Aerin looked down at Marli, who was drifting off to sleep. 'I'm the last one of our group who isn't married or in a long-term relationship.' She looked back up at Harper. 'I can't bear being the only singleton. Everyone always asks me if I'm dating anyone. I always feel like such a pariah. I'll be thirty next birthday. What am I going to do?'

'So don't go. Why torture yourself?'

'I have to go,' Aerin insisted. 'We've always had perfect attendance since we left school.'

'It won't be perfect attendance next year unless your friend flies back from Australia.'

'No, which is why I don't want to wreck the track record this year—our final year of all being together.'

'So, I guess you have to find a partner in a hurry.'

Aerin looked down at the baby again and sighed. 'Yes…'

'Do you have anyone in mind?'

'No.'

Silly question. At last count, Aerin had an eight-point checklist on what she wanted in a partner. No such perfect man existed as far as Harper knew. 'So what will you do? Pay someone to go with you?'

Aerin's head came up and her grey-blue eyes widened. 'You mean…a male *escort*?' She whispered the word in a shocked tone.

'No, not an escort but someone who could be a stand-in.'

'You mean I should convince someone to *pretend* to be my partner?'

'It's just for a couple of hours and it would certainly stop everyone carrying on about you being single. Surely you know someone who would do it for you? What about one of your brother's friends? The hot-shot lawyer one—Drake Cawthorn.'

A vivid blush crept over Aerin's cheeks. 'Oh, I could never ask *him*.'

'Then you'll have to go to the catch-up alone and face the violins.'

Aerin winced as if the thought horrified her and quickly changed the subject. 'Have you heard from Jack?'

'Yes, he calls every day.'

'How are things between you? The same?'

'The same.'

Aerin gave another sigh. 'I still think you did the right thing. I know Ruby doesn't agree with me but you have to be sure he loves you. How could you build a future on anything less than true love?'

How indeed?

Jack walked through the house he had bought before Harper had called time on their relationship. It had been repainted and recarpeted throughout and the interior designer was in the process of organising curtains and other soft furnishings. The house still needed a bit of work but it was taking shape. What a pity he wouldn't be needing it after all. Or should he keep it so Marli had somewhere to grow up rather than in a hotel? But the house was too big for a single dad and an only child.

A single dad.

How those words were like a punch to the guts. He had planned to be married to Harper by now but she had refused to accept his offer of a secure future. He had been so confident she would fit in with his plans…well, reasonably confident. Harper wasn't the sort of person who could be forced to do things she didn't want to do, which was one of the things he admired about her. One of the many things. Things that made it hard for him to get through a day without thinking of her, without missing her, without wanting her. And the nights were worse, way worse. He had turned in bed several times to reach for her, only to feel the crushing blow of realisation that the other side of his bed was empty.

Harper was gone and she was not coming back.

And somehow he would have to get used to it.

CHAPTER TWELVE

HARPER WAS AT home a couple of days later with Marli when the doorbell rang. She wasn't expecting Jack back until the end of the week and she knew Aerin and Ruby had other commitments. Poor Ruby had even mentioned postponing her own wedding so they could keep up with everything. She and Aerin had taken on so much extra work because of her taking maternity leave, something that worried her deeply. It wasn't just her who had been blindsided by the arrival of Marli but her business partners too. But how could she leave her baby in the care of strangers in order to get back to work? And did she even want to go back to full-time work? She was enjoying being a mother, far more than she'd ever expected to. It wasn't always easy—Marli had occasional colic and it was harder to get her into a routine than all the baby books and parenting blogs said. But Harper loved seeing her grow and her heart melted every time Marli smiled or cooed at her. She was so like Jack in colouring, with those big blue eyes and ink-black hair.

Harper juggled Marli along one of her arms and checked the security monitor Jack had insisted on installing a few days ago. Jack's mother was standing outside with a basket balanced on one arm. Harper opened the door even though she could have done without an impromptu visitor right then, especially one as critical and judgemental as Liz Livingstone. It was four in the afternoon and Harper hadn't had a shower, for Marli had been fractious for most of the day.

'Is it a good time to call in? I know you must be busy with the wee one,' Liz said.

Harper shrugged as if she didn't care either way. 'It's fine. Come in. Sorry the place is a bit of a mess. Marli's not had a decent sleep all day and…' She had to stop before her emotions got the better of her. The last thing she wanted to do was burst into floods of tears in front of Jack's mother.

'Are you okay, dear?' Liz's softer maternal tone only made it harder for Harper to keep control. 'Here, let me take her for you.' She put the basket on the floor and reached for the baby.

Harper handed Marli to her grandmother, her eyes misting over, her chin developing a distinct wobble. 'I'm okay. Just a bit tired.'

Liz rocked from side to side, her hand gently stroking Marli's back in a rhythmic fashion. 'But of course you'd be tired. Looking after a baby on your own is hard work. And the lack of sleep really gets to you. I remember being an emotional wreck most days until I got Jack into a routine.'

'Was he a difficult baby?'

Liz gave a wistful smile and glanced at the baby now settling in her arms. 'Not really. I was the problem, to be honest. I wanted to be the best mother in the world. I set unrealistic expectations for myself.' She sighed and continued in a reflective tone, 'I was missing my work but I felt guilty about it. I thought I should've been happier being a full-time mother like my own mother and my mother-in-law. But I was so *bored* a lot of the time. Of course, I couldn't talk to anyone about it. All of my mum friends seemed happy being at home all day with a baby, but I nearly went out of my mind.'

'I think I have the same problem,' Harper said, only realising it at that moment. The older woman's honesty about her experience had helped Harper to gain more insight into her own see-sawing emotions and increasing stabs of guilt. 'I'm not used to spending so much time at home. I'm usually flat out with my photography, if not taking photos, then editing and formatting and consulting with clients. I want to be a good mother but I also want my career, and I don't know how to manage both.' Tears began to leak from her eyes and her shoulders shook with the effort of trying to keep control.

'Oh, you poor darling,' Liz said, patting one of her shoulders in a soothing manner, whilst still managing to settle Marli. 'And you'll be missing Jack, I expect.'

Harper stretched her mouth into a don't-feel-sorry-for-me grimace. 'I'm the one who broke things off.'

'Yes, but I think you did the right thing.'

'Because you would prefer someone a little more acceptable as your future daughter-in-law?' Harper couldn't quite remove the cutting edge to her tone.

Liz gave a hefty sigh. 'I probably deserve that. But I was so shocked when Jack said he was getting married to someone he didn't love. Every mother wants the best for their child and I'm no different. But I worry it's because of me that he resists falling in love.'

'How could it be your fault?'

Liz gave a sad-looking smile and laid the now sleeping Marli in the bassinet. She turned to look at Harper. 'I loved Jack's father so much and we were happy in the early days, but then he got sick and…and well, I lost the man I fell in love with. I nursed him for years, always hoping he would come back to me, but he didn't. I think Jack was deeply affected by that. It made him feel I had given away too much of myself and got nothing in return. But I don't see it that way. I loved my husband, and I took my wedding vows seriously—in sickness and in health, for richer, for poorer, till death do us part.' Her voice trembled on her last sentence but she continued stoically, 'If you love someone with your whole heart and soul, then you love them for ever. I may have lost the man I loved to illness but I didn't lose him, not really. I still have those precious memories of our first years to look back on. No one can ever take that away from me.'

Harper didn't bother hiding her own emotions now. Tears rolled down her cheeks and she stepped closer to hug the older woman. Liz's arms came around her and held her the way a mother would do an adult daughter.

'If you love my son like that, then you're the perfect person for him.'

Harper stepped out of the older woman's embrace and tried to smile, but it fell short of the mark. 'I want to do the best for Marli but I can't marry Jack unless he loves me. I just can't.'

'And you shouldn't,' Liz said. 'You deserve to be loved—everyone does. I wish I could say Jack might change but I'm reluctant to give you false hope. But he is a good person, a loyal and hardworking man who has sacrificed a lot for his family. You've blessed him with a beautiful daughter. Maybe by loving Marli he will learn to open his heart to you.'

'Maybe…'

Liz gave her another warm hug and then released her and smiled. 'Let me help you with Marli. I can babysit while you work. I think I might make a better grandmother than I was a mother.'

Harper smiled in return. 'I would love that. It will be nice for Marli to spend time with you. And it will help me not feel so guilty about letting my business partners down during our busiest season. Marli's arrival blindsided them as well as me and Jack.'

'Well, that's settled, then.' Liz picked up the basket off the floor. 'I brought you a meal and a teddy bear Jack used to have as a baby. I hope you don't mind? I washed it and sewed on new eyes.'

'Of course I don't mind,' Harper said. 'What a lovely thing to do.'

Liz handed her a tattered old teddy bear with only one ear. 'I'm afraid our dog Chester chewed off poor Ted's ear when he was a puppy. But I couldn't bring myself to throw him away.' She gave a self-effacing grimace and added, 'I'm a bit sentimental that way.'

Harper held the old bear against her chest. 'There's nothing wrong with being sentimental.'

'Well, then, I'd better leave you in peace…'

'Why don't you stay and share the meal with me?' Harper said.

'Are you sure?'

'Of course, but if you could mind Marli while I have a quick shower first, I'd be so grateful.'

Liz beamed. 'I would be thrilled to do that.'

Jack finally solved the problem at his Brussels hotel and was at the airport when his flight was delayed by a couple of hours. He cursed himself for not using a private jet but he was trying to do his bit for the environment. He hated killing time, especially now as he was desperate to get back to see his baby girl.

And equally desperate to see Harper.

Only the day before he had stumbled across an olde-worlde toy shop and happened to come across a teddy bear that played the lullaby Harper had mentioned was played by the teddy she had lost in foster care. He wasn't sure why he was buying it for her rather than for Marli. It was kind of like the London house—it seemed the right thing to do. Her childhood had been so lonely and miserable and he had hoped to make her life with him more than make up for the heartache she had experienced growing up. But he was unable to do that now because she'd refused to accept his offer of marriage.

Jack decided waiting around a crowded airport where all he could see was couples and young families was a form of torture. He'd never used to notice kids in prams or babies in front carrier pouches when he was in transit before, but now they were everywhere he looked, striking a deep pang in his heart. And then there were the loved-up couples walking around hand in hand, or greeting each other with deep affection. There was even an older couple who were walking along arm in arm, the old man making sure his frail wife didn't trip on luggage as they made their way along the line to the check-in counter.

Jack hadn't been able to stop thinking about his conversation with his mother a few days ago. Love had always seemed to him a terribly painful exercise, one he didn't want any part of. There were too many sacrifices to make, too much freedom to be lost, too much distress if the love wasn't returned or was blighted by illness as in his father's case. The dementia component of his father's Parkinson's Disease had taken away the man Jack's mother had loved, and yet she had willingly kept loving him and nursing him till his death. She *still* loved him.

What would it be like to be loved like that?

To be loved so deeply you always knew the person had your back? You always could rely on them to want the best for you. That nothing would destroy the commitment they had made to you.

Jack glanced back at the older couple who had now checked in and were walking towards the security checkpoint. The old woman smiled at her husband and the old man smiled back. Their faces were lined with age and their bodies not anywhere near as vital as they had probably once been, but the love they had for each other was there for all to see. A love that would get them through the winter years of their marriage and beyond...beyond to the scary unknown.

Jack realised then that, no matter who you loved, there was a risk you would lose them one day. Age, illness, tragedy—there was no way of escaping the pain of loss unless you didn't love in the first place. But what sort of life would that be?

Your life.

The words dropped into his head and he couldn't get them out. He had resisted feeling the way that old couple felt for each other. He had resisted feeling what those young couples felt as they walked hand in hand. He had resisted feeling what his mother felt for his father.

He had resisted his true self, his true nature. He had shut it down, locked it away so he could keep himself safe. But Harper's coming into his life had changed everything. From their first night together something had shifted in him but he had refused to face it until now.

He was in love with her.

Deeply in love for the first time in his life. That was why it had terrified him so much, that was why he had stubbornly refused to acknowledge it. Harper had told him she loved him and yet he hadn't told her he loved her back. He hadn't said those words to anyone in his life. Not to his father or his mother. And to his eternal shame, not even to his baby girl. What sort of man did that make him? A scared man. A man running from fear. Fear of loss, fear of being hurt, fear of experiencing emotional pain.

But that was about to change.

If only he could get on a damn flight back to London.

Harper was working on an advertisement at her flat for an assistant to help her with her workload. Liz Livingstone had suggested it over dinner the other night and she had finally decided it was the best way forward. Liz was still going to babysit but it would mean Harper wouldn't be too overwhelmed with the pressure of work when she finally got home each day. It was a matter of balance, something Liz had encouraged her to aim for instead of being so all-or-nothing as Liz herself had once been. Harper was enjoying the new-found friendship with Jack's mother, not only because it gave her an insight into Jack and his family life, but also because Liz was becoming like a mother figure to her. Liz was warm and supportive towards Harper and she absolutely adored Marli and loved being a grand-mother. And interestingly, Marli had stopped being so unsettled and fractious and seemed to enjoy being cud-dled by her grandmother. And as a result, Harper had found it easier to relax as a mother, not trying too hard to do everything perfectly but allowing that some days were better than others and just enjoying each moment for what it was.

The doorbell rang just as Harper was thinking about going to bed. She checked the security camera and saw Jack standing there looking a little travel worn. He was carrying a toy shop bag in one hand. She ignored the leap of her heart, the race of her pulse, the rise of her hopes. He was coming to visit his baby girl, not her.

Harper opened the door and stepped back, barely able to look at him without wanting to throw herself into his arms. 'It's late. Couldn't you have waited until morning to drop by to see Marli? I've not long put her down.' She wasn't proud of the resentful note in her tone but she didn't want to seem too eager to see him. Let him think she was over him. That her love for him had withered and died for lack of encouragement.

Jack stepped over the threshold and closed the door. 'No, it couldn't wait. I had to see you as soon as possible.'

'Me? Why me?'

A crooked smile formed on his lips and the spark she loved so well was back in his dark blue eyes. 'I've missed you so much. I can't believe it has taken me so long to realise this, but I love you.'

Those three little words hung in the air for a long moment because Harper couldn't decide whether he had actually said them or she had imagined he had.

'Pardon?'

His smile widened and he dropped the bag he was holding and reached for her, taking her by the hands and drawing her close. 'My darling girl, I've been such a damn fool. I think I fell in love with you that first night at the Tenterbury wedding. You caught my eye and you captured my heart. I love you with all of my being. I have fought it, resisted it, denied it, but I can do so no longer. I can't be the man I want to be, the man I was meant to be, without you by my side. Will you please think again about becoming my wife? Please?'

Harper stared at him speechlessly, her heart thudding so excitedly in her chest until she was sure her ribcage would be bent out of shape or permanently damaged. 'You're not pretending to be in love with me so I will agree to marry you?'

'No, darling. I was pretending *not* to be in love with you all these months,' Jack said. 'Pretending to you, pretending to my mother, but, most foolishly of all, pretending to myself. I've always thought loving someone was a dangerous thing to do. I watched my mother love my father and it always seemed so one-sided to me. But she has no regrets about that. She was all in from the moment they met and she never stopped loving him, even when his illness changed him. I want to be loved like that. I want to love like that. I *do* love you like that.'

Harper wrapped her arms around his neck and lifted her face to be kissed. 'Kiss me, Jack. Convince me this is really happening.'

Jack placed his mouth on hers and kissed her deeply, holding her so close she could feel every firm plane of his body. A few breathless minutes later, he pulled back to gaze down at her with so much love shining in his eyes it took her breath away. 'No one has ever made me feel the way you do. It's not just about having Marli. I would have fallen in love with you even if she hadn't come along the way she did. It's why I couldn't date anyone else. I didn't want to feel anyone else's touch in case it made me forget yours. I guess that's why my mother has never dated anyone since my father died. I want us to grow old together, to bring up our little family. We will face whatever we have to face together. There are no guarantees that we won't be touched by tragedy or illness, but I promise to be there for you no matter what.'

'Oh, Jack, I can think of nothing I would love more than to be your wife and partner in life,' Harper said. 'I've been hungry for love all my life but, like you, I pretended for so long that I didn't want it because I was protecting myself from disappointment in case I couldn't have it. Meeting you that night at the wedding turned my world upside down, not just because of getting pregnant, because I didn't even realise that had happened. But also because I knew if I allowed myself to fall in love with you, I would be opening myself up to certain heartbreak. You were a playboy. I was a career girl who wanted no complications in my life—I'd had enough of them in my childhood. But I fell in love with you anyway. I couldn't help it.'

Jack kissed her soundly again, his mouth so tender and yet so passionate it made her blood sing in her veins. He lifted his lips off hers and looked down at her with twinkling eyes. 'I was sitting at the airport in Brussels because my flight was delayed. I saw all these loving couples and families walking past—old ones, young ones and everything in between. It really made me think about why I was avoiding love. It made me realise that before you my life was empty of everything but work. My relationships were shallow and temporary and completely transactional. You're the first person I've ever wanted to commit to. You opened my heart, my love, and I can't thank you enough.'

Harper's heart was so full of joy she could barely speak. She placed her hand on the side of his stubbly face and gazed into the midnight-blue of his eyes. 'My love for you is so deep and all-consuming it will take me a lifetime to show you.'

He smiled down at her. 'A lifetime sounds good.' He bent down and picked up the toy shop bag. 'I bought this for you in Brussels.'

Harper took the bag from him and pulled out a teddy bear. 'I thought that must've been for Marli.'

'No, it's for you to replace the one you lost.'

Harper turned the bear over and found a gold key in its back. She turned it a few times and the sweet cadences of her favourite lullaby filled the air and filled her heart with even more love for this sensitive man who had made her dreams come true. 'Oh, Jack, it's so sweet of you. I missed that bear for years.'

He gathered her close again, the bear crushed between them. 'I missed you more than I can say. I kept searching for you in my sleep, only to wake up bitterly disappointed.'

She gazed up at him. 'I missed you too. So very much.'

'I was at the London house the other day,' Jack said with a crooked smile. 'It's like me—it still needs a bit of work, but I think it will be fine in the end.'

'I can't wait to see it. I've never lived in a proper house before.' She stroked the length of his strong nose and added, 'I have a confession to make.'

'What?'

Harper smiled. 'I've fallen a little bit in love with your mother as well.'

'Have you really?'

'She's been amazing while you've been away. She's going to help me with Marli so I can get back to work part-time. I feel comfortable leaving Marli with her because she loves her so much.'

'Oh, my darling, I'm so glad,' Jack said. 'That's such wonderful news.'

'Jack…will you promise me something?'

'Anything, my darling.'

'Will you promise to paint me a picture? I would love to be the first person to own a Jack Livingstone watercolour.'

His eyes lit up and a wide smile spread across his face. 'It's a deal. I'll bring some brushes and paints on our honeymoon. Who knows what fun that could be?'

'The paints and brushes or the honeymoon?'

'Both.' He bent down to plant a kiss on her lips.

'Waa-waa-waa!' came Marli's piercing cry from the bedroom.

Jack grinned and released Harper. 'I almost forgot I have something to say to our baby girl.' He took her hand and led her to where Marli was wide awake and wailing in her bassinet.

Jack reached down and scooped the baby out, and she immediately stopped crying and blinked up at him with eyes the same colour as his.

'I love you, little one. Your daddy loves you so much.' He smiled at Harper and added, 'And I love your beautiful mummy too, more than words can ever say.'

* * * * *

COMING SOON!

We really hope you enjoyed reading this book. If you're looking for more romance, be sure to head to the shops when new books are available on

Thursday 24th November

To see which titles are coming soon, please visit

millsandboon.co.uk/nextmonth

MILLS & BOON®

Coming next month

WEDDING NIGHT WITH THE WRONG BILLIONAIRE
Dani Collins

"It's just us here." The words slipped out of her, impetuous. Desperate.

A distant part of her urged her to show some sense. She knew Micah would never forgive her for so much as getting in Remy's car, but they had had something in Paris. It had been interrupted and the not knowing what could have been had left her with an ache of yearning that had stalled her in some way. If she couldn't have Remy then it didn't matter who she married. They were all the same because they weren't him.

"No one would know."

"This would only be today. An hour. We couldn't tell anyone. Ever. If Hunter found out—"

"If Micah found out," she echoed with a catch in her voice. "I don't care about any of that, Remy. I really don't."

"After this, it goes back to the way it was, like we didn't even know one another. Is that really what you want?" His face twisted with conflict.

"No," she confessed with a chasm opening in her chest. "But I'll take it."

He closed his eyes, swearing as he fell back against the door with a defeated thump.

"Come here, then."

Continue reading
WEDDING NIGHT WITH THE WRONG BILLIONAIRE
Dani Collins

Available next month
www.millsandboon.co.uk

MILLS & BOON

THE HEART OF ROMANCE

A ROMANCE FOR EVERY READER

MODERN

Prepare to be swept off your feet by sophisticated, sexy and seductive heroes, in some of the world's most glamourous and roma locations, where power and passion collide.

HISTORICAL

Escape with historical heroes from time gone by. Whether your passi for wicked Regency Rakes, muscled Vikings or rugged Highlanders, the romance of the past.

MEDICAL

Set your pulse racing with dedicated, delectable doctors in the high-sure world of medicine, where emotions run high and passion, comf love are the best medicine.

True Love

Celebrate true love with tender stories of heartfelt romance, from th rush of falling in love to the joy a new baby can bring, and a focus c emotional heart of a relationship.

Desire

Indulge in secrets and scandal, intense drama and plenty of sizzling action with powerful and passionate heroes who have it all: wealth, s good looks…everything but the right woman.

HEROES

Experience all the excitement of a gripping thriller, with an intense mance at its heart. Resourceful, true-to-life women and strong, fearle face danger and desire - a killer combination!

To see which titles are coming soon, please visit

millsandboon.co.uk/nextmonth

LET'S TALK
Romance

For exclusive extracts, competitions
and special offers, find us online:

 facebook.com/millsandboon

 @MillsandBoon

@MillsandBoonUK

Get in touch on 01413 063232

For all the latest titles coming soon, visit
millsandboon.co.uk/nextmonth